FAR
from the
TREE

D1113518

Also by Robin Benway:

Emmy & Oliver

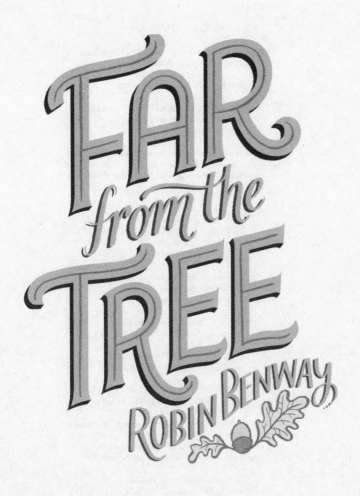

FAR from the TREE

ROBIN BENWAY

SIMON & SCHUSTER

First published in Great Britain in 2018 by Simon & Schuster UK Ltd
A CBS COMPANY

Originally published in the USA in 2017 by HarperTeen,
an imprint of HarperCollins Publishers

Text copyright © Robin Benway 2017

This book is copyright under the Berne Convention.
No reproduction without permission.
All rights reserved.

The right of Robin Benway to be identified as the author of this
work has been asserted by her in accordance with sections 77 and
78 of the Copyright, Design and Patents Act, 1988.

3 5 7 9 10 8 6 4 2

Simon & Schuster UK Ltd
1st Floor, 222 Gray's Inn Road
London
WC1X 8HB

www.simonandschuster.co.uk
www.simonandschuster.com.au
www.simonandschuster.co.in

Simon & Schuster Australia, Sydney
Simon & Schuster India, New Delhi

A CIP catalogue record for this book
is available from the British Library.

PB ISBN 978-1-4711-6433-0
eBook ISBN 978-1-4711-6434-7

This book is a work of fiction. Names, characters, places and
incidents are either the product of the author's imagination or are
used fictitiously. Any resemblance to actual people living or
dead, events or locales is entirely coincidental.

Typeset in the UK by M Rules
Printed and bound by CPI Group (UK) Ltd, Croydon, CR0 4YY

Simon & Schuster UK Ltd are committed to sourcing paper
that is made from wood grown in sustainable forests and support the Forest
Stewardship Council, the leading international forest certification organisation.
Our books displaying the FSC logo are printed on FSC certified paper.

For my brother

Thank you for being my bungee buddy

FALLING

GRACE

Grace hadn't really thought too much about homecoming.

She knew that she'd go, though. She figured that she and her best friend, Janie, would get dressed together, get their hair done together. She knew that her mom would try to be cool about it and not get excited, but she'd make Grace's dad charge the fancy, expensive camera—not the iPhone—and then Grace would take pictures with Max, her boyfriend of just over a year.

He'd look great in his tux—rented, of course, because what would Max do with a tux hanging in his closet?—and she didn't know if they'd slow dance or just talk to people or what. The thing was that she didn't make any assumptions. She thought it would happen, and it'd be great.

Grace thought like that about everything in her life. Homecoming was something that she knew she'd do. She didn't question it.

Which is why it was so surprising that she ended up spending homecoming night not in a fancy dress, not sipping out of Max's flask and dancing with Janie and taking cheesy photos of each other, but in the maternity ward of St. Catherine's Hospital, her feet in stirrups instead of heels, giving birth to her daughter.

It took Grace a while to figure out that she was pregnant. She used to watch those reality shows on cable TV and yell at the screen, "How did you *not* know you're pregnant?!" as actors re-created the most unbelievable scenarios. Karma, Grace thought later, really bit her in the ass on that one. But her period had always been erratic, so that was no help. And she had morning sickness the same time as the flu was going around school, so that was strike number two. It wasn't until her favorite jeans were tighter during Week Twelve (which she didn't realize was Week Twelve at the time) that she started to suspect something was off. And it wasn't until Week Thirteen (see earlier comment about Week Twelve) that she made her boyfriend, Max, drive them twenty minutes away to a store where they wouldn't see anyone they knew so they could buy two pregnancy tests.

It turned out that pregnancy tests were expensive. So expensive, in fact, that Max had to check his bank balance on his phone while they stood in line, just to make sure that he had enough in his account.

By the time Grace realized what had happened, she was in the fifth day of her second trimester.

The baby was the size of a peach. Grace looked it up on Google.

* * *

After that day, Grace knew that she wasn't going to keep Peach.
She knew that she *couldn't*. She worked part-time after school at
a clothing boutique that catered primarily to women forty years
older than her who called her dear. She wasn't exactly earning
baby-raising money.

And it wasn't even that babies cried or smelled or spit up or
anything like that. That didn't seem terrible. It was that they *needed*
you. Peach would need Grace in ways that she couldn't give to her,
and at night, she would sit in her room, holding her now-rounded
stomach, and say, "I'm sorry, I'm sorry, I'm sorry," a prayer and
a penance, because Grace was the first person who Peach would
ever need and Grace felt like she was already letting Peach down.

The adoption lawyer sent over a huge folder of prospective families, each of them more eager looking than the next. Grace's
mom and she looked at them together like they were shopping in
a catalog.

No one was good enough for Peach. Not the prospective dad
who resembled a hamster, or the mom whose haircut hadn't been
updated since 1992. Grace nixed one family because their toddler looked like a biter, and another because they hadn't ever
traveled east of Colorado. Never mind that *she* hadn't even traveled past Colorado, but Peach deserved better. She deserved *more*.
She deserved mountain climbers, international voyagers, people
who searched the world for the best things, because that's what
Peach was. Grace wanted intrepid explorers who mined for

gold—because they were about to strike it rich.

Catalina was originally from Spain and she was fluent in both Spanish and French. She worked for an online marketing firm but also ran a food blog and wanted to publish a cookbook someday. Daniel was a website designer who worked from home. He would be the stay-at-home parent during the first three months, which Grace thought was pretty badass. They had a Labrador retriever named Dolly, who looked both affectionate and stupid.

Grace chose them.

She never felt ashamed, not with Peach inside her. They were like a little team. They walked, slept, and ate together, and everything that Grace did affected Peach. They watched a lot of TV on her laptop, and Grace told her about the shows and about Catalina and Daniel and how she would have a great home with them.

Peach was the only person Grace really talked to. All her other friends had fallen away. Grace could see it in their eyes, their uncertainty about what to say about her rapidly expanding stomach, their relief that it was she and not they who had gotten pregnant. Her cross-country teammates had tried to keep her updated at first, talking about meets and gossiping about other teams, but Grace couldn't handle the way her jealousy pushed against her skin until it felt like she would explode. Even nodding silently became difficult after a while, and when she stopped responding, they stopped talking.

Sometimes when she was almost asleep, when Peach pushed up into her rib cage like it was a safe little space for her, Grace could feel her mom standing in the doorway to her room, watching her. She pretended to not know she was there, and after a while, her mom would leave.

Her dad, though. He could barely look at Grace. She knew she had disappointed him, that even though he still loved her, Grace was a different person now, and she would never be the same Grace again. He must have felt like they swapped out his daughter for a new model ("Now with baby inside!"), a Grace 2.0.

Grace knew this because she felt the same way.

Grace was forty weeks and three days when homecoming rolled around. Janie had kept asking her to go, saying they could go in a group with friends or something, which was probably both the dumbest and sweetest thing she had ever said to Grace. Her words were always tinged with apology, like she knew she was saying the wrong thing but didn't know how to stop herself. It'll be fun! she texted Grace, but Grace didn't respond.

When school had started up that year, Grace hadn't gone back with everyone else. She was too pregnant, too round, too exhausted. Also, there was the risk of her going into labor one day during AP Chem and traumatizing everyone in the junior class. She wasn't exactly disappointed by this decision. By the time summer vacation had rolled around, she had grown tired of feeling like a sideshow freak, people giving her so much room in the hallways that she couldn't remember the last time anyone had touched her, even accidentally.

Peach was born at 9:03 p.m. on homecoming night, right

when Max was being crowned homecoming king because, Grace thought bitterly, boys who get girls pregnant are heroes and girls who get pregnant are sluts. Leave it to Peach to steal Max's thunder, though. The first thing Grace's daughter ever did and it was genius. She was so proud. It was like Peach knew she was the heir to the throne and had arrived to claim her tiara.

Peach came out of her like fire, like she had been set aflame. There was Pitocin and white-hot pain that seared Grace's spine and ribs and hips into rubble. Her mother held her hand and wiped her hair back from her sweaty forehead and didn't mind that Grace kept calling her Mommy, like she had when she was four years old. Peach twisted and shoved her way through her, like she knew that Grace was just a vessel for her and that her real parents, Daniel and Catalina, were waiting outside, ready to take Peach home to her real life.

Peach had places to be, people to see, and she was done with Grace.

Sometimes, when it was late at night and Grace let herself drift to that dark place in her brain, she thought that she would have been okay if only she hadn't held Peach, if she hadn't felt her skin and smelled the top of her head and seen that she had Max's nose and Grace's dark hair. But the nurse had asked Grace if she wanted to, and she ignored her mother's worried eyes, her lip caught between her teeth. She reached out and took Peach from the nurse, and she didn't know how else to explain except to say that Peach fit, she fit into Grace's arms like she had fit beneath her rib cage, nestled there soft and safe, and even though Grace's body felt like soot and ashes, her head felt as if it had been washed clean for the first time in ten months.

Peach was perfect. Grace was not.

And Peach deserved perfect.

Catalina and Daniel didn't call her Peach, of course. No one knew about that nickname except for Grace. And Peach. They called her Amelía Marie instead. Milly for short.

They had always said that it could be an open adoption. They wanted it to be that way, Catalina especially. Privately, Grace thought Catalina felt a little guilty that Peach was becoming her baby. "We can set up visitation," Catalina said one day when they met in the adoption counselor's office. "Or send you photos. Whatever makes you comfortable, Grace."

But after Peach—*Milly*—was born, Grace didn't trust herself. She couldn't imagine seeing her again and not taking her back. Right after she was born, Grace was flying on the sort of adrenaline that she imagined only Olympic athletes could experience, and she was half ready to jump up, tuck Peach under her arm, and run like a linebacker toward the end zone. She probably could have run a marathon with her, and what scared her was that she knew she wouldn't have brought Peach back.

Grace didn't remember giving Peach—*Milly*—over to Daniel and Catalina. One moment, her daughter was in her arms, and the next, she was gone, riding away with strangers, someone else's daughter and lost to Grace forever.

Her body remembered, though. It had ushered Peach into the world, and it mourned her when Grace got home from the hospital. She locked her bedroom door and writhed in agony, one of Peach's receiving blankets clutched in her fist as she choked into it, sobs pressing down on her chest, her heart, crushing her from the inside. She didn't want her mother anymore. This wasn't a pain that she or the doctors could take away. Grace's body twisted on the bed in a way that it hadn't during her labor, like it was confused about where Peach had gone, and her toes curled and her hands flexed. Grace had delivered Peach, but now it felt like she had truly left her. She was untethered, floating away.

Grace stayed in her bedroom for a while. She lost track after ten days.

After two weeks of staying in the dark, she went downstairs and interrupted her parents' breakfast. They both stared at her like they had never seen her before, and in a way, they hadn't. Grace 3.0 ("Now with no baby!") was here to stay.

And then she said the words that her parents had dreaded hearing for the past sixteen years, ever since the day Grace had been born. Not "I'm pregnant" or "my water broke" or "there was an accident."

Grace went downstairs, her stomach empty, her hair wild, and she said to her parents, "I want to find my birth mother."

Grace had always known that she was adopted. Her parents had never made a secret of it. They didn't really talk about it, either. It just *was*.

At the breakfast table, Grace now watched her mom reflexively screwing and unscrewing the lid on the peanut butter jar. After the third time, her dad reached over and took it from her. "We should set up a family meeting," he said as her mom's hands moved to her paper napkin.

The last time they had had a family meeting, Grace had told them she was pregnant. At the rate they were going, her parents would probably never have a family meeting again.

"Okay," Grace said. "Today."

"Tomorrow." Her mom had finally found her voice. "I have a meeting today and we should . . ." She glanced at her dad. "We should get some paperwork for you. It's in the safe."

There had always been an implied agreement between Grace and her parents. They would tell her everything they knew about her biological family, but only if she asked. She had been curious a few times—like when they studied DNA in freshman-year biology, or that time in second grade when she found out Alex Peterson had two moms and Grace wondered if maybe she could have two moms, too—but it was different now. Grace knew that somewhere in the world was a woman who had maybe hurt (and maybe was still hurting) like Grace was hurting now. Meeting her wouldn't bring Peach back to Grace, or fill the cracks that were threatening to shatter her into pieces, but it would be something.

Grace needed to be tethered to someone again.

Her parents knew very little about her mother. Grace wasn't entirely surprised. It had been a private adoption, through lawyers and courts. Her mother's name was Melissa Taylor. Grace's parents had never met her. Melissa hadn't wanted to meet them.

There was no picture of Melissa, or fingerprints, or note or memento, just a signed court document. The name was common enough that Grace suspected she could Google it for hours and not find anything, but it seemed like maybe Melissa had never wanted to be found. "We did send a letter to her through the lawyer," Grace's mother said, passing her a thin envelope. "Right after you were born, us telling her how grateful we were, but it was returned." She didn't need to add that last part. Grace could see the red "Return to Sender" stamp slashing across the white paper.

And right when she started to feel a new, different (though no worse) despair, that there wasn't a woman who had wanted her, who had craved her the way Grace craved Peach, who had writhed and ached and wanted to know anything about her, Grace's parents said something that immediately closed the black hole that was threatening to swallow her up.

"Grace," her father said gently, like his voice could hit a trip wire and destroy them all, "you have siblings."

After Grace was done throwing up in the downstairs guest bathroom, she got herself a glass of water and came back to the table. The look of anxiety on her mother's face made her twitch.

They laid out the story in careful and obviously rehearsed words: Joaquin was her brother. He had been one year old when Grace was born, and had gone into foster care a few days after her

parents brought her home. "They asked us if we wanted to foster," Grace's mother explained, and even now, sixteen years later,
Grace could see the lines of regret that Joaquin had etched on her
face. "But you were a newborn and we—we weren't prepared for
that, for two babies. And your grandmother had just been diagnosed . . ."

Grace knew that part of the story. Her grandmother, Gloria
Grace, the woman who Grace shared her name with, had been
diagnosed with stage 4 pancreatic cancer a month before Grace
had been born, and died right after Grace's first birthday. "The best
year and the worst year," Grace's mother described it, when she
talked about it at all. Grace knew not to ask too many questions.

"Joaquin," Grace said now, rolling the word over in her mouth.
She realized that she had never known a Joaquin before, that she
had never said the name before.

"We were told that he was placed with a foster family that was
on track to adopt him," her father told her. "But that's all we know
about him. We tried to keep track of him, but it's a . . . complicated system."

Grace nodded, taking it all in. If her life had been a movie,
this was where the reflective, orchestral music would swell. "You
said *siblings*? Plural?"

Her mother nodded. "Right after Gloria Grace"—no one ever
called her anything except that—"died, we got a phone call from
the same lawyer who helped us get you. There was another baby,
a girl, but we couldn't . . ." She looked to Grace's father again,

someone to help her bridge the gap between words. "We couldn't, Grace," her mother said, her voice wavering before she cleared her throat. "She was adopted by a family about twenty minutes away. We have their information. We agreed that whenever one of you wanted to contact the other, we would let them know."

They slid an email address across the table to her. "Her name is Maya," her father said. "She's fifteen. We talked to her parents last night and they talked to her. If you'd like to email her, she's waiting to hear from you."

That night, Grace sat in front of her laptop, the cursor blinking at her as she tried to figure out what to write to Maya.

~~Dear Maya, I'm your sister and~~

Nope. Way too familiar.

~~Hi Maya, my parents just told me about you and wow!~~

Grace wanted to punch herself in the face after reading that sentence.

~~Hey, Maya, what's up? I always wanted a sister and now I have one~~

Grace was going to have to hire a ghostwriter.

Finally, after almost thirty minutes of typing, deleting, and typing again, she came up with something that seemed reasonable.

Hi Maya,

My name is Grace and I recently found out that you and I have the same biological mom. My mom and dad told me about you today, and I have to admit that I'm kind of in shock, but excited, too. They said that you knew about me already, so I hope you're not too surprised to get this email. I also don't know if your parents told you about Joaquin. He might be our brother. It'd be nice if we could try and find him together?

My parents also said you live thirty minutes away, so maybe we could meet for coffee or something? If you'd like to get to know me, I'd like to get to know you. No pressure, though. I know this has the potential to be super weird.

Hope to hear from you soon,

Grace

She read it three times and then hit "send."

All she could do was wait.

MAYA

When Maya was a little girl, her favorite movie was the Disney version of *Alice in Wonderland*. She loved the idea of falling down a rabbit hole, of plummeting into something that she wasn't expecting, and of course, the idea that a small white rabbit could wear a tiny waistcoat and glasses.

But her absolute favorite scene was the part when Alice grew too big to fit inside the White Rabbit's house. Her legs and arms went out the windows, shattering the glass, and her head crashed through the roof, while people yelled and screamed all around her. Maya *loved* that part. She used to make her parents rewind it over and over again, laughing herself sick at the idea that a roof could go and resettle itself.

Now, when her parents would fight and the walls on her house felt too small and she wished she could smash the glass windows and escape, the idea of a house blowing apart didn't seem so funny.

Maya didn't really remember a time when her parents weren't fighting. When she and her sister, Lauren, were younger, it was done behind closed doors, muffled voices and tight smiles the next morning at breakfast. Over the years, though, the quiet words became raised. Then came the shouting, and finally screaming.

The screaming was the worst, shrill and high-pitched, the kind of noise that made you want to cover your ears and scream right back.

Or run and hide.

Maya and Lauren chose the latter. Maya was thirteen months older than Lauren, so she felt responsible. She would jump for the remote and turn up the TV volume until it was too hard to tell what was louder, who wanted to win the noise battle more. "Would you turn down that TV?" her dad had yelled more than once, and it felt so unfair. They had only turned it up because he was too loud in the first place.

Maya and Lauren were fifteen and fourteen now.

The fights were louder than ever.

The fights were all the time.

You're always working! You're always working and you don't—

For you! For the girls! For our family! Jesus Christ, you want everything and yet when I try to give it to you—

Maya was old enough to understand that a lot of those angry words had to do with the wine: a glass before dinner, two or three during dinner, and a fifth sloshed into the glass when Maya's dad was away on business. Maya never saw empty bottles lying in the recycling bin, and the pantry shelves always seemed to be stocked with unopened bottles, and she wondered who her mom was hiding the evidence from: her daughters, her husband, or herself.

Then again, she would have let her mother drink three *bottles* a night if it kept her calm, complacent. Even, Jesus Christ, *sleepy*.

But the wine only served to rev her parents up like cars before a race, gunning at each other until someone waved a flag and *vroom!* They were off. Maya and Lauren had learned to be out of the way by then, safely stashed away upstairs in their bedrooms, or at a friend's, or even just saying they were at a friend's and then hiding in the backyard until the coast was clear. It wasn't that their parents' fights got violent or anything like that; words could shatter harder than a glass breaking against a wall, hurt more than a fist plowing through teeth.

It was easy to follow their pattern. Maya was fairly certain she could even write out their dialogue for them. Once the yelling began, it was always about fifteen minutes until her mother accused her father of having an affair. Maya didn't know if it was true or not, and honestly, she didn't even really care that much. Let him, if it made him happy. Maya suspected that her mother would be thrilled if it were true. Like she'd finally win a race she'd been running for decades.

Would it kill you to be home before eight o'clock at night? Really? Would it?

Oh, well, remind me again who wanted to redo the kitchen? Do you think that just pays for itself?

A knock at her door made her look up. She half expected it to be Claire, even though she knew it wasn't possible. She had been dating Claire for five months, and her arms were a place safer and better than all the backyard hideouts in the world. Claire was security. Claire, Maya sometimes thought, felt like home.

It was Lauren at the door instead. "Hey," she said when Maya opened it. "Can I hang out with you for a bit?"

"Sure," Maya said.

At some point, and Maya wasn't sure when, their conversations had gone from riotous giggles to whispered secrets to short sentences, and then just one- or two-word responses. The thirteen-month difference between them had spread them apart like a gulf, growing only wider with each passing month.

Maya had always known she was adopted. In a family of redheads, that fact was pretty obvious. At night when Maya was little, in order to get her to sleep, her mom would tell the story of how they had brought her home from the hospital. She had heard it a thousand times, of course, but she always wanted it told again. Her mom was a good storyteller (she had been a radio DJ in college), and she'd always ham it up and do these big exaggerated gestures about how scared they were to put Maya in the car seat for the first time, and how Maya's parents had bought pretty much every single bottle of hand sanitizer that Costco had.

But Maya's favorite part was always the ending. "And then," her mom would say, pulling the covers up over her and smoothing the blankets down, "you came home with us. Where you belong."

At first, it hadn't seemed to matter that Maya was adopted and Lauren wasn't. They were sisters and that was that. But then other kids had explained it to her.

Other kids could be real assholes.

"They probably wouldn't have gotten you if Lauren had been born first," Maya's third-grade best friend, Emily Whitmore, had explained to her one day at lunch. "Lauren's *biological*"—she said the word like someone had just taught it to her—"and you're not. That's just facts." Maya could still remember Emily's face as she explained the "facts" to her, could still remember the sharp, cutting way she'd wanted to put her eight-year-old fist right through Emily's smug little mug. Emily had been super into *honesty* that year, which was probably why she didn't have many friends now that they were sophomores in high school. (Her face was still smug, though. And Maya still wanted to punch it.)

But Emily had been right about one thing: Three months after her parents brought Maya home from the hospital, their mother had discovered that she was pregnant with Lauren. They had tried for almost ten years to have at least one baby, and now they were blessed with two.

Well, *blessed* wasn't always the word that Maya would have used.

"Which one of you was adopted?" people would sometimes say to her and Lauren, and both girls would just blink at them. At first, they hadn't understood the joke, but Maya caught on a lot quicker than Lauren. She had to. She was the only one who stood out, the only one who wasn't pale with freckles and amber-colored red hair, the only dark brunette stain in every single family photo that lined the stairs.

When their parents were fighting, Maya sometimes imagined torching their entire house. She always thought she'd spray the most gasoline on those family portraits on the stairs.

By the time she was five, Maya got that she was different. When she'd been Star of the Week in kindergarten, all the kids had asked questions about why she was adopted, where her "real mommy" was, if she had been given away because she was bad. Not one of them asked anything about her pet turtle, Scooch, or her favorite blanket, which her great-grandma Nonie had knitted for her. She had cried afterward. She hadn't been able to explain why.

She loved her parents, though, with a desperation that sometimes scared her.

Sometimes she dreamed about the ones who'd given her away, and she woke up running from faceless brown-haired people, their arms reaching out for her, Maya sweating from the effort it took to escape. Her parents—minus the wine, the fighting, the suffocating *adultness* of kitchen renovations and mortgage payments—were good people. Very good people. And they loved her deeply and wholly. But Maya always noticed that the books they read about child rearing were about adopted kids, not biological ones. They spent so much time trying to normalize her life that Maya sometimes felt like she was anything but normal.

She cleared a space off her bed for Lauren. "What are you doing?"

"Math homework," Lauren said. Lauren was terrible at math, at least compared to Maya. They were only a year apart in school, but Maya was three years ahead in math classes. "What are you doing?"

Maya just waved in the general direction of her laptop. "Essay."

"Oh."

To be fair, Maya *was* working on an essay. It was just that she wasn't working on it right then. She had been working on it for a week and it had been due three days ago. She knew her teacher would give her a pass, though. Teachers loved Maya. She could wrap them around her fingers, and by the time she was done, she had extra-credit points without even having to do the work. And besides, it wasn't like the world was waiting with bated breath to read yet another essay about the importance of characterization in *Spoon River Anthology*.

Instead, she was chatting with Claire.

Claire had been a new student at their school last March. Maya could still remember her walking up the front lawn, backpack slung over one shoulder instead of both, like how everyone else on campus wore it.

Maya liked her immediately.

She liked that her nail polish was always, always chipped, but her hair never had a split end. She liked that Claire's socks never matched, but she had the best shoes. (Maya coveted her Doc

Martens and cursed the fact that her feet were two sizes bigger than Claire's.)

She loved the way Claire's hand felt in hers, how her skin could sometimes feel like the softest, most electric thing that Maya had ever touched. She loved Claire's laugh (it was deep and, quite frankly, sounded like a goose being murdered) and Claire's mouth and the way Claire would pat her hair like she was something sweet and precious.

Maya loved the way that she had spent her entire life trying to figure out where she fit, only to have Claire snap right into place next to her, like they had been waiting their whole lives to find each other.

Maya's parents, because they weren't antiquated dinosaurs, didn't care that she was gay. Or, more to the point, they weren't just fine with it. They were *proud*. Her dad even put a rainbow sticker on his car, which scandalized the neighborhood for a bit until Maya gently explained that a rainbow sticker on your car usually meant that *you* were gay, and maybe the neighbors were getting the wrong idea?

But still, it was a sweet gesture. They gave money to PFLAG and she and her dad ran a 10K together. Maya had all the support she needed in that particular arena, and she was grateful for it. She just wished sometimes that her parents would pay attention to their own relationship, rather than focusing on hers.

Another door slammed and Lauren jumped. Not too much, but enough for Maya to notice.

Do you even care *about seeing your daughters?*

How dare *you say something like that to me!*

You didn't even ask Maya about—

Both girls looked at each other. "Did you get anything from that girl yet?" Lauren asked after a beat.

Maya shook her head. "Nope."

The night before, Maya's parents had sat her down—the first time in months that she had seen them together at home when they weren't at each other's throats—and they had told her about a girl named Grace. She was Maya's half sister, who lived with her parents twenty minutes away. For the first time ever, it seemed, Grace had asked about her biological family. There was a boy, too, a supposed half brother named Joaquin, but no one seemed to know where he was anymore, like a set of keys someone had misplaced. "Is it okay if we give Grace your email address?" her father asked.

Maya had just shrugged. "Sure, okay."

It wasn't okay, not really, but she didn't entirely trust her parents to be strong for her anymore. They could barely keep it together around each other—what sort of energy did they have left over for her? She had no desire to cry in front of them, or ask questions, or give them even the smallest glimpse into her brain. She didn't trust them with her thoughts, not when they acted like two bulls in a china shop. She would have to keep herself at a remove—safe from that sort of damage.

Last night, she had woken up from a horrible nightmare: the tall, dark-haired people were reaching out for her, trying to pull her through the window of her bedroom, and she had woken up gasping, her hands shaking so bad that she couldn't even text Claire on her phone. She wasn't sure what had been scarier: the strangers trying to spirit her away or the fact that she wasn't sure she wanted them to fail.

She never fell back to sleep.

You know Maya. She won't tell you things, you have to ask her! She's not like Lauren! If you spent any *time with them—*

It wasn't like Maya was thrilled she was adopted, but in times like that, she was sort of glad that these people weren't biologically related to her. (*Sucks to be you, Laur,* she would sometimes think when the fights got too loud, too close.) It was easier to imagine a world of possibilities, a world where literally anyone could be related to her. But then, sometimes, that just made the world seem too big and Maya started to feel untethered, like she could float away, and she'd reach for Claire's hand and hang on tight, shocking herself back down to earth.

"Do you think they're going to get a divorce?" Lauren had asked her a few months ago, after their dad had stormed out of the house and their mom hadn't even come to check on them. The girls had slept in the same bed that night, something they hadn't done since they were little.

"Don't be stupid," Maya had said, but then the thought kept her awake all night. If her parents split up, who would they pick? Lauren was biological, just like Emily Whitmore had pointed out. Maya wasn't.

It was a ridiculous idea, obviously.

And yet.

That night, after everyone had drifted back upstairs, after Lauren had gone back to her room and shut the door behind her and Maya had texted with Claire way past when she was supposed to be off her phone (my parents are totally getting a divorce lol) and no one came to stop her, Maya lay awake in bed.

Everything seemed more terrible at three a.m. That was just a fact.

Her phone suddenly dinged, an email notification, and she opened it. She read somewhere that for every minute you spent on your phone in bed, you lost an hour of sleep. She had thought that was bullshit, but now it seemed possible.

Sister? the email header read.

It wasn't from Lauren.

Maya opened it up.

JOAQUIN

Joaquin always liked early mornings best.

He liked the pink sky that slowly turned yellow and then blue on clear mornings. When it wasn't clear, he liked the fog that folded into the city like a blanket, curling itself over the hills and freeways, so thick that sometimes Joaquin could touch it.

He liked the quiet of those mornings, how he could skateboard down the street without worrying about dodging slow tourists or toddlers making a sudden break from their parents. He liked being alone without anyone around him. The aloneness felt more like his choice that way. It was easier than feeling alone while surrounded by people, which was how he always seemed to feel once the rest of the world started to wake up, before reality settled in and the fog blanket was melted away by the sun.

Joaquin leaned his body to the left as he careered down the hill toward the arts center. The wheels on his board were new, a "just because" gift from his eighteenth set of foster parents.

Mark and Linda were good people, had been his fosters for almost two years, and Joaquin liked them. Linda had taught him how to drive on their ancient minivan, ignoring the small dent that Joaquin had put in the back passenger-side door; Mark had taken him to six baseball games last summer, where they sat next to each other and watched the games in silence, nodding in agreement whenever the ump made the right call. "Nice to see a dad and son at the game together," one older man had said to them at the end of one game, and when Mark had grinned and hooked his arm around Joaquin's shoulders, Joaquin had flushed so deeply that he felt almost feverish.

He knew some basics about his early life, but not too many things. He had gone into foster care when he was one, put there by his mother. He knew from seeing his birth certificate once that her name was Melissa Taylor, and that his father's last name was Gutierrez, but that had been about ten social workers ago, and Melissa's parental rights had long been severed. She had never shown up for any visitations when he was a baby. Sometimes Joaquin wondered if he had been the worst baby in the world if his own mother didn't even want to come to see him.

He didn't know anything about his bio dad, other than his last name and the fact that Joaquin only had to look in the mirror to know that his mysterious father hadn't been white. "You look Mexican," one foster brother had told him after Joaquin had to explain that he didn't know where he was from. No one had ever said anything to argue against it, so that was that. Joaquin was Mexican.

As far as foster parents and foster homes went, they had been good and bad. There had been the foster mom who once lost her temper and whacked Joaquin in the back of the head with a wooden hairbrush, making him feel like one of those cartoon characters who literally saw stars; the elderly couple who, for reasons that Joaquin never understood, would tape his left hand shut, forcing him to use his right (it didn't work, Joaquin was still a lefty); a foster dad who liked to squeeze Joaquin by the back of the neck, literally grinding his vertebrae together in a way that Joaquin could never fully forget; the parents who kept the fosters' food on a separate pantry shelf, the generic store brands lined up right below the brand-name cereals for the biological kids.

But then there had also been Juanita, the foster mom who stroked his hair and called him *cariño* when he had the stomach flu one winter; Evelyn, who organized water balloon fights in the backyard and used to sing Joaquin a song at night about three little chicks who curled up under their mother's wing and fell asleep; and Rick, the foster dad who once bought Joaquin an entire set of oil pastels because he thought that he was "pretty goddamn talented." (Six months later, after Rick had too much to drink and got into a fistfight with the next-door neighbor, Joaquin had been forced to leave that foster home and his pastels behind. He still wasn't quite over losing them.)

Mark and Linda were the latest foster parents, and they wanted to adopt Joaquin.

They had asked him last night, when he was sitting at the kitchen table putting his new wheels on his board. They sat down across from him, holding hands, and Joaquin knew immediately that they were asking him to leave. It had happened seventeen times before, so he knew the signs well. There would be excuses, apologies, maybe even tears (never Joaquin's), but it always ended the same way: Joaquin putting his few things in a trash bag and waiting for his social worker to pick him up and take him somewhere new. (Once, a social worker had brought him an actual suitcase, but that had gotten ruined at the next home when two of the other kids got into a fight. Joaquin preferred the trash bags. That way, he had nothing to lose.)

"Joaquin," Linda started to say, but Joaquin interrupted her. He liked Linda and he didn't want one of his last memories of her to be full of quivering excuses and weak reassurances.

"No, it's okay," he said. "I get it, it's okay. Just—is it because of the car door? Because I could fix it." Joaquin wasn't sure how he could do that—his job at the arts center wasn't exactly making him into a millionaire, and he had zero idea of how to fix a car dent himself, but hey, wasn't that what YouTube was for?

"Wait, what?" Linda said, and Mark scooted his chair closer to Joaquin's, which made Joaquin sit back a bit. "Don't worry about the car, sweetheart, that's not what we want to talk to you about."

Joaquin rarely felt off-kilter. He had gotten good at predicting what people would do, how they would react, and when he couldn't predict their behavior, he knew how to provoke it instead. The therapist Mark and Linda made him see had called it a defense mechanism, and Joaquin thought that sounded exactly like something that someone who never needed a defense mechanism would say.

But Linda wasn't saying the lines in the script that Joaquin had come to know by heart.

Mark leaned forward then, putting his hand on Joaquin's forearm and squeezing a little. That didn't bother Joaquin—he knew Mark would never hurt him, and even if he tried, Joaquin had three inches and about thirty pounds on him, so it would be a fast fight. Instead, he couldn't help but feel like Mark was trying to keep him steady. "Buddy," Mark said. "Your m— Linda and I wanted to talk to you about something important. If it's all right with you, and you're okay with it, we'd like to adopt you."

Linda's eyes were shiny as she nodded along with Mark's words. "We love you so much, Joaquin," she said. "You . . . you feel like our son; we can't imagine not making it permanent."

The buzzing in Joaquin's head almost made him dizzy, and when he looked down at the skateboard wheels in his hands, he realized that he couldn't feel them. He had only felt like this once before, when Mark and Linda had (casually, oh so very casually) told him that he could call them Mom and Dad if he wanted. "Only if you *want* to, of course," Linda had said, and even though she had been turned away from Joaquin at the time, he could still hear the tremble in her voice.

"Your call, buddy," Mark had added from the kitchen island, where he had been staring at his laptop. Joaquin noticed that he wasn't clicking through websites, though, just scrolling up and down on the same page.

"'Kay," Joaquin had said, and pretended to ignore their disappointed faces that night at dinner when he called her Linda, like nothing had happened that morning.

Joaquin had never called anyone Mom or Dad. It was either first names or, in some of the stricter homes, Mr. and Mrs. Somebody or Other. There were no grandparents, no aunts or uncles or cousins like other foster kids sometimes had.

And the truth was that he wanted to call Linda and Mark Mom and Dad. He wanted it so bad that he could feel the unspoken words sear his throat. It would be so easy to just say it, to make them happy, to finally be the kid with a mom and dad who kept him.

They weren't just words, though. Joaquin knew, in a way that he knew every true thing, that if he spoke those two words, they would reshape him. If those words ever left his mouth, he would need to be able to say them for the rest of his life, and he had learned the hard way that people could change, that they could say one thing and do another. He didn't *think* Mark and Linda would do that to him, but he didn't want to find out, either. He had once dared to call his second-grade teacher Mom one afternoon during their math lesson, just to feel how the word felt in his mouth, how it sounded in his ears, but the resulting embarrassment from the other kids had been so sharp and acute that it still burned hot when he thought about it all these years later.

But that had been just a mistake. To call Linda and Mark Mom and Dad on purpose would mean that Joaquin's heart would form into something much more fragile, something impossible to put back together if it broke, and he could not—would not—do that to himself again. He still hadn't managed to pick up all the pieces after last time, and one or two holes remained in his heart, letting the cold air in.

But now Mark and Linda wanted to adopt him, and Joaquin felt the skateboard wheels rumble under his feet as he took a hard right past the library. Mark and Linda would be his mom and dad whether he called them that or not. He knew they couldn't have children ("Barren as a brick!" Linda had once said in that super cheerful way that people do to hide their worst pain), and Joaquin wondered if he was their last chance to finally get what they wanted, if he was just a means to an end.

The library had a sign for a Mommy & Daddy & Me Story-time! on one of its windows as he sailed by.

Joaquin had long gotten over not having parents. He wasn't as dumb as he had been when he was little, when he'd tried to be charming and funny like those kids he saw on sitcoms, the ones with the stupid laugh tracks and the parents who just sighed when their children did something idiotic like drive a car through their kitchen wall. He changed foster homes so many times when he was five years old that he went to three different kindergartens, which meant he managed to dodge that brutal Star of the Week bullet, where kids talked about their homes and families and pets, all the things that Joaquin was already painfully aware that he lacked.

Once, in tenth grade, Joaquin had had to write an essay in his English class about where he would go if he could travel back in time. He wrote that he'd go back to see the dinosaurs, which was probably the biggest lie he'd ever told in his life. If Joaquin could go back in time, of course, he'd go find his twelve-year-old self and shake him until his teeth rattled and hiss, "*You are fucking everything up.*" That's when he had been *really* bad, when he would give in to the fury that bubbled up under his skin. He would writhe and scream and howl until the monster retreated, satiated for the time being, leaving Joaquin wrung out and exhausted, beyond comfort, beyond punishment. No one wanted a kid like that, Joaquin knew now, and they especially didn't want one who wet the bed nearly every night.

By the time Joaquin turned eight, he knew the game. His straight baby teeth had given way to buck teeth and gaps, his chubby cheeks had thinned into his approaching adolescence. He wasn't baby-cute anymore, and it was a hard-and-fast rule that prospective parents wanted babies.

He understood that there probably wouldn't be anyone at his parent-teacher conferences at school, listening as the teacher told them what a good artist he was. There was no one to take a picture of him standing under the blue ribbon that someone had pinned to his drawing at the school's art fair in fourth grade, or to drive him to that one birthday party across town in fifth. Some of his foster parents had tried, of course, but it wasn't like there was a ton of money or time to go around, and Joaquin had long ago figured out that if he didn't expect people to be there, then he wouldn't be disappointed when they didn't show up.

He still had that blue ribbon, though. He kept it buried at the back of his sock drawer, its edges frayed from the eighteen months that Joaquin had slept with it under his pillow.

He hadn't had that many strokes of good luck in his life, but Joaquin knew he had gotten lucky by not having any siblings. He had seen what that had done to other kids, how hard they fought to stay together and how destroyed they were when they were inevitably pulled apart. He had seen the older brothers try desperately to be adopted by families who only wanted younger sisters; he had seen older sisters wrenched away from younger brothers because there wasn't enough room for three kids in a foster home, and social services sometimes separated siblings by gender. It was hard enough for Joaquin to keep himself together, keep his heart and mind above water in a tide that wanted only to drown him. He could never have kept someone else afloat, too. He was *glad* he didn't have to, that he was untethered, even if he sometimes suspected that without that tether, he could just float away and no one would even know he was gone, that no one would ever look for him again.

Mark and Linda would probably look for him, Joaquin realized as the arts center came into view, as the sun broke through the clouds. But they would not adopt him, he had decided.

Joaquin had been adopted once before.

And he was never going to let it happen again.

GRACE

After Grace's parents had found out that she was pregnant, they had met with Max's parents. "It's a discussion," her dad had said. "We just want to discuss our options." But at fourteen weeks pregnant, Grace knew that there weren't a lot of options on the table to discuss.

Max's parents didn't want to discuss "options." They all met in her living room, the one that Grace and her parents hardly ever used because the TV wasn't in there; it was in the den. Nevertheless, there in the living room Max and Grace sat across from each other like they had when they'd first met in Model United Nations. To say that she and Max had united and become a single country was a joke that Grace kept thinking, but never said. She didn't think anyone's parents—or Max—would appreciate it. And it probably wasn't that funny in the first place.

Max's dad was so angry that he was shaking. Even on a

Saturday afternoon, he was wearing a collared shirt and a jacket, and he never took his hand off Max's shoulder, but not in a comforting way. More like in a "you will sit here under my command" way. Max hated his dad. He always called him an asshole behind his back.

"I don't know what your daughter has done to my son—"

"I don't think that blame is going—" Grace's mom started to say, and her hand was on Grace's shoulder now, too. It was warm, though, too warm, and Grace already felt crowded enough with Peach continuing to grow inside her. She shook her off. She didn't want anyone touching her, not even Max.

Especially not Max.

"Max has a future," his dad said, while his mom sat silent. "He's going to go to UCLA. This is not a part of his plan."

Grace's parents didn't say anything. She had plans to apply to Berkeley next year, but they weren't talking about going up for a campus tour anymore. (Also, Grace knew that Max had cheated on his AP French exam, but she didn't say anything about that, either.)

"Grace has a future, too," her dad said instead, speaking over Max's dad. They looked like two hockey players about to start brawling on the ice. "And she and Max are both responsible—"

"I don't know what she said to get my son in this situation, but if you think you're getting any of my money . . ." Max's dad trailed off. His nostrils were flaring. Max shared that same trait when he was angry. Sometimes Grace called him Puff the Magic Dragon, but only in her head, and only when she was really mad at him.

"It's about the baby," her mother interrupted. "And Grace and Max."

"There's no Max *and* Grace," Max's dad said. His mom didn't say anything. It was creepy. Grace guessed that you really got to know a guy's family once you got pregnant with their son's baby. "Max is dating a good girl now."

A good girl. The words hung in the air as Grace looked to Max, but he was looking down at the floor. "Max?" she said.

He wouldn't look at her. Or at Peach.

Stephanie was the good girl, of course. Grace had no idea if she was a good person or not, but Max's dad obviously equated "good girl" with "person whose womb is currently unoccupied." So, if they were going by his definition, then yes, Stephanie was 99.99 percent a good person. Grace was 100 percent not.

And that, in a nutshell, is how Grace and her boyfriend broke up.

Max and Grace had dated for almost a year, which, if she thought about it, was about the same amount of time that it took Grace, later on, to grow Peach. But she couldn't think about it that way, not at all. She couldn't think about Peach without feeling a pain that sliced through her, splitting her open just like it did in the delivery room. Grace didn't think it could be worse than that night, her mother gripping her hand, nurses urging her to push, but it was.

Janie used to call Max Movie Guy because he was pretty

much the guy in the movies: football player, white straight teeth, friend to all . . . but a better friend to some. She didn't realize it at the time, but Grace liked him just because he liked her, and that wasn't a strong enough tree to hang on to when the storm came. She knew that now, of course, because both Max and Peach were gone and her hands were empty, scratched from clinging too tight to something that should never have been held in the first place.

"You're fidgeting," Grace's mom said.

"I'm not fidgeting, *you're* fidgeting," she replied.

"You're *both* fidgeting," her dad said. "Stop it."

"But you have lint on your—" her mom interrupted him, reaching for his shirt. He playfully batted her hand away.

"*Fidgeting*," he said.

The three of them were standing on a stone front porch, huddled together even though there was plenty of room to spread out. Grace probably could have done a cartwheel without taking out either one of her parents. That's how big the porch was.

And it wasn't just any front porch. It was Maya's front porch. Or, more accurately, Maya's family's front porch. A week after she and Grace had exchanged emails, Maya's parents had invited her family to dinner, and they had accepted because, well, how exactly does one turn down *that* invitation?

Maya and Grace had talked a few times, starting with Maya's response to Grace's first email: *Well, it's about time.* It had been short and to the point, which Grace was starting to realize was Maya's usual mode of response. And she didn't use emojis or smiley faces made of semicolons and parentheses, either. Grace was beginning to wonder if her sister was really a humorless robot, but she assumed that even robots knew how to send the winking emoji. Maybe Maya was just super serious about technology. Or maybe she was one of those people who collected typewriters and longed for a landline like they used thirty years ago.

Grace had a lot of questions for (and about) Maya, and she wasn't sure how to ask any of them.

When they pulled up to the house, Grace's dad whistled under his breath and her mom said, "Oh my God, I knew you should have worn a suit."

"Dad hates wearing suits" is what Grace would have said if she hadn't been busy staring at the house. It was a sort of stone mansion—only one turret short of being something out of a Disney movie.

And it was where Maya lived.

"I hate wearing suits," her dad said. The three of them were still sitting in the car. Grace's breath was fogging up the glass; that's how close she was to the window. It took them another few minutes to make it to the epic front porch, and when her mom rang the bell, the sound of chimes that came from inside the house played "Ode to Joy."

"Did we accidentally go to church instead?" Grace whispered.

"You okay?" her dad said, turning to her as the doorbell continued to sing out.

"Yeah, fine."

"You sure?"

"Ask me again in an hour," Grace whispered, just as the door was flung open and a smiling couple greeted them. They were both redheads. The man was wearing a suit.

Grace heard her mom swear very softly behind her.

"Well, you found the place!" the woman said. "Come in, come in!" She was A Lot, as Janie used to say. (And as she probably still said. Grace hadn't talked to Janie in . . . a long time.)

"It's so nice to meet you!" the woman said. "I'm Diane, this is Bob."

They were both smiling at Grace like they wanted to eat her.

Grace smiled back.

She followed her parents into the house, which shone and gleamed and had the vague air of a mausoleum, thanks to all the marble. There was a double spiral staircase that wound up to a second-floor landing, also marble, and along the staircase, Grace could see a large portrait wall covered in professionally framed pictures.

There was not a dust ball in sight.

"Your home is so lovely," said Grace's mother, who read *Architectural Digest* the way—well, Grace had never met anyone who consumed anything the way her mom read *Architectural Digest*. Anyway, Grace's mother was *dying*. Grace could see her mentally ripping out the carpet in their living room, adding a second wing, or quite possibly abandoning Grace's father and her to live in this house instead. "This is just magnificent."

Grace had never heard her mother use the word *magnificent* before.

Her dad took over. "Yes, thanks so much for having us over. Grace has really been looking forward to it."

Grace had, in a way, like the way she would look forward to a drop in a roller coaster. Only she wasn't sure how good the seat belts were on this ride, or when was the last time anyone had done a safety inspection of the track.

Luckily, her manners snapped into place, and she stepped forward and offered her hand to Diane. "Hi, I'm Grace," she said. "It's so nice to meet you."

Diane's eyes looked wet as she shook her hand. "Grace," she said, her voice cracking a little. "It is so, so lovely to meet you. I know Maya is looking forward to it, too. I think this'll be really good for her."

Good for her? Grace saw trouble just around the bend.

"She looks just like her," Bob said. "Isn't it uncanny, Di?"

Grace smiled again, not sure what to say. She had no idea if that was true or not. She and Maya still hadn't exchanged pictures yet, and she had been scared to look her up on social media.

Grace wasn't sure why.

Just then, a girl came around the corner, also a redhead. Grace took a deep breath without realizing it. *Did Maya have red hair? Was this her?* Bob had said she looked just like Maya, but this girl and Grace couldn't have looked more different.

"Oh, this is our daughter Lauren," Diane said, reaching an

arm out to the girl and hugging her close. "She's Maya's sister."

Lauren smiled and Grace smiled back. Lauren was so obviously biological that it was ridiculous. Grace wondered what that
was like, living in a house where the other three inhabitants looked
nothing like you, like you were in a forever game of One of These
Things Is Not Like the Other.

"I thought Maya was on her way down," Diane said, then took
a step toward the stairs, Lauren still in tow. "Maya! Grace and her
parents are here!"

After a beat or two, Maya appeared at the top of the stairs.
She was wearing cutoff denim shorts and a loose tank top, and her
hair was in one of those topknots that Grace had tried to create
many times but had never succeeded at because her hair wasn't
long enough. Maya looked like someone had dropped her into a
life with these three well-dressed, redheaded strangers.

And in a way, Grace realized, someone had.

"Hi," she said, waving a little. "I'm Grace."

"Hi," Maya said. Her voice was oddly flat, but maybe she was
playing it cool.

When she got down to the end of the stairs, they both stood
there looking at each other. Grace could hear the quiet sniffles
from all four of their parents behind them, watching their two
children meet for the first time. Maya looked like Grace, that
was for sure. Eye color, hair color, even the same weird, ski-slope
nose. She was a little bit shorter than Grace, but give or take a few
freckles, it was like looking in a mirror.

And Grace felt absolutely nothing.

"Hi," she said again. "Sorry, I don't know what to say." She giggled nervously, which she hated, but the whole thing was starting to feel so bizarre. They were in a house that looked like a princess's castle! She had a biological sister who was staring at her, and who looked just like her! The dad was wearing a *suit*!

Maya just looked at Grace, then turned to her dad. "Why are you wearing a suit?"

"Because we have company," he said, taking her by the shoulders and steering her toward the living room. Grace got the feeling that he was used to steering Maya away from things, like a distraction technique people used on toddlers. Redirection, that's what it was called. Grace had seen it once when she'd dared herself to pick up a parenting book, in a bookstore fifteen miles away, where no one would recognize her.

"Appetizers are this way!" Diane said, gesturing to Grace's parents as she kept an arm around Lauren's shoulders. Neither sister acknowledged the other, Grace noticed. As an only child, she had always studied how siblings interacted with one another. It was like watching one of those nature shows about weird animal species on TV that her dad always got obsessed with.

"After you," Grace's mom said, following them into the (also white, also flawless) living room. "C'mon," she said to Grace, and she walked between her and her dad.

Grace's dad leaned down to whisper in her ear as they walked. "You say the word," he murmured, "and I'll bring the car around.

We'll blow this fancy Popsicle stand."

Grace smiled and kind of swatted at him before her mom heard.

Dinner was excruciating.

The food was fine, of course; it wasn't like they served sweetbreads or anything. (Grace had tried sweetbreads exactly once, before she realized that the words *sweet* and *bread* were the two worst possible ones to describe that particular food.)

But they were basically seven strangers sitting in a dining room that was fancier than almost any restaurant Grace had ever set foot in, and two of them were related and had just met twenty minutes earlier. To make it even worse, the room had high ceilings, which seemed to make the silence echo around them, forks scraping against plates and sounding like someone yanking the needle off a record player over and over again.

"Well, we're just so glad that the two of you could meet," Diane said, her voice a bit louder than necessary.

Grace's mom took the ball and ran with it, as moms often do.

"Oh, same here!" she said, smiling at both Maya and Grace. "You both look so alike, too. I know Grace has always wanted a sister."

Grace looked at her mom, raising her eyebrow a little. *Since when?* But then she caught Maya glancing at her and quickly reset her face.

"If you'd like a sister, may I offer a suggestion?" Maya said, then gestured toward Lauren. "We'll even throw in a set of free steak knives, but you have to act now. Operators are standing by."

Lauren glared at Maya, and even though both Bob and Diane laughed, Grace could tell that they sort of wanted to murder Maya with their eyes. She laughed anyway, though. She couldn't help it. Now she knew why Maya never wrote emails or texts like a normal human being: her humor was too dark.

"Maya and Lauren are either best friends or worst enemies," Diane said, picking up her wineglass and then setting it down while Maya took a bite of chicken. "We actually found out that I was pregnant with Lauren three months after we brought Maya home. I mean, we tried for almost ten years to have a child, and then that? Two miracles in three months! We couldn't believe our good luck."

Grace saw her dad glance between Maya and Lauren, and she wondered if he was thinking what Grace was thinking: that those two were one dessert course away from a full-fledged cage match. Diane was either delusional or, more likely, trying to keep her children from ruining dinner.

"So what's it like being an only child, Grace?" Lauren asked her. "Is it amazing? It sounds *amazing*."

Maya's mom cleared her throat and took a long swallow of wine.

"Um." Grace looked at her plate for a second, then back at Lauren. "It's . . . quiet?"

Every adult at the table laughed, and Grace smiled.

"It's okay, I guess. I don't know, it's fine."

Maya looked at her but spoke to her parents. "Can Grace and I be excused?" she asked. "We have, like, fifteen years of bonding to catch up on."

"Sure, I suppose so," her mom said. "Take your food with you, though? You don't eat enough."

"You know that's a line straight out of the *How to Give Your Daughter an Eating Disorder* manual, right?" Maya said, but she was already pushing back her chair, grabbing her plate, and motioning to Grace to follow her.

Grace glanced at her mom, the roller-coaster train climbing farther up the track. "It's fine, go ahead," her mom said, and she left her plate and scampered up the stairs behind Maya, slipping a little on the marble.

The portrait wall Grace had seen when they'd first entered the house was more striking up close, and she found herself walking more slowly as she looked at the photos. They were candids and professional portraits from over the years, from Maya and Lauren as babies up until what looked like the most recent shot, taken last Christmas. Maya stood out in every single photo, the one brunette in a family of redheads, her smile getting less and less full over the years.

The minute they were in Maya's room, Maya shut the door and let out a huge sigh. "Oh my God, I'm so sorry, that was brutal," she said, untwisting her hair out of the bun. Grace realized that it was way longer than her hair, and she wondered if maybe she should grow hers back out, too.

"Oh, it's—yeah, it's cool." Grace looked around the room, at the blue ribbons won for . . . something sporty, probably. "Your parents seem nice."

Maya shot her a look in the mirror. "You know those ribbons are just participation awards, right?"

"Oh," Grace said.

Maya pulled her hair over her shoulder, then tossed it back again. "I told my parents, like, a *million* times, don't do a fancy dinner, let's just get pizza or something, don't make it weird. And what do they do? They make it weird."

"It's not *that* weird."

"My dad is wearing a suit, Grace."

"Okay, that's a little weird," she admitted.

Maya's room, as opposed to the rest of the house, looked like there had been an explosion at a color factory. One wall was dark blue, another pale yellow, and then two white ones. Posters were up all over the walls, mostly of bands, plus dozens of Polaroids that had been stuck to the wall with bright blue tape. "Did you take these?" Grace asked, leaning in to look at one of Maya with her arms around a girl, kissing her on the cheek as the girl smiled with her eyes closed.

Maya glanced over at her. "Yeah," she said. "That's my girl-friend, Claire."

"She's cute," Grace said. "She looks like Tinkerbell."

Maya paused. "You know I mean *girlfriend*, right? Not, like, girl, period. Friend, period."

Grace nodded. "No, I got it." She suspected this was a test for Maya to see whether or not her newly discovered biological relative was a homophobic nightmare. "Girlfriend. One word. How long have you dated?"

"Almost six months," Maya said, and for the first time, she looked almost relaxed, not like a lab rat in a cage, waiting to see what would happen next. "She's amazing. We met at Catholic school."

"You're Catholic?"

"Nope." Maya flopped down on the bed and pressed her thumb against Claire's face in the photo, scrunching up her nose. "It's just the best private school around, so my parents sent Lauren and me there anyway. We're basically sinning our way through religious school. It's great."

Grace sat down on the edge of the bed, still looking at Maya's Polaroids. There were overexposed shots of roses, hands pressed together in prayer, more selfies of Maya and Claire together. "So do you and Lauren, like, hate each other?"

"You mean the Redheaded Golden Child?"

Grace guessed she had her answer.

Maya rolled over so that she was looking at Grace upside down. "So, no siblings for you, huh?"

"Nope," Grace said. Maya's duvet was soft against her leg, the worn material reminding Grace of all the days and nights she had spent in her own bed after Peach, huddled up in her own sheets and blankets like they could protect her.

"Why do you look sad?" Maya cocked her head at her. From

that angle, she sort of looked like a parakeet.

"Um, just because . . . it *was* sort of a bummer growing up an only child," Grace said, covering.

Maya groaned and flopped down on the other side of the bed. "Do you want *my* sister?" she asked. "A two-for-one deal?"

"That's the second time you've offered her. Is she that terrible?" Grace asked. For all the photos on the bedroom wall, she realized that there wasn't a single shot of Maya's family.

"She's not terrible, just annoying," Maya said. "You know that smart kid that's in your class and always knows the answers and the teacher leaves her in charge whenever she has to step out of the classroom for a minute?" Maya arched her back so she could look at Grace upside down again. "That's Lauren."

"That sounds fun to live with," Grace said.

Maya smiled. "So we both inherited the sarcasm gene. Good." Then she sighed and sat back up. "My parents don't really get it when I'm sarcastic. It complicates things."

"Um, speaking of inheriting," Grace said, and Maya looked over at her, suddenly still as a deer. "I mean, not money or anything, but I'm trying to find our biological mom."

Maya let out a huge sigh and slumped back down on the bed. "Ugh. Have fun."

"You don't want to?"

Maya rolled back over so they were face-to-face. She had a lot of energy, and Grace suddenly wondered if Maya was nervous. "Look," she said, "I know we're in the same boat here, so you do you or whatever, but she gave us away. She gave us *up*. Like, fly, little chickadees. Why would I want to find a woman who didn't want me in the first place?"

"You don't know that, though!" Grace said, louder than she meant to. The room felt very warm all of a sudden. "What if she was young, or scared? What if her parents *made* her give us away?"

"Well, then, how come she hasn't come looking for us?" Maya asked, in a way that Grace knew meant she wasn't waiting for a response. "Point, me."

"Maybe she doesn't want to upset us or—"

"Grace, look, if you want to find her, go for it. But I'm out. I just want to graduate, go to New York with Claire, and move away from here and finally start my life. I'm not interested in going backward, okay?"

Grace knew right then that Maya was angry—at their bio mother. And that as a result, she could never tell Maya about Peach.

"But it's cool if we hang out," Maya added, and Grace wondered what her face looked like if Maya felt the need to add that part. "You seem nice, your parents seem fine, and you know, if I ever need a kidney or a blood transfusion, it wouldn't hurt to have you in my contacts." She smiled a little. "And vice versa, of course, although I faint around needles."

Grace nodded. What was she going to do, force this new person to go on a wild-goose chase with her? "Okay," she said. "If that's how you feel."

"Really?" Maya picked up her pillow and hugged it to her. "God, that was easy. Lauren would just whine and whine until I finally said yes."

"Well, that's a sister thing. Give me some time—I'm sure I can work on it."

"I would maybe be interested in finding our brother, though," Maya said.

Grace nodded. She hadn't told anyone—and she had no plans to, either—but she kept having nightmares that Peach's new parents gave her away, that she was suddenly gone all over again, lost in the system that had ensnared Joaquin. But instead of saying any of this, she dug her phone out of her pocket. "I talked to his social worker last week. My parents helped me track down her info, and she said that we could email him."

"She did?" Maya set her pillow down, leaning forward. "Why does he have a social worker?"

"Because he was, um . . ." Grace squirmed a little, the duvet no longer as comfortable. "Because he wasn't adopted. Like, ever? He's been living with this family about an hour away from here, but he's been in a lot of different homes since before then."

Maya's eyes grew wide, and Grace finally saw the little-sister potential in her. She could imagine Maya toddling after her, annoying her, pulling her hair and borrowing her clothes without asking first. She didn't tell Maya about all the people she'd talked to on the phone, trying to follow a seventeen-year-old trail of bread crumbs that had mostly blown to the wind and taken Joaquin with them. She didn't mention that some people had been rude, others had been so helpful that it made Grace's heart hurt, that Joaquin's family tree seemed to have way too many scraggly branches and not enough roots, not the kind of roots you would need when the storm was strong.

"We should totally email him!" Maya said, then threw her pillow at Grace in excitement. "But you do it. You write really good 'Hello! I think we might be related!' emails."

"I took it as an elective freshman year," Grace said, then smiled when Maya laughed at her joke.

So that's how Grace ended up drafting yet *another* email to a sibling she had never met.

> Hi Joaquin,
> You don't know me, but I think we share some family. I know your social worker mentioned that we might email you. A girl named Maya and I recently found out that we're biological sisters. We were both adopted and met each other for the first time and, after doing some research, realized that you might be our brother.
> Would you be interested in meeting up with us? We live about an hour away so we could meet you anywhere.
> Best wishes,
> Grace & Maya

"Best wishes?" Maya said when she saw the email. "Seriously?"

"It's warm without being personal," Grace explained, shrugging her shoulders.

"Warm without being personal?" Maya repeated. "Wow, okay."

"So what's it like being in a family of redheads?" Grace asked, trying to change the subject.

Maya huffed out a laugh. "Did you see the Sears Portrait Studio out there?" she asked, then sang, "One of these things is not like the other . . ."

"Are your parents cool with you being gay?" Grace suddenly felt oddly protective of her, like she had with Peach.

"Are you kidding? This is basically their claim to fame. They pretty much joined PFLAG before I even finished telling them that I was a lesbian. My dad—get this—he wanted to go to a gay pride parade with me."

Grace couldn't help but giggle, oddly relieved that Maya wasn't in some awful, oppressive home. "Well, that's good, right?" she said. "That they're supportive?"

"No, it's totally good. It's just like . . ." For the first time since they had been upstairs, Maya seemed at a loss for words. "It's good," she finally said, and Grace decided not to push it anymore.

They exchanged phone numbers and listened to music (Maya's) and talked about Claire. It was a good thing Grace didn't want to tell Maya about Peach or Max, because she could barely get a word in edgewise. And by the time she and her parents were driving off in their car, she savored the relative silence of their Toyota Camry (squeaky brakes excepted).

"So!" her dad said after a minute, clapping his hands together. "Highs and lows!"

Grace groaned. Her parents used to do Highs and Lows at night after work and school, where they'd each have to talk about the high and low points of their day. That had pretty much stopped after Grace had announced she was pregnant. (Low.) "Dad, please . . ."

"I'll start!" he said. "My high was seeing you meet Maya, Grace. That was . . . well, it just meant a lot to me, as your dad."

"Dad, please, I can't cry anymore this month. I'm tapped out."

"Okay, okay, fine. But my low was realizing that I might have to wear a three-piece suit every single time we get together with their family." He sighed. "I felt like a farmer at the table."

Grace clapped him on the shoulder from the backseat. "You took one for the team, big guy."

He patted her hand in response.

"Okay, my turn, my turn," her mom said from the driver's seat. "My high was listening to you talk to Maya upstairs and hearing you laugh. It's been a long time since we've heard you laugh, Gracie."

"Maybe you're just not as funny as you used to be," Grace said, but she knew her mom would know she was joking. She was pretty hard to offend.

"And my low was knocking my chicken off my plate with my knife. I wanted to die." Grace's dad started to laugh. "I seriously did, Steve! That entire house looked like a mausoleum—"

"That's what I thought, too!" Grace cried.

"—and who's the first person to get gravy on the tablecloth? Me." Her mom groaned. "Diane was very gracious about it, though."

"Where's *our* tablecloth?" Grace asked. "Do we even have one?"

"Not since your dad accidentally set it on fire last Thanksgiving."

"Oh, yeah." The highs and lows on that particular holiday had been intense. And smoky.

"Okay, your turn," her mom said, glancing at Grace in the rearview mirror.

"Well, I guess the high was meeting Maya. And she's normal. I mean, at least she's not homicidal or anything."

"And the low?" her dad asked after a minute.

"Well, she's kind of annoying," Grace said. She hadn't even known it was true until she said it. "She kept interrupting me, she only talked about herself, and she was sort of rude, too, honestly."

"Honey?" Grace's mom said.

"Yeah."

"Welcome to having a sister."

MAYA

It took Joaquin almost a week to respond to the email.

Maya was not amused.

She finally got his response while she was at home. She was always at home these days, since she had gotten grounded for sneaking out to see Claire one night when her dad was out of town on business and she had thought her mom was asleep. And by *asleep*, she meant *passed out*, but it didn't really matter because her mom hadn't been asleep *or* passed out when Maya had snuck back in downstairs at two in the morning. They had just looked at each other before Maya's mom pointed at her and said, "Grounded. One week," and then went upstairs. Maya suspected that if she had been dating a boy, there would have been a much bigger scene involving yelling and threats and being found dead in a ravine somewhere and teenage pregnancy statistics. Like Maya would have ever been stupid enough to get pregnant, anyway.

She guessed that dating a girl was a lot less threatening to her parents.

Lucky her.

Maya opened Joaquin's email.

Hey Grace and Maya,
Sure, that sounds cool. Let's meet up next weekend? I'm working that day at the arts center, but I'm free after 1 p.m. Cool to meet up with you and talk.

"That's it?" Maya said as soon as she got Grace on the phone. She was using her parents' landline. Part of her punishment was the surrender of her phone. She felt like someone in an eighties movie. It was humiliating. "'*Cool* to meet up with you'? What does he think this is, a date?"

"God, I hope not," Grace said. She sounded like she was doing something in the background, which bugged Maya. She had only met Grace once, and Joaquin never, and already her siblings were annoying her. Typical.

"We've got even bigger problems if he thinks it's a date," Grace added. "Hey, why are you calling me instead of texting?"

"What, I can't call you and talk, voice to voice? Have a human connection?"

"Nice try. Are you grounded?"

"Yep. My parents took my phone. I can only use the computer for school." Maya sighed heavily as her mom walked past the kitchen, then one more time for good measure. "My *jailers* let me use the landline for five minutes. The fucking *landline*. Like I'm on the Oregon Trail or something. I told them I had a question about homework."

"So how did you get the email from—you know what, never mind. I don't want to know. So do you want to meet him?"

"Hell yeah, I want to meet him." Maya wrapped the phone cord around her finger. It was oddly soothing, being able to do that. The tip of her finger started to turn red, and she loosened the cord, then did it all over again. "You have to drive, though," she told Grace. "Shotgun."

"There's not even going to be anyone else in the car. Why do you have to call—"

Maya felt bad for Grace sometimes. Imagine being raised without a sibling and not understanding the importance of yelling "Shotgun!" at every single opportunity. Grace was really missing out. Maya wondered how she played Slug Bug on car trips.

Maya's mother came back through the kitchen this time, and Maya immediately put on her most innocent face. (She had practiced it in the mirror. It was sort of necessary when she snuck out as much as she did.)

"Oh, is *that* the quadratic equation?" Maya's voice suddenly changed into a sweet and dopey imitation of herself. "Oh, that makes sense. Okay."

There was a pause on the other end of the line. "Are you having a mathematically based stroke?"

Sweet, innocent, naïve Grace. Maya was definitely going to have to toughen her up.

Maya's mother widened her eyes at her, then pointed at her watch. "One minute," she mouthed.

"I know, I know," Maya said, and her mom gave her a warning glance before she left the room.

"Do I even want to know *why* you're grounded?"

Maya could hear Grace tapping on a keyboard in the background. How dare she? "I snuck out last week to practice devil worship with these kids I met in a cornfield." Maya wrapped the phone cord around her whole fist this time. "They're not the best conversationalists, but they're pretty nice once you get past all the ritual sacrifice."

Grace laughed this time, which made Maya feel pleased. Her family was so used to her weird brand of humor that they had stopped acknowledging it a long time ago. Hearing Grace laugh made Maya feel like a comedian who had finally found her perfect audience.

"Okay, I'm going now," Grace said. "I'll pick you up at noon on Saturday. Don't be late. Good luck with the ritual sacrifice."

It warmed Maya to hear Grace tell her not to be late. She felt like she had spent her entire life watching out for Lauren, herding her from place to place, telling her to hurry up. It was nice to have another person take the reins, even if that person was still basically a complete stranger.

"I'll put in a good word for you with the cornfield kids," Maya said, then hung up before Grace could respond.

* * *

Maya didn't tell her parents much about going to meet Joaquin, mostly because she didn't want to answer questions about it. Her parents were super into discussing *everything*. It made Maya feel anxious, the way she was supposed to put her emotions into words, like it was an easy thing to do. Lauren was good at it, being able to say whatever was on her mind so that other people could understand, but for Maya, it was like describing colors: the sunset pinks and reds of first love, the stormy blues that clouded her brain when she was hurt or angry.

Claire had always seemed to see the palette of her brain, had been able to sort the colors through a prism so she could understand how Maya felt without Maya having to say a word. The night she had gotten caught sneaking out, she had met up with Claire in the park, smoking a joint that Claire had stolen from her older brother, Caleb. (They also had two younger siblings, Cassandra and Christian. Their parents were Cara and Craig, but Craig had taken off five years ago, so he didn't count. It was the first time that alliteration had made Maya feel like barfing.)

They had smoked in silence for a while, which was one of Maya's favorite things.

Afterward, they had lain down in the damp grass, Maya's head pillowed on Claire's stomach. "I think the stars are moving," she told Claire. Her own voice sounded syrupy to her, like she could pour it out.

"We're moving, not the stars," Claire pointed out. Her hand was soft against Maya's hair. "That's how the world works."

"Do you think Joaquin even wants to meet me and Grace?"

"I don't know," Claire said. "He's the only one who can answer that."

"I wouldn't want to meet me," Maya said. "I'd hate me if I were him."

"Good thing you're not him, then," Claire said, then bent down to kiss Maya, making yellow sparks shine behind her eyes.

Maya's parents always wanted to talk about her adoption, especially when she had been younger. Maya suspected that they were doing a lot of preventative work to make sure that they hadn't monumentally screwed her up. That if one day she suddenly went berserk and slaughtered a roomful of people, they could hold up their hands and say, "We tried, really we did." She had been to therapists, group sessions with other adopted kids, guided one-on-one discussions with her parents when Lauren was at friends' houses. "Do you think about your birth mother?" they asked her, and Maya said, "Yes?" because she thought that was the correct answer. But the truth was far deeper. The truth was every single color in a rainbow spectrum, and Maya didn't have the words to say what she felt.

So she didn't say anything. It was just easier that way.

Grace picked Maya up just before noon on Saturday. The plan had been to meet at eleven thirty, but Maya had overslept, and when she eventually came downstairs, she felt like a cranky tornado, a swirl of grays. (She was pretty sure there was a *Fifty Shades* joke in there, but she was too tired to make it.) "Starbucks," she said to

Grace, her Ray-Bans already over her eyes even though they were still inside.

"Okay," Grace said. Maya was pretty sure she agreed only because she was too scared of Maya's uncaffeinated state to argue.

"So do you have a boyfriend?" Maya asked once they were in the car, a giant Frappuccino clutched in her hand.

"Nope," Grace said in a sort of clipped way. There was something there pressing against the surface of her words, but Maya couldn't tell what it was.

"Girlfriend, then?" she asked. "Did you inherit the same gene as your little sister?"

Grace smiled this time. "Nope. That's all you."

"Well, have you, though?"

"What?"

"Had a boyfriend. Or girlfriend."

"Yes. And no."

Maya wondered if Grace was lying. Grace seemed like the kind of girl who would wait her whole life so she could lose her virginity on her wedding night, who would read *Cosmo* articles about *how to give him the best blow job of his life!* but never actually say the word *blow job*. Which was *fine*—Maya wasn't about to start telling someone what they should do with their body or whatever—but being next to someone that perfect made Maya just want to be messier, dirtier, louder.

For God's sakes, Maya thought, her posture was perfect even while she was *driving*.

"But you don't want to talk about this boyfriend?" Maya asked.

"Who said I don't want to talk about him?"

"Well, you're answering me like it's a deposition."

'Well, you're quizzing me like a lawyer."

"Touchy, touchy," she muttered, pushing her sunglasses up her nose. "Bad breakup?"

"You could say that." Grace laughed again. "You could definitely say that."

Maya nodded in agreement. "Yeah, I had a bad breakup, too, before I met Claire. There was this girl, Julia? Ugh, she was the worst. I don't know what I saw in her."

"Hmm," Grace said, which is what Maya's mom usually said to her dad whenever he was talking about something that didn't interest her.

"I mean, I know what I saw in her," Maya continued, rolling down her window. "It's just that I saw the wrong things, you know?"

Grace glanced at her. "She was hot?"

"She was hot," Maya confirmed. "Hey, speaking of. Can you put the AC on? You drive like my mom."

"Pretty sure that's not a compliment," Grace said.

"You would be right."

Grace sighed and reached over to turn on the air. "Any other requests?"

"Can we change the radio station?" Maya started pressing buttons on the dashboard. "I don't know if you noticed, but I'm not fifty-five years old. I don't exactly want to listen to NPR, Grandma."

Maya had no idea why she couldn't stop talking. She liked Grace. Grace was *fine*. She had done nothing but drive Maya to meet their brother and buy her Starbucks on the way. But Maya had done the same thing when she and Grace first met at Maya's house, her words coming out rapid fire, talking and talking, making fun of Lauren and her parents, never letting Grace get a word in edgewise. *Please like me* was what she had wanted to say. *Please be my friend.*

Maya didn't have a lot of friends. There were girls she knew at school, but they mostly just said hello in the hallways, sometimes talked before class began and the teacher hadn't yet arrived. Her old school had been kindergarten through eighth grade, and that was back when she and Lauren were inseparable, even dressing alike when they were really young. She hadn't needed many friends because she had Lauren.

That had changed on the first day of ninth grade, when they were suddenly in two different schools and Maya found herself the odd girl out, surrounded by girls who had been learning together since preschool.

And having a mom who drank made it hard to bring anyone home after school, or to invite them over for pool parties or slumber parties. Maya hadn't brought a friend over in years. Claire was the exception, but even *she* was rarely there.

Maya had eaten a lot of lunches alone those first few months.

The sound of other girls giggling would make the hair stand up on the back of her neck. *Are they making fun of me?* she would wonder.

It turned out she wasn't the only gay kid at school, and she was never harassed or teased—but she found she didn't know how to be affectionate with friends. Would they think she was hitting on them if she just hugged them hello? Would she make it weird just by being herself? It hadn't mattered with Lauren, but at her new school, Maya found herself holding back, using sarcasm as affection until it became habit, until it became who she *was*.

"Are you *always* like this?" Grace said, interrupting her thoughts. "Seriously, *are* you? Because I swear I'm going to pull over and put you in the trunk if that's the case."

Maya just sipped at her drink. If Grace thought she was the first person who had threatened to put her in the trunk for being a brat on a car trip, she had another think coming. "Am I like what?"

"Annoying," Grace said.

Maya shrugged, turning her face toward the passenger window. "Yes."

"Maybe you should cut back on the caffeine."

"You're just not used to having a sister," Maya told her, then sat back in her seat and put her feet up on the dashboard. Grace swatted them down.

"Did you hear yourself?" she said. "You just called me your sister."

Maya pretended to sigh happily. "Next thing you know, we'll be going to Sephora and talking about boys—well, *you* will, at least—and sharing clothes. It'll be like a movie." She sipped at her drink again. It was getting to the perfect stage of meltiness, where the sugar and caffeine came together in a glorious adrenaline spiral. Another five minutes and Maya could probably launch herself to the moon.

"Are you serious?" Grace said.

"About the clothes sharing? No, I was just exaggerating." Her eyes moved from Grace's shoes (flip-flops from Target; Maya had the same pair, but in blue) to her jeans (way too big, what the hell?) to her sweater (the beigest color of beige that Maya had ever seen). "But if you ever want to go clothes shopping, I can help you. I helped Lauren. Changed her life."

"You need to stop talking."

"I'm just saying—"

"In. The. Trunk."

Maya held up her hands. "Okay, okay. I'll just sit here. Quietly. Not talking. At all. Maybe I'll even *learn* something from NPR. Oh, wait—"

"Five minutes!" Grace cried. "That's all I ask!"

"But—"

"Maya, I swear to God—"

Maya pointed out the window. "That's our exit."

"What? Oh, shit!" Grace immediately pulled the car across four lanes of traffic, swerving past two cars and exactly zero cops. Maya just grabbed onto the handle over the passenger door, hanging on as they zoomed onto the off-ramp, but when she saw herself in the side mirror, she had a wild grin on her face.

"That's more like it!" she cried. "Those were some straight-up *Fast and Furious* moves!"

Grace looked at her.

"Shutting up now," she said, then pretended to lock her lips and throw away the key.

The beach was crowded for a Saturday, and their pace slowed to a crawl as they got closer to the arts center. "Ugh, traffic," Maya said, but Grace shot her a look and she immediately went quiet again. No one had ever *really* locked her in the trunk before, and she didn't quite know Grace's limits well enough to push them yet. Silence was definitely golden.

It was almost one p.m. by the time they parked, and Maya groaned as they crawled out of the car. "It wasn't even an hour and a half," Grace said, squinting into the sun. Maya had no idea why she didn't just get some sunglasses.

"Whatever, I'm young, I'm still growing. I *hope*." Maya was sort of sensitive about being short. (Well, short*er*.) She looked around. "Yep. Lots of art."

"So the fact that it's called an arts center isn't just a clever disguise."

"Hey, sarcasm is *my* job," Maya said, tossing her bag over her shoulder as Grace slammed her door shut and checked to make sure that the car was locked.

"What sarcasm? I'm just—" Grace started to say.

Maya lowered her sunglasses long enough to look at her.

Grace sighed. "I'm just stressed."

"I kind of figured that out when you threatened to lock me in the trunk," Maya scoffed.

"It's . . ." Grace took a deep breath and shook out her arms. "You're seriously not even a little nervous to meet him?"

Maya shrugged, tossing her empty Starbucks cup into a recycling bin. She wasn't sure what she felt, but it was bright orange, like a warning, like a question. "Not really. The way I see it, if he's a big weirdo or a psycho killer or something, then we can just be like, 'Oops, sorry, the lab screwed up the DNA results, *later gator*,' and then we just block his calls and emails. Oh, look, they made a whale out of gum wrappers! That's pretty cool."

Grace followed Maya's gaze to see that yes, someone *had* in fact made a whale out of gum wrappers. "So you're ready to just bounce on our biological brother. Were you going to do the same thing with me?"

"Well, yeah, but only if you were a weirdo who drove alternately like a grandma and a *Fast and Furious* extra *and* listened to NPR." Grace's face stayed the same and Maya wondered if Grace's interest in her sense of humor had been a one-time thing. "Just kidding!" she finally said. "C'mon, let the family bonding begin!"

They paid the admission fee ("Do you have a friends and family discount?" Maya asked the woman at the box office), then made their way into the center. It was hot and crowded, and it took a few minutes to find the information booth. "Hi," Maya said, sidling up to the window and pushing her sunglasses up on her head. "Do you happen to know Joaquin?"

"Oh, yeah," the guy said. "He's over at the pottery tent."

"Pottery. Ooh, so *real*," Maya said, then looked at Grace. "He must take after me."

Grace moved so that she could block Maya out of the information window entirely. "And where's the pottery tent?"

He pointed over Grace's head toward the center of the festival. "Just follow the line of kids," he said. "You can't miss it."

"Thanks," Maya said. "You've been a pal."

"Hey, wait! Are you his sisters?"

Maya shoved her way back into the window. "Maybe," she said. "What have you heard?"

The man smiled. "Just that he said that he had two sisters coming to see him today."

Maya stuck her hand through the window. "Hi! I'm Maya. This is Grace."

"Hi," Grace said, but only after Maya nudged her in the side.

"Gus," the man said. "Lucky ladies, having Joaquin for a brother. Yeah, he's working in the pottery booth."

"Would you say he has artistic ability?" Maya asked Gus. "On a scale of normal to Manson family, how would you rate his—"

"Thank you so much," Grace said, shoving Maya out of the window again. "We'll go find him now." She took Maya's arm and led her away a few feet before she shook her off. "You know, you might not want to share your concern that Joaquin's a psychopath with people we just met."

"Whatever, Gus seems cool. We could hang." Maya readjusted her sunglasses, then glanced around. "And you never know, maybe the whole point of meeting Joaquin is so we can become friends with Gus. You've got to look at the big picture, Grace. Now where's the pot throwing?"

They eventually found the tent, and Gus hadn't been wrong: there was a huge line of kids wrapped around it, all of them looking in to where there were two volunteers, each with a kid, carefully turning clay on a pottery wheel. One of the volunteers was older looking, like she could have been a grandma, and the other volunteer had dark hair that he had pulled back from his face in a short ponytail. Even though he was sitting down, Maya could tell he was tall.

When he looked up at Maya and Grace, both of them gasped a little.

It was Joaquin.

"He looks like *you*," they both said at the same time, and Maya supposed that neither of them was wrong.

The three of them stood looking at one another for a long minute, children and parents carrying clay pots weaving between them. Joaquin was definitely not white like his sisters, that much was obvious, but he had Maya's brown eyes and curly dark hair and Grace's tight, set jaw, and Maya felt something in her rib cage catch and pull tight, like a muscle that had never been used before. Her feeling was green, like grass, like a seed coming up through dirt, sprouting and growing toward the sun.

Maya smiled at him and he smiled back. They had the same crooked teeth in front, one front tooth slightly overlapping the other. Well, Joaquin still had his, but Maya's parents had put her through two years of braces in order to correct it. She regretted that now. She wanted to look like the people who shared her blood. She wanted people to stop them on the street and say, "You must be related." She wanted to belong to them, wanted them to belong to her the way that no one else in the world could.

Grace was sniffling next to her. "Seriously?" Maya whispered to her just as Joaquin made the international gesture for *Give me one minute and I'll be over*. "Do we really need the waterworks right now?"

"Shut up," Grace mumbled, wiping at her eyes. "I'm hormonal."

"Are our cycles already syncing?" Maya said, her eyes widening. "Because I'm totally going to start my period, like, *tomorrow*, and—"

"Hey," someone said. Maya looked over—and up, way *up*, her hopes of being tall in at least one family dashed—to see Joaquin standing next to them. "Hey, I'm Joaq." He pronounced it like *wok*.

Maya tried to hide the fact that her hand was shaking when he shook it. She wasn't used to touching boys, and she wondered if all of their hands felt this dry. Next to her, Grace was still wiping her eyes, and when Joaquin turned toward her, she reached out and hugged him around his waist. "Hi!" she said. "It's so good to meet you!"

Joaquin looked like an animal who had just realized that he was prey instead of predator, but he did a good job of hiding it. "Hey," he said, his hand awkwardly patting her shoulder. "Hey."

"Why didn't you cry when you met *me*?" Maya demanded, putting her hands on her hips and turning toward Joaquin again. "She didn't get teary even once. You should feel lucky."

"I do! I mean, totally. I do," he said, still patting Grace's shoulder. Finally, Maya yanked her away from him.

"You're freaking him out," she whispered. "Pull it together, seriously."

"Maybe we can go get something to eat?" Joaquin asked, gesturing toward the exit. "I'm done for the day, so I can get lunch or . . . ?" He left the question hanging in the air, like he wasn't sure if it was the right one to ask.

"No, yeah, that's perfect," Grace said. "Let's go."

And Maya watched as all three of their shadows turned at the same time, heading in one direction.

JOAQUIN

Joaquin knew even before he met his sisters that they would be white.

His social worker, Allison, had approached him and Mark and Linda about it several weeks ago. They sat at the kitchen island and ate chips and salsa while Allison carefully explained the situation—that Joaquin had not one but *two* sisters, that they all shared a mother, that the girls had been adopted at birth but had just found out about him and were looking to get in touch.

That's when Joaquin knew.

He wasn't naïve about the ways of the world. He knew that white baby girls were first-ranked on most people's list of Children We Would Like to Have One Day. He knew they were more expensive, too, that people paid almost $10,000 more in legal fees for babies who were white, so he knew that these girls' adoptive parents had some money. Well, good for them. Joaquin couldn't resent his sisters for that.

His *sisters*.

Holy shit.

Joaquin had sat very still and steady while Mark and Linda nodded and Allison kept talking. "Yeah, it's cool," he said when Allison asked if maybe Grace and Maya could email him, and then said he had homework and went upstairs and listened to music and worked with some charcoals on his new sketch pad and didn't do any homework at all and definitely did not think about the fact that there were at least two people in the world who were related to him, and that one of his biggest fears had come true not once, but twice.

Mark and Linda knew not to push him, so they didn't. And when Joaquin got the email, he read it three times before filing it away, then read it twice more and put it away again. He wasn't sure if he should reply. By lassoing himself to these girls, he might pull them down from the sky and out of their perfect elliptical orbit, throwing everything off-balance.

"Did you hear from Grace and Maya?" Linda asked one night while they were loading the dishwasher. Joaquin could tell that she and Mark had practiced this conversation, but it didn't bother him. He liked that they practiced things for him, that they wanted to get it right for him. It was a nice gesture. Sometimes he felt like someone's parent at a school recital whenever Mark and Linda did that, like he should be giving them a thumbs-up and whispering loudly, "Good effort!" the way he had seen other parents do for their kids.

"Yeah," Joaquin said, then turned on the garbage disposal.

When he couldn't run it anymore, he turned it off. Linda was still standing there.

"Did you write back?" she asked.

Joaquin just looked at her.

"Okay, fine, busted," she said, then playfully smacked his shoulder with a rubber glove. (She had done that the first week that he had lived with them and Joaquin had almost flown out of his skin.) "Mark and I were just wondering, that's all."

"They sound nice," Joaquin said, passing her some spoons. "Pretty girly."

"Well, sometimes girls are girly," Linda said. "Nothing wrong with that."

"You think they want to meet me?"

Linda paused. "I'm pretty sure that when someone emails you asking to meet them, that's a good sign."

Joaquin just shook his head. "No, I mean, like . . . meet *me*."

Linda paused again, but there was a gentleness between her words. "I think lots of people want to meet you, kiddo," she said, then put a warm, soapy hand on his shoulder. "You just don't know it yet."

So he wrote back.

He tried to keep it casual, like he had tons of practice emailing his biological siblings about getting together. He wondered if he'd managed to pull it off, but they wrote back the very next day (Grace seemed to be the spokesperson for their little group, so Joaquin guessed she was the older one) and said that they'd be happy to meet him on Saturday at the arts center.

Well, then. That was that.

Joaquin had a hard time sleeping the night before. He hadn't looked them up online, didn't want to know who they were until he actually met them, but that left his brain with too much space to fill, so it felt like he was floating instead of sleeping. At three a.m., he went downstairs to eat cereal because that's what Mark always did when he couldn't sleep, and that's where Mark found him fifteen minutes later.

"Any Golden Grahams left?" was all Mark said, and Joaquin passed him the box. "Can't sleep?"

"Nope." Joaquin shook his head, then pushed the milk toward Mark.

Mark, to his credit, managed to eat half the bowl before asking another question. "Nervous about meeting Grace and Maya?"

Two years ago, Joaquin would have answered "Nope" to that question, too, but it wasn't two years ago anymore. "What if they don't like me?" he asked before shoveling a huge spoonful of cereal into his mouth.

Mark just nodded thoughtfully. "Well, if they don't like you, then the unfortunate fact is that you're related to idiots. I'm sorry. A lot of us are, though. You're in good company."

Joaquin tried to hide his smile by eating again, but Mark caught him. "Seriously," he said. "Meeting people for the first time is hard. But they're your . . . well, you're related to them. You all deserve to get to know one another. At least meet them first and then decide who likes who."

Joaquin wrinkled his nose.

"Not like that, you perv." Mark reached for the cereal box again, then looked at him. "Did you already finish the box?"

"Night!" Joaquin said, putting his bowl in the sink and taking the stairs two at a time.

He got so busy at the pottery station the next day that he actually forgot about Maya and Grace for a few minutes. He was working with Bryson, a little boy who refused to make anything except vases that would eventually become pencil holders, but his parents seemed to be thrilled with each and every one. Joaquin wondered if they had an entire room in their house dedicated to lopsided pencil holders, and just when he was picturing what that would look like, he looked up and saw two girls staring back at him. One of them teary-eyed and the other one just, maybe, scared.

It was the first time that Joaquin had looked at someone who was related to him.

They were white—he was right—but the shorter one had piles of curly hair that looked a lot like his own, and a nose that leaned to the left like his did. The taller one, the one who was trying desperately to not look like she was crying, had his tight jaw. He could tell just by looking at her that she had a secret. Her posture was too straight, her backbone too rigid. Well, good for her. Joaquin had secrets, too. Maybe they'd respect each other's privacy and not go around trying to dig things up.

He was the one who said they should go and eat, and he sort of regretted the words as soon as they were out of his mouth. But Maya, the younger and shorter one, didn't seem to regret any of the words that came out of her mouth. And there were a lot of them.

"So I was totally freaked out at first," she was saying as they walked, Maya strolling in between Joaquin and the other girl, Grace, who still hadn't said much other than her initial outburst.

"Because I already have one sister, Lauren? She's like their miracle baby—they had her right after me, *oh joy*—and sometimes she's crazy annoying and I was like, 'Another one? I don't know about this.' But then they told me about you, *too*? And I was like, 'Get. Out.' I mean, it's like insta-family, right? Just add water. Like sea monkeys."

Joaquin nodded. It was like listening to a cartoon character talk while sucking helium and he was only really hearing every third word. *Baby, miracle, insta-family.*

"Maya," Grace said.

"Sorry, I talk when I'm nervous," she said. She stuffed her hands in the pocket of her hoodie.

"It's all good," Joaquin said, then pointed down the street. "There's a burger place right around that hill. Fries are pretty good. Unless one of you, um, doesn't eat meat? Or fries?"

"Bring on the cow," Maya said.

"Fries sound good," Grace said, smiling at him. Her nose wrinkled when she did that. Joaquin knew that he did the same thing because his girlfriend Birdie used to love that about him.

Wait. *Ex*-girlfriend Birdie. He kept forgetting that part.

Which was weird, because he was the one who'd broken up with her.

Joaquin had known who Birdie was for approximately 127 days before they'd actually talked. He wasn't used to knowing other kids for that long since he moved around so much, but Mark and Linda had gotten him into a magnet high school in his junior year, and on his first day, Birdie was in his math class. Not that she knew who he was, of course.

That year, right before Christmas break, the teacher's aide in his U.S. history class had pulled him aside and handed him a twenty-dollar bill. "Hey, Joaquin," she said, smiling at him. Her name was Kristy and she had always been pretty nice to him. Joaquin was sort of a sucker for people who were nice to him. It was his greatest downfall.

"I was wondering," she said, "could I buy some tamales from your family this Christmas?"

Joaquin didn't say anything at first. Mark and Linda were the closest thing he had to family, and Mark was Jewish and didn't eat pork and Linda went to a drumming circle down at the beach every month during the full moon. Neither of them could have made tamales if they'd had an instructional YouTube video and a sous chef at their side.

And then Joaquin realized that Kristy didn't realize that he was a foster kid. She thought he had a big Mexican family that made tamales on Christmas Eve.

He didn't bother to correct her. He couldn't bring himself to tell her the truth.

The next day, he found himself on his computer, researching the best tamale places, and on Christmas Eve, he went down to stand in line with a bunch of other people, Kristy's twenty-dollar bill stuffed safely in his hoodie pocket. The guy at the counter spoke to him in Spanish and Joaquin had to say, *"No español,"* which he had gotten used to saying whenever someone greeted him that way. "You're too much and not enough," one of his old foster siblings, Eva, had told him once. "White people are only gonna see you as Mexican, but you don't even speak Spanish." It was clear from her tone of voice that this was a huge black mark in her book.

Joaquin hadn't been able to disagree.

Joaquin eventually carried his tamales home, then stowed them in the very back of the freezer, where he knew Mark and Linda would never see them. When he took them to school the Monday after their holiday break, Kristy had been so delighted— and Joaquin hated her, *hated* her for putting him in that position.

And that's when Birdie spoke to him.

"You make tamales?" she said as soon as Kristy disappeared off to the teachers' lounge. (Joaquin had been in the teachers' lounge exactly once. It had been hugely disappointing.)

"No," Joaquin said. He hadn't even realized that Birdie had been behind him. She had been as quiet as a hawk on a branch, watching, and he suddenly felt like a very small mouse. "I just bought them for her."

"Well, aren't you nice?" Birdie said, then smiled at him. "Happy New Year, Joaquin."

They were together for the next 263 days.

It was the happiest Joaquin had ever been.

Birdie liked people, liked when they did embarrassing things like talk too much when they were nervous, or act shy because they didn't know how to hide it. She laughed a lot, but never in a mean way, and sometimes if she didn't sleep enough, she got really snippy and cranky, which only made Joaquin like her more.

He hadn't realized how much he had missed liking something, *anything*. He had numbed himself, according to Ana, the therapist who Mark and Linda sent him to, so that he wouldn't feel any future pain. But it wasn't until Birdie came along that Joaquin realized he had stopped feeling happiness, too, that the small curls of warmth that wound up his spine when she smiled at him burned and felt good at the same time. Like holding ice in his hand and having it melt against his skin. Joaquin wasn't used to that.

He fell in love with Birdie a step at a time, going from one stone to the next until he made it safely into the shore of her arms, and he had thought that maybe now he could understand what people meant when they said that home was a person and not a place. Birdie was four walls and a roof and Joaquin would never have to leave.

But Birdie wanted things, things that Joaquin couldn't get for her. She was going to move to New York and work in finance, she said. She was going to get her MBA from Wharton. She wanted to learn Italian and live in Rome for at least one year. She said all these things to him like she knew they would happen, and that he would be right there with her when they did. But when Joaquin looked forward, he could barely see anything at all.

One night, he had gone to dinner at her parents' house. They were always really nice to him, and Joaquin called them Mr. and Mrs. Brown even though they kept asking him to call them Judy and David. After dinner, Mrs. Brown brought out some photo albums, and even though Birdie kept saying, "Oh my God, *Mom*," it was obvious that she was pleased.

Joaquin looked at every baby photo, every first day of school, every Christmas morning, every Halloween. Birdie with her top two teeth missing, Birdie dressed like a cheerleader one year, a scientist the next. Birdie, whose smile never looked fake, who never wondered if anyone would show up at her academic decathlon, who never woke up in one house and went to sleep in another.

And Joaquin had the horrible, terrible feeling that he would never be able to give this kind of life to her. There was no one to tell her about him, no one to share embarrassing stories about him that Birdie would love, or show her baby pictures of him. Mark and Linda had photos around the house, sure, but it wasn't the same. Birdie wanted—no, *needed*—the world. She was used to it. These photos were her map, and Joaquin knew then that he was rudderless, that he would only lead her astray.

He knew what it felt like to be held down.

He loved Birdie too much to do that to her.

He broke up with her the next day.

It was pretty terrible. At first Birdie had thought he was kidding, then she had cried and cried, and yelled and yelled, and Joaquin didn't even say "I'm sorry" because he felt that apologizing for something meant that you had done wrong, and he knew he wasn't wrong. He had tried to hug her, but she had slugged him in the arm. It felt worse than almost anything else in his life, and when he went home, he had gone straight up to his room and pulled the covers over his head.

Mark and Linda came up later that night, one of them sitting on either side of his bed, like bookends that kept him from falling over. "Judy Brown just called," Mark said quietly. "You all right?"

"Yeah," Joaquin said, not bothering to uncover his head. He wished they would go away, because nothing was worse than someone wanting you to talk when the words you needed to say hadn't even been invented yet. And after a while, they left him alone, which somehow made him feel even lonelier, but at least that was familiar. Comforting, almost.

He saw Birdie in school, of course, but she only glared at him in the hallways, swollen eyed and furious. "You're a real asshole, you know that?" her best friend, Marjorie, had said to him one morning when he was at his locker, and when Joaquin said, "I know," she just looked surprised, then stormed off.

The next day, his social worker, Allison, came over and told them that he had two sisters who wanted to meet him.

Two empty branches where the bird had been.

"This is weird, right?"

Grace was sitting next to Joaquin now, and Maya was up at the counter getting napkins while they waited for their order. "Like, we just met each other and now we're eating burgers like it's a normal day."

Joaquin sat up a little straighter. Grace's posture was making him feel like a slouch. "Do you not want burgers?" he said. "There's a burrito place across the street, or . . . ?"

"No, no, that's not what I meant," she said. There was a steeliness in Grace's smile, like it had been forged in a fire. Joaquin could respect that. He also knew not to ask about it.

"I just meant that it's strange, that's all," she continued as Maya came back, holding napkins under her arm and a bunch of tiny paper cups filled with condiments in her hands. "I feel like I should know what to say, but I don't."

"I know," Joaquin said. Maya plopped down on his other side with a sigh, then tucked one of her legs under her. "I, um, I actually Googled," he admitted.

"Did you really?" Maya giggled. "Me, too."

Joaquin was pretty sure their Google searches had looked a little different, but he didn't say anything.

What's it like to have sisters?

Will my sisters hate me?

Will I hate my sisters?

How does it feel when someone is your sister?

Why did someone want my sisters instead of me?

How do you talk to your sisters so they like you?

"Yeah, Google was pretty useless in that regard," Maya said as she arranged her condiments in front of her.

"Hey," Joaquin said, pointing at them. "You got mayonnaise. You got two of them."

"Oh, I know, it's gross," Maya said. "Everyone in my family always makes fun of me for it, but I love mayonnaise for my fries. It's weird because I *hate* mayonnaise on everything else, but—"

"No, that's not—I like mayonnaise on my fries, too," Joaquin said. It was hard to interrupt Maya. She talked like a run-on sentence, no pauses or periods.

"No way," Maya said.

"Me, too," Grace piped up. "It's my favorite. My parents think it's disgusting."

There was a quiet space after that, the three of them looking at one another before Maya broke into a huge smile. "We're bonding!" she said. "Over condiments!"

"It's a start," Joaquin replied, and Grace got up to get more mayonnaise cups for all of them.

It was simpler once the food came and they could eat instead of talk. Joaquin still had no idea what to say, but they were easy to listen to, chirping to each other about families and school. He mostly just nodded.

"Ugh, I have to go back to *school* on Monday," Grace said, using two fries like chopsticks to pick up a piece of pickle.

"Were you on break or something?" Joaquin asked. He was also really good at asking open questions, making other people talk about themselves so he wouldn't have to say anything about himself. His therapist called it a coping skill, but Joaquin just thought it was polite. They agreed to disagree on that one.

Grace's face became one big "Oh no!" Like something had slipped past the drawbridge at the castle, but then her forehead smoothed out. "I was out for over a month," she said. "Mono."

"Lucky," Maya said. "I'd kill for a month out of school."

"Yeah, *super* lucky," Grace said. "It was just like going to Hawaii."

Maya rolled her eyes. Joaquin couldn't believe how easy it was for them already. It was like they had a rhythm. Maybe it was because they were girls? Or maybe it was because there was something broken in him, something that everyone could see except him and—

His therapist called that negative thinking. Joaquin thought that was a pretty obvious term.

"Well, I'd still kill for a month off." Maya shrugged. "School's the worst. I mean, the only saving grace is that my girlfriend goes there."

Joaquin knew his cue.

"How long have you been dating?" he asked. He could tell that Maya was ready for a fight about it, but she wasn't going to get one from him.

"Around six months," she said, shrugging a little even as her cheeks flushed.

"And your parents are . . ." Joaquin swirled what was left of his Coke in his cup. "You know, they're cool with it?"

Maya sat up a little straighter. "Oh. Oh, yeah, they're totally fine with it. It's, like, made them the cool parents in our neighborhood."

"One of my favorite foster sisters ever was gay," Joaquin said. "We did time together for about six months in this one placement, but then our foster mom found out that she was gay so she kicked her out and took her back to the agency."

Maya looked smaller in her seat. "Because she was gay?"

Joaquin nodded, suddenly aware that he had maybe picked the wrong anecdote to tell Maya. "She was cool, though," he said. "I still miss her. Meeka. She left her iPod behind and I still listen to it sometimes. Good playlists. She wanted to be a DJ."

Maya just nodded, her eyes round like pennies. "Oh. Cool."

"Tell Joaquin how you and Claire met." Grace said, and Joaquin turned back to his drink.

He could see Maya's cheeks flush as she talked about Claire, the way she bit her lip and smiled almost to herself, even though the restaurant was packed and Joaquin and Grace were sitting right there. He wondered if he had looked that goofy, that sappy, when he talked about Birdie. "Oh, you've got it *bad*," Mark had said to him the night after his and Birdie's first official date (they'd gone to the movies and then gotten frozen yogurt afterward), and

Joaquin had wondered how Mark knew because he hadn't even said anything.

Watching Maya talk about Claire now, he understood what Mark meant.

And it hurt so bad that Joaquin wished he had never let that ice cube melt.

It wasn't until after they were finished eating (and all three mayonnaise sides decimated) that the question came. They were down on the beach. Joaquin knew it was inevitable. That's why he didn't tell people that he was a foster kid. Their curiosity always got the best of them, making him feel like a science experiment, a cautionary tale.

"So what's it like in foster care?" Maya asked as they walked. Maya and Grace had left their shoes back by the steps, but Joaquin carried his. He didn't have a lot of things and he wasn't in the habit of leaving them for other people to take.

"Maya," Grace groaned.

"It's okay," he said, shrugging a little. He knew that's what they wanted him to say, that it wasn't as bad as the news always made it out to be, that no one had ever hit him or hurt him, that he had never hit or hurt anyone. People always thought they wanted the sordid details, Joaquin thought, until they actually had them. "I like my foster parents now, Mark and Linda. They're pretty cool." That part, at least, was the truth.

Maya looked up at him, her eyes worried. "I feel bad that you didn't get adopted," she admitted. She had her camera app open on her phone, snapping a photo every so often as they walked. "Is that bad to say? Because it's true."

"No, it's not bad," he said, and it wasn't. No one had ever actually said that to him before. "I was almost adopted when I was a baby. They put me with this family right after I went into the system and they were going to adopt me, but right before the paperwork went through, the mom got pregnant, and they only wanted one kid, so."

Joaquin shrugged again. He didn't really remember the Russos, but he had seen the case file.

Maya, though, looked horrified. "But weren't you practically, like, their kid already?"

"Bio trumps foster," Joaquin told her. In a world where the rules kept changing from house to house, there was one hard-and-fast one. Joaquin could still remember the placement where the oldest biological son would greet each foster kid by saying, "I decide whether you stay or go." He hadn't been wrong, either. Joaquin had only lasted a month there.

Maya didn't look comforted at all, though. "Well, that's . . . Wow."

Joaquin wasn't quite sure when he had crossed that invisible line of too much information, but apparently he had. "I mean, that was just one home. There were others. They're mostly fine."

"Then why haven't you been adopted? You're nice."

Joaquin made a decision to lie to them. Joaquin didn't think of himself as a liar, not really, but he was good at knowing when to hold back information. "I don't know," he said. "Probably just too old. Most people want babies. Or girls."

"Like us," Grace murmured.

"It seems to be that way," Joaquin said. "But your homes are good, right? Like, people are nice to you and stuff?"

He hadn't even realized it until he said it, but Joaquin thought that if anyone had ever hurt either one of these girls, he would grind them into dust.

"Oh, we're fine, we're fine," Grace said, Maya nodding at him from his other side. "Our parents are nice."

"Well, mine are probably getting divorced," Maya said, kicking at the wet sand a bit with her toe. "But they're still pretty nice. When I came out, my dad actually put a rainbow sticker on his car for a few days. The whole neighborhood thought he was the one who was gay until I explained it to him."

Joaquin couldn't even imagine what it would be like to swing with that kind of net waiting to catch you. He thought of his foster sister again. She had cried when she had been kicked out of the home, had begged to stay. No one ever liked being sent back to the agency, of course, entering into the Russian roulette of a brand-new home. Maya had really gotten lucky, but Joaquin wasn't going to say that to her. Sometimes it was better to not know how lucky you were.

"That's good" was all he said now. "That's good."

"Can I, um, do you remember our mom?" Grace asked. "At all?"

Joaquin stopped walking then, not so much because of the

question but because they had gotten to the end of the path. It was either go back or climb over a pile of slippery-looking boulders. Maya and Grace stopped walking, too, and the three of them looked out at the water for a moment. They had gone past the tourists and beachgoers, and the water was flat so there weren't many surfers, just a boy and a girl on their boards way out in the distance. The girl was laughing about something, but Joaquin couldn't hear her.

"I sort of remember our mom," he finally said. "Like, the space of her. Not so much her."

"Do you remember what she looked like?" Grace asked. She sounded so hopeful that Joaquin couldn't let her down.

"She had brown hair," he said. "Curly, like us. And she smiled a lot." Joaquin was making it up, but he had pictured those features every time he had thought of his real mom. He had dreams about her, this woman smiling at him.

"Did you ever see her after, um . . . ?"

"You can say it," Joaquin told Grace. "After she gave me up."

"Yeah," Grace said. "That."

"We had some visitations before she lost her rights." What Joaquin didn't tell them was that she had never shown up to any of those visits. Joaquin could remember wandering the room, looking for this person who he probably wouldn't have recognized anyway. His foster mother at the time had tried to placate him with candy from the vending machine, but he had just cried under the table until she dragged him out and they went home.

Joaquin still hated candy. And vending machines.

"She was beautiful," Joaquin said now. "Really beautiful."

By the time they got back to the arts center, where they had left the car, Joaquin could feel the sunburn on his nose and the beach tar stuck to the bottoms of his feet. He'd have to peel it off before he went home. Linda really liked her hardwood floors. He didn't want to mess them up.

"So I wanted to say something," Grace suddenly piped up, and Maya turned to look at her. Joaquin already knew what she was going to say, though. He had known from the minute she'd mentioned their bio mom, and he wished that she wouldn't bring it up.

"I think we should look for our bio mom," she said. She literally wrung her hands together in front of her as she said it. Joaquin had read about people doing that in books, but he had never seen someone actually *do it* before. It seemed painful.

Next to him, Maya was quiet. Joaquin was pretty sure that silence wasn't a good sign. It felt more like that space between seeing a gun fire and hearing the shot.

He was right. He usually was.

"That's *stupid*," Maya snapped. "Why do we even want to find her? She gave us *away*. She gave Joaquin to *strangers*."

"But that was almost eighteen years ago," Grace protested. "She was basically my age, right? Or Joaquin's age? She was just a kid! Maybe she wants to know how we're doing. I mean . . ." She paused before adding, "I'm sure she still loves us."

Joaquin laughed. He couldn't help it. He envied Grace's belief that someone would wonder about her. "Sorry," he said when both girls looked at him. "It's just . . . I don't want to look for her. You two can do it if you want, but I'm out."

"Ditto," Maya said.

Grace looked like she was about to cry, and Joaquin felt a small well of panic rise up in his chest. Then she blinked and her face smoothed out into a steely veneer. "Fine," she said. "You don't have to. But I'm going to look for her myself."

"You do you," Maya said.

"That's fine," Joaquin replied.

"Fine," Grace said.

The whole day ended on a strange note after that. They weren't sure whether to hug or shake hands or just wave good-bye, so it ended up as an awkward combination of all three.

Joaquin wasn't that great at hugging, but he tried.

GRACE

It took a while for Grace to figure out what to wear back to school on Monday morning.

Mostly because everything she had was either super baggy, super maternity, or way too tight. Her stomach was still a little . . . well, *floppy* was the only real way to describe it. She wanted to wear pajama pants, but she was pretty sure that it didn't matter how many babies she had, her mom wasn't going to let her go to school in plaid flannel PJs.

In the end, she put on a pair of boyfriend jeans and then a maroon shirt that she found in the back of her closet. The maroon matched the stress hives that were starting to appear on her chest and neck.

Her mom, of course, noticed.

"Are you sure you want to go back?" she said, holding a travel mug of coffee and her car keys. "I know it's been a busy week, what with meeting Maya and Joaquin and all."

"I'm going back," Grace said, picking up her backpack, which felt way too light. "I can't stay home anymore, and Maya and Joaquin don't have anything to do with it." Grace could barely say their names without wincing. She had lied to them both. She had barely known Joaquin for an *hour* and she had lied to them. The worst part was that they had believed she'd had mono. They were *sympathetic*.

Grace wondered if she could give up her sister duties or if someone would just come take them from her, like when beauty pageant winners got caught in a sexting scandal.

Her mom played the radio the whole way to school, laughing at some joke the DJ made, then glancing at Grace to see if she thought it was funny, too. It wasn't (the DJ was a misogynistic jerk, and Grace had never thought he was funny), but she smiled back at her mom, her carefully practiced "I am a normal person and this is my normal smile" smile. Definitely not the smile of someone who'd had a baby four weeks earlier.

"Honey," her mom said, when they pulled up to the school, "do you want me to come in with you?"

"Are you serious?" Grace asked. "No. Oh my God, *no*."

"But—"

"Mom." Grace cut her off. "I have to go at some point. You just have to let me."

Grace had meant it literally, but it was pretty clear from her mom's face that she took it metaphorically, and Grace could see her eyes fill with tears behind the sunglasses, even as she leaned in to kiss her good-bye. "Okay." Her mom sniffled, then cleared her throat. "Okay, you're right. Your dad told me not to cry this morning and here I am, crying." She laughed to herself. "Call me if you need me, okay?"

"Okay," Grace said, even though she knew she wouldn't. Her mom didn't really know the extent of the things kids at school had said to her when she was pregnant. *Slut, baby mama, Shamu*—the list went on. Grace didn't tell her because she knew she would tell the principal and then the teasing would get even more brutal, but Grace also didn't tell her because she knew her mom would feel bad for her.

Pity wasn't strength, and Grace had had a hard enough time holding it together. She didn't want both her parents *and* her to crumble, not at the same time.

Grace carefully got out of the car, heaved her empty backpack to her shoulder, and headed toward English, her first class of the day. It felt a bit like she was heading toward a firing squad, except worse, because she knew that instead of dying, she was going to have to stay alive through the whole day. And then the next one after that.

And she couldn't help but think as she saw the first set of staring eyes fix upon her that a firing squad might have been preferable.

Grace had already been excused from all her homework—she just had to make it up before the end of the year, which okay, fine—but as she walked past students, she could see highlighters, flash cards, all of the things that she normally used during crazy study sessions. Her best friend, Janie, used to even make fun of her for all of her mnemonic devices.

"Now," Janie would say, imitating Grace studying for their European History final. "Napoleon was short, which reminds me of an octopus. An octopus is purple, which is the color of my family's couch, and we got that couch from a store that was next to a pretzel store. And pretzels are German, which . . ." Grace would laugh and laugh, clutching her then-flat stomach.

"Grace."

She stopped short, her reverie broken. "Janie," she said. "Hi."

She hadn't seen Janie since she'd come over to visit two days after Milly was born. Grace didn't remember much of that visit, other than that they had watched *Friends* on Netflix. But Grace had been pretty whacked out and the all-encompassing grief of loss. Details were fuzzy, to be honest.

"Hi," Janie said now, her head cocked to one side. Grace had the distinct feeling she had done something wrong, something that violated friend code, but she didn't know what it was. Or, probably more accurately, *how many* violations there were.

"You didn't tell me you were coming back to school."

Ah. There it was.

"Um, yeah," Grace said. She tried to smile, but it felt more like she was baring her teeth at her friend, a warning signal to stay away. "I just decided last night. I got tired of staying home, you know?" Grace shrugged, like it was a totally casual thing to have a baby and forget to tell your best friend that you were returning to school.

"Oh," Janie said. "Well, it's good to see you! You look good."

Janie never used the word *good*, and definitely not twice in a row. This was, well, *not* good.

"Thanks," Grace said, then looked at the girl standing next to Janie. They both had purses slung over their shoulders, holding their books and binders on their left hips, while Grace's backpack hung limp from her shoulder. When had Janie gotten rid of her backpack?

The girl next to her was Rachel. "Hi," Grace said to her. "I'm Grace."

"I *know*." She replied in a way that made Grace feel like she had introduced herself as Rasputin or Voldemort, a name that must not be said.

"It's really good to see you, Grace," Janie said again.

The third *good*. Grace couldn't help thinking, *Three strikes and you're out*. "If you're around at lunch, eat with us, okay?" She smiled at Grace; then she and Rachel walked away.

Grace hadn't thought as far as lunch. Now she was wishing she had. She had been friends with Janie since the third grade, so she had never worried about who to eat with, or where she would sit. But now that she was thinking about it, the school campus suddenly felt bigger, way too big, like it had no end. She had had dreams like that before, wandering around in a strange place and not being able to find her way out.

Janie and Rachel walked away, and Grace hitched her thumbs under her backpack straps, which suddenly felt like they had betrayed her. She unhooked them, then continued walking up the hill to English class. For some reason, it was even harder now that she wasn't pregnant. She had spent her last month at school huffing and puffing everywhere (and also making approximately 982,304,239 trips to the bathroom, since Peach had enjoyed using her bladder as a cozy pillow), but now her legs felt heavy, like they didn't want to go into English class and were trying to warn her brain to *stay away*.

Grace realized, too late, that she should have listened.

Everyone stared at her when she walked into the room right before the bell rang, but Grace was prepared for that. As much as anyone could be prepared for thirty sets of eyeballs suddenly locked on them. She smiled at the wall behind Zach Anderson's head, just so they would think she was smiling at someone, and then Mrs. Mendoza came over and put her hand on Grace's shoulder and said, "It's so nice to see you, Grace," and Grace silently told herself, *Do not cry, do not cry* until it worked and the tears slipped from the edge of her throat and back down into the pit of her stomach.

"Thanks" was all Grace said out loud, though, then went and took her seat. Someone had carved SLUT into the fake wood desk, but she wasn't sure if that was for her, some other girl, or just the product of some bored junior who had a limited vocabulary and too much time on his hands. *I mean,* Grace thought, *it's English class. You think he'd have a stronger grasp on synonyms. Harlot, maybe, or floozy or strumpet?*

"Grace?"

She looked up. Mrs. Mendoza was smiling down at her, the way priests do when they're visiting sick people at the hospital. Benevolent, but also silently wishing for hand sanitizer.

"I was just saying that if you'd like to spend the next few days in the library doing makeup work just so you can catch up a little, that's fine."

"Oh," she said. "No, that's okay."

There were snickers behind her. It sounded like Zach. And Miriam Whose-Last-Name-Grace-Could-Never-Remember. You know people have been laughing behind your back for a while when you can identify each giggle's source. "Too bad *I* couldn't have a baby," the voice said. Grace was right—it was Zach. "Get out of homework. Score, man."

"Ugh, you are the worst." That was Miriam. At first Grace thought she was defending her. She was about to turn around and smile when she really *heard* what Miriam said. She said "You're the worst" in the way girls say things when they want boys to think that they're teasing, like, "You're the worst, but I still like you enough to hook up with you, even though you're the emotional equivalent of dirt."

Then again, who was Grace to judge? The last boy *she'd* liked got her pregnant, left her alone, and took another girl to homecoming on the same night she gave birth.

She couldn't exactly blame Miriam for poor life choices.

She couldn't help but wonder what Maya would say to Zach if *she* were in this situation. Grace hadn't known Maya that long, but she was pretty sure that Maya would have thrown herself back into school the way lions ran into the Colosseum during Roman times: teeth sharp and claws out.

Grace channeled that energy. "Wow," she said, turning around to look at Zach. "Nothing gets past you, does it? You're *very* observant."

Grace was pretty sure that instead of a lion, she was the equivalent of a mewling kitten.

Zach just smirked and took his baseball cap off, smoothing down his hair before putting it back on. "Whatever, Baby Mama," he said.

"Zach, seriously," Miriam joked. Grace would have given her kingdom to grab Miriam by the shoulders and shake her until her head wobbled on her neck.

But then Mrs. Mendoza started talking ("Zach, take off your hat, you know the rules in my classroom"), and Grace found her pen and opened her notebook. *Just act normal*, she told herself.

She acted normal through English and second period (AP Chem), but third period was where it all fell apart. If, by *fell apart*, you meant *crumbled into oblivion*.

Third period was U.S. history.

Third period was with Max.

Janie wasn't the only person who hadn't realized Grace was coming back to school, judging by the look on Max's face. He was laughing with Adam, one of his friends, and when Grace walked into the room, his eyes got so big that he looked like a cartoon. If Grace hadn't hated him so much, it would have been funny, but the only thing she felt was a sick thrill for surprising him. She liked the idea of keeping him on his toes, popping up where he least expected her, a flesh-and-blood ghost to haunt him for the rest of his life.

Grace knew it wasn't possible, but it felt like everyone in the room stopped talking when she walked in, their heads swiveling between her and Max. As if this period was suddenly the new episode of a soap opera, and the long-thought-dead evil twin had just sauntered back into town.

She sat down in her normal assigned seat, which, unfortunately, was right across from Max. She had chosen that seat back at the beginning of the year because it was easier to talk to him that way. Now she cursed Past Grace for making such a terrible decision. Past Grace, it turned out, was a real idiot.

Adam was giggling and saying, "Dude, dude," quietly, the way you do when you have a secret.

"Shut up," Max hissed at him. Adam had been (and, Grace assumed, still was) as dumb as concrete, one of those guys who thought he was a football star when he really just watched from the sidelines and high-fived other people when they made the winning touchdowns. Grace had never liked him, and Max knew that.

Unlike her first two teachers, Mr. Hill ignored Grace and got down to business, which she appreciated. Sympathy was sometimes worse than being ignored. "Okay, bodies," he said loudly. (Mr. Hill always referred to his students as "bodies." It was a little distressing at times. Grace couldn't help but picture a roomful of corpses.) "Let's focus!"

Grace dug her pen out of her bag, willing herself to not even look at Max. She could see his feet, though, and he was wearing new shoes. That blew her mind. Somewhere in the time between when she'd had his daughter, met her half siblings, and returned to school, Max had gone shopping and bought new shoes, like his life was still normal; like it hadn't changed at all.

And the truth was that it hadn't. Somewhere in the world, another couple was raising Max's biological child. And *he* had new shoes.

By the time Grace found her pen, her cheeks were bright red. The urge to use it to scribble all over Max's shoes was strong, painfully so, but she just set it down on her desk and looked forward.

"Hey," Adam whispered across the aisle as Mr. Hill turned toward the whiteboard at the front of the classroom. "Hey, psst! Grace!"

She didn't turn around. She knew Adam wasn't going to ask about how she was feeling, or wish her a good first day back, or see if she needed anything.

"Grace! Hey, are your boobs all saggy now?"

Someone—Grace didn't know who—giggled behind her, and

over the rushing sound in her ears, she heard Max say, "C'mon, dude." Grace would have preferred if Max had, oh, gone all *Game of Thrones* on him and mounted his head on a stick, but Max just said, "C'mon, man," again.

Grace gripped her pen and wondered when Max had become such a weakling, with a spine made out of cotton candy. Maybe it had happened while they'd waited in line at Target that day, buying pregnancy tests, or maybe it was that day when his dad talked about the "good girl" Max was dating instead of Grace. Or maybe it had happened at homecoming while Grace was squeezing a baby out of her body and he danced, wearing a cheap plastic crown.

This version of Max wasn't the boy Grace had dated, or slept with, or loved. And it seemed crazy to her that, somewhere out there, there was a child who was half him and half her, when she suddenly couldn't stand to be in the same room with him anymore.

"Grace!" Adam hissed again.

Mr. Hill was still up at the whiteboard, apparently writing out an entire soliloquy, so Grace turned to look at Max. Even his face looked weak. How could she have ever dated someone with that jawline? Thank God Peach hadn't inherited it.

"Would you tell your friend to shut the fuck up?" Grace hissed at Max. She could tell that he was sorry, it was written all over his (pathetic) face, and she spun back in her seat, cheeks flaming like she had a fever.

That's when Adam's phone made the noise. It was a baby's

cry—a newborn baby's cry. It sounded like Peach, like the first sound Grace had ever heard her make, that crazily desperate wail that announced her arrival into the world.

Grace didn't know what moved first, her body or her hand, but then she was flying over her desk like she was running the hurdles in gym class, her fist out so it could make clean contact with Adam's face. He made a sound like someone had let the air out of him, and when he fell backward, his desk trapping him against the floor, Grace pinned him and punched him again. She hadn't had this much adrenaline since Peach had been born. It felt good. She even smiled when she punched Adam for the third time.

It eventually took Max, Mr. Hill, and this guy named José (who really *was* on the football team) to pull her off Adam. José sort of spun Grace away, setting her down on her feet so hard that her teeth rattled together, and then Grace was gone, leaving her backpack, Adam, Max, and U.S. history class behind.

She stumbled toward the bathroom at the end of the quad, the one that no one ever used because it was near the biology classroom and the smell of formaldehyde sometimes leaked into the vents. It was disgusting, but she didn't care. She just needed somewhere to contain the hurricane inside her chest when it eventually burst out of her.

The sound of Peach roared through her ears as she cried out.

She sank down on the floor under the sink farthest away from the door, hugging her knees to her chest. The floor was cold, which was good, because Grace was fairly sure that her skin was on fire, and also, her hand was throbbing. Punching someone in the face, it turned out, hurt like hell, and she pressed her knuckles against the tiled wall, hissing a little.

It was hard to catch her breath. Like it had been when Peach was being born, like her body was working separately from her brain, and she closed her eyes and tried to breathe. The room was cool and quiet and there were probably twenty people now looking for her, but Grace didn't care.

She just wanted it to stay quiet.

After a few minutes, the door swung open and a boy walked in. Grace had never seen him before, but it wasn't like she had been super present during her last few months at school.

Either way, it was pretty obvious that the guy wasn't expecting to see her on the floor.

"Oh, sorry, I didn't know that anyone was . . ." he said, then glanced back at the door. "Wait, is this the girls' bathroom or . . . ?"

Grace shook her head, still crying. She hadn't even realized she was crying, but her cheeks were wet and her hair stuck to them when she moved her head.

"Are you . . . ?" The boy backed up, then took a step forward, a slow-motion cha-cha. "Shit, I'm sorry, I'm so bad when people cry. Are you . . . okay?"

"I'm fine," Grace said, and apparently it was Opposite Day in her head, because *fine* was definitely not the word to describe her at that moment.

He continued standing by the door. "I'm not calling you a liar or anything, but you don't look fine."

Grace started crying again.

"What'd you do to your hand?"

"I punched Adam Dupane in the head three times," she told him. There was no way to make it sound nicer than that, so Grace didn't bother trying. It wasn't like he wouldn't find out, anyway. There was probably already video online. Grace was going to get expelled, she realized, and was surprised by how nice that sounded to her.

"Wow." The guy's eyes widened. "Well, I don't know who Adam Dupane is, but you seem like a nice person, so he probably had it coming."

"He's a dick," Grace said.

"A total dick," the guy agreed. She couldn't tell if he was humoring her or teasing her, but Grace didn't care.

"Um, you probably need to put something on that," he said, motioning to her swollen hand, then set his backpack down and pulled some paper towels off the machine and ran them under the cold water. "Here." He passed them to Grace. "It's not exactly an ice pack but it'll help."

Grace just stared at him. "Who are you?" she finally asked. Her nose was starting to run and she felt disgusting and snotty— and embarrassed for feeling disgusting and snotty.

"Oh, sorry. I'm Raphael. Raphael Martinez. But you can call me Rafe, you don't have to be, like, formal or anything. I'm very nonthreatening, don't worry. Well, I mean, since you're the one who just punched someone, maybe you're not worried. Maybe *I* should be worried. Trust me. I'm a total wimp." He wetted another paper towel as he talked, then passed it to her. "I mean, I faint at the sight of blood, I really do. Not exaggerating. Hey, can I ask you a question?"

This Rafe person was making her head start to spin. "Yeah?"

"What is that *terrible* smell in here?"

"Formaldehyde." Grace wasn't sure when she had stopped forming complete sentences. "Dead cats. Next door."

"Anatomy class?" he guessed.

She nodded.

"Got it."

Grace winced as her hand throbbed under the cold towels. Everything hurt now—her head, her arm, the base of her spine— and she tried to keep from tearing up, with no luck.

And Rafe, Hero of the Day, flipped the lock on the bathroom door and came to sit down next to her. Grace could tell that he was being very careful not to touch any part of her, and for some reason, that just made her sad. "So," he said conversationally, like they were talking about the weather, "Adam's a dick."

"Max just sat next to him the whole time and didn't even say anything," Grace said, and she wasn't crying again, not exactly. Her face was just wet and there was a lump of something terrible stuck in her throat.

"I know," Rafe said with a sigh. "What an asshole."

"You don't even know who I'm talking about!" Grace cried. "Why are you *agreeing* with me?"

"Well, you're sad," Rafe said, sounding a bit confused. "Do you want me to argue with you? Because I will if it'll make you stop crying. Here, okay." He cleared his throat. "You are *so* wrong. Adam's the best."

"No," Grace sniffled. "I just . . . I just want to be quiet, okay?"

"Got it," he said. "Whatever you want." But Grace couldn't stop hearing that baby noise, the very first sound that Peach had ever made, a battle cry that had somehow triumphed over everything else, including her heart, and when Grace started crying again, Rafe carefully leaned his body toward hers so that their shoulders were touching.

He was very, very quiet.

Grace lost track of how long she sat on the floor and cried, but after a while, there was a knock at the door and someone saying, "Gracie?"

"That's my mom," Grace explained, wiping at her eyes.

"Are you in trouble?" Rafe asked. "I'll hide you in a stall if you want."

Grace suddenly wanted her mom so bad that it hurt. "No, you can let her in," she said. "It's okay."

"Oh, honey," her mom said when she saw her. "Let's go home."

And that was the last day of Grace's junior year.

MAYA

After meeting Joaquin, Maya had a hard time sleeping.

Our foster mom found out that she was gay so she kicked her out. Bio always trumps foster.

And yes, Maya knew that she was adopted, not fostered, that she had been adopted out of the hospital, that her parents had chosen *her*, wanted *her*. That's what they always said, that *she was chosen because she was special*.

And yet, she wasn't Lauren.

Three a.m. would come and Maya would lie awake in bed and watch lights from the cars outside pass across her ceiling, lighting her room before it fell dark again. She would look at websites on her phone. (She had done the "Which Hogwarts House Do You Belong To?" quiz at least three times, and got Hufflepuff each time, which infuriated her.)

Then she would scroll through old messages from Claire,

emojis and xoxo's and notes that were so private that Maya would throw her phone into a toilet before she let anyone read them. She would look at the very end of the messages and hope that the little bubbles would pop up that meant Claire was texting her, that she would somehow know that Maya was alone in the world and that the middle of the night felt lonelier than any other time of day.

But of course Claire was sleeping, and it was stupid to be upset about it. Claire needed to sleep. *Maya* needed to sleep. She could feel the sleeplessness starting to unravel her brain like a kitten with a blanket, pulling at important threads until it wasn't even functional anymore. She had fallen asleep in history class two times that week, which, to be fair, probably had more to do with her history teacher's nasal, droning voice than with her exhaustion.

That was what she told herself, anyway.

At lunch, she put her head in Claire's lap and let her stroke Maya's hair as they sat in the grass in the sunshine. Maya thought that if everyone had to die eventually, this wouldn't be the worst way to go, with the sun on your face and your head in the lap of someone you loved.

"Hmm?" Claire asked.

"I didn't say anything," Maya said, her eyes closed. The sun made the space behind her eyelids as red as blood, made her think of lineage and dynasties, of rightful places in families.

She opened her eyes and rolled over so she could bury her face in Claire's thigh instead.

"No, you didn't *say* anything," Claire agreed. "But you're thinking."

"I'm always thinking," Maya told her. "I'm very smart that way. That's why you love me."

"Hmm, jury's still out," Claire said, but then she put her hand up the back of Maya's shirt, pressing her palm against Maya's skin, anchoring her down to earth. "Come back, come back, wherever you are," she whispered.

Wherever Maya belonged, she was here now.

That was enough.

Maya found the wine bottle a few days later.

She had texted with Grace a few times, mostly responding to Grace's somewhat awkward sentences. "Hi! How's school?"

"Sucks donkey balls," Maya had written back, then regretted it when Grace didn't respond for a few days.

She didn't text with Joaquin, but not because she didn't want to. Maya just didn't know what to say. It was hard to find words when you were adopted and your brother wasn't, and it was pretty clear that you had been chosen because of things beyond your control. It was stupid to feel guilty, Maya told herself sometimes when the clock crept past three a.m. toward four a.m., and the lights from the cars hadn't slowed down. But then she would picture Joaquin as a baby, waiting for someone, a family, a person, and that terrible feeling would push its way past her heart and into her throat, choking her.

In her worst place, in the darkest part of her brain, Maya didn't want the same thing to happen to her, and just like Joaquin, she didn't know how to keep it from happening.

Maya's European History class was restaging the French Revolution (which Maya felt was extremely appropriate, given the number of people in that class who she would have gladly beheaded), and because she couldn't act her way out of a paper bag, she had been assigned to costumes. *Easy-peasy*, she had thought, and then gone upstairs to rummage through her mom's closet.

The wine bottle (or *bottles*, actually, but one of them hadn't been opened yet, so Maya decided that it didn't count) was wedged in the back of the closet, nestled into a pair of old boots that Maya thought would look spectacular on whoever played Marie Antoinette. They were heavy when she pulled them out, though, way heavier than any boots should have been, and by the time she'd wrestled them out of the closet and into the bedroom, the bottle of merlot had fallen out.

Maya looked at it for a long minute before reaching into the other boot and pulling out a half-full bottle of red zinfandel. It was cheap—Maya could tell by the label—which for some reason upset her even more. If her mom was going to hide wine in the closet, she could have had at least bought the good stuff, rather than this convenience-store shit.

"Hey," someone said, and Maya whirled around so fast that she almost dropped the bottle. Lauren stood in the doorway, tugging on her lower lip. Maya *hated* when she did that. "What are you doing?"

"Nothing," Maya said, which was easily the dumbest thing she could have said, considering that she was standing in her parents' bedroom, going through her mom's closet without permission, and holding a bottle of half-drunk wine. "It's nothing," she amended. Somewhat better.

"Why are you holding wine?" Lauren asked. "Are you *drinking*?"

They were only thirteen months apart, but Lauren was younger. Maya knew that in her bones, the way she knew that Grace and Joaquin were older than she. It didn't matter if they were related by blood or not: Maya was responsible for her little sister. She had to protect her.

"Get out," she said to her. "Get *out*, Lauren, I'm serious."

"But why are you—"

"Get out," Maya said, gesturing with the wine bottle (bad idea) toward the door. "This isn't about *you*, for once in your life."

Maya would remember the look on Lauren's face for a long, long time after that. Three a.m. would get a whole lot lonelier the next time she saw it against the backs of her eyelids.

"Is that . . . is that Mom's?" Lauren asked.

Maya tightened her grip on the bottle and said nothing.

"Did you find it in her closet?" Lauren pressed on—and then dropped a bomb. "Because I found a bottle in the garage."

Maya felt so stupid, standing there listening to her, holding the evidence while trying to hide it at the same time. Lauren finished, "It was in an old shopping bag. I think she drank most of it yesterday."

The two sisters stood across from each other for a long few seconds before Lauren finally walked into the room. "There's another bottle downstairs in that old Crock-Pot," she said.

Maya sank down onto the bed because she wasn't sure if her knees were going to support her. "How long have you known that she . . .?"

"A month, I guess? Maybe longer? I don't know."

"Why didn't you tell me?"

Lauren shrugged. "Because I knew you were meeting Grace and Joaquin, and—I don't know—I didn't want to burden you. You've got a lot going on."

Lauren sat next to her, their shoulders slumped together. "You should have told me," Maya said after a minute.

"Why?" Lauren asked, and Maya didn't have an answer to that.

"Do you think Dad knows?" Maya asked.

"No," Lauren replied. "Dad travels. He's not looking in Mom's boots during his free time."

"Do you think she's driving?" she asked. "You know, after?" She shook the bottle in her hand. Maya wasn't used to asking Lauren questions like this. Usually she was the sister who knew everything, the one who was in charge, who made up the rules for the games and decided who won or lost.

"I don't know," Lauren said. "I don't think so. She picked me up from school yesterday and she seemed okay."

Mom could drink at lunch, though, Maya thought. Two glasses of wine with a salad and some bread from the bowl. That would be pretty easy to hide.

She was still holding the bottle of zinfandel and she carefully set it down on the floor, like it could suddenly shatter and stain the carpet with all of their secrets.

"Should we put it back?"

"Give it to me," Lauren said instead, and Maya handed it over. When Lauren went downstairs and didn't come back, Maya followed her and found her standing in the kitchen, one hand holding the cork and the other hand dumping the bottle down the drain.

"What are you—" Maya started to say.

"What's she going to do?" Lauren said. "Get angry at us for dumping out her contraband? She's not going to do that. She *can't*. Because then she'd have to admit what she's been doing."

Maya watched her for a long minute, then went upstairs and brought back the second bottle. Lauren opened it and they dumped it out, watching it swirl down the sink before turning on the faucet and rinsing it all away.

When their parents finally made their big announcement, it really wasn't that much of a surprise. Maya later thought that it was more like ripping off a huge bandage—inevitable, but you still knew it would hurt like hell.

She had been doing physics homework when the knock came

at her door. It had been quiet that night, way too quiet, and Maya had done the same problem four times and still hadn't gotten the right answer. She wondered how fucked up it was that she worked better when her parents were fighting. If she was ever going to make it through high school, she'd probably need a nuclear explosion every night.

Great.

When she said, "Come in," her parents were both standing there, looking apprehensive and nervous. Like children, in a way. Maya had never seen that kind of look on their faces before. Lauren was behind them, and Maya didn't need to look in a mirror (or at a birth certificate, for that matter) to know that her own expression was similar to her sister's.

"Your dad and I want to talk to you," their mother said, and Lauren pushed past her parents and went to sit on Maya's bed. Maya, who had actually been doing homework at her desk for once, got out of her chair and went to sit down next to her sister. She suddenly found herself wishing that her *other* sister was there, too, and her brother. And Claire. She wished for an army of people to stand behind her, swords at the ready.

Of course, no one actually came.

"We'd like to talk downstairs?" Their mom's voice sounded a bit strangled, and Maya felt like someone was pushing down on her throat now, too, that three-a.m. feeling creeping back in. "It's okay," her mom said quickly. "We just need to have a family meeting."

They hadn't had a family meeting since Maya was eight and Lauren was seven and accused Maya of killing her goldfish. (Maya would still swear on a stack of Bibles that she hadn't touched that creepy, scaly thing. Lauren was paranoid and a terrible fish parent, that was all.)

"I've got this homework," Maya started to say. She suddenly prayed for inertia. *An object in motion stays in motion until acted upon by an outside force*, the words said in her physics textbook. She wanted things to keep going the way they had. For all the terrible fights, it was still familiar. Maya wasn't ready for that to change, and she wasn't ready for what would potentially take its place.

"Maya," her mother said. "Please."

She didn't need to say anything else.

Downstairs, Maya and Lauren sat next to each other on the couch while their parents explained things.

You know we haven't been getting along.

It's going to be so much better this way.

You get to spend time on the weekends with Dad now, just you and him.

You girls will be so much happier.

Lauren cried, of course. She had always been the emotional one (see: family meeting about a dead *goldfish*), the one who had to be taken out of the movie theater during sad scenes because she would sob too loud and disturb everyone else.

Maya, though, just sat there quietly while her parents explained that Dad was moving out, that they loved both of their girls so, so much, that it had nothing to do with them at all, that it wasn't her or Lauren's fault.

"Of course it isn't," Maya muttered, because that was the stupidest thing she'd heard in a while. "*We're* not the ones who have been fighting for the past ten years." *And hiding wine in the closet,* she almost added, but thought better of it. Lauren was still crying and Maya didn't want to hurt her sister any more.

Her mother blinked while her father cleared his throat. "That . . . is true," her dad finally said. "That's very true."

"You girls will stay here with me, in the house," their mother said. "But you can visit your dad whenever you want."

"What if we want to live with Dad?" Maya asked. She wasn't even sure she wanted to, but she felt the overwhelming need to put herself in between them, to see which one of them would tug her closer. To know if either of them would fight to keep her after trying so hard fifteen years ago to get her.

"We can figure that out," her dad said. Maya's mom couldn't answer; she was too busy blinking back tears and moving to put her arm around Lauren. She tried to put her arm around Maya, too, but Maya moved down on the couch so that there was space between them. She didn't want anyone touching her.

"We're going to try and make this as easy as possible for you two, don't worry," her dad added.

Maya laughed, short and sharp and bitter. She couldn't help it. "I think we sailed past *easy* a long time ago," she said.

"Maya," her dad started to say, but she held up her hand.

"No. I don't—" The words suddenly got caught in her throat, the walls were too close to her, the air too thin. She felt like a character in a movie running away from an explosion, with the road crumbling into gray ash just steps behind her, struggling to stay ahead of the abyss that pulled at her like hands, sucked her in like a tar pit, like a black hole that only wanted to absorb the light.

"I have to go," she said, and then she was grabbing her phone and running out the front door, down the grass and their driveway. It wasn't until she reached the end of the street that she realized she was barefoot, and that her feet were throbbing even from that short a distance, but it didn't matter.

She texted Claire. *Meet at the park? I need you.*

Her heart pounded through her body as she waited for the response bubble, and then Claire was there, as steady and sure as she always was. *On my way. Everything ok?*

Maya didn't bother answering. She just ran. Once she hit the park, it felt like green, sharp and cutting against the soles of her feet. Her lungs burned like gray, like smoke that she couldn't breathe out.

She just ran faster.

Claire was just climbing out of her car when Maya rounded the corner and into the parking lot. "Hey," Claire said, and when Maya ran into her arms, she stepped back only a little bit, Maya's momentum throwing both of them off.

"Hey, hi . . . hey, *hey*," Claire said, and then Maya was crying and she couldn't say anything, not because she didn't know what to say, but because there was too much of it. She could have every dictionary in the world and it wouldn't be enough to begin to explain the darkness of that space, the fear of being alone like Grace, unwanted like Joaquin.

Claire held her for long minutes in the parking lot. "Don't go" was the first thing Maya managed to whisper when she could speak again.

"Not going anywhere," Claire whispered back.

Her voice was as soft as a prayer.

JOAQUIN

The first time Joaquin had met with his therapist after moving in with Mark and Linda, it hadn't gone well.

They had met in an office that was in a high-rise building, so high that Joaquin could see all the way to the ocean. That alone had made him a little woozy, but the office itself was clean and white and modern. The only color in the room had been a purple orchid (in a white pot, of course) on his therapist's, Ana's, desk, and all that glaring white had reminded Joaquin too much of thin white sheets on a bare cot, of restraints and chafing on his wrists, of that drugged-up sleepiness that had made him feel like he wasn't really sleeping at all. It was so quiet in the office that he could hear the whoosh of the air-conditioning when it came on.

Joaquin made it all of two minutes in there before walking out, the sweat beading at his hairline, his hands shaking.

"I'm not going back in there," he told Linda and Mark at the time, which was the first time he had actively told them something that they didn't want to hear. He had tried so hard to make them happy, to make them *want* him, but he couldn't set foot back in that room.

They had sat with him on the curb while he got his breath back, Mark's hand resting carefully on his shoulder as his heart slowly returned to a normal pace. They had sat with him for the better part of twenty minutes, waiting silently for him to explain, and when Joaquin didn't—*couldn't*—explain, they started asking questions. Sometimes he liked when they asked him questions, sometimes he didn't. Sometimes it felt like they cared too much; other times, it felt like they wanted to *know* too much.

"Too much like the hospital," Joaquin finally managed to say. He hadn't minded the questions that time.

"Ah," Linda said.

"Got it," Mark agreed.

The next week, he and Ana met in a diner closer to Mark and Linda's house. (Joaquin still hadn't and still didn't think of it as "my house" or even "our house," just "their house." It was okay, though, because it was still a nice house. It didn't have to be his for him to like living there.) "Is this spot okay?" Ana had said, sliding into the booth across from him. "I heard my office is a little too antiseptic-looking."

"It's fine," Joaquin said.

"You do know that the word *fine* is basically kryptonite to a therapist's ears, right?" Ana said, then signaled the waiter for a lemonade. "Fucked up, insecure, neurotic, emotional," she recited, ticking the emotions off on her fingers. "Therapy 101."

Joaquin knew all that, of course. One of his older foster brothers had actually gotten a tattoo that said "I'm Fine" across his shoulder blades. Joaquin knew all the tricky ways the phrase worked. "Well, it's accurate," he told Ana, who smiled.

Joaquin hadn't wanted to see her, even if she was nice and didn't tell Linda when he drank three Cokes in a row. (Refills were free.) But then he had figured out that Mark and Linda were paying for Ana out of their own pockets, and Joaquin guessed that he owed it to them to at least go. Foster parents weren't always crazy about spending their own money on things. Joaquin didn't want to push his luck.

Eighteen months later, Ana and Joaquin were still meeting in the diner every Friday after school. They always got the same thing—Cobb salad and lemonade for Ana; veggie burger, fries, and a Coke for Joaquin—and sat in the same booth at the back of the restaurant, where the acoustics made the restaurant sound way busier than it actually was.

"So," Ana said as she slipped into the booth across from him the Friday after he first met Maya and Grace. "How did it go?"

It had taken Joaquin a while to appreciate Ana's no-bullshit approach to therapy. She also dropped a lot of f-bombs, which he liked. Most therapists treated him like he was his own bomb, about to explode, which, to be fair, was how he had felt for most of his life.

But still.

"It was fine," Joaquin said, then grinned when she glared at him. "Just kidding. It was nice." If *fine* was Ana's gold-medal word, then *nice* definitely took the silver.

"They're white," Joaquin added, tearing the paper off his straw as the waitress brought their drinks. She knew their orders by heart now; Ana and Joaquin hadn't seen a menu in three months.

"You thought that might be the case," Ana said. "What about them? Were they *nice*?"

Joaquin smiled to himself. "They're funny. They get along really well already. And that made me feel," he said, beating Ana to the question, "fine. I'm glad they like each other."

"And did they like you?"

Joaquin shrugged and took a sip of his Coke. "Guess so. We have a group text now. We're meeting on Sunday again."

"That's good," Ana said. *Good, nice, fine.* Ana was trying to pave a very rocky road, Joaquin could tell.

"It's just—" he started to say, then reached for his Coke.

Ana raised an eyebrow. "It's just . . . ?" she prodded.

Joaquin ran his thumb down the glass, leaving a dry stripe down the center of condensation. "They were both adopted, you know? Their parents paid a lot of money to get them."

Ana nodded. "Probably so, yes."

When Joaquin didn't respond, she added, "Does that bother you?"

"It doesn't bother me for them," he said, then made another

stripe on the glass. "It's just . . . people got *paid* to keep me, and that still wasn't enough."

Ana looked at him across the table. "How does that make you feel?"

Joaquin shrugged. He didn't want to talk about his sisters anymore. He was still finding the words to describe how he felt about them, and he knew that Ana would wait for him to discover the right ones.

"I broke up with Birdie," he said instead. He hadn't brought it up at their last meeting because of the Maya and Grace decision. And also because he hadn't wanted to talk about Birdie. Discovering two new sisters had been *really* helpful when it came to avoiding difficult subjects.

Ana blinked at him. It took a lot to surprise her. Joaquin had seen her composed face many times over the past year and a half; surprising her felt like a weird sort of victory, a Pyrrhic one. "Wow," she said after almost a full ten seconds, during nine of which Joaquin questioned his decision to bring Birdie up at all.

"Want to tell me why?" The surprise was gone and Ana's face had smoothed back into its normal therapist mode. "I thought you really liked her."

"I do," Joaquin said. "That's why I broke up with her."

Ana cocked her head at him. "You know, that sounds like something the Joaquin I met eighteen months ago would have said."

"I'm the same person," Joaquin told her. He hated when Ana

tried to sort his past from his present. Joaquin knew that that was impossible, that he would always be intertwined with the things he had done, the families he had had. He knew this because he had spent years trying to outrun them. "I just realized that it was a bad idea, that's all."

"You told me last month that Birdie made you happier than any other person in your entire life."

Joaquin sometimes wished that Ana didn't have such a good memory.

"She does—she did," he corrected himself. "I just . . . She has all these baby pictures."

Ana sank back against the booth and reached for her lemonade. "And you don't."

Joaquin shifted a little in his seat and wondered where their food was. He was starving. He was always starving. Mark and Linda used to joke about how much food he ate, so he took the hint and scaled back on eating. When they realized what he was doing, they were horrified. No one joked about food anymore. They even kept extra bread in the freezer just for him.

"Joaquin," Ana said. "Just because you don't have baby pictures doesn't mean that you don't have a past."

"I know that," Joaquin said. "You think I don't know that? We meet here every single week because of my past. I just don't want that for Birdie."

Ana waited a beat before saying, "What about what you want for you?"

"That's not important. She's more important."

"You're *both* important, Joaquin. Did you ever tell Birdie about what happened before you came to Mark and Linda's?"

Joaquin scoffed, rolling his eyes. "Yeah," he said sarcastically. "I told her all about how they put me on a psychiatric hold when I was twelve. Girls *love* that story. Especially the pretty ones."

"What about—"

"Birdie wants things, okay?" Joaquin said, interrupting her. Sometimes it was so frustrating talking to Ana, because she refused to see it from his perspective. If anyone was an expert on Joaquin's life, it should be Joaquin, after all. "I mean, not *things*, but just a *life* . . . I could never give her what she wants."

"Did she say that?" Ana shot back. "Or did *you* say that?"

Joaquin looked away. They both already knew the answer.

"What about Maya and Grace?" Ana asked him. "Are you going to tell them about what happened?"

"Nope," he replied, popping the *p* sound at the end and look-ing out the window. An entire van full of kids drove past them, some surfboards sticking out of the back. Joaquin was pretty sure some of them went to his school. He both envied them and never actually wanted to be them.

"You don't think they would understand?" Ana asked now, pulling Joaquin's attention back to the restaurant, to the waitress setting their food down on the table.

"Of course they're not gonna understand!" Joaquin said as soon as he was gone. "They live with these perfect families, they have these perfect lives. What am I going to say, that their older brother who looks nothing like them is *crazy*?"

Ana raised an eyebrow. She hated that word.

"Sorry," Joaquin said.

"I don't know either one of them, but I can tell you that their lives aren't perfect," Ana said gently. "Your problems may not be the same, but they have their own shit, I guarantee it."

Joaquin crossed his arms over his chest.

"Are you upset that your sisters were adopted and you weren't?"

"Why should they have bad lives just because I did? That's stupid. They should have good families. They *have* good families." He paused before adding, "Grace—she's the older one—she wants us to look for our bio mom."

"And what did you say to that?"

"Thanks, but no thanks. So did Maya. Well, she actually said, 'She gave Joaquin to *strangers*.'" Joaquin tried to mimic Maya's indignance, the way she had spit out the word like a swear, like it was the worst thing in the world to not know your family. "Grace is on her own for that one."

"Did Grace say why she wanted to look for her?"

Joaquin shrugged. "Don't know. She can talk to her own therapist about that shit."

Ana smiled at him, and Joaquin smiled back. "Can we go back to Birdie for a minute?" Ana asked.

"Sure. Metaphorically."

"Touché. Do you miss her?"

Joaquin missed every single thing about Birdie. He missed the smell of her skin, the way her hair would fall across and down his arm whenever she would rest her head on his shoulder. He missed her laugh, her furious anger whenever someone said something she disagreed with.

"A little," he said. "Sometimes."

He missed her every single minute of the day.

"So what about your sisters, then?" Ana asked. "Are you just going to push them away when you get to know them better? Run away like you did from Birdie because you think you're not good enough for them, for anyone?"

Joaquin ate a french fry and didn't answer. French fries were really terrible when they were cold, but these were hot and crispy. He ate another one.

"Because I've got news for you," Ana continued. "You can't just push family away. You're always going to be connected to them."

Joaquin drew a pattern on the table from the condensation of his glass. "Really?" he said. "Tell that to my mom."

"Joaquin," Ana said, and now her voice was gentle. "You deserve to have these people in your life. Mark and Linda, too. You have to forgive yourself for what happened."

"I can't," he said before he could stop himself. "I can't forgive myself because I don't even know who I was when I did it. I don't know that kid at all. He's a fucking idiot who fucked everything up."

Ana's eyes were a little sad as she looked at him. She knew the truth, of course. She had seen the hospitalization records, the police reports, the statement from Joaquin's adoptive family, the Buchanans.

"I just want to pretend it didn't happen," he said after a minute.

"Oh, yeah?" Ana said. "And how's that working out for you?"

"Really shitty," he replied, then laughed before he could stop himself. "But at least I'm the only one getting hurt this time."

"You sure about that?" Ana asked.

Joaquin looked out the window and didn't answer.

The nightmare woke him up later that night, his sheets and T-shirt damp with sweat, his blood pulsing so hard through his skin that it felt like something was shaking him from the outside.

"Kid, kiddo. Hey, it's okay." Mark's hand was warm on his back, his fingers pressing down and grounding Joaquin. "It's okay, just wake up a little."

"'M fine," Joaquin managed to say. The colors behind his eyes had been too bright, too sharp, like they could pierce his skin.

Linda was standing next to Mark, and she handed Joaquin a glass of water. She always looked softer in the middle of the night, her hair down, her makeup gone.

"Sorry," Joaquin said. "Sorry, I'm fine. Sorry I woke you up."

Mark and Linda sat down on either side of him on the bed. Joaquin should have known that they wouldn't leave him. He had spent seventeen years trying to get someone to stick around for him, and now that they did, he just wanted them to go.

"Want to talk about it?" Mark asked. In the beginning, Joaquin couldn't even handle Mark being in the room with him after a nightmare. He guessed that this was what Ana would call *progress*.

"Just . . . I can't remember," Joaquin said, rubbing his hand over his face. He needed a clean, dry shirt. He needed a brand-new brain. "It just woke me up."

That wasn't true, of course. He had seen his sisters in the dream, Maya and Grace standing on the edge of the ocean, calling for him as the waves crashed harder onto the sand. He tried to get to them, but his feet were stuck in the ground, and he could only watch as they were washed out to sea.

"You were yelling for Grace and Maya," Linda said gently. "Did you dream about them?"

Joaquin shrugged. "Dunno."

He didn't have to look up to know that Mark and Linda were exchanging a look over his head. If he had a dollar for every time they did that, he could move out and get his own place. And a car.

Two more people shoved away.

"Think you can get back to sleep?" Mark asked after a minute of silence. His hand was still steady on Joaquin's back. Joaquin liked both of them, but he liked Mark's ability to be quiet, to not always need an answer right away. Mark sometimes realized that Joaquin could say a lot more without using words.

"Yeah, I'm good," Joaquin said, sipping at the water again. "Sorry I woke you up."

"Don't be sorry," Linda said. "Mark was still awake. Reading something stupid on the internet, I'm sure."

Joaquin smiled, more because Linda expected him to smile than because he actually wanted to.

GRACE

Adam's mom decided not to press charges against Grace, which was nice of her. The school had a zero-tolerance violence policy, but it also had a zero-tolerance bullying policy, and since Adam had started all the drama, the school decided that he was technically responsible. (Also, Adam's mom was a single mom and she was pretty upset with him for taunting Grace with the sound of a baby crying. There may have been some shouting coming from the principal's office soon after she arrived at the school. Grace may or may not have heard it as her mother signed her out in the office.)

Of course, the school wasn't thrilled with Grace, either, but she heard her mom say something about "hormones" and "baby" on the phone to them while she stood just outside Grace's room, and apparently those were words that terrified school administrators. Grace was also fairly certain that she was the first pregnant girl in the history of the school, and she also knew that schools didn't exactly get great ratings for having a high teen pregnancy rate.

In the end, they compromised. Grace would do home schooling for the rest of the year and then go back for her senior year in the fall. It sounded less like a compromise and more like a present, honestly. Grace would have been fine if she'd never had to walk down those hallways again. She almost hoped that her parents would send her off to one of those East Coast boarding schools that were always in movies. She could start over, surrender her old self, every single wrong decision she had made, and become someone else.

But she knew she couldn't outrun her past. Or Peach. She would never be able to outrun Peach.

Her mom called Grace downstairs around eleven that Saturday morning. Grace was fairly certain that her mom had hit the limit of her patience for Grace's stay-under-the-covers-and-binge-watch-bad-TV habit. The day before, her mom had made Grace change the sheets and clean out from under her bed, and "open a window—it smells like a hobbit hole in here." (Grace's mom wrote a thesis on Tolkien in college, so she referred to a lot of things as "hobbit holes." Grace's dad and Grace had learned to roll with it.)

"Here," she said when Grace came downstairs. "I need you to return this for me." She handed her a bag from Whisked Away, a cooking-supply store.

Grace let go of the banister, catching herself before she fell down the last step, and peeked in the bag. "What is it?"

"Something that needs returning."

Grace poked around at the tissue paper, ignoring her. "What are these?"

"You ask a lot of questions."

Grace ignored her some more. It was a tiny ceramic fried egg nestled in an equally tiny ceramic skillet. "Are these . . . ? These are salt and pepper shakers!" Grace held up the egg. "I can't tell if these are terrible or amazing."

"They're an insomnia purchase," her mom said. Her insomnia caused her to buy a lot of things online around three in the morning, things that were often returned as soon as they arrived, once she'd seen them in the cold, harsh light of day. (Grace suspected that insomnia was also how her mom had made it through all the Tolkien books.)

"They're terrible," Grace finally decided. "Dad will hate them."

"Dad *does* hate them!" her dad yelled from the kitchen.

Her mom raised an eyebrow at Grace as if to say, *Do you see what I'm dealing with here?* "Just please return them," she snapped, handing Grace a twenty-dollar bill. "You can get yourself a giant fancy coffee or frozen yogurt or something."

Luckily for Grace's mom, Grace was easily bribed. She took the salt and pepper shakers. And the money. And the car keys.

Once Grace pulled in at the shopping center, though, she

realized that she had made a huge mistake, one much bigger than salt and pepper shakers. It was a Saturday, also known as a non-school day. The parking lot wasn't too crowded, and she didn't recognize any of the cars from her school's parking lot, but that didn't make her suddenly nervous stomach feel any better. After all, the last time Grace had seen any of her classmates, she had been punching one of them in the face. She wasn't exactly looking to repeat the experience.

If Grace's mother had done this on purpose just to "get her out of the house," Grace was going to kill her.

Grace put on sunglasses as she skulked across the parking lot, then took the back way to the store rather than go past all the pretty fountains with the splash pads for the little kids. Grace didn't think she could handle seeing them, hearing them shout about the water, without thinking of what Peach might look like at that age. Just seeing a baby on TV made her change the channel. It was like her heart was being stabbed with the most immense kind of love, and regardless of its source, the pain was still too much to handle.

Whisked Away was pretty much empty when Grace finally made her way there (she guessed browsing for kitchen appliances wasn't everyone's ideal thing on a Saturday morning). She got in line behind a woman who was paying with a check. A *check*.

Grace wondered if the woman's cart and oxen were double-parked outside.

Just as it was her turn to get up to the register, though, Grace saw a few people come in. She didn't know their names, but she recognized them from school. Two girls who had always seemed nice enough, but Grace suddenly wanted to fall down a hole like Alice, disappear into Wonderland before anyone could see her, and her heart started beating a pattern that felt like a gun going off at the start of a race, over and over again, telling her to run.

She didn't run, per se, but she left the line and did a ridiculously fast walk toward the back of the store, near the clearance section, where they did their cooking classes. It was deserted back there, and cooler, too, and she stood under the draft of an air vent and tried to catch her breath.

It was so stupid. They probably didn't know who she was, and even if they did, who cared? It wasn't like they had caught her trying to rob the store at gunpoint.

Grace *knew* all this, of course, but it was taking her heart a little longer to catch up with her brain.

"Can I—oh. Hi."

Grace turned around, ready to tell the salesperson that she was fine, that she didn't need help, she was just browsing, anything to get them away from her, when she realized who it was: Rafe, the guy from the dreaded formaldehyde bathroom.

Of course it's you, Grace thought. *Of course it is.*

"Oh, hi," Grace said instead. "Hey. I was just, um, yeah. I'm returning some stuff."

"Cool," he said, but he didn't move. The green apron he had to wear made his eyes look even more brown, but it might have just been the light. Or the reflection from the Teflon cookware display case. That was probably it.

"Yeah," Grace said again. She sounded super intelligent. This was easily her best conversation ever. "You, uh, you work here?" Gold medal–winning conversation, for sure!

"No, I just like aprons," Rafe said. He said it so seriously that she blinked, wondering if maybe she had accidentally struck up a conversation with a psychopath who had a thing for baking. Then he smiled. "Kidding!" he said. "Sorry, no one gets my humor. I'm kidding. I work here. But I do like the apron. Don't tell anyone."

Grace nodded, trying to figure out how to get out of both the conversation and the store as soon as possible. "It has pockets," Grace said. "That's always nice."

"It is," Rafe said, then stuck his hand in the front pocket and flapped it a little. "Room for all my secrets. Sorry, that's me attempting humor again, in case you couldn't tell."

He was somewhere between embarrassing and charming. Grace couldn't decide if she liked him or just felt bad for him. "Got it this time," she said.

"So, you're returning something?" he asked, and okay, Grace had to give him credit. It couldn't be easy trying to make conversation with a girl who he had last seen crying on the floor of a bathroom because she had just punched another boy, all while dead animals were being hacked up next door in the name of science.

"I am," Grace said, then held up the bag. "For my mom. She has insomnia and buys a lot of stuff online, then returns it."

"Ah. I can help you with that. The return, not the insomnia."

Grace glanced up toward the front of the store. "Could you, um, maybe do it back here?" she said.

Rafe followed her gaze, then looked back at her. "Is there a terrible customer up there or something?" he asked. "Does someone smell?"

"No, just . . . you know, some people from school."

"Ah," he said. "You spend five days in a row with them, and now it's the weekend and you *still* can't get rid of them."

"Something like that," Grace said, but he smiled at her in a way that made Grace wonder if he knew the real reason she didn't want to go up there.

"I'm glad to see you again," he said as he led her toward the back register. "Only, you know, without the formaldehyde smell this time."

"I tried to warn you about that," she told him. "You wouldn't listen."

"Yeah, that was just an interesting experience all around." He took the package from Grace without looking up at her. "What *are* these?"

"Salt and pepper shakers," she said. "I told you, insomnia. She makes some weird choices around three a.m."

"I can't tell if these are terrible or amazing."

"That's what I said!" Grace cried. "My dad voted for terrible, though, so . . ."

Her phone buzzed in her back pocket, but she ignored it.

"Soooo," Rafe said as he started to do the return. "Who else have you been punching? You gotta stay sharp, you know. A ninja never rests."

"I'm not an actual ninja."

Rafe pushed a bunch of buttons on the keyboard in front of him. "How do you know you're not?"

"Don't you need some kind of . . . certification? Like a badge or a diploma?"

"Dunno. They never stick around long enough for me to ask."

Grace smiled despite herself. "Haven't punched anyone since," she admitted. "That was just a one-off."

"Did your parents ground you for the rest of your life?"

"No." She watched as he rang up the return, expertly flipping the tiny egg in the frying pan like he was actually cooking it. "My parents are sort of tiptoeing around me right now."

"Oh yeah?" He glanced up at her from the register. "Why? Afraid you'll punch them, too?"

"Has no one told you?" Grace finally asked. "Seriously?" Her phone buzzed again. She ignored it *again*.

"Told me what?" Rafe handed her the receipt. "I just credited your mom's account."

"So wait, you seriously don't know why I punched that guy and . . . ?"

"See, that's one of the things that sucks about being a new kid at school. You don't have any friends to fill you in on all the dirt."

Grace felt her heart sink. No wonder he was being so nice to her. He had no idea. "Consider yourself lucky."

"I'll do one better. I'm supposed to go on my break right now. You want to get frozen yogurt or something? You can catch me up on everything I should know. Be my very own TMZ."

Grace hadn't had frozen yogurt since before Peach. Just the thought of that tart berry taste had made her stomach ache with nausea, but now it didn't sound so terrible.

Getting frozen yogurt *with someone else*, on the other hand, was a different story. A bad story. A story that sounded *very* terrible.

"Look, I need to tell you something," Grace told Rafe, facing him head-on. She had a really hard time looking people in the eye lately. It was almost like it made her head feel heavy, like she had to look down or away in order to keep her equilibrium.

"Well, *that* sentence never leads into anything good."

"I just . . . I'm not really looking to hook up with or date anyone right now, okay? I don't want to."

"Whoa, whoa, *whoa*." Rafe held up his hands and looked around like Grace had just threatened him with a gun and told him to empty the register. "Who said anything about hooking up or *dating*? I said *yogurt*. They don't even rhyme!"

He was making Grace smile despite herself. Max had done the same thing, too, once upon a time.

"I just like eating frozen yogurt and I thought that *you* might like eating frozen yogurt, too," he continued. "And my break's only fifteen minutes, anyway, so that would be a really cheap date. You *shouldn't* date me—I'm obviously terrible at it."

"You're very odd," Grace said after a minute.

He shrugged. "My siblings are way older than me. I'm basically an only child. I spend a lot of time talking to myself."

"Me, too," Grace said, before suddenly realizing that she kind of *wasn't* an only child—not anymore. "Well, sort of. Long story."

Rafe raised an eyebrow at her but didn't push. "Frozen yogurt?"

"Fine," Grace said. "But I'm paying for myself."

"Duh. I work at a kitchen supply store—how much money do you think I make?"

There wasn't a line at the yogurt place, which was nice. Grace wasn't sure what she would do if she recognized someone from school. Or Janie. Or Max. The thought made nervous sweat pop up along her spine.

In front of her, Rafe squinted at the toppings. "What do you think? Yogurt chips?"

Grace shook her head. "No, they get stuck in your teeth."

"Wise, so wise." He reached for the Fruity Pebbles, shaking some onto his yogurt, then gummy bears. Grace took some pomegranate seeds, then some strawberries, before realizing that she was choosing things that would be healthy for Peach. When things had felt so out of control, all Grace could do was make sure she was healthy, so she had learned about antioxidants and omega-3s and folic acid.

Grace set down the strawberries and reached for the cookie dough bits instead.

"You know that that has raw egg in it, which could give you salmonella and—"

Grace looked Rafe right in the eye this time, then popped some dough in her mouth.

"Okay then," he said. "Moving on."

When they got to the register, Grace handed the cashier the money her mom had given her. "Wait, I thought this wasn't a date!" Rafe yelped. "You can't pay."

"Courtesy of my mom," Grace told him. "And her insomniac ways."

"Nice," Rafe said. "Tell her thanks. And now I wish I had gotten extra gummy bears."

"You don't mind?" Grace took her change from the cashier. "The last boyfriend I had always paid for everything." She led them to a booth as far away as possible from the shop's windows.

"Fancy guy. Does he go to our school?"

Grace nodded.

"And he's your ex?"

Grace nodded again.

"I'm really enjoying this game of charades, by the way. First word, sounds like?"

Grace smiled and took her spoon out of her mouth. "The guy that I punched? It was his best friend."

Rafe's eyes widened. "Wow. You're ice cold."

"He deserved it." Grace watched as a mom pushed a stroller past the window, hustling to get wherever she was going.

Rafe started stirring the Fruity Pebbles into his yogurt, making the colors bleed into a rainbow swirl. "So, are you going to tell me why you punched your ex-boyfriend's best friend and why your parents didn't ground you for it and why you don't come to school anymore?"

"How do you know I don't go to school anymore?" Grace's phone buzzed again, a reminder notice.

Rafe shrugged. "I notice things."

"You *really* want to know?"

He nodded.

Grace took a breath, looking out the window again. The mom and the stroller were gone. "Because I got pregnant and had a baby last month." The words rolled out of her mouth like they had been waiting to escape.

Rafe blinked. "You have a baby?"

"I *had* a baby. I gave her up for adoption." Grace had to force those words out. "She's with a really good family, though."

That sharp, piercing love pain stabbed her right between the ribs.

Rafe nodded to himself. He was still stirring the yogurt, and it was turning a pinkish shade of gray. "Wow. Okay. Wow."

"The guy I punched, it was Adam—my ex Max's best friend—and on my first day back, he played the sound of a baby crying on his phone." Grace shrugged, like that was something that happened to normal, average, *nice* people every single day. "I just lost it."

"What was her name?"

Grace looked up. No one had asked her that question. No one had ever asked about Peach since the day she had been born. "Milly," she said. "Amelía. But I called her, um, Peach. In my head, that's what I call her."

"Do you miss her?"

Grace nodded and took a bite of yogurt before Rafe could see her chin wobble. "Every day."

"And your ex?"

"He didn't want anything to do with her. His parents, they pretty much said no way. He signed away his rights about two seconds after he found out about her."

"This is the same guy who paid for everything on your dates?" When Grace nodded, Rafe sat back in his chair and let out a long sigh. "Well, chivalry is *officially* dead. Who wants a guy who can buy you frozen yogurt but not take care of a baby?"

"*You* didn't even buy me frozen yogurt," she pointed out.

"Fair point," he said. "You can't count on anyone anymore." His tone was soft, though. Grace knew that he wasn't being mean. She had gotten good at being able to tell the difference in people's voices, the ones who had said, "Oh, you're pregnant!" versus "Oh. You're pregnant."

Rafe popped one of her cookie dough bites into his mouth. "Well, now I'm glad you punched that guy. You should've punched your ex, too."

Grace raised her plastic spoon. "Hear hear," she said, and he clinked his spoon against hers. "Next time for sure."

"So is it weird . . . you know, now? After?"

Grace lowered her spoon. "Do you always ask strangers questions like this?" Her own parents hadn't asked her that question. Come to think of it, nobody had asked her any questions at all. Though she guessed that was the smart move. Rafe was basically chipping away at the Hoover Dam, and there was a *lot* of water behind that wall, just waiting to get out.

He shrugged at her question, though. "Do you always *answer* strangers' questions like this?"

At that point, Grace would have answered questions about the clothes dryer's lint trap from the lady behind the makeup counter. She was starved for conversation.

"It's not weird, it's just that everything is different. I mean, I don't have any friends anymore, my parents are on eggshells around me, nobody texts me—"

"Really? Because your phone keeps buzzing at you."

"That's probably just my mom. Or Maya. She's my . . ." *Sister.* Another word that felt strange in her mouth. "It's a long story."

Rafe paused with his spoon halfway to his mouth. "My favorite kind."

"She's my biological sister. We just met each other. And our brother, Joaquin."

"Your bio— Wow." Rafe started to laugh. "Look, Grace, I don't know what you're planning on doing next year to top this year, but it's going to have to be immense. Like, skydiving-while-being-devoured-by-piranhas immense."

"I'll take a rain check on that experience," Grace replied. Her yogurt still wasn't sitting right with her, even though Peach was gone. She pushed the cup toward Rafe. "But Maya's basically the only person who texts me now."

"No friends, no texts. Your life sounds a lot like mine."

"Pretty pathetic."

"Yep." He bit a head off a gummy bear, then sighed. "We can't even get dates. Terrible."

Grace smiled despite herself.

"Well," Rafe said, looking at his phone. "I have exactly four minutes before I have to get back to the store and clock in. Want to walk me back?"

Grace pretended to think about it.

"I'll let you wear the apron if you want."

"Pass," she said, but stood up and followed him out.

He held the door for her. Max had once done that, too.

Grace waited to look at her phone until she was back in the car, the doors locked and the windows rolled up. It was hot in the car, the air too still, the outside sounds of people muffled from the windows being rolled all the way up.

Grace almost felt like she couldn't breathe.

It was a text from her mom.

There's something in the mail for you.

Grace drove home at the pace of the snail, if a snail could get its driver's license and didn't really want to go back home. She knew what was waiting for her in the mailbox, she just knew it, the same way she had known from the beginning that Peach was not hers to keep.

When she got home, her mom was standing in the kitchen. There was a small manila envelope on the kitchen counter, glaring against the white tiles, and Grace looked at it and then at her mom.

"It's for you," her mom said, and Grace knew that her mom was all too aware of the envelope's return address, the adoption agency's address. Daniel and Catalina had promised to update Grace on Peach's progress every month for the first year via emails and pictures, and Grace wasn't surprised to see the first update.

Grace ignored her mom's look, then picked up the envelope and took it upstairs. She knew her mom wanted her to open it in the kitchen, wanted to see everything that was in that envelope, but Grace was afraid that as soon as she slit it open, she would shatter across the floor, and she wanted to be alone if that happened.

It had been over thirty days since she had given Peach to Daniel and Catalina. Thirty days to take Peach back, contest the adoption, grab her daughter, and bring her back into her arms. On that thirtieth day, Grace had huddled in bed and watched the clock tick down. When her phone flipped to 12:01 a.m., something in Grace wilted.

Thirty days had passed. The adoption was official. Peach was truly gone.

Once in her room, Grace cleared a space in the debris on the floor—laundry that she hadn't done, books and magazines that she hadn't read—then sat down cross-legged and slit the envelope open with her thumb, ignoring the sting of the inevitable paper cut that followed.

A letter and two photos tumbled out, and Grace caught one of the photos before it could hit the floor. It was a picture of a baby, fat and not as red and wrinkly as Grace remembered her being.

It was Peach, her eyes cool and clear as she looked at the camera, and she was so perfect.

Grace stared at the photo for a full minute before picking up the piece of stationery that had tumbled to the floor. It was personalized, *Milly Johnson* scrawled in a trendy pink-colored font at the top, and it took Grace a beat before realizing who Milly Johnson even was.

Peach had her own stationery. Grace would have never thought to give her that. She wondered how many other things she would have forgotten, both big and small, things that she wouldn't have even known that Peach needed until it was too late.

Dear Grace, the letter began.

We know we agreed to send emails regularly, but we thought our first update should be a handwritten letter for you. Anything else seemed a bit too impersonal.

From the depths of our hearts, we cannot begin to thank you for the beautiful, precious gift that you have allowed us to bring into our lives. Milly has been a joy from the very first moment we laid eyes on her, and our love for her has only grown deeper and more vast as the days have progressed. We can't wait to see who she becomes, how she changes. Our hearts are too full, our cups runneth over, as the saying goes.

Within that love, however, is an immense gratitude for the love that you have also bestowed upon Milly, and for the sacrifice you made for our family. We tell Milly every single day that her biological mother is brave and beautiful and loved her in ways that we will never be able to describe to her, and we will always want her to know you, to know <u>about</u> you and the selfless way that you have brought her into this world.

We can only imagine the conflicting emotions that you might have had in the past thirty days, but please know that we cherish and adore Milly more than anything else in the universe, that she is our baby girl, but that she was once yours, too, and that the grace of your gift will never be forgotten.

With our warmest wishes and deepest gratitude for you and your family,

Daniel, Catalina, and Amelía (Milly)

Grace read it again, and then once more. Each word felt like it was being engraved at the base of her heart, cutting into her, burning, and she picked up the second photo and turned it over. "Amelía Johnson, four weeks old" had been written in careful script on the back. On the front, Peach was wearing a little sailor outfit, complete with a teeny hat and itty-bitty boat shoes, and

Grace picked up both photos and carefully tucked them under her shirt, pressing them against her stomach, where Peach had once been.

She knew it was ridiculous, that they were just photos, that Peach would never be anchored to Grace the way she once had been, but she tried to feel it again anyway, tried to remember the press of her tiny foot against Grace's ribs, the way she would drum her fists at three in the morning.

But in the end, they were just photos, and Grace finally took them away and placed them in a drawer, feeling foolish. She wanted to look at them forever, and she never wanted to see them again. The letter she folded up and tucked into the back of her sweater drawer, right where her favorite sweater was, the one she had worn when she was pregnant, its knit soft and warm.

Grace knew that she couldn't go back, but as she stood in her messy room, one hand over her stomach as if to keep Peach there, she also realized that she had no idea how, exactly, to go forward.

MAYA

Maya's dad moved out on Sunday morning.

At first, he had promised that he wouldn't move out for a while, that they were still in the beginning phase of "planning the separation," which Maya thought made it sound like her parents were about to extract something out of the ground instead of divorce.

But then he found an apartment in a neighborhood ten minutes away, and there was a good deal on the rent, and he signed the papers and came home one night with a bunch of collapsed cardboard boxes under his arm and disappeared upstairs without saying anything.

The apartment was a two-bedroom, so Maya guessed the conversation about whether she and Lauren would have separate bedrooms was out of the question. "Can you have dogs in your building?" she asked him one night, leaning against the doorjamb while he placed books in a half-open box. Maya had always wanted a dog, but her mom said that they shed and drooled and barfed on the rug. "So did Lauren, but you kept her," Maya had pointed out more than once, but the joke had worn thin by now and she had stopped asking for a dog.

"No pets, unfortunately," her dad said. "Maybe a goldfish?"

"Goldfish don't have such a great track record at our house," Maya pointed out, then watched as her dad stood on his tiptoes to reach the books from the highest shelf. When she had been little, she had thought that he was the tallest man in the world. When she would wake up in the middle of the night now, she always thought that at least her dad was in the house, that he would always be able to frighten any burglar, bear, monster.

She wasn't used to seeing him look so small now, reaching with his fingertips for the book at the far edge of the shelf. It made her hate him suddenly, hate him for leaving so fast, so soon, like he couldn't wait to get away from all of them.

She wondered if he knew that there was currently a bottle of room-temperature sauvignon blanc in one of the dresser drawers. She wondered if she should tell him. Would he still move out? Would he take her and Lauren with him? Who would watch out for her mom if that happened?

The day he left, Maya had planned to meet up with Grace and Joaquin. They'd agreed to meet every Sunday—that was their plan. Maya couldn't help but wonder how long it would be before someone couldn't make it, until someone had something better to do, better people to see. She wondered when the novelty of having new siblings would wear off. And then they'd drift apart just as easily as they had come together.

Her money was on Grace bailing first. That girl seemed nervous *all the time*. Typical only child, Maya thought. Used to having everything for herself, not wanting to share. Then she felt terrible for thinking that about someone who had only ever been nice to her.

Maya wasn't sure why, but she could feel a spiral of darkness starting to weave around the people she loved. Lauren grated on her nerves, to be sure, but now it had a sharp edge of annoyance to it, the edge of an envelope that caught your fingers when you slit it open, slicing deeper each time. Her mom—Maya could barely look at her without thinking of all the bottles that were currently in their house, both obvious and hidden, the contents of all of them dwindling at a steady, fast pace. Her dad—he was weak for leaving, and for forcing Maya and Lauren to pick up the pieces behind him.

The worst, though, was Claire. Maya loved her with all her heart, loved every single cell of Claire's body like it was a puzzle made only for her to put together, but Maya was starting to feel like she could easily rearrange those pieces, too, smash her fist down on the finished picture and scatter everything to the wind, leaving nothing but the shards of who Claire had been with her in her wake.

Maya had never realized how much power there was in loving

someone. At first, she thought it was a source of strength, but now she was realizing that, in the wrong hands, on the wrong day, that power was strong enough to destroy the very thing that had built it. Maya looked at Claire and wanted to say, "Run away, get out while you can," but instead she said nothing and felt the dark vine swirl up around her, trapping her legs, keeping her in the same place while everyone else seemed to only drift farther away.

When Maya's dad moved out, she thought she would cry.

She didn't.

Lauren did, though, huge gulping sobs like when she had been little and infuriated that Maya wouldn't play with her. Lauren was the baby, after all. She was used to getting her way.

But their dad just packed up the car with his clothes and boxes and books, then came over and hugged Lauren tight, whispering something into her hair before letting her go and embracing Maya. The vines held her steady, though, keeping her quiet and immobile as her dad whispered into her hair, too. "I love you so much," he said. "I'll see you soon. I'll call you tonight. I love you, I love you."

Maya felt herself nod against his chest, then pulled back. The whole thing felt so forced, so cheesy. She half wondered if she was starring in a movie, or dreaming, or maybe even dreaming about starring in a movie. Behind her, she could feel the presence of her mom standing on the porch, watching the scene with her bathrobe still clutched tightly around her. Maya knew she was hungover by the way she winced against the sunlight, the way her shoulders seemed pulled too tight against her robe.

She wondered if the sauvignon blanc was still in the dresser, or if it was all gone now.

Maya's dad tried to hold on to her, but she just kept stepping back until her feet hit the porch's front step. Next to her, Lauren was wiping at her face with the sleeve of her hoodie, and all Maya could think was, *Gross*.

"Take care of your sister," her dad said, and then she could see his own chin wobbling. She had seen her dad cry before, of course, but that had been during movies or really sad TV commercials, not during real life. She wondered if he had cried when he'd first seen Maya, or Lauren, or even their mom. Probably not on that last one. That would be super weird to date a guy who cried when he first saw you. Maya hoped her mom had had better sense than that.

"My," Lauren said, nudging her out of her thoughts.

"What?"

Lauren pointed toward her dad, who was handing them both a package. "Oh," Maya said, then took it from him.

"You can open it after I leave," he said. "I just want you to remember me, that's all."

"You're not *dying*," Maya said. She meant to sound funny, to ease the mood, but her words sounded sharp, like not dying was an accusation instead of a good thing. "You're just moving out. We could have dinner with you tonight, even."

She waited for him to say, *Have dinner with me tonight.*

He didn't.

Instead, he kissed them good-bye one more time, his unshaved cheek scratchy against Maya's, and then climbed into his car and drove away. Lauren waved, but Maya didn't. A trail of blues floated across her mind as his car turned the corner, drifting away and then disappearing, just like him.

"Girls," her mom started to say, but Maya just brushed past her and went back inside. She didn't want a speech from her, not now, not ever.

"So," Maya said, Joaquin and Grace sitting across from her at the coffee place. "My parents are getting divorced."

She had practiced saying that sentence in the shower that morning. At first it had been hard to get the words out, but then she just turned off the hot water, and the cold water shocked the words out of her. By the time she had gotten through the sentence, her teeth were chattering and her lips were blue.

"Whoa," Joaquin said, but he didn't seem too amazed. Maya thought that, objectively, her half brother was a pretty handsome guy, but his eyes watched everything in the room, constantly flitting from person to place to thing. It reminded her in a way of those cats who followed the laser point on the ground, trying forever to trap it between their paws, but she didn't tell Joaquin that. She wasn't sure he would see the humor in it.

"Wow, really?" Grace said, and okay, she looked pretty taken aback. She hadn't stopped chewing on her iced-coffee straw, and now it was stained with her pink lip gloss, the top starting to fray into pieces. "When did they tell you?"

"Last week," Maya admitted. "My dad just moved out this morning." She shrugged, then reached for a piece of the cookie that they were ostensibly supposed to share, but Maya had eaten most of it already.

"Yeah, he got a place that's about ten minutes away, or that's what he said. I guess he was pretty eager to leave." She had practiced saying those words out loud, too, but no amount of icy water had been able to pull them from her. Even now, they hurt coming up.

"Is your mom freaking out?" Joaquin asked, just as Grace said, "Does that affect the adoption at all?"

"What?" Maya screeched. "Why would that affect the adoption? For fuck's sake, I'm fifteen years old! The deal is *done*!"

"I just meant—" Grace was wide-eyed with guilt, not innocence. "Like, that doesn't invalidate it, right? Your parents can get divorced and it doesn't mean anything in the long run."

Maya rolled her eyes skyward. "Joaquin, help me out here," she said, pointing to Grace. "Tell her that it doesn't affect the adoption."

Joaquin glanced from one sister to the other. "It doesn't affect the adoption," he said. "At least, I don't think so. But I'm not exactly the best person to ask."

Both Maya and Grace looked away. It was too easy to forget sometimes that Joaquin hadn't always lived with Mark and Linda, his foster parents. They were the ones who had dropped Joaquin off at the coffee place that afternoon. They had said that they needed to do some shopping nearby, but Maya was 99 percent sure that they just wanted to scope her and Grace out for themselves.

Still, they had been really nice. Mark was tall, way taller than Maya had ever even imagined her dad being when she was little. He had shaken both girls' hands and smiled like you would expect someone's proud dad to smile. Linda had seemed warm and kind, squeezing Joaquin's arm a little just before they left the three of them alone. "Stay as long as you like," she had said, and Joaquin had nodded. They seemed like parents. Joaquin seemed like their kid.

Now, though, he was methodically shredding his napkin into evenly square pieces. Maya wondered if she was the only sibling to escape these disgusting habits. *Dodged that bullet,* she thought, as Grace stuck her straw back in her mouth and continued to chew it to oblivion.

"I'm sorry," Grace said to her, and in her defense, she really did look contrite. "I just wanted to make sure that you were okay, that's all."

"I'm fine," Maya said, and watched as Joaquin looked up and raised an eyebrow. "I am," she said. "They fought like crazy. It'll be nice to have a night when people aren't screaming at each other so loud they shake the walls. I might actually sleep again."

Grace nodded but didn't look convinced, and Maya threw a glance at Joaquin, desperate to have the subject changed. "So how are you?" she asked. "What's new?"

"Mark and Linda want to adopt me," Joaquin said.

Maya choked on her cookie.

"What?" Grace said, yanking the straw back out of her mouth. "Are you serious? Joaquin, that's amazing!"

Joaquin just shrugged, though. "Yeah. They're cool. They're nice."

"They're *really* nice," Maya said, leaning forward a little. She had the urge to wrap a blanket around Joaquin for some reason. He always looked cold, hunched in on himself. She wondered what he had been like before Mark and Linda, then quickly realized that she didn't want to know.

"Seriously, Joaq, they're crazy nice," Maya said again.

"You like them, right?" Grace added. "Like, they're good to you and all of that?" She looked like the fate of the entire world hung on his answer.

"No, yeah, they're great," Joaquin said. "It's just . . . yeah. It's a lot. Still trying to process it."

"Seventeen years is a long time to wait for a family," Maya said, trying to sound encouraging, the way Claire always did when Maya felt down or ragged, and Joaquin's mouth curled up into a smile that didn't make him look either happy or sad.

"It is," he agreed, then laughed. "It's a fucking long time."

"So do you have to do all the paperwork?" Grace asked. "Can we come to the ceremony?"

"Grace, pump the brakes," Maya told her.

"Sorry."

"I don't know that I'm going to say yes," Joaquin admitted. "They asked me a month ago, but it's my decision."

Grace and Maya exchanged a glance between them. "Why . . . wouldn't you?" Maya dared to ask. "You just said that they're great."

Joaquin shifted in his seat, opened his mouth, closed it, and opened it again. "Not sure," he said. "Just a lot of things to figure out."

Maya wondered whether, if she shook Joaquin, all the thoughts he'd been holding in would fall out of him like candy out of a piñata. It was a tempting image.

Grace was the first to speak. "Why wouldn't you want them to adopt you?" she asked. "It's not . . . You can say anything. I'm not judging, I'm just curious."

Joaquin looked like he wanted a car to drive through the shop window and interrupt the entire conversation. "It's just hard to explain," he said. "It's a lot. There's a lot."

Maya could see Grace starting to open her mouth again, so she gave her a tiny pinch, the same way she used to pinch Lauren when they were kids.

"Ow!" Grace yelped.

"My hand slipped," Maya said.

"It did not. You pinched me!"

Maya shrugged. "You're verbally assaulting Joaquin. Leave him alone already."

"Oh," Grace said. "Sorry." She was still biting her lip, though, and Maya knew that she was about to say something else—something equally delightful.

"I still think we should meet our bio mom," Grace said.

There it is, Maya thought wearily.

"Fuck. No," she told her. "Absolutely not. Stop bringing it up—it's ridiculous."

"It's not ridiculous," Grace shot back. "It's totally reasonable."

Maya looked at Joaquin, who seemed like he'd rather be stuck in a broken-down car on the freeway than between the two of them. "Please back me up on this," she said.

Joaquin just looked at Grace while pointing at Maya. "What she said."

"*Thank* you," Maya sighed, sitting back in her seat and reaching for her drink.

"No," Grace said, and now she seemed annoyed. "You tell me why *you* don't want to, Joaquin. Don't just say 'what Maya said.' That's not fair. She's your mom, too."

"No, she's not," Joaquin murmured. "She stopped being my mom a long time ago."

Maya raised an eyebrow at Grace as if to say, *See?*

"If you want to go for it, Grace, do it," Joaquin told her. "I'm not holding you back. I don't really care. I just don't want to be involved. I don't want to know about her. I know when I'm not wanted, you know?"

"Grace, why don't you tell us something about *your* week

instead?" Maya suggested. "My parents are divorcing, Joaquin's parents want to adopt him, so you better have a good story. And don't say, 'I want to find my bio mom,' or I'll pinch you harder this time."

Grace's face changed from annoyed to thoughtful before she finally said, "I punched a guy at school and now I have to be home-schooled until the end of the school year."

If Grace had said that she had been arrested for running an elephant-breeding program in her backyard, Maya would have been less surprised.

"You *what*?" Maya said before she could stop herself. "No, you didn't. I don't believe you. Joaquin doesn't believe you, either."

"I believe her," Joaquin said gently, then pointed to Grace's right hand. Her thumb was bruised, Maya suddenly noticed, and one of her fingers had a scabbed-over cut. "You didn't tuck your thumb. Nice."

Grace just shrugged. "It all happened pretty fast."

"You seriously punched a guy?" Maya wished she had known this fact before pinching her just a minute ago. "What's thumb tucking? Is Grace some secret boxer now?"

Grace laughed in a way that didn't sound funny, then ran a hand over her eyes. "Definitely *not* a secret."

"When you punch someone, you have to put your thumb over your first two knuckles. Here, like this." Joaquin held up his hand to show Maya. "You can hit better and make more of an impact without hurting yourself."

"There's not going to be a next time," Grace insisted, but next to her, Maya nodded, pleased by this new piece of information.

Maya was impressed that Joaquin knew all that. She wondered if this was what it would have been like to grow up with him, a big brother protecting her, teaching her how to protect herself, someone else to carry the burden, unearth the empty wine bottles from under the bed and inside the refrigerator. Maya had found another one in the bucket of cleaning supplies under the bathroom sink. She hadn't told Lauren.

"Why'd you do it?" Maya asked instead. "Did he touch you?" If that was the case, Maya wasn't sure that she could stop herself from finding the guy and punching him again on behalf of Grace. (She'd remember the thumb trick, too.)

"He just . . ." Grace looked as uncomfortable as Joaquin had earlier, squirming and biting her bottom lip. "He just said some pretty terrible things about my family, that's all. I couldn't let him get away with that."

"Family's important," Joaquin said.

Maya nodded. She wondered how important it could be, though, when hers just seemed to keep fracturing into pieces.

That night, she climbed into bed, the blissful silence ringing out throughout the house. Lauren had already gone to sleep. She and Maya had watched TV that night while their mom was upstairs on the phone. Maya could hear her voice but not her words, which made it hard to tell if she was slurring or not. Lauren had slumped next to her on the couch and didn't argue when Maya changed the channel from a wedding show to a cheesy movie, some romantic comedy that they had both seen at least fifty times before.

She had tried to text Claire, too, but she hadn't responded, and Maya felt that dark vine climbing up around her phone now, almost like it was keeping Claire's response away. She knew that there were a million good reasons why Claire wasn't writing back—she had homework, she was grounded, her phone was dead, she was at the movies with her grandmother, anything—but Maya kept checking it anyway, feeling angrier each time her text that read my dad moved out today went unanswered.

By the time her head finally hit the pillow, Maya was exhausted. How nice, she thought, to be able to fall asleep without the muffled sounds of fighting, but after an hour of tossing and turning, she realized that the silence in their house was too loud, too still. Now that it was quiet, Maya could *hear* almost everything, including every tiny noise that sounded like someone was breaking into their house. It was ridiculous, of course. They pretty much lived in the safest (some people—like Maya, for instance—might say *most boring*) neighborhood in America. No one would actually break into their house. But Maya hadn't ever really worried about the potential threat before. Her dad had always been there to protect her. Even when he had been gone on business trips, she'd known he would come back eventually.

Now?

She never thought silence could sound so scary.

She eventually fell into a restless sleep, woken only by the buzz of a text message on her phone. It was Claire. I'm so sorry! it said. I was camping with my family. We just got back to civilization. Are you ok?

Maya had forgotten about the camping trip, and she felt dumb for being upset about Claire's absence. She held her thumb over the keyboard for a long time. It felt like there weren't enough letters in the alphabet for everything she had to say, for all the words that wanted to tumble out of her.

Where were you?

I needed you.

I need you.

I'm scared of how much I need you.

Instead she wrote back, I'm fine. Going to bed now. Chat tomorrow. Then she found a song on her phone that she hadn't listened to in years, one that she had heard even before she had met Claire. She fell asleep to it, the words filling the silence in her room, the sudden cavity that seemed to be steadily growing, burrowing its way into her heart.

JOAQUIN

So how were Maya and Grace?" Mark asked from the front seat. Linda didn't like driving on freeways, not if she could help it. She said they made her feel jittery. Joaquin thought that when Linda drove on the freeway, *everyone* in the car felt jittery.

"They're fine," Joaquin said, then added, "Maya's parents are getting a divorce," because he knew that *fine* wasn't going to suffice, not with Mark and Linda. They expected more from him.

"Well, that doesn't sound fine," Linda said, turning around in her seat. Joaquin didn't know how she could do that. He always got nauseous whenever he faced backward in a car.

"I mean, not *fine* fine," Joaquin explained. "I just meant that they weren't missing any limbs or anything."

"Your standards for *fine* are pretty low." Mark laughed as he changed lanes.

"And Grace punched a guy," Joaquin told them.

"You sure you don't want to rethink that 'fine' statement?" Linda asked, just as Mark said, "Grace *punched* a guy? She looks like the human equivalent of a kitten."

Joaquin had no idea what that meant, but he decided not to ask. Sometimes Mark's brain worked in weird, creative ways. "I guess someone at school said something bad about her family, so she clocked them."

Later that night, though, when he was upstairs in his room, Joaquin regretted what he had said. Not the part about Grace, but the part where he'd told his sisters that he knew how to punch. Maybe Linda and Mark would think he was violent now. Maybe they would wonder why he was even capable of throwing a punch in the first place.

Joaquin hadn't actually been in a fistfight before. But he had lived with a family when he was ten—two foster sisters, an older biological one, and Joaquin. The mom was an executive assistant in Long Beach and the dad was an amateur boxer. At first, Joaquin had worried about the potential ramifications of having a fighter in the family, but the dad had been really nice. He would even show Joaquin how to punch the bag that hung in the garage, which was too packed with stuff to park any cars in it.

"Like this," he said to Joaquin one afternoon, and had tucked his thumb carefully around Joaquin's small hand so that it was a perfect, solid fist. "Now hit the bag. Hit it hard."

Joaquin had punched, hard. He suspected that the foster dad just liked having a son to do things with (the girls weren't

interested in punching things in the dusty garage, apparently).
The home had been pretty good, too, one of his best, but then one
of the social workers had figured out that they had too many kids
for the square footage of the house, and because Joaquin had been
the last one in, he was the first one to go out.

That's when he had ended up at the Buchanans'.

Joaquin had learned a lot of things in his seventeen years. One
of the things that came from moving from family to family was
that he learned how to adapt, how to change his colors like a cha-
meleon so that he could blend in to his surroundings. He always
hoped that if he did the correct things, said the correct things, no
one would realize that he was a foster kid. Everyone—neighbors,
people at school, the person who bagged their groceries—would
just think that he was one of the bio kids, as permanent as blood,
someone who could never be traded in, swapped out, sent away.

So he had learned boxing from one family. He also knew how
to make great chocolate chip cookies and loaves of bread from
when he lived with the family whose dad was a pastry chef at a
fancy restaurant in Los Angeles. Another mom taught him callig-
raphy, and then he had an older foster brother who was super into
early punk music and used to greet Joaquin at the door holding
an album and saying, "Wait until you listen to *this*." Joaquin had
loved the attention. Not so much the music, though. It jangled his
nerves.

He didn't mind adapting like that. It felt like hopping from
stone to stone, picking up tricks of the trade along the way,

leveling up on his way to the final battle. He would watch the families to see if they waited to say grace before dinner, if they put their napkins in their laps and kept their elbows off the table. Whatever they did, Joaquin did it, too.

It was when people assumed that he *didn't* know things that he got upset. He still remembered one foster mother, an older woman who had smelled like cloyingly sweet powder, like someone had pulverized rose petals and sprinkled them on her clothes. She had crouched down in front of Joaquin upon his arrival at her house, smiled with her yellowing teeth, and said, "Do you know what *iced tea* is, sweetheart?"

Joaquin knew immediately that she'd asked him that because he looked Mexican. He knew that tone of voice, the slow speech in case he didn't understand English (like speaking more slowly would somehow be more effective), the assumption behind the question that he had never experienced something as basic as *iced fucking tea* before. When he had nodded and said, "Yes," she had seemed almost disappointed, like someone else had planted their flag in Joaquin before she could get the chance.

Since that day, Joaquin had hated iced tea.

That night at dinner, both Mark and Linda kept glancing at each other. Joaquin felt like he was watching a tennis match, glancing back and forth between both of them.

He finally couldn't take it anymore.

"What?" he said, spearing a piece of broccoli with his fork.

(At Mark and Linda's, Joaquin had adapted to eating vegetables at every meal. Broccoli and spinach were fine; brussels sprouts were death, even when they were cooked in butter.)

"What what?" Mark replied, mostly because that was their routine.

"You keep looking at each other," he said, gesturing with his fork at them. "Something's up."

Mark and Linda looked at each other again.

"See?" Joaquin said.

Linda smiled at that. "We just wanted to talk to you about what we discussed last month."

Joaquin set his fork down and readjusted his napkin. (In his lap.) "Oh," he said.

Mark cleared his throat. That's how Joaquin knew he was nervous. Mark had all sorts of tells, but that was a big one. "We just wanted to know if you had had time to think about it. We know this has been a busy month for you, what with finding Maya and Grace and getting to know them."

"But," Linda quickly added, "we're fine with waiting if you need more time to think about it. We don't want to pressure you at all, sweetheart."

Joaquin had thought about it so much that he didn't think there was any possible way to have new thoughts about it.

"I'm still thinking," he said. "Don't worry."

Mark cleared his throat again. Linda tried not to look hopeful, but she didn't have much success at hiding the expression that flitted across her face.

Joaquin thought about Grace defending her family, about Maya's parents splitting up, her dad moving out. "I have a question," he said.

Mark and Linda sat up at the same time like nervous rabbits, their ears pricking up. "Of course," Mark said. "We imagined you would. You know we're always here to answer questions if you need it."

"And we'll answer them truthfully," Linda added. She knew that was important to him.

"Okay," Joaquin said slowly, sitting back in his chair. "So if I say no, that I don't want to be adopted, do I have to leave?"

Linda seemed to wilt, while Mark looked like one of those helium balloons that Joaquin had gotten from a birthday party when he was seven. He had been so excited to bring it home and keep it, but the next day it was sunken and deflated, almost to the ground. Seeing Mark that way made Joaquin feel as bad as when he had woken up and seen the balloon.

"I mean, I'm not saying no," he quickly added. "But I just wanted to . . . yeah. I just wanted to know." Now Joaquin was the one clearing his throat.

"Joaquin," Linda said, and her voice was as soft as it was whenever he had a nightmare, like it could be a protective barrier between him and any bad thing that would possibly happen. "No matter what you decide, no matter what happens going forward, there will always be a place for you in our home."

Joaquin nodded and ignored the tightness in his throat.

"Have you talked to your therapist about it?" Mark asked.

Joaquin nodded.

He had not. He knew that Ana would be 100 percent in favor of the adoption, and he didn't want her to sway him. Joaquin had realized early on that he needed to figure out things in his head before he brought them up to Ana. Otherwise, she just muddled up his thoughts until he wasn't sure how *he* felt anymore.

"I told her I needed to think about it on my own for a while," Joaquin said instead, which he considered a half-truth and therefore not really a lie. "But I just wanted to know what would happen if I said no, that's all."

Mark was quiet for a few seconds before asking, "Are you afraid of what will happen if you say yes?"

One of the things about adapting, Joaquin had learned, was that you could get so comfortable in a family that their tells would become *your* tells, too, and then they would know the things that could scare you before *you* even knew about them.

"I mean, it's a change either way, right?" Joaquin said, then started to stand up. "Can I be excused?"

"Joaquin," Linda said, and he froze halfway up. "We're not scared of adopting you, if that's what you're worried about. Mark and I love you. We know you. We *trust* you. Implicitly."

Joaquin wondered if Linda was thinking about the Buchanans, the hospital reports, the X-ray of Joaquin's broken arm.

"I'm not scared," he said, then cleared his throat. *Goddamnit.*

"It's okay if you are," Mark started to say, just as Linda said, "We really do want you."

"I know," Joaquin said to both of them. "I know that."

He *did* know that. That's what was freaking him out so bad.

Joaquin saw Birdie the next day at school.

Truth be told, the potential to see her at school *every* day was there. (Joaquin had carefully floated the idea of maybe going to a different high school after he had broken up with her, but Mark and Linda had shot that idea down flat.) Instead, he had changed his routine, going down different hallways, taking the long way to English class instead of the shortcut through the quad, where he used to hold Birdie's hand before kissing her good-bye. "Gutierrez," the vice principal would say sometimes if he saw them kissing, glaring warningly at Joaquin.

"Why don't you ever say *my* last name?" Birdie had shot back once.

The vice principal left them alone after that.

Joaquin thought he had gotten pretty good at avoiding her, but that morning during their snack break, he went past the back side of the gym, trying to get to calculus early so that he wouldn't see Birdie while she was walking to her AP Civics class. (He almost wished he had a tracking device on her so that he could know where she was at any given time. He would have wished it, if he hadn't realized immediately how creepy that sounded.)

But that morning, apparently, Birdie was early to class or late leaving wherever she had been before, because Joaquin rounded the gym just as she did. They didn't bump into each other—that would have been too perfect, too cute—but they both stopped when they saw each other.

"Hi," Birdie said.

"Hey," Joaquin replied, jamming his hands into his hoodie pockets and looking down at his shoes. Looking at Birdie was too hard, too *much*. She still looked like she wanted to murder him, which made him nervous. He couldn't blame her, though. Sometimes he wanted to murder himself for doing something so terrible to her.

Birdie didn't move, and Joaquin started to go around. "Wait, Joaq, no," she said, putting her hand on his arm. Her hands were always cold; he could feel it even through his hoodie sleeve.

Joaquin froze when she touched him, but Birdie didn't let go. The very first time she had kissed him, he had panicked at how soft she was, how hot her mouth felt, and he didn't understand how someone with such cold hands could have such a warm heart. "I have to . . ." he started to say, but he didn't have anything he had to do.

"Wait," she said again. "Just . . . I miss you so much, Joaq. I really . . ." Her voice started to drift away, and when Joaquin dared to look up, he saw that she was crying.

In almost ten months of dating, Joaquin had never seen Birdie cry, not even once.

"I miss you, too," he said.

"Can you just tell me why, please?" she said, her face struggling to smooth itself back into control. "Please—we never lied to each other. I don't want this to end because of a lie *now*."

Joaquin looked down again. He hated this feeling, the feeling that all the words that he wanted to say would just tangle themselves into a giant ball, wound so tight that nothing could manage to escape. The words would just sit on his chest, pressing down on his lungs, pulling the air out of him.

"I didn't lie" was all he finally said. He wanted to touch her so bad, pull her into his arms, make her stop crying. He knew what it was like to cry by yourself, after all. He didn't want that for Birdie.

"Then why? I keep going over and over it again in my head, and I can't understand why!" Now she was getting mad. Joaquin had seen Birdie mad many times. It rarely ended well for the person she was mad at.

"Because I think you *did* lie to me!" she yelled. "I think you lied and said that you wanted to break up, but I think you just got scared, that you ran away because it was easier than being left again!"

Joaquin kept looking down at his shoes, letting her words bounce off his chest. Nothing could get to him, not even Birdie, who always seemed to be able to untangle the words that he struggled to find.

"Is that what it is?" she asked, stepping toward him. "I'm right, aren't I? You bailed because you got scared."

"It's not—" he started to say, taking a step back from her.

"I don't care if you're scared!" she cried, and now she really was crying again. Joaquin hoped none of Birdie's friends would find out about this. They would murder him in the hallway after school, no questions asked.

"You can be scared!" Birdie was still shouting. "Don't you get it? That's what happens when you love someone: they're brave when you can't be! I can be brave—for you, for both of us!"

"You can't," Joaquin said, laughing a little. It wasn't funny, though. None of this was funny at all.

"Yes, I can!" Birdie closed the space between them, pulling his hands out of his pocket and holding them in hers. She was freezing. "You can trust me. Don't you know that?"

Joaquin nodded. He tried to make himself let go of her hands. She clung on, though, and he took another step away.

Birdie looked hopeful for the first time in their conversation. "So what is it? What's wrong, Joaquin?"

The words suddenly pushed themselves out of Joaquin's lungs, making him feel lighter, freer. "I don't trust myself," he said. "And there's no way you can fix that, Birdie. So leave me alone."

She was still crying when he finally let go of her hands and walked away.

GRACE

For days after meeting up with Maya and Joaquin, Grace was a mess.

She felt on edge, sleep deprived, and overcaffeinated. She kept dreaming of Peach in her little sailor outfit, sailing away on a boat, crying as lustfully as she had the day she had been born, and Grace couldn't get to her, couldn't reach out, couldn't hold her baby.

She woke up gasping, her arms outstretched, the sound of Peach still ringing in her ears.

Grace knew what it was, of course. She was convinced that she had chosen the wrong parents for Peach, that Daniel and Catalina wouldn't stay together and that they would divorce, just like Maya's parents had. She still felt bad about asking Maya whether or not the adoption would be invalid. That had been a supremely stupid thing to say, Grace knew that, but she couldn't help herself at the time. The idea that she had picked the wrong parents, the wrong home, for Peach sent her into a panic that clawed at her back whenever she was alone—whenever her mind was quiet. *You did it wrong,* a voice would say, and Grace would shiver. *You had one job as Peach's mom, and you completely, royally fucked it up.*

Before Peach, Grace hadn't really given her biological mom much thought, but now this strange woman kept dominating her mind. She wondered if her bio mom had ever worried about her, or Maya, or Joaquin. She must have, though, right? Even if Maya and Joaquin disagreed with her, Grace knew more than they did. She had lived it. They couldn't possibly understand the pull that Grace felt.

She wished she could ask her mom about it, or even her dad. They had always had an agreement that if Grace wanted to know anything, all she had to do was ask, but that put all the pressure, all the responsibility, on Grace. There were questions she didn't even know how to ask, and sometimes she felt that if her parents really wanted her to know things, they would just tell her. Why did she have to ask the questions, anyway? Weren't *they* the parents? Wasn't *she* the kid?

But now, in a way, she was the mom. And Grace hadn't quite figured out how to make up the difference between the two spaces yet.

One thing she did know, though: staying home with her parents was slowly beginning to drive her insane.

Grace knew they were trying to keep her occupied, keep her from feeling completely left out from friends who never called anymore. (Grace suspected that they just didn't know what to say, and honestly, she wouldn't have known what to say in response.) But they were her *parents*, after all. They were boring, and plus, they had actual jobs. Grace found herself home in the mornings, watching talk television with her untouched history textbook in front of her. She especially liked all the courtroom judge shows. Those people's problems always seemed much worse, yet much more easily solvable, than her own.

When her parents were home, they tried to keep her busy. "Come with me to yoga," her mom had suggested one morning, and Grace had just rolled over in bed and pulled the covers back over her head. "Wanna learn how to golf?" her dad had asked one day, and Grace didn't even reply to his question because it was so ridiculous. (Later, though, he made her help him wash the cars, and Grace sort of wished she had said yes to golf instead.)

One of the reasons Grace had given up Peach was because she hadn't wanted her life to stop ("You're so *young*," her parents had implored over and over again), but nobody had told Grace that her life might stop anyway, that she'd be trapped in the amber of her pregnancy, of Peach, while the rest of the world continued to change around her.

One afternoon, when her mom was working from home, Grace leaned her head into the office. "Hey," she said. "Can I borrow the car?"

"May I ask why?" her mom said without looking up from her laptop.

Grace thought fast. "Um, Janie called. She wants to know if I want to meet her at the mall."

Her mom looked up from her laptop.

Fifteen minutes later, Grace was driving to the mall, all the windows down so she could feel fresh air again. Her mom hadn't asked too many questions after that lie, and Grace hadn't bothered to explain anything beyond the basics. Nobody needed to know that she hadn't talked to Janie since that ill-fated day back at school, that Janie hadn't so much as texted her since Grace had punched Max's friend in the face. Grace couldn't even be that mad at Janie about it, though. She hadn't been a good friend to Janie. She had stopped calling and texting. She'd ignored Janie's calls and texts because she didn't know how to explain how she felt, how to explain the rawness of this new world. If the situation was reversed, maybe Janie wouldn't have called or texted her, either. Grace had no idea. She only knew who she was now, and that was a girl who didn't have friends anymore.

But she did have Rafe.

"Hey!" he said when he saw her wandering down the gadget aisle of Whisked Away. "Let me guess—your mom got insomnia again and bought that thing that cooks salmon in the microwave."

"I hope not," Grace said, wrinkling her nose.

"Okay, good, because it doesn't work. I didn't want to say anything," he added as Grace smiled at him. "I work here. I shouldn't trash our amazing gadgets and supplies, but it's really bad. Your microwave will never recover."

Grace laughed at that. "Well, we don't have a microwave. My

parents don't believe in them."

Rafe widened his eyes at her, then walked over and carefully put his hands on her shoulders. "Grace," he said quietly. "Is this a cry for help? Just blink if you need me to make a call."

She laughed again. "Are you hungry?"

"Yes," he said, moving his hands from her shoulders and taking that warmth away. "Starving. I had to take a make-up quiz during lunch. Did you eat already? Please tell me your parents at least believe in eating lunch. Otherwise I might actually have to call Child Protective Services."

Grace laughed a little less this time. It wasn't as funny now that she knew Joaquin. "I'll buy," she said. "But I only have enough cash for me to eat."

"You sweet talker," Rafe replied, then started to take off his apron. "Give me two minutes."

They ended up at a sandwich place just down from the store. (Grace tried to keep the distance short. The last thing she needed was to see anyone she knew from school.) "Can I ask you a question?" Grace said as they tucked into their sandwiches.

"No, you may not have any of my Doritos," Rafe replied. "Get your own if you want them."

Grace just wrinkled her nose. She'd never be able to eat Doritos again, not after what she'd read about preservatives and food dyes when she was pregnant with Peach. "I don't want your Doritos," she said. "Keep that fake cheese to yourself."

"It's not really cheese until it's spelled with a z," Rafe told her. "But I digress."

"Are your parents divorced?"

"Yep," he said before popping a chip into his mouth. He crunched. "Am I mutating yet?"

Grace threw a piece of lettuce at him, which he caught before it hit the table. "Masterful reflexes," he said. "Just FYI."

"Your parents?" Grace said.

"Yes, ma'am. Split up when I was five. I'm pretty sure the world is only turning because they got divorced. Otherwise their fights would have probably made the planet implode."

The idea of parents fighting was so foreign to Grace. Her parents had always argued behind closed doors, whatever battle they had smoothed over by the time the sun rose next morning. She had never even heard them yell at each other.

"What about you?" Rafe asked.

"No, they're still married."

"Throw the rice."

"But Maya, she—"

"Is that your sister?"

Grace paused.

"The sort-of sister?" Rafe amended.

"No, she's my actual sister," Grace said, and was surprised by the bristle in her own voice. "Maya's not 'sort of' anything."

"I'm sorry," Rafe said, and he both sounded and looked sorry. "That was an asshole thing to say. Carry on with your tale of woe."

Grace rolled her eyes. "Never mind."

"No, wait. Shit," he said, then set down his chips. "Okay, I'm really sorry. You were telling me something serious and I blew it.

Let's have a do-over, okay?" He pretended to hit a rewind button. "Aaaaand back."

Grace had to give him points for effort. "Okay," she said. "So Maya's parents—"

"The parents of your real, true, actual, one hundred percent sister, yes, go on."

"—are getting divorced."

"Well, that sucks. Is she upset?"

"It's hard to tell with her," Grace replied, reaching for one of her apple slices. "She sort of plays it cool a lot of the time."

"That sounds healthy," Rafe said. "She's probably super upset on the inside. You should talk to her."

"I'm still trying to figure out *how* to talk to her. And Joaquin, too. They're both just . . . They're different."

"Well, yeah, welcome to having siblings," Rafe said. "My dad actually had two kids way before he met my mom, so my brother and sister are both in their twenties. It's like having four parents. I don't recommend the experience, by the way."

"But do you think . . ." Grace tried to choose her words as carefully as she could. "Do you think that . . . like, okay, when your parents divorced, did it . . . Are you . . ."

"Did it completely fuck me up?" Rafe asked. "Is that what you want to know?"

"Yes," Grace said with a sigh of relief. "Exactly that."

"Well, you better hope not, since you're the one who asked me to lunch." Rafe reached over and swiped one of her apple slices.

"Relax, I'm just trying to counteract the Doritos."

"I don't think that's how science works," Grace said.

"Whatever, Bill Nye." Rafe stuck the slice into his mouth, then chewed. "And to answer your question, no, it did not fuck me up. It made things more difficult, of course, and I still get two Christmases, two birthdays, all of that good stuff, but I'm not fucked up."

"But do you think that you could have had a *better* experience?"

Rafe was eyeing her carefully. "Why do I feel like you want me to say what you want to hear?"

"Because maybe I do," she admitted, and then she realized that she had chewed the top of her straw into two separate pieces.

"Wait, no, let me see if I can follow your train of thought," Rafe said, sitting back in his chair. "I'm taking AP Psych at school, so don't worry, you're in good hands."

"Great," Grace said. "My brain feels super safe right now."

Rafe just waved away her concerns, staring at her for almost thirty seconds. Grace hadn't realized how long thirty seconds actually was.

"You're worried that the adoptive parents you chose for Peach are going to split up," Rafe finally said. "That's why you're asking all these questions. You're not worried about Maya, you're worried about the baby. God, I'm so going to get a five on this AP test. I'm going to *clobber* it."

Just hearing the name fall from Rafe's mouth made her eyes fill with tears. "That's it," she said, her voice wobbling.

Rafe, however, went from looking triumphant over his future AP test to looking absolutely horrified. "Oh, shit," he said. "I made you cry. Ohhh, shit, this is not good."

"No, it's fine, it's fine," Grace said, waving him away, but Rafe was already climbing out of his side of the booth and coming over to hers. "It's fine, it's just . . . no one's ever said that name before. I'm the only one who calls her Peach." She used one of the paper napkins to wipe at her eyes, suddenly mortified. This was probably why she had a hard time staying in touch with her friends. She didn't want them to be there for the all-too-frequent waterworks.

Rafe was sitting next to her now, his thigh pressing against hers. No boy had been this close to Grace since the night she and Max had had the sex that produced Peach, but she didn't scoot away from him. "I know I've told you this before," Rafe said gently, "but I am *terrible* when girls cry. I'm awful. I'm going to really screw this up, so do you think you could stop crying before it ruins our beautiful friendship?"

Grace was laughing even as she kept wiping her eyes. "No, you're fine, it just got me," she said. "That's all. I'm fine, really."

Rafe seemed dubious, but he let it go and just handed her a fresh napkin instead. "Feel better?"

Grace nodded. "It's just that I basically had one job as her mom, you know? I had to pick her parents, and I thought I did a really good job, but—what if I didn't? What if fifteen years later, Daniel and Catalina split up and it ruins her life?"

"Why does it have to ruin her life, though?" Rafe said. "My parents split up—it didn't ruin my life."

"I don't want anything to be hard for her," Grace admitted. "I just want to say that I did the right thing for her, that's all."

"You did," Rafe said. "You *know* you did. And nobody has an easy life, Grace. Not me, definitely not you. I mean, you had a baby at sixteen, right? But your life's not *ruined*."

"I don't have any friends," Grace said, and now she was crying again. "Nobody texts me or calls me or stops by to say hi. I don't run cross-country anymore with Janie—"

"You ran cross-country?"

Grace nodded. "Varsity. But now I spend all day with my parents and they act like I'll break if they say the wrong thing to me—"

"I mean, to be fair, you *are* sort of breaking because I said the wrong thing to you."

"—and I had to find parents for my baby and I did it all wrong and Max was fucking homecoming king!"

People were starting to look over their shoulders at her. "She's fine," Grace heard Rafe say. "Contact lenses. The *worst*, am I right?" Then he leaned so that he was blocking people's view of her. "Look," he said. "You know what nobody cares about the day after homecoming? Who was homecoming king. Like, anyone who introduces themselves as 'homecoming king' after the actual homecoming dance is a complete asshole, so don't worry about that." Then he paused. "Max was the dad, right?"

Grace nodded, reaching for another napkin.

"Okay, so that's one problem solved. As for this baby—"

"You can say Peach—it's okay."

Rafe looked dubious. "As far as her, her life's not going to be easy. As long as she's living it correctly, there's going to be hard times for her. And anybody who cares this much about the kind of parents she has probably picked a pretty good set for her.

"Now, as far as friends, you've got me, right? I mean, we're eating lunch together. Pretty sure that's what friends do. And the only reason I don't text or call you is because I don't have your phone number." Rafe raised an eyebrow. "You *do* have a phone, right? Your parents aren't forcing you to communicate via carrier pigeon, are they? Because that might be why no one's calling you."

Grace smiled, looking down at her half-eaten sandwich on the table. "Cell phones are fine," she said. "We're not pioneers."

"Well, great then. Just give me your phone and I'll text you and you'll text me back. Wham bam, thank you, ma'am. Metaphorically, I mean. I'm not going to wham bam you."

Grace looked at him. "Do you talk a lot when you get nervous?"

"I talk *so* fucking much when I'm nervous." Rafe grinned at her. "What gave it away?"

"Call it a hunch. And it's just . . . I don't know if I want to date anyone right now, that's all."

Rafe pretended to draw back in horror. "Okay, honestly, Grace? Why do you keep insisting that I'm trying to date you? This is sexual harassment, that's what this is. In my place of *employment*, even."

Grace was giggling now. She couldn't remember the last time she had actually giggled. "Platonic texting?" she said. "That's all?"

Rafe held up one hand. "Scout's honor," he said. "Even though I was never a Boy Scout. But you can still trust me. You have to stop harassing me at work, though, or I'm going to file a complaint with HR and then you're going to be up to your eyeballs in paperwork."

Grace just held out her hand for his phone, then input her number. "Do they even have HR at Whisked Away?" she wondered.

"Wouldn't you like to know?" Rafe said, taking his phone back. "Are you done crying? Did I fix you?"

"At ease, soldier," Grace said, and Rafe ruffled her hair before sliding back into his own side of the booth.

She got home an hour later, the other half of her sandwich wrapped up in a paper bag. "Is that you?" her mom called from her office.

"No!" Grace yelled back. "It's a serial killer!"

"Can you ask him to check to make sure I turned off the coffeemaker, please?"

"How do you know it's a him?"

"Odds are!"

Grace checked the coffeemaker. "You're good!"

She tried to sneak past her mom's door, but her mom stopped her. "Wait," she said, and Grace took half a step backward. "Have you been crying?"

"Oh, no, no," Grace said as she headed for the stairs. "Contact lenses. The *worst*, am I right?"

MAYA

It wasn't that Maya meant to break up with Claire.

It just sort of . . . happened.

Maya couldn't stop being mad at her for not answering her texts the night that Maya's dad moved out. She knew that it was stupid, of course, but still, it hung around her like a jacket she couldn't shrug off.

It didn't help that Claire didn't seem to get why Maya was so upset.

"I told you," Claire said the next day at lunch. Maya didn't have her head in Claire's lap this time; instead, she was sitting across from her, their lunches spread out between them like a wall, a barrier made up of bread crusts and orange peels. "I was camping, I didn't have my phone, I—"

"Who doesn't have their phone?" Maya asked, exasperated. "I'm fairly sure that mine is pretty much grafted to my hand!

How do you *not* have your phone?"

"Okay, so let's say I had it," Claire said, sitting up a little. "And I'm camping with my family, and there's basically zero reception, and you text me that your dad just moved out. What am I supposed to do?"

Maya thought that the sun was exploding behind her eyes.

"Oh, I don't know," she said, aware of how much she sounded like Lauren right then, high-pitched and obvious. "Maybe *text me back*? I'm just spitballing here, though."

"But then what? I couldn't talk to you, I couldn't come over. I mean, Maya, your dad didn't die, he just moved ten minutes away."

Maya started to gather up her bag.

"No, wait, My, no." Claire reached out for her, grabbing her by the wrist. "I'm sorry, I didn't mean that."

"You *so* meant that," Maya said, but she stopped moving, her bag dangling from her hand.

"I just meant——" Claire sighed, took a deep breath. "Look, you know my dad's not around. At least yours is, okay? You can still see him every day if you want. You could text him right now and he'd probably text you back in less than thirty seconds."

This was all true. Maya was always slightly pleased and slightly embarrassed by how fast her dad responded to her texts. (Her life got considerably more difficult when he discovered the emoji keyboard.) Maya knew that she didn't have a lot of room to complain, that she still had it way better than most kids. Look at Joaquin! He didn't even have parents.

But that didn't make her feel any better.

"It's all just because this is new," Claire continued, still holding on to Maya's wrist, anchoring her in the grass. "And I'm sorry I wasn't there that day, okay? If I could have been, I would have been there in a second. I swear. Okay? Okay?" she repeated when Maya didn't respond. "I hate fighting with you. I'd rather make out with you. It's so much more fun."

Maya's mouth perked up at the corners. "It is way more fun," she said. "But I'm still mad."

Claire started to pull her back down to the grass, and Maya fell to her knees, her bag thudding down heavily next to her. "You wanna make-up make out?" Claire said, smiling against Maya's mouth. "I've heard it's pretty hot."

Maya smiled again, her teeth bumping against Claire's mouth. "Because nothing's more hot than making out behind the gym at school," she said, winding her arms around Claire's neck.

"Let's find out," Claire replied, and they tumbled into the grass.

The breakup happened five days later.

Looking back, Maya realized that it wasn't really either of their faults. It was a Saturday, and they should have been hanging out, but Claire had to watch her little brother and Maya was up to her neck in physics homework. Their make-out session in the grass at school had been pretty great, but it didn't solve anything. Maya couldn't help but think of it as like the Hello Kitty Band-Aids she and Lauren had had when they were little: super cute, but not so great when it came to fixing major wounds.

When they finally got together that afternoon, Maya was cranky from homework and Claire was exhausted from watching her little brother. They were supposed to go to the movies, but the one they wanted to see was sold out and they couldn't agree on anything else.

"What about that one?" Maya suggested, pointing at the board.

"That looks dumb," Claire said, squinting up.

"It's literally just a title. How do you know it looks dumb?"

"It *sounds* dumb."

Maya sighed. "Okay, what about—"

"No aliens."

"How do you even know there are—"

"It literally says *aliens* right there in the title."

"What if it's a metaphor?"

Claire just raised an eyebrow at Maya.

"Fine," Maya said. "Let's just get coffee. No aliens there."

But Claire was sulky about not being able to see the movie, and the weather was the sort of warm that became uncomfortable and sweaty after more than five minutes of sitting in the sun, and Maya's dad had texted her and Lauren saying that his business trip to New Orleans had been extended by two days and could they grab dinner on Tuesday night instead of Sunday? He loved them and was really, *really* sorry.

"Figures," Maya said, tucking her phone back into her pocket without answering him. Let Lauren handle that part. What was the point of having a younger sister if you couldn't make her do your dirty work, after all?

Claire eyed her as she sipped at her drink. *There's way too much whipped cream in that cup,* Maya thought, then wondered when things like that had started bothering her about Claire in the first place.

"What figures?" Claire asked, talking around her straw. "Who was that?"

"My dad," Maya said. "He's stuck on a business trip in New Orleans. He can't have dinner with me and Laur until Tuesday."

"Oh. Well, that sucks."

Maya glanced at Claire. She could feel a sunburn starting to spread across her bare shoulders. She hadn't put on sunscreen since they were supposed to have gone to the movies. "Go ahead, say it."

"Say what?"

"Say what you're really thinking."

Claire paused before saying, "Well, I mean, that sucks, but at least you'll see your dad next Tuesday, right? It's just a few days. Maybe you can spend more time with him next weekend."

It was a perfect reasonable response, Maya knew, and it was exactly the sort of response that infuriated her. Claire was too measured, too reasonable, too Claire. Even her goddamn *name* sounded calm. Maya wanted someone to be as angry as she was, someone to be at her level so that she wouldn't feel all alone up at the top of her volcano, red lava spewing everywhere inside her.

"Why do you have to do that?" Maya said. She would have sipped at her drink, but she had finished it a long time ago. On top of everything else, Claire was a slow drinker, too.

"Do what?"

"Always be so freaking calm," Maya said. They had been sitting on a wall by the fountain, and Maya hopped down, too agitated to sit still. "Why do you always have to be like my mom?"

"Your mom?" Claire said, starting to laugh. "You think I'm like your *mom*? That's pretty fucked up, My."

"Why can't I just be angry?" Maya continued. "I miss my dad, okay? I miss. My. Dad. And I'm sorry you don't get to see yours anymore, but just because I have a better situation than you doesn't mean that it still doesn't make me feel bad!"

Claire sat up straight, making Maya think of a cobra rising up to strike. "Because you have it *better* than me?" she said slowly.

"That's not what I—"

"Yes, it is. That's exactly what you said." Claire hopped down off the wall as well, so now they were eye to eye. "Look, Maya, don't try to hang your shit on me, okay? You've had a really rough couple of months, I know—your dad moving out, Grace and Joaquin and that whole thing—"

"I think you mean me finding not one but *two* biological siblings," Maya shot back, "not 'that whole thing.'"

"And I know you're worried about your mom—"

"Do *not* bring up my mom!" Now Maya was yelling. She wished she had something to throw, something to ricochet off buildings with the kind of force that she felt building up behind her heart. "Leave her out of it!"

"But I can't, My! That's the problem! You're angry at all these other people but you can't tell them, so you just take it out on me instead!"

"Oh, I'm sorry! I didn't realize you had become my therapist instead of my girlfriend. That's a surprise. Do you take insurance?" Maya didn't actually know much about therapists and insurance, but she had heard her parents talking about it. Her mom had always said couples therapy was too expensive because they didn't take insurance, but her dad had offered to pay anyway. It hadn't worked.

"Maya!" Claire yelled. "God, you're so *annoying* sometimes! You act like a little kid!"

"And you act like some know-it-all!" Maya yelled back. "You don't know anything about my family, okay? So stay out of it!"

"I don't know anything because you don't tell me anything!" Claire cried. "You keep dropping all these little bread crumbs and you expect me to trace them back to you, but you don't leave enough."

Maya blinked. "That is a terrible metaphor."

"Fine, how's this? You shut me out because you don't want me to find out too much about you. You think that if I know too much about your family, I'll leave you."

Maya started to laugh. "You are so terrible at this," she said. "I'm sorry, how much have I told you about my dad? All of it. All of it!"

"What about your mom?" Claire said, and Maya looked away. "Exactly, My."

"That's private," Maya said. "That's about her, not me."

"Bullshit. It's about all of you. You just don't realize it. And who cares if it's private? I'm your *girlfriend*. You can tell me this stuff."

Maya could feel herself careering down the hill, the wheels starting to come off the cart even as she continued to pick up speed. "Well, then, if you don't think I tell you enough, then maybe I shouldn't be your girlfriend anymore."

Claire had been about to yell something back, but Maya's words stopped her short. They stopped Maya short, too, for that matter. She hadn't even known that that was something she was going to say.

"You want to break up with me?" Claire said, her voice suddenly low and quiet.

"Well, it sounds like you want to break up with me." That wasn't what it sounded like at all, not to Maya. Who was this stranger inside her who kept speaking on her behalf? Whoever she was, she was really fucking things up in a colossal way.

"Is this what you do?" Claire said, and now her voice was dangerous. "Just poke and poke and poke?" She stepped toward Maya, poking her in the shoulder. "Make yourself meaner and meaner until you make me break up with you because you don't have the guts to break up with *me*?"

Maya had nothing to say to that. Instead, she just stared at

Claire. Maya had learned this trick a long time ago, the art of staying quiet and letting the other person dig themselves into a hole. She had just never thought that she would use it on Claire.

"Are you seriously not even going to say anything?" Claire said. "We're basically breaking up and you just go silent?"

Maya shrugged. Lauren would do that to her sometimes when they were fighting, her impassivity sending Maya through the roof.

"Oh my God," Claire said, starting to laugh. "You're such a fucking baby." She took a step away, then circled back. "You know what? Never mind. You want to break up, you're going to say it to me. I'm not saying it to you."

It was a dare, Maya knew, and she was so mad and so frustrated and so furious at herself that she took the bait.

"I'm breaking up with you," she said to Claire, then watched as Claire seemed to wither right in front of her eyes.

"Are you serious?" Claire whispered. "Goddamnit, Maya. Why do you have to burn down the house with everyone inside it?"

Maya had no idea what Claire was talking about. She was too busy trying to keep her mouth still, her eyes dry. She could cry once she was home, but there was no way she was going to fall apart in front of Claire.

She wouldn't give her the satisfaction.

"You know what?" Claire said. "Find your own ride home. I'm out."

"Fine," Maya said. Her house was only a couple of miles away. She would have somersaulted home on bare gravel before she got back into Claire's car.

Claire laughed again, short and sharp and bitter, and then spun on her heel. Right before she turned the corner, she threw her empty coffee drink in the trash with such force that Maya half expected it to bounce right back out, but it stayed put.

Claire was the one who kept going.

Maya had been right. She had a hell of a sunburn.

Her shoulders were bright pink, and her nose was an interesting shade of rose. "Hey, Rudolph," Lauren said later that afternoon, when she found Maya examining her face in the bathroom mirror.

"Shut up. Do we have any aloe?"

Lauren came into the bathroom and reached past her into the medicine cabinet. "Here," she said. "I think there's some Noxzema in Mom and Dad's—I mean, Mom's bathroom, too."

"Noxzema is disgusting," Maya said, ignoring Lauren's slip-up.

"Why are you so sunburned?" Lauren asked, sitting down on the closed toilet.

"Flew too close to the sun," Maya muttered, trying to spread the goo on her nose without it dripping on the rest of her face.

"What?"

"Nothing. Just went outside and forgot sunscreen. Did you get Dad's text?"

Lauren nodded, resting her elbows on her knees.

"Question," Maya said. "Why are you hanging out in the bathroom with me?"

"Because there's nothing on TV."

Maya glanced at her in the mirror. "Where's Mom?"

Lauren shrugged again.

"Laur," Maya said.

"She's asleep," Lauren said quietly.

Maya sighed to herself. Asleep at five thirty in the afternoon. More like passed out. Fantastic. She had been "asleep" the day before when Maya came home from school. There had been more empties than usual that week, and both Maya and Lauren had started recycling them without even saying anything to each other. Their mom must have noticed.

Right?

"What do you want for dinner?" Maya asked Lauren instead.

"Pizza."

"Pizza's boring."

"You asked me what I wanted. And the Greek place doesn't deliver."

Maya sighed. She had already had one disastrous fight with someone that day. She wasn't up for another.

"C'mon," she said to Lauren. "Let's just walk to the Greek place. Mom can sleep it off. We'll bring her back something."

"You're not going to invite Claire, are you?"

Maya froze. "Why?" she asked, her voice sounding strangled to her own ears.

Lauren didn't seem to notice, though. "Because then you're just going to be all lovey-dovey and canoodly with each other and I'll have to sit there and watch—like a big weirdo."

The fracture in Maya's heart split a bit wider. "No canoodling," she said. "Claire's hanging out with her family tonight." None of that, Maya thought, was actually a lie.

Lauren went to find her shoes while Maya tiptoed into their parents'—their mom's—bedroom. The room seemed even bigger now that their dad wasn't there, the bed emptier. Her mom was curled up on the far side of the mattress, her breaths deep and even, and Maya watched her for a minute before reaching down and pulling the blanket up over her shoulders.

Then she went over to the dresser and opened the top drawer, finding the wad of twenty-dollar bills that she knew would be there. She took out two, then counted the rest. Assuming her mom planned on sleeping through the rest of the week's dinners, she and Lauren could eat out at least four more times. Five if Maya gave in to the pizza idea.

At the Greek restaurant, she and Lauren sat side by side at the counter facing the windows, eating pita and tzatziki and kabobs. (Steak for Maya, chicken for Lauren. Neither of them would even consider the lamb. It just seemed too mean to eat a baby lamb.) Maya wondered if it would ever be like this with Grace and Joaquin, the ability to just sit quietly side by side, content in the knowledge that no matter what happened with your parents, or your girlfriend, that your siblings will still be there, like a bookend that keeps you upright when you feel like toppling over.

When they got home, the house was still dark, and Maya turned on lights as she made her way into the kitchen, then stashed her mom's takeout chicken souvlaki in the refrigerator. "Mom?"

she yelled. The car was still in the driveway, at least. Her mom wasn't *that* stupid.

"Mom!" she yelled again. "Wake up! We brought you food!" Secretly, she hoped the idea of Greek food would make her hungover mom nauseous. Then she wondered when she had become such a mean person. "Mom!"

There was silence from upstairs, and then she heard Lauren scream, "Mom!"

Maya was running up the stairs before she even realized she had left the kitchen.

"Mom!" Lauren kept screaming, and Maya followed the sound of her voice down the hall and into her parents' bathroom. Lauren was on the floor next to their mom. She was crumpled like a baby bird that had fallen out of its nest, and there was blood coming from her head, staining the marble floor that was freezing cold under Maya's bare feet.

"I just found her in here!" Lauren cried. "We need to call Dad!"

Maya grabbed for Lauren's phone, which was still in her hand. "We need to call nine-one-one!" she said. "Jesus *Christ*, Lauren, what's Dad going to do from New *Orleans*?"

It took her three tries to type in 911 because her hand was shaking so bad.

At her feet, her mom was moaning. Lauren had a towel pressed against her head, trying to mop up the blood. The 911 dispatcher promised to stay on the phone with her until the paramedics arrived, and Maya put the phone on speaker and set it down on the countertop.

"Maya?" her mom moaned.

"I'm right here," Maya said, but she didn't crouch down. She didn't want to get too close to her mother. She didn't want to break her. Instead, she just dug her own phone out of her back pocket and started to call Claire, getting halfway through the motions before remembering with a cold shock that Maya was the last person Claire would want to hear from at the moment.

"Shit," she whispered to herself. Lauren was stroking their mom's hair, holding the towel to the underside of her temple, and Maya forced herself to think straight, to not cry, to figure out this problem.

She called someone else instead. At first, she was afraid that she wouldn't answer, but she suddenly picked up on the fourth ring. "Hello? Maya?"

"Grace?" Maya said, and then she started to cry.

JOAQUIN

Joaquin was pretty used to receiving random texts from Grace. *Hey, how was your day?* he would get sometimes after school, or a *Did you see that new movie?* last weekend. He wasn't sure if it was because she was genuinely curious or because she just wanted to check the boxes when it came to bonding with him, but it was nice either way. He usually sent back a pretty standard answer—*good, how about you* or *nope, did not*—because he didn't always know what to say. Grace was basically a stranger, after all. Blood relative or not, they had only met twice before with their other blood relative/stranger. It wasn't exactly *the warmest of fuzzy situations*. (Joaquin once had had a younger foster sister who used to say that all the time. The phrase had stuck with him, even if he thought it made him sound like an idiot.)

All that changed on Sunday.

It started with—what else?—a text from Grace, and Joaquin

rolled over in bed, rubbing the sleep out of his eyes so he could read it. Hey, it said, and already he could tell that this text was different. I know we're supposed to meet for coffee today, but could you come over to Maya's instead?

That was weird.

sure okay. why?

Long story. Can you come over this morning?

Joaquin thought for a minute, then rolled back over onto his side, closing one eye so he could see the screen. okay, he wrote back. see you at ten?

Cool. Thanks, Joaq.

He stayed in bed for another minute or two, then went to the foot of the stairs. "Hey, Linda?" he yelled.

"Yeah?"

"Can I borrow the car?"

Linda came to the foot of the stairs. "Mark and I thought we'd go to the store while you were meeting Maya and Grace."

"Grace just texted me," he said, holding up his phone. "She wants to meet at Maya's house." Then he paused before adding, "I think something's wrong."

An hour later, Joaquin swung Mark's car into Maya's very, very spacious driveway. Grace's car was already parked there. Joaquin suspected that they could have also parked a sixteen-wheeler and there still would have been room to play basketball.

"Shit," he said softly to himself, looking up at the house

through the windshield. He had suspected that his youngest sister's family had money, and looking up at the tall front doors, the high windows that framed the front of the house, and the bougainvillea that climbed up one side of the brick wall, he realized that he had been right.

Grace opened the front door before Joaquin could even use the huge brass door knocker that was shaped like a trophy. "Hi," she said.

She looked terrible.

"You look . . ."

"I look awful, I know." Grace stood back, waving him into the house. "I don't even live here, but I'm inviting you in anyway. Welcome to Maya's home."

Joaquin stepped onto the marble floors. There was a pile of shoes to the side, so he toed off his sneakers, glad that he had worn clean socks, at least. "Why are you here?" he asked her. "Where's Maya?"

Grace jerked a thumb over her shoulder. "She's outside with Lauren. Her sister," she added when Joaquin raised an eyebrow, not recognizing the name. "She's the one who was born right after they adopted Maya."

"Oh, right, right," he said, but his eyes had already traveled to the massive staircase, and the huge number of family photos that lined the wall next to it. It was like watching a timeline of Maya's life, from baby pictures to school photos set against a fake forest background. There were vacation snapshots, candids, and posed portraits, and Joaquin could find Maya in every single one within seconds. She was the short brunette in a sea of tall redheads, and for the first time, Joaquin was sort of glad that he didn't have a ton of baby photos. He didn't need the constant reminder that he was different from everyone else.

Grace stood next to him, following his gaze. "I know, right?" she said after a minute. "Imagine walking past *this* every single day. It freaked me out the first time I saw it, too."

"Do you think they even know that it's weird?" Joaquin asked her, crossing his arms over his chest as he leaned closer to look at one of the baby pictures, an infant Lauren propped up in toddler Maya's lap. Maya didn't look thrilled. Joaquin realized that she still made that same face whenever she was annoyed.

Grace just shrugged. "I don't know. Maybe they just wanted her to think that she was one of them, regardless of how she looked."

Joaquin huffed out a laugh before he could stop himself. That was one of the first things that Mrs. Buchanan had said to him when he first moved into their home. "We don't see skin color," she had said, leaning down to put a hand on his then-bony shoulder and smiling so wide that Joaquin could see her back teeth. "We're all the same on the inside."

He had thought that was pretty funny. Everyone else seemed to be able to see skin color just fine.

"Trust me," he said to Grace. "Maya knows she doesn't look like them."

"Well, that's the least of her problems right now." Grace sighed. "C'mon, they're out by the pool."

Of course there's a pool, Joaquin thought as he followed her outside. Maya and a red-haired girl who Joaquin guessed was Lauren were sitting across from each other by the pool. Lauren was tucked under the shade of an umbrella, but Maya was sprawled out on the cement by the pool, sunglasses over her face and her feet in the water. She sat up when she heard them come outside. "Hi," she said, waving to Joaquin. "Welcome to the latest episode of *Real Housewives.*"

Joaquin looked at Grace, who was rubbing her temples. "What?" he asked.

"Nothing," Maya said. "Thanks for coming over. You want to put your feet in the pool?"

He kind of did. Their patio area was warm, warmer than it was at Mark and Linda's house by the beach. But first, he went over and offered his hand to Lauren. "Hi," he said. "I'm Joaquin."

"Oh, sorry," Maya said, sitting up again. "This is my sister, Lauren. Lauren, this is my . . . this is Joaquin. Neither of you are related to each other."

"Hi," Lauren said, shaking his hand. Joaquin remembered that they were only a year apart, but Lauren seemed younger, more fragile. It was clear she had been crying, too. Joaquin wondered if that was why Maya was wearing such huge sunglasses.

"Wait," Maya said. "*Are* you related?"

"No," Grace said, sitting in the chaise lounge across from Lauren in the shade.

"No, but . . ." Maya trailed off as she started to think again. "There's some mathematical property at work here, right? Like, the transitive property? The brother of my sister is my brother?"

"I don't think that's how it works," Joaquin said, pulling off his socks.

"Math isn't biology," Lauren added. "Even though I suck at both."

Maya just waved her hand in the air. "Congratulations on your two new friends, Lauren," she said. "And don't say you suck at math and science. That's such a cliché when girls say that. Even if it's true, just lie." She sighed heavily, like Lauren lying about her intelligence was the biggest of her problems.

Joaquin looked at Grace again. She simply shook her head in response.

"So," Joaquin said, sinking down next to Maya and easing his feet into the pool.

Maya waved at him again without looking up. "How's the water feel?"

"Good," he said. "Blue."

She raised her sunglasses up so she could look at him. "That's what I always say," she said, her brown eyes wide. "Do you feel color, too?"

Joaquin had no idea what she was talking about. "You want to tell me why I'm sitting in your backyard instead of our normal coffee shop?"

"Because this is so much better," Maya said, then reached out and patted his arm. No one had really touched him like that, not since Birdie and their fight several days ago. "Just relax. Enjoy the blue."

Joaquin didn't need convincing.

"Hey, My!" Lauren called after a few minutes. "Can I ride my bike to Melanie's house?"

"Why are you asking me?" Maya replied. Her arm was draped over her eyes now. "I'm not Mom. Thank God," she added under her breath.

Lauren paused. "So is that a yes?"

"Yes."

But then Maya pushed herself up off the ground and walked over to hug Lauren. They hung on tight to each other, longer than Maya had ever hugged Joaquin or Grace, and then let go. Lauren, who was almost a full head taller than Maya, patted her sister's hair as she walked away. "I'll be back by three," she said.

"You better," Maya replied, "or I'll run over you with a truck. Not a metaphor."

"You don't even have your license." Lauren didn't sound too threatened.

"I know. That makes it worse. Think of the damage I can do." But she reached out and squeezed Lauren's arm before letting go and heading back to sit next to Joaquin at the pool.

Joaquin felt like he had walked into a play midperformance. He had no idea what was going on. He was tempted to pull Grace inside the house to ask her, but she was reading something on her phone, her own sunglasses pushing her hair back as she frowned at the screen.

Oh, well. At least the pool was nice.

As soon as Lauren pedaled away, Maya went inside. She came back a few minutes later with something clutched in her palm. "I love Lauren and everything," she said with a sigh as she sat back down by Joaquin, "but I can't do this in front of her."

"Is that—oh, shit," Joaquin said, looking at the joint and lighter in her hand. "Are you supposed to be smoking weed?"

"My glaucoma," Maya said, putting the joint up to her lips. "Relax, it's fine. My parents have no idea."

"Oh my God. Is that weed?" Grace asked, sitting up on the chaise lounge.

"Ding ding ding," Maya said, tapping her sunburned nose. "You want some?"

Grace hesitated, then came to sit down at Maya's other side. "What about you?" Maya asked Joaquin as she lit it. "You in? Sunday Funday?"

"No, thanks," he said. "I have to drive."

"Fair enough," Maya said as Grace settled next to her, putting her bare feet in the water. "But I go first since it's mine."

"Aren't you, like, twelve?" Joaquin said. "Where did you even get this?"

"From my girl—excuse me, ex-girlfriend. Claire."

Joaquin and Grace looked at each other over Maya's head, and Joaquin had a flash of Mark and Linda doing the same thing to him. "You broke up?" Grace asked as Maya inhaled.

"Yes, ma'am," Maya said, her voice rough, and she held the smoke before passing her joint to Grace.

Grace took it, holding it for a minute. "It's been, like, a *really* long time since I smoked." She had an odd smile on her face, and Joaquin couldn't tell if she was happy or sad. "Oh, well, whatever."

"Never mind," Joaquin said automatically, then felt pleased when both his sisters smiled at him. "So is anyone going to tell me why we're here?" he asked. "Or do I have to guess?"

"Ooh, guess, guess!" Maya said.

"Maya, stop," Grace said, passing the joint back to her. "Wow, that's strong."

"Yeah, Claire doesn't—didn't—mess around."

"Are we here because you broke up with Claire?" Joaquin asked. If they were going to make him dig for the information, then that was fine. He had asked tougher questions before. "Is that it?" Personally, all he had wanted to do was die after he had broken up with Birdie. He couldn't imagine hosting a pity party about it. Maybe girls were different that way, huddling together like penguins instead of just staying under the covers and watching Netflix all day.

Maya laughed, short and sharp. "You know what? I actually forgot for a minute that Claire and I broke up. That's how terrible yesterday was."

Joaquin waited for more explanation. When none was forthcoming, he sighed. "So what else happened yesterday?"

Maya took the joint back from Grace. "You tell him," she said, gesturing to Joaquin. "I bet you'll tell the story so much better."

"What the hell happened yesterday?" he said. "And why aren't any of your parents here?" Joaquin had always imagined Maya's and Grace's parents following them around like ducklings, caring for them, cleaning up after them, holding out an eternal net so that they would never fall, never get hurt. "Did you overthrow them or something?"

Maya started to giggle, then laugh, but Grace just looked somber, and Joaquin suspected that he had either said the most perfect thing or the most terrible thing.

When Maya started to cry, he realized it was the latter.

"Oh, shit," he said, just as Grace moved to put her arm around her. Maya was still holding the joint, its smoke rising up in a long, smooth line before curling up at the top, and when Grace moved, her arm cut through the smoke, sending it scattering. "Oh, shit, Maya," Joaquin said. "I'm sorry. I was only kidding."

"Stop, it's fine," she said, but she was still sniffling. Joaquin was new to having siblings, but he was pretty sure that making your little sister cry was at the top of the Do Not Do This Ever list.

"Just tell him," Grace said, her voice quiet even as she pressed her cheek against Maya's hair.

Maya took a deep breath, then took another hit off the joint. "So," she said, her voice ragged with both tears and smoke. "Maybe you already knew this, but my mom's a pretty big alcoholic?"

Joaquin felt his spine straighten up like the line of smoke in front of him. He had spent time with an alcoholic foster parent once. It hadn't been great. If anyone had hurt Maya like that, Joaquin was pretty sure that he would have to do something about it.

Judging from Grace's face, she felt the same way.

"Anyway, she's not really dealing with the divorce that well?" Maya continued. Her voice kept going up on the end of her sentences, like she was asking if the things she was saying were really true. Joaquin could understand that. "And she's been drinking a lot this week, even for her? And then last night, Lauren and I"—Maya gestured in the general direction of where Lauren had left—"went out to dinner and when we got back, my mom was . . . she was on the floor. She fell and hit her head. There was a lot of blood. There's probably a lot of blood still. We might need to hire someone to clean that up. It looks like a crime scene in there. Do you ever watch those shows on TV, the ones about murderers where they re-create the crime scene?"

"My." Grace reached over and put her hand on Maya's knee. "We got it."

Maya nodded. "Anyway, yeah. She had to stay in the hospital overnight because she had a concussion."

"Where's your dad?" Joaquin asked. "Is he with her?"

"Nope. He's in New Orleans. Well, actually, he's probably flying home right now from New Orleans. Grace's parents called him last night."

"And does he know about . . . you know . . . ?"

"The drinking?" Maya said, and Joaquin nodded. "Well, he does now, I guess. I don't think he knew how bad it was. But he knows now."

"Maya called me last night," Grace said "And we—my parents

and I, I mean—met everyone at the hospital."

"Lauren and I rode in the ambulance," Maya said. "Lots of sirens, lots of lights. You'd think it'd be loud inside the ambulance, but it wasn't. The movies lied."

Joaquin watched Maya raise the joint to her mouth again, then set it down without taking another hit. He felt like he was watching a little kid drive a car, her legs too short to reach the pedals, her eyes too low to see over the steering wheel. "So when does she get to come home?" he asked.

"She's not," Maya said, her voice clipped. "At least, not yet. She's going to *rehab*. My dad found a place in Palm Springs and he's going to take her out there tonight, once she gets released. Oh, and yeah, my girlfriend and I broke up yesterday. So I've got that going for me. I should probably wrap Lauren in Bubble Wrap or something, because people are dropping like flies all around me." She gestured to both Grace and Joaquin with the hand that was holding the joint. "Definitely look both ways before crossing the street, you two. I'm bad luck."

"You're not bad luck," Joaquin snapped, and both girls looked up at him in surprise. "Don't say things like that. Shitty things are just happening around you. It's not your fault."

Maya suddenly looked very woebegone. (Joaquin had read that word in a book once and had never forgotten it. It made him think of Dickensian orphans, old widows, puppies abandoned in the rain.) "No, I'm pretty sure it's me," she said, wiping at her eyes again. "In fact, I'm one hundred percent sure that the breakup with Claire was my fault. I pushed her away."

"Well, is it permanent?" Joaquin asked. "Can you apologize?"

"Nope," Maya said.

"That's not true," Grace told her.

Maya started to cry again.

Joaquin and Grace looked at each other once more; then Joaquin moved over until he could put his arm around Maya's waist. He knew what it felt like to cry alone. It felt terrible, like you were the only person alive in the world. He didn't want that for Maya.

"What if she doesn't stay in rehab?" Maya sobbed. "What if she thinks she's okay and signs herself out and then hits her head again?"

"She's going to stay," Grace soothed. "Your dad will make her stay."

"She might not," Joaquin said, and ignored the angry glance that Grace shot him. "I mean, it's true, right? She might not."

"The rain cloud to Grace's sunshine," Maya sniffled. "You're a good team."

Joaquin hadn't thought of anyone being on his team before, not since Birdie. He wondered if Maya was right. "Look," he said. "You can't control what your mom does. But you can control what *you* do."

Maya wiped her eyes on the back of her arm before looking at him. "Do you . . . go to *therapy*, Joaq?"

Joaquin startled a little. "I . . . Yeah, I do. Mark and Linda pay for it, but yeah."

"I've been trying to keep her sober—well, less drunk," Maya said. "She has wine hidden all over the house. Lauren and I were trying to keep track of that."

"Does your dad know about that part?" Grace asked. "Maybe you should tell him."

"How could he not know?" Maya said. "And if he does, he obviously doesn't care. I mean, he just left us here with her. He found a place and moved out last week. He's going to move back in now while my mom's gone, but . . . yeah." She tossed the joint into the pool, where it quickly burned out and then floated on the blue water. "Everything is so fucking fucked up. My mom's a drunk and my ex-girlfriend hates me."

"Well, my ex-girlfriend hates me, too," Joaquin admitted, and both of his sisters' heads swiveled toward him, their eyes wide. "If it's any consolation."

"You had a girlfriend?" Grace asked.

"Why'd you break up?" Maya asked.

"How long were you together?"

"What was her name?"

"Did you break up with her or did she break up with you?"

"I broke up with her," Joaquin said. "And her name was Elizabeth but everybody calls her Birdie."

"Birdie." Maya looked unimpressed. "Is she twee? Does she buy things on Etsy?"

Joaquin had no idea what Etsy was. "It was her grandmother's name," he explained. "What does *twee* mean?"

"Nothing," Grace said. "Why'd you break up with her?"

Joaquin laughed a little, then watched as the joint started to sink to the bottom of the pool. "It's stupid."

"No, it's not," Maya said. It was the softest Joaquin had ever heard her sound. "You obviously still like her."

"How do you know that?" he asked her.

"You're blushing," both girls said, and Joaquin realized that they were right.

Goddamnit.

"Fine," he said. "Since we're all doing deep confessions right now, I broke up with her because I wasn't good enough for her."

"She *said* that?" Grace gasped.

"I'll punch her right in her stupid bird face," Maya growled.

"No, no, she didn't . . . oh God." Joaquin raised up his hands. "I figured that out on my own. She has a lot of dreams and goals and stuff. She should get to have them."

Joaquin watched as the girls' faces went from furious to perplexed. "Wait," Maya said after a few seconds of silence. "Did *you* think that you weren't good enough for her?"

"Oh, Joaquin," Grace sighed.

Joaquin was getting used to the way people seemed to be disappointed in him all the time. "You don't understand," he said. "You two, you grew up with families. You've probably lived in this house since you were born, right? Right?" he said again when Maya didn't respond, and she reluctantly nodded. "Okay, the same with Birdie. That wall of pictures on the staircase? She has that, too. And I don't have that. I have nothing like that. It's like . . ."

Joaquin tried to remember what Ana had said to him once. "There's no foundation for the house. And you need a foundation if you want to build anything that lasts." That wasn't exactly what Ana had said, but that's how Joaquin had heard it.

Maya just looked at him. "Are you kidding me?" she said. "My foundation is basically *crumbling* right now. My mom's going to rehab, my parents are getting a divorce. Just because you don't have some perfect TV family doesn't mean you're not a good person, Joaquin."

That's when Joaquin knew that he would never tell Grace and Maya what had really happened: why he had left the Buchanans, why he really *wasn't* a good person. Instead, he said, "It's hard to explain. You wouldn't understand. Birdie, she had all these baby pictures."

Grace sat up straight, her mouth in a hard line. "You don't have any baby pictures," she said quietly.

She looked so sad all of a sudden, and Joaquin wanted to take the sadness away. He was so tired of making the people around him sad when he all he wanted to do was keep them safe. "No. And you have to buy school pictures, those packages that they sell." Joaquin shrugged. "Birdie had all these photos. Someone had saved them for her. I saw those and I thought . . ." Joaquin's voice trailed off as he remembered how the photos had made his stomach feel like it was collapsing in on itself. "We would never be equal. She would always have more than me. Always need more than me. She needs someone who understands things like she does."

"Joaquin." Maya put her hand on his arm. "I think you're a fucking idiot."

Grace covered her eyes with her hand. "Maya," she sighed.

Maya just kept her hand on his arm. "No, I mean it," she said, and Joaquin didn't know if she was just super upset or super high, but the earnestness on her face made him smile a little. "Did you *see* those pictures on the stairway when you came in? Really see them?"

Joaquin nodded. "Pretty intense."

Maya's eyes were starting to well up again. She was definitely high. "I mean, my parents read all these books about adoption, and adopted kids, and how to accept and love your adopted child, but I've never seen them read a single book about their biological kid, you know? They don't read books about *Lauren*. Just me. Because I'm different. I'm *work*.

"So I'm just saying, maybe don't break up with Birdie just because you think you can't give her things. Maybe that's not what she even wants from you, you know? Maybe she just wants *you*. Pictures are the past, that's all. Maybe you're her future."

Joaquin could feel that same shaky feeling that he had gotten when he'd broken up with Birdie, watching her face crumble and knowing that it was, as Maya had said earlier about her own breakup, 100 percent his fault. "Okay," he said after a minute. "So what about you and Claire, then?"

Maya rolled her eyes. "Nice segue."

"No, I'm serious," Joaquin said. "You should call her."

"She probably deleted my phone number."

"Probably not. You think I should get back together with Birdie? Well, then, I think *you* should get back together with Claire."

"It's been less than twenty-four hours," Grace pointed out. "You should at least tell her about what happened last night."

Maya's lower lip was wobbling a bit. "She said that I shut her out and don't tell her things because I think that if I tell her the truth about things, she'll leave me."

Joaquin let out a breath he hadn't realized he was holding. "Fuuuuuck," he said, pressing the heels of his palms against his eyes and laughing to himself. "Did we inherit the same dysfunction or something?"

Maya was giggling now, too, even through her tears. "Why don't *you* call Claire and *I'll* call Birdie?" she said. "We'd probably have better luck."

Joaquin smiled. He knew that he would never call Birdie again, but it was a nice thought just the same. Sometimes people broke too hard and you could never put them back together the same way. Birdie would never fit back in his life the way she used to, and it would only make him feel worse if she tried and failed.

"What about you, Gracie?" Maya said. "Why'd you break up with your boyfriend? Since we're doing group therapy right now, 'fess up."

But Grace's eyes were lost in a way that Joaquin recognized

from a few foster kids, the ones who had been transferred so many times that they were rudderless, adrift in the storm. She blinked, though, and it disappeared. "Long story," she said, then started to get to her feet. "I'm hungry. Do you have food?"

Maya and Joaquin watched as she started to walk away. Then Maya pulled her feet out of the water and followed her in. "C'mon, Joaquin," she said. "Maybe we can draw mustaches on the family photos."

He laughed at the idea. What a luxury to be able to do that. "Be right there," he said as the girls disappeared indoors. Once they were gone, he grabbed the pool skimmer and ran it across the bottom of the pool, catching the joint in its net before tossing it out over the fence and then following the girls inside.

"Hey," Joaquin said. "Do you have a minute?"

Both Mark and Linda looked up. "Yeah, buddy," Mark said. His hands were in the soapy sink water, rinsing off the last of the dishes while Linda bagged up the trash for Joaquin to take outside. "What's up?"

Joaquin leaned against the doorjamb, knocking his knuckles against it as if for luck. "I just wanted to talk to you about, um, the adoption thing?"

He watched as Mark's jaw tightened, as Linda's eyes grew hopeful. "Yeah, I was just thinking. About it. And um, yeah, maybe we shouldn't do it."

The light in Linda's eyes disappeared so fast that Joaquin could have sworn someone blew out the flame behind them. "It's not that I don't— I really, really like living here."

"We really like you living here, too, Joaquin," Linda said. "That will never change, you know that."

Joaquin *did* know that. His brain knew it 100 percent. It was the rest of him that had trouble sorting through it. "I just think that things are really good right now? And maybe we shouldn't mess with it?" His voice had started doing the same uptick that Maya's had done earlier that day, a question instead of a statement.

Linda was chewing on her lower lip, but Mark just nodded. "Absolutely, bud," he said. "We always want you to feel comfortable here. Whatever you want, that's what we want, too."

Joaquin felt the load lift off his heart. He even smiled a little. "Cool," he said. "Great. Thanks. And, I mean, I do really appreciate it. I'm not lying."

"You're not a liar, Joaquin," Linda said, her voice tight. "We've never thought that."

"Cool," Joaquin said again, because he didn't know what else to say. "I'm gonna take the trash out, then. Is this everything?"

He had almost made his getaway through the back door when Mark's voice stopped him. "Joaq?" he said, and Joaquin turned to see Mark standing next to Linda, his arm around her shoulders, his knuckles tight and white.

"Yeah?"

"The Buchanans. Joaquin, we would never . . . we would never do what they did. You know that, right? We love you. You're ours, no matter what."

Joaquin forced himself to nod. "Yeah, totally," he said. "I'll be right back."

He stood next to the trash cans for a minute longer than necessary, trying to get his heartbeat back under control. *You control what* you *do,* he had told Maya earlier that day, and he knew he was right. He loved Mark and Linda too much to let them adopt him, so if the decision was his to make, Joaquin would make it.

It was, he reminded himself as he went back inside, the right thing to do.

GRACE

"So over here," Rafe said, loudly enough for his coworkers to hear, "we have our finest assortment of slicer-dicers. They slice *and* dice. It's not just a clever name. And over here— Are they gone?"

Grace peeked around the corner. "Um . . . yes. All clear."

"Whew." Rafe's shoulders visibly sagged. "Pretending to work is way more exhausting than actually working."

"Funny that," Grace said, patting one of the oven mitts in the shape of a chicken. "These are cute."

"To some people," Rafe replied, then slipped his apron over his head. "Thanks for coming to visit me after work, by the way."

"Well, thanks for texting me," Grace said. "It was nice to have a reason to blow the dust off my phone."

"Oh, go on, I know your mom texts you all the time," Rafe said with a wink. He was one of the few people Grace had ever met who could actually wink, instead of doing something that looked like a halfhearted blink. She liked that about him. "Where do you want to eat? The same dark booth at the sandwich place around the corner, I assume?"

Grace nodded. She wasn't ashamed of Rafe, of course. She was only ashamed of herself.

"Well, good, because day-old sandwiches taste way better when you eat them in semidarkness." Rafe folded up his apron, then gestured toward the Employees Only door. "Let me go clock out and then the night is ours." He waggled his eyebrows suggestively at her, and Grace punched him in the shoulder in response. "I love a woman with a violent streak," he said, then disappeared before she could really clock him.

"So it turns out that Maya's mom is an alcoholic," Grace said as they walked, positioning herself between Rafe and the wall just to keep anyone from catching a glimpse of her.

"Wow," Rafe said. "Did she tell you all of this?"

"Her mom fell and hit her head, so she called me. My parents and I ended up at the emergency room with them." Grace could see Maya's pale face, her eyes blown wide open from shock, the way she had clung to Lauren's arm even after Grace and her parents had arrived. "Her mom went to rehab the next day. Pretty scary stuff."

"Indeed," Rafe said. "So let me guess. You're worried that Peach's parents are now going to get divorced *and* become alcoholics?"

He was kidding, though, and Grace knocked her hip against his without thinking. "No," she chided him. She thought again of the letter, of the photo of Peach wearing the sailor outfit. "They actually sent me a letter last week. I know Peach is in good hands."

Rafe raised an eyebrow at her. Grace had never met anyone whose eyebrows were so expressive. She wondered if it was maybe just a muscle twitch. "Really?" he said. "Like a thank-you letter?"

"Kind of. They were just telling me how much they appreciated what I had given them, how much they loved Peach. They sent a photo, too. She was wearing a sailor outfit."

"That sounds cool of them."

"Yeah, they said they would send letters and photos for the first year." Grace could hear the measured calmness in her own voice. "It made me start thinking about maybe finding my mom. Our mom."

"Do Maya and Joaquin want to find her, too?" he asked.

"God, no," Grace said. "They basically said that she abandoned them, so why should they look for her? Especially Joaquin, what with the foster care and everything."

Rafe was still stuck in the same place, staring at her. "They said that to you?" He gaped. "Even though they know about Peach?"

Grace suddenly wished that she had never brought up the subject in the first place. "Well . . . they don't actually know about Peach. I haven't told them yet. I might not tell them at all."

Rafe closed his eyes, dragging his hand over his face and letting out a low groan. "Okay," he said, opening his eyes again, and then took Grace's arm and turned her around. "Cancel sandwiches. This conversation needs french fries."

"It's not that bad," Grace said, but she let herself be led past the fountain anyway.

"Trust me," Rafe said. "It is."

"So how long do you think you can keep your biological daughter—who, by the way, you have nicknamed after a *fruit*—a secret from your biological siblings? Asking for a friend."

Grace rolled her eyes, then dipped her fry in her side of mayonnaise.

"That's disgusting, by the way," Rafe said, gesturing to her french fry with one of his own. "Mayonnaise, it's the devil's condiment."

"More for me, then," Grace said. She popped it into her mouth and winked at him. She wasn't as good a winker as Rafe was, but it was a nice effort. "Maya and Joaquin like it, too, just so you know."

"Must be a recessive gene," Rafe replied, then pulled the ketchup bottle closer to his plate.

"I like the name Peach," Grace said, ignoring his question.

"You're ignoring my question," he pointed out.

"Everyone likes peaches," Grace continued. "They're universally beloved. And she'll be the same."

Rafe opened his mouth, then closed it again. "There's no way to argue that point without insulting your biological child, so I'm not going to try. Well played, by the way."

Grace shrugged.

"So you're not going to tell them?"

"You think it's a bad idea?"

"I think it's a terrible idea. Secrets always get out."

"But it doesn't even affect them."

"She's their niece."

"Not anymore. She has a new family."

"Okay, forget about Peach then. What about *you*? They could be supporting you and you're not even letting them in."

Grace laughed and signaled the waitress for more mayonnaise. ("Disgusting," Rafe said under his breath.) "Well, seeing as how they think our mom is basically a demon for giving all of us up, I'd rather not get their opinion on how I did the same thing to Peach."

"I'm sorry. Why Peach again?" Rafe asked.

"That's how big she was when I found out I was pregnant with her. When you're pregnant, they always describe the size of the baby in utero in relation to food. Bean, lime, peach, grapefruit. . . . Peach is what stuck."

He nodded thoughtfully. "I just think that if you tell Maya and Joaquin, they'll be a lot more understanding. None of you knows why your mom—"

"Bio mom," Grace interrupted.

"What?"

"My *bio* mom. I have a mom. She's back at my house probably wondering why I'm not texting her back."

"Got it. None of you knows why your bio mom did what she

did, but Maya and Joaquin would probably understand why you did it. You should tell them."

"Maybe it's none of their business."

"Well, using that logic, then no one would tell anyone anything about anything."

"So if you got pregnant, you'd tell your sister?"

Rafe smirked. "If I got pregnant, I'd have a pretty hard time keeping it a secret from *anyone*, much less my older sister."

"You know what I mean," Grace said, shooting him a look.

"I know, I know, I'm just kidding. But yeah, I'd tell my sister. I tell her everything. And you can't just assume how they'll react. That's not fair to them."

Grace looked at him over their shared trays of french fries and hamburgers. "I just met them, you know? I don't want them to hate me before they even get a chance to know me."

"Does it count as knowing you if they don't know one of the most important things that's happened to you?"

Grace didn't have an answer for that.

"So you tell your sister *everything*?" she asked instead. "Really?" Grace tried to imagine having someone like that in her life.

"Everything," Rafe said, stealing some of Grace's fries, pulling them away before she could swat at his hand. "Such an only child," he chided her. "Not even willing to share."

Grace smiled despite herself. "And she doesn't judge you or anything?"

"Are you kidding? She judges the hell out of me sometimes. But she's still my sister. She'll still talk to me for an hour about something even if she thinks I'm being stupid about it. Maybe that's *why* she talks to me for so long, now that I'm thinking about it."

"I think you're the only person I've actually told about Peach," Grace admitted. "Everyone else either already knew or saw me when I was pregnant."

"And did I judge?" Rafe asked, his voice innocent. "No, ma'am, I did not."

"Everyone else did."

"Grace." The joking tone fell away from Rafe's voice, and he set down his fries on his tray. "You don't have to tell anyone. But it'd just be a shame if you had all these people willing to support you, and you never let them."

"But what if they're not?"

Rafe smiled at her. "What if they *are*?"

After she got home that night, Grace sat down in front of her computer. Her hair still smelled like french fries from the restaurant, and she tied it back as she opened her search engine.

She waited almost a full minute before typing in her first search term.

MELISSA TAYLOR.

It was way too broad, of course, and pulled up a million sources, all of which Grace immediately knew were not *her* Melissa Taylor. She tried **MELISSA TAYLOR BIRTH MOTHER**, but even that was too big, too vast, and Grace suddenly felt again like

Alice in *Alice in Wonderland*, when Alice became too small and fell inside a bottle that was washed out to sea, carried away on a current that she couldn't control, too small to see past the waves in front of her, too insignificant to make a difference.

She closed her computer and sat back in her chair.

"Grace!" her dad called from downstairs. "Can you come down here, please?"

Grace knew that *that* wasn't a good tone. It wasn't as bad as the tone had been when she'd told her parents that she was pregnant, but she was pretty sure that it would never sound that bad again. Everything after that would be an improvement.

"Yeah?" she called instead.

"Downstairs!" her mom replied.

Two parents. It was times like this that Grace wished she had grown up with a sibling, someone to balance the scales a bit. It seemed a lot easier to be in trouble when you could point to someone else and say, "Wait till you hear what *they* did, though." Grace thought it would be nice to not always be the only person in the house who kept screwing up.

She went downstairs, poking her head into the kitchen. "Yeah?"

"We need to talk," her mom said. "Elaine from down the street called and said that she saw you with a boy at the shopping center?"

Grace frowned. "I didn't realize that Elaine from down the street was running a police state."

Grace's dad raised an eyebrow at her. (Grace couldn't help but think that Rafe was a much better eyebrow raiser, but she decided it wise to keep that information to herself.)

"It was Rafe," she said instead. "He works at Whisked Away."

Grace's mom crossed her arms over her chest. "Are you dating him?"

"No," Grace said. "We're friends, that's all."

Grace's parents exchanged a glance, and she once again wished for a partner in crime. Even a dog would have sufficed at that point.

"We really don't think you should be dating right now," her dad said. "You need some time to focus on yourself."

"Well, good, because I'm not dating anyone," she said. "Like I said, Rafe's my *friend*."

"Grace," her dad said, "you have to understand. We just want to protect you. You've had a rough couple of months and—"

Grace could feel her temper starting to rise along the back of her spine, forcing her stand up straighter. "No, wait. Let me guess. Elaine from down the street called you because she's worried that I'm slutting it up all over town again!" Grace's face felt too hot, her pulse too fast. "Right?"

"Language," her mother said.

"Oh, let's just say what Elaine and everyone else is thinking!" Grace exploded. "I got pregnant, I had a baby, and now I can't even look at a guy without everyone thinking I'm about to pop out three more rug rats!"

"Grace," her dad said again. "We're worried about you, that's all. We—"

"Because if memory serves," Grace continued, ignoring her dad, "the whole point of me giving up P— *Milly* was so that I could live my life, right? 'Oh, Grace, you have your whole life ahead of you!' How many times did I hear *that* come out of your mouths? And now everyone reminds me that I had a baby, I can't go to school, I can't make friends with a boy—"

"You can make friends—" her mom started to say, but Grace kept going. She felt like someone had released a steam trigger on the top of her head.

"Okay, let's say he's *not* a friend, then," Grace said. "Let's say that Rafe is a boy that I *do* like. Do I not get to date? Do I not get to kiss a boy ever again? Did I blow my big chance at falling in love and starting a family because I made one mistake?"

"Grace," her mom said, and Grace could hear the wobble in her voice. "You did *not*—"

"Well, good!" Grace shouted. "Because if I can't move forward and *like* someone and make friends and, God forbid, fall in *love* again, then I don't understand why I gave up my baby in the first place! Unless it was only to make everything okay for *you*!"

She didn't even realize she was crying until she went to move her hair off her face and realized that her cheeks were wet. Her parents looked shell-shocked, stricken. Grace suspected they would have looked less horrified if she had slapped them.

"I think we need to meet with a counselor," Grace's dad said after almost fifteen seconds of near silence, Grace's breath the only sound in the room. She felt wild, feral, like she had when Peach had forced her way out of her. She felt, Grace suddenly realized, alive.

"Fine," she said. "Make an appointment. Because I have a lot to say and I'm tired of not saying it. And," she added, "you can tell Elaine from down the street that what I do is none of her damn business. I mean, that's what you would have told her *last year*, right?"

Grace didn't bother to wait for a response. Instead, she turned and ran back upstairs, locking herself in the bathroom and turning on the faucet as hard as it would go. She waited until she was sure no one could hear her before she started to cry.

MAYA

Maya kept trying to think of a word that would describe how it felt to have their dad back in their house full-time while her mom was in rehab. She tried to come up with something, but at the end of the day, all she had was one word.

Weird.

It was weird to see her dad making breakfast in the morning, eggs that looked too slimy to eat but both Maya and Lauren choked them down anyway. By the end of the day, all of them were too tired to figure out dinner, which led to pizza boxes on the coffee table while the three of them sprawled out, gnawing on the crusts while watching reruns of *House Hunters*.

Their mom went to rehab straight from the hospital, her head bandaged, her hands shaking. Maya thought she looked like a frightened child, what with her big eyes and small bones, and Maya hugged her good-bye and couldn't decide if she wanted her mom to come home soon or stay away forever.

The counselor at the hospital said that it was better if she didn't come home in between the hospital and rehab, that she might see her house and suddenly decide not to go, conclude that she could just drink less at home and not need any sort of counseling. "Yeah, no," Maya had said when the counselor said that. This was after Grace and Joaquin had come over the morning after the accident, when the three of them had sat side by side and put their feet in the water and smoked a joint that, Maya later realized, was one of the only items she had left from Claire.

The rehab was in a place that, according to the pamphlets, looked more like a spa vacation. But their dad assured them that it was "a wonderful facility" that "will finally give your mom the help she needs. That's great, right?" Maya and Lauren had sat next to each other on the couch in the hospital lobby and nodded. What else could they do?

Their dad had been horrified to hear about the wine bottles hidden around the house, the empties stashed at the bottom of the recycling bin in the backyard. He had sat between Lauren and Maya on their living room couch while Maya explained everything in a monotone that didn't even sound like her own voice. "How long has this been going on?" he asked.

"A while?" Lauren finally offered, and their dad had let out a long, low sigh before lowering his head into his hands. Maya wasn't sure if she was supposed to comfort him, so she didn't do anything.

"Okay," he finally said. "We're making some changes around here."

And now it was the three of them rattling around in the house that suddenly felt too big. Maya had never realized how much space their mom had taken up. One afternoon, she found herself automatically going upstairs to suss out the latest stash of wine bottles, and only realized upon opening the closet that that wasn't a problem anymore.

Their dad wanted Maya and Lauren to start going to therapy, too. "Why?" Maya had asked. "We're not the ones with the drinking problem." Privately, she thought that was yet another result of her mother's selfishness: she was the one with the drinking problem, so why did *Maya* need to waste a hour of her week in therapy?

"Dad's being weird," Lauren said one night. They were doing homework in Maya's bedroom, Lauren sprawled on the floor while Maya sat cross-legged on her bed. Neither one of them thought about using the desk, and even if they had wanted to, Maya's laundry was spread all over it. Laundry felt like a luxury at this point, something that people with fewer worries and more time did for themselves.

"Dad's weird because he's afraid we're going to be cripplingly and emotionally damaged," Maya replied, her pen between her teeth as she flipped back and forth between her physics textbook and her lab book. "Plus, dads are weird in general."

"Are you going to go to counseling?" Lauren asked. From the floor, she sounded very far away.

"Fuck no," Maya said. "Mom's the one with the problem. She can use her own precious time to sort it out."

Lauren was quiet for another long minute before she said, "How come you're always home right now?"

"What?" Maya shut her textbook and went back to her workbook. Why couldn't they put all the information in one book, instead of making you need at least three for each class?

"Where's Claire?"

Maya ignored the dull pain that shot up her spine whenever someone mentioned Claire. "We broke up."

"What?" Lauren sounded scandalized. "Why? I thought you two were totally in love with each other."

"*Were*. Past tense. Love is fleeting, things change, et cetera."

"Why?"

"Because we had a fight and we both said mean things to each other." Maya left out the part where she was mostly the one who said mean things, and Claire was mostly the one who said the truth.

"Well, that's stupid," Lauren said. "You two were really cute together."

"Yeah, Grace and Joaquin already told me that I'm being an idiot. You don't need to tell me, too, okay?"

There was a pause from the floor before Lauren said, "Grace and Joaquin? You told them?"

"Of course I told them. When they were here the other day, after you left to go to your friend's house."

"I thought you were only talking about Mom, though."

"We talked about a lot of things, okay? For example, the fact that Grace thinks that we should find our biological mom."

Maya had been trying to steer the conversation away from Claire, from how bad it felt to even say her name, the dullest grays and blacks that her mind could ever envision, plumes of choking smoke left over after a fireworks show. But judging from Lauren's silence on the floor, she had sent the conversation down the wrong road entirely.

"What, so you're just going to abandon your family now?"

"What?" Maya looked up from her physics homework. "What are you talking about?"

"Mom goes to rehab and you decide to swap her out for a new model? Is that what you're doing with Grace, too? We're too much trouble, so you decide to find something better?"

"Lauren, what the hell are you—"

"Never mind." Lauren stood up, gathering her computer and books in such a hurry that one of her notebooks fell to the floor. Maya started to reach for it, but Lauren stepped in front of her, blocking Maya with her back. "Leave it alone," she said.

"You're in *my* room," Maya pointed out. "I'd be happy to leave you alone, but *you're* the one who needs to leave, not me."

Lauren had always been like this, explosive as a toddler, screaming tantrums when she didn't get her way. "It's that red-headed gene," her parents had explained, dragging her out of restaurants, movie theaters, bookstores, leaving Maya, the one thing that was not like the others, with a smile on her face and as the unexpected recipient of double the popcorn, ice cream, and books.

But when Lauren stormed out, Maya realized that she hadn't left anything behind, and what used to feel like a victory now felt like a sad, hollow loss.

It was Thursday before Claire finally cut Maya off on her way to history class.

"Um, excuse me," Maya said. "You're making me late."

That's not what she had been planning to say to Claire, of course. Maya had thought of a thousand different things to say to her: apologies and confessions, tears and mea culpas, detailed explanations of how stupid Maya could be, how stubborn she was.

But then she saw Claire and the hurt bubbled over, taking over all the smart things she wanted to see in a jealous, green-fueled fury.

"How come you didn't tell me your mom was in rehab?"

Maya went still. Nobody was supposed to know about that. Did everyone know? Was everyone at school watching her, judging her? "How—what? How did you—"

Claire held up her phone. She was taller than Maya, but for the first time, her height felt intimidating instead of safe. "Because *Lauren* texted me, that's why. Your little sister was the one who had to tell me."

Maya felt herself regroup, her insides steadying themselves

against the nervous sloshing feeling in her stomach. "It's none of your business."

"Bullshit."

Maya tried to step around her, but Claire stepped in time with her, blocking her path. "You and me are going to talk. Right now."

"I have class."

"Oh, suddenly you're a perfect student who never ditches? Nice try. Let's go."

Maya stumbled after her, following Claire past the gymnasium and the theater that everyone referred to as Little Theater, even though it was the only one on campus and pretty sizable. Finally they were back on the same spot of grass that Maya had always thought of as theirs. It seemed strange that the grass still looked so green and lush, even though they had broken up.

"Okay," Claire said. The late bell had already rung and the school felt strangely empty, like they were the only two people left on campus. If this were a TV show, Maya thought to herself, this would be when the zombie invasion started. "Spill it."

"Spill what?" Maya asked, deliberately not looking at Claire. "You already know everything."

"I know one basic fact, that's it." Claire's face suddenly softened, and she put her hands on Maya's shoulders. "My," she said, and her voice was so quiet that it hurt Maya more than if she had been shouting. "What happened? Lauren said she was in the hospital. She said that you rode in the ambulance."

Maya gnawed on her lower lip, looking everywhere but at

Claire. "She hit her head, that's all. She had a concussion. And then my dad took her to rehab in Palm Springs and moved back in with us."

"Why didn't you tell me any of this?" Claire's hands were moving her hair back from her shoulders now, and Maya couldn't tell if she wanted to step closer to her or run away and never look back. She felt so exposed, and they weren't even her secrets. They were her mother's, for fuck's sake.

"Because we broke up," Maya said, trying her best to put the perfect "duh" tone in her voice.

Claire sighed in a way that made her sound like a disappointed parent. "Maya, seriously? You think everything has to just stop? We had a fight. Why does that mean it has to be over?"

Maya found herself thinking about Joaquin and Birdie, how Joaquin had said that he and Maya had the same dysfunction. For all the times that Maya had thought about her biological family, she had wondered whether or not they looked alike, if they had the same laugh or smile or double-jointed thumbs. She never thought they'd share the same stupid breakup stories.

"I don't want to talk about this," Maya said, trying to step around Claire again. "I'm serious, Claire. I need to go to class."

"Lauren also said that you were going to look for your biological mom."

"She what?" Maya had been a step away, but she whirled around, red like a wound exploding, sending blood straight into the sky. "Look," she said, "let's get one thing straight. I don't need you and my little sister gossiping about me, okay? If you want to know something, you can ask me—"

"No, I can't, Maya!" Claire shouted back. "That's the problem! You keep everything from me! You didn't tell me about your mom, you never talked to me about finding your brother and sister, and now you want to find your bio mom and you don't even bring it up, not even once?"

"If I wanted to talk about it, I would!"

"I don't believe you! I think you've been keeping your mom's secrets and now *her* secrets are starting to ruin *your* life."

Maya was shaking, literally trembling with the force of her anger. But was it anger? Was this what it felt like to be truly angry, or was it something bigger, more complicated? Was this what it felt like to be exposed, for all of her private thoughts to be laid bare in front of the one person who she had wanted to be perfect for?

"Stop texting with my sister," Maya said instead, her teeth gritted so tight that her jaw pulsed a little. "I mean it!"

And then she turned and started walking toward her class. "Maya!" Claire yelled after her, but Maya hugged her bag tighter and started to run. It felt good to move, to have her lungs ache and her chest heave. She wanted the pain to match how she felt.

She wanted it to hurt.

The next Sunday, when Maya met with Grace and Joaquin, everybody was cranky.

One look at Grace's straw pretty much told Maya that she was not in a good way. Maya had no idea how she could drink out of it without cutting up her mouth. "Have you thought about maybe just sipping straight from the cup?" Maya asked at one point.

Grace glared at her, then glanced over her shoulder. They were at a Starbucks at the outdoor mall near Grace's house, sitting out on the patio, and Grace looked like she was waiting for a sniper to take her out. Just watching her made Maya feel edgy. "*God*, Grace," she said at one point. "No one's out to get you."

Grace huffed out a laugh that made Maya wonder if her sister perhaps had Mob ties.

Joaquin just looked sullen, his eyes heavy. Not that he was the most talkative person, of course, but Maya was used to a little more, especially after last weekend, when they had talked about things that were actually important. "So," she said after nearly a minute of complete silence. "My mom went to rehab."

"That's great," Grace said.

"Really good," Joaquin agreed.

"And my dad moved back in with us," Maya continued.

"Really great," Joaquin said.

"That's good you have him," Grace added. "Really good."

Maya narrowed her eyes a bit. "And my sister, Lauren? She finally got approval for the surgery to remove those horns from her forehead."

"Awesome," Grace said, glancing past Joaquin's shoulder.

"Wait, what?" Joaquin said. "Your sister's having surgery?"

"Finally," Maya sighed. "You two are zombies, you know that? You're both being so weird."

"Sorry," Grace said. "I just . . . I *really* hate this mall, that's all."

"And I'm actually a zombie," Joaquin replied. "My secret is out, I guess. God, I feel so much lighter." He took a deep breath and sighed it out, which made both Grace and Maya laugh despite themselves.

"You're so bizarre," Maya said.

Joaquin just pointed at himself. "I told you. *Zombie*."

"That explains the rotting flesh smell," Maya replied, then ducked when Joaquin threw a napkin at her.

Grace, however, had just gone still next to them. "The zombie's definitely going to eat you first," Maya said to her, giving her a nudge.

"Shut up," Grace just whispered in response, looking past Joaquin's shoulder, and Joaquin turned to see what had her attention.

There were two boys coming into the Starbucks, and from the looks of it, they knew who Grace was. They were snickering between them, and then one of them said something to the other and they both burst into laughter before fist-bumping each other.

"Do you know those frat-boy wannabes?" Maya said. She herself had zero patience for dudes who wore their baseball caps backward and always talked about "getting girls," even though Maya was pretty sure that they had never even touched one.

"I think we should go," Grace said.

"Wait, Grace," Joaquin said, sitting up a little. "Are you *shaking*?"

"Hey, *Grace*."

Now the boys were standing next to their table. It was almost empty on the patio outside, just a few older people sipping teas in the far corner, and their voices sounded loud. "New boyfriend?" one of them asked. He was tall and skinny and made Maya very glad that she had been born a lesbian.

"Just go *away*, Adam, okay?"

"What's up? You just hanging out?" Adam looked like the cat that had caught the canary.

"You move pretty fast," the other guy said. "You and Max just broke up, right?"

"Grace," Maya said slowly. "Let's just go, okay?"

Across from them, Joaquin was sitting up very straight. Maya had never seen him look so alert before, and it didn't make her feel any better about the situation.

"So you tell your new guy about what you were up to in the last year?" Adam said, and his smile reminded Maya of the Cheshire Cat's, too big to be sincere, a crescent moon too sharp at the edges. "All your big . . . *changes*?"

Grace started to stand up, shoving her chair back so hard that it crashed into the table behind them. That just seemed to make the boys laugh, though, and before Maya or Joaquin could do anything, Adam leaned forward and said, "Does he know what a slut you are? Or is that what he likes best about you?"

Maya was about to do something, say something, anything to release the pressure that she felt exploding in her chest, when suddenly Joaquin was up and moving so fast that no one saw him coming. In one smooth motion, he had Adam up against the wall, his forearm pressed across his chest, and Adam looked wide-eyed and scared, a fish out of water.

"Listen, you asshole," Joaquin hissed, and now Maya was standing up next to Grace, hanging on to her arm. "That's my *sister*, okay! You think it's cool to talk to my sister like that? Do you?!" Adam didn't say anything. Maya felt the pressure in her chest go straight into her heart, bursting with a sudden, vicious love for him.

"Joaquin," Grace started to say, but it sounded like her voice had died in her throat.

"No!" Adam yelped. His hat had tumbled off in the fracas, and now he just looked like a little kid. "No, man! I'm sorry, okay? I didn't even know she had a brother!"

"You talk to her again, you even *think* of looking at her again"—Joaquin pressed his arm harder across Adam's chest, sliding it up toward his throat—"and you're going to have to talk to me. You got that?"

Adam nodded nervously, his pupils dilated. Next to him, his friend was standing silent.

So was Grace.

"Now get the fuck out of here," Joaquin said, and Maya thought it was more of a growl, a bear on the attack. "If I see you again, you and me, we're going to have problems."

Adam nodded again, and Joaquin gave him one final press before locking eyes with him, then letting him go. He and his friend scurried away as Joaquin seemed to slump, all his bravado slinking away and leaving him like a shell.

"Joaquin," Grace said. She was panting now. So was Joaquin.

"Joaquin," Maya said when he didn't answer.

"I—I'm sorry," he said, his breath coming in short gasps, and then suddenly he was leaving the patio, running down the street, sprinting away from them, trying to escape.

JOAQUIN

Joaquin thought that he was going to be sick.

He wasn't quite sure what had happened. One minute, he had been sitting with Maya and Grace, thinking about Mark and Linda, and then that fucking weasel had come up to Grace, had make her shake in her shoes, had called her a slut, and Joaquin felt himself slip into that white-hot space that he had spent years trying to avoid.

He'd be lying if he said it didn't feel good to feel that kid's pulse beating fast against his arm, his breath short, his eyes blown wide open. It was a powerful thing to literally hold someone's fate in your hand, and Joaquin hadn't had that sort of power in a long time.

The problem with power, though, is that having it doesn't always make you a good person. Sometimes, it makes you the bad guy.

Joaquin ran until he hit the edge of the park that bordered the mall, one that was usually used only by toddlers and their attentive parents, and it wasn't until he stopped that he realized his sisters were hot on his trail. "Joaquin!" they were shouting, dashing after him. "Joaquin, wait!"

Joaquin turned, his chest heaving as he tried to catch his breath. He hadn't run like that in a long time. He felt as if he could keep running forever. "Just—go away, okay?" he said to his sisters, holding out his hand as if to keep them at bay. "I'm sorry, I ruined our day."

"You're shaking," Grace told him. She was still trembling, too. Maya was the only one who seemed steady, her eyes wild and alive. "You should sit down."

"I'm fine," Joaquin spat out. "I just got upset, that's all. I'm sorry."

Grace just shook her head at him. "I'm not," she said. "He deserved it."

"Joaquin." Now Maya was stepping toward him. "Let's go sit down at least, okay? You don't look good."

Joaquin didn't feel that great, either. "Okay," he said.

"Okay," Maya said, holding out her hand to him. "Let's sit. Sitting is great. Everyone likes sitting, even active people. Do you run competitively or something? Because you were hauling ass across the parking lot. I think you outran a Tesla at one point."

Somewhere in the back of his brain, where it was fuzzy with memories, Joaquin remembered Maya saying that she talked a lot when she was nervous. *He* had made her nervous, Joaquin realized, and that only made him feel worse.

By the time the three of them sat down on a bench, Joaquin bookended by his two sisters, his breath was starting to come back a little. Grace still looked pretty shaky, though, and Joaquin noticed that she kept her hands clenched tightly in her lap.

"Okay," Maya said as soon as they were settled. "What the hell was *that*?"

"He called Grace a slut," Joaquin said. He could barely get his voice above a murmur. "He shouldn't have said that."

"No, I don't mean that," Maya said. "I mean the sprint across the parking lot, Joaq. You ran like a scared rabbit."

That wasn't exactly the image that Joaquin had of himself, but maybe Maya was right. He had never seen himself run, after all.

When he didn't say anything, Grace unclenched her hands and reached over to take one of Joaquin's. "Joaquin," she said quietly. "What happened?"

He wrapped his fingers around hers, clenched and unclenched her hand until he felt like he could speak again. Grace was fine, he reminded himself. No one had gotten hurt. He hadn't hurt anyone.

Maya was pressed against his other side, her hand on his shoulder. "You're okay, Joaq," she said quietly. "It's fine. Just take a deep breath."

He nodded, trying to get his heartbeat back under control, tried to put the tiger back in its cage. "When I was twelve," he said before he could stop himself, and then he couldn't start again. He had only told the story once before, to Ana and Mark and Linda, but that had been in Mark and Linda's living room, where he was surrounded by people who—well, if not *loved* him, then definitely cared about him—and the room had been soft with sunlight and specks of dust dancing between the rays.

The sun poured through the trees of the park, and Maya and Grace waited for Joaquin to speak again.

"When I was twelve," he said again, "this family adopted me. The Buchanans." Just saying their name made his mouth feel funny, and he paused and waited until he could talk again. "They became my foster parents when I was ten, and they decided they wanted to adopt me."

"Did you want them to adopt you?" Grace asked when he paused. He wouldn't have thought that her hand could be so strong, but she was holding on to him, not letting go.

"I thought I did," he said. "They had a couple of other foster kids who they had adopted, and they had an older daughter and a, um, a baby, later." Joaquin could still see her, bowlegged with dark curls hanging like a halo around her head. It made him sick to even think about her.

"Were they nice to you?" Maya asked.

"They were fine," he said. "I don't know if they were nice. They weren't *not* nice, though. Sometimes that's enough. I had my own room, my own bed. We went shopping and they let me pick out sheets. That was a big deal."

Joaquin's heart still felt like it was vibrating in his chest, and he took another deep breath, Maya's hand still warm on his shoulder. "Living with them was fine, the kids were nice, all of that. They had a baby"—Joaquin could hardly bring himself to say her name—"Natalie, and that was cool. I was like . . . I thought that it was the real thing, you know? I thought that this was my family."

"What happened?" Grace asked, and Joaquin could hear a deeper kind of fear in her voice, different from when Adam had called her a slut.

Joaquin bit the inside of his cheek, waiting until he could say words again. "I just started . . . I don't know, I just started having these tantrums. They called them meltdowns. I would just black out with this anger. It felt like my skin was exploding, you know? Like I couldn't even breathe. And the closer we got to the adoption, the worse it got. I was starting fights with everyone except Natalie and I couldn't even explain why. The Buchanans still went through with the adoption, though."

Joaquin wondered if they regretted that, if they sat up late at night and reminisced about that time they'd made a terrible decision by bringing Joaquin into their home.

"I knew something was wrong, though," he said now. "I couldn't even call them Mom and Dad. Two years later and I only called them by their first names. It felt like . . ."

"Like what?" Grace asked softly.

Joaquin sagged a little, leaning against both girls. They were strong enough to hold him up, he realized. "Like once the adoption went through, then that was it," he said. "It'd be final. I just thought that if our mom ever came back, if she actually, finally just came fucking back and showed up at the house and saw that I had a new mom, a new dad, that she . . . she'd think I replaced her. It's stupid, I know, it's so fucking stupid. I was such an idiot."

"No, *no*," Maya said, leaning into him. "It's not stupid, it's not stupid at all. You were a kid, right? That wasn't your job to figure all that out."

Joaquin laughed a little. "Well, I haven't actually told you the bad part yet."

The girls were quiet, waiting for him to speak again.

"So one day, about six months after the adoption went through, Natalie was almost two, and it was a Saturday afternoon, and I was having this epic meltdown." Joaquin tried not to feel the carpet on his back, the way his hair tangled against it as he writhed on the floor, howling for something, for someone, that was always just out of reach. "No one could even touch me. I wouldn't let anyone get close. And then the dad, Mr. Buchanan, he tried to pick me up and set me on my feet, right? Like, to stand up. And I just started throwing everything that I could get my hands on. We were in his office and there was a stapler on the desk. . . ."

Joaquin paused. He could still feel the cool metal of the stapler in his hand, the heaviness of it as he picked it up. His hands were shaking again, and Grace just held his fingers even more tightly between hers.

"What happened?" she whispered.

"I threw it," he said, and then there were tears on his cheeks, sliding down his throat, burning him all over. "I threw it," he said again, clearing his throat. "I threw it at him, but it went out the door and Natalie . . . Natalie was coming around the corner right then."

Joaquin dropped his head, closed his eyes, sick with shame. "It hit her in the head." He gestured her up toward his temple. "Right here, and she just dropped. And Mr. Buchanan, he let out this . . . it was like a roar, like a lion, and he grabbed me and threw me backward, and I flew into the bookshelf. Broke my arm." Joaquin could still hear the crack of bone, one white-hot pain replacing another, but nothing was as loud as the sound of Natalie falling to the floor.

Joaquin was crying steadily now. He hadn't even cried when he told Mark and Linda and Ana the story. *They* had wept, but Joaquin had been unmoved, like it had happened to someone else. "I would have never hurt the baby," he sobbed. "I loved Natalie. I didn't want to hurt her. I didn't want to hurt anybody."

Grace was holding him now, and Maya's arm was around his shoulders, and Joaquin put his hand to his forehead and rested his elbows on his knees. "What happened after that?" Grace asked him.

"Emergency room," he said. "They signed me back into foster care that night."

"People can do that?" Maya asked. Joaquin was pretty sure that she was crying now, too.

"People do it all the time," he said. "They said I was a danger to the other kids. And if you're violent in a home, they put you on a psych hold for a few days, and then I went to this group home out in Pomona. I was 'special needs,' they said. I was too old, too violent." He thought of his foster sister Eva's words. "Too much and not enough. I think people were scared of me."

Grace cleared her throat before speaking again. "And Natalie, was she . . . ?"

"She was fine, ultimately," Joaquin said. "I asked my social worker as soon as she showed up at the hospital. It was a concussion, but . . ." Joaquin couldn't even finish the sentence. "She's fine," he said again.

"But you broke your arm?"

"It was a clean break," Joaquin said, like that made the story better. "The Buchanans weren't allowed to have any more foster kids after that."

"Good," Maya spat out.

"I just sort of went from group home to group home," Joaquin said. "After that, I couldn't stay with just any foster family. They had to have special training to be able to handle kids like me. They got paid more, too, because of the danger, but yeah."

"And Mark and Linda have that?" Grace asked.

"They got it after they met me," Joaquin said. "When I was fifteen, almost sixteen, they came to this adoption fair thing at one of the group homes. They liked me, they said." Joaquin still didn't entirely believe them, but it was a nice thought, all the same.

"I think they *love* you, Joaquin," Maya murmured.

"Is this why you won't let them adopt you?" Grace suddenly asked. "Because you're afraid they'll give you back like the Buchanans did?"

Joaquin wiped his eyes, glancing over at her. "I don't care about going back," he said. "I just love them too much to hurt them—to hurt *anyone*—like that. Once was enough."

Both of his sisters seemed to sag against him. "Oh, *Joaquin*," Maya sighed.

"No," he said, before she could start telling him how he felt, how he should feel. "You don't understand, okay? You saw me with that asshole. It just came up out of me—it's like I can't contain it. I could have really hurt him."

"But you didn't," Grace said. "You *didn't*, Joaquin. You were defending me. He said something really terrible that he knew would hurt me, and you defended me. That's not the same thing at all.

"And," she continued before he could argue with her, "remember how I told you that I punched a guy at school?"

Joaquin waited for her to continue, and when she didn't, the realization dawned on him. "That was *him*?"

Grace nodded, her face grim.

"Wow. Okay." Joaquin felt a tiny bit less terrible about wanting to murder Adam.

"Then that guy is an even bigger idiot than I thought!" Maya said. "When do I get to punch him?"

Joaquin smiled at that, and Maya hugged him, pressing her face against his arm. "You're not a bad person, Joaq," she whispered. "You're not."

"I threw a metal stapler at a baby," he replied. He had thought that by saying it out loud, he would diminish how terrible it was, like ripping off a Band-Aid, but it was the completely opposite feeling, the words cutting his mouth as he said them.

"You threw a stapler because you were scared," Grace corrected him. "The baby happened to be there. It was an *accident*. They shouldn't have hurt you, too."

"You were a just a kid yourself," Maya added.

Joaquin had to close his eyes at that, felt like he was going underwater, his sisters the only thing buoying him.

His *sisters*. Holy shit.

"Is it okay that I said that?" Joaquin asked, glancing over at Grace.

She frowned. "Said what?"

"You know. I called you my sister."

The edges of Grace's mouth trembled even as she started to smile. "That's fine," she said. "That's what I am, right?"

On his other side, Maya rested her head on his shoulder. "Me, too," she said quietly.

When he could talk again, Joaquin swiped at his eyes with the sleeve of his T-shirt. If Linda had been there, she probably would have handed him a packet of tissues.

"So—I'm a monster," he said. He was trying to keep it light, trying to bring them back up after almost drowning in the tide, but it felt forced. He didn't even believe his own tone.

"I think anyone who's been in that much pain must have a pretty big heart." Grace's voice was thoughtful. "And no matter what, Maya and I won't give you back."

"Nope," Maya added. "This was a final sale. No returns, no backsies."

Joaquin smiled a little. "But what if—"

"Nope!" Grace said. "You heard Maya."

"But maybe—"

"No!" both girls cried this time, and Joaquin laughed, clear and sharp in the cooling air, the sound echoing back in his ears and filling him up.

GRACE

Grace nervously bounced her leg in the waiting room of the therapist's office. There was a half-done puzzle on the table in front of her, but she had no interest in fitting the rest of the pieces together. She just wanted to get this over with and get the hell out of there.

Next to her, Grace's mom leaned over and gently pressed down on Grace's knee with her hand.

Grace started bouncing her other leg instead.

She had been dreading this appointment for the better part of a week. She knew she was going to have to talk about Peach, talk about her biological mom, her siblings—basically everything that had blown up in her life over the past few months was about to be fair game to a stranger, and all Grace wanted to do was circle the wagons and head back home to the safety of her bedroom and her loneliness. Her only consolation was that at least her parents looked as ill at ease as she felt.

Grace wished that Rafe were there with her. If nothing else, at least he could make her laugh.

By the time they got into the office, Grace thought she might throw up. *How does Joaquin do this every week?* she wondered, and then she thought of the last time she'd seen Joaquin and felt sad all over again. After he had told her and Maya everything, Grace had started to drive herself home, then pulled the car over halfway there so she could cry. More than anything, she wished she had known Joaquin back then, wished she had known him her whole life so that he would have been a little less lost. She thought of Alice again, tossed in the bottle and riding through the storm on the ocean.

The therapist's name was Michael, and he seemed nice enough. His tie was in a perfect Windsor knot, which Grace had only seen in pictures on the internet, and that made her trust him a little bit more.

Just a little bit.

"So, Grace," Michael said as soon as they were seated, "your parents told me some things about you when they first called to make this appointment. Sounds like you've had quite a year."

Grace raised an eyebrow. "I shoved a baby out of me, if that's what you're asking."

Grace's mother covered her eyes with her hands and groaned.

"What?" Grace said, annoyed. "You were there, Mom. That's basically what happened."

Michael, to his credit, seemed pretty unfazed. Grace liked him a little bit more. "And your parents mentioned that you put the baby up for adoption, correct?"

Grace nodded. "With Daniel and Catalina, yeah. They're really good parents."

"And you're okay with that decision?"

Grace shrugged. "I mean, it's a done deal, right? It's not like I could get her back if I wanted to."

"So you would like to have her back?"

"That's not . . ." Grace took a deep breath, forced herself to keep her hands in her lap. "I miss P— Milly very much. Of course I do. I carried her for almost ten months. But she's in a much better home, a better family for her. I did the right thing. My parents agree."

"Your mom also mentioned that you recently spent time with a boy, and when they tried to discuss that with you, you got a little upset."

"She tried to tear the roof off the house," Grace's dad clarified, but he sounded like he was trying to make a joke.

Grace wasn't laughing.

"I got mad," she said, shooting a look at her dad, "because Elaine from down the street called them to tell them that I had lunch with a boy, like it was a freaking crime or something."

"Grace," her mom said, "we weren't upset. We're just worried about you. You seem so . . . you're not yourself, sweetheart."

"Of course I'm not myself!" Grace cried. "I had a baby and

then gave her away! I don't even recognize who I am anymore! You act like I'm just going to go back to high school and go to dances and prom and everything, but none of that has happened. I can't even go to the mall without people whispering about me, calling me a slut! You want a daughter back who doesn't exist anymore."

"Sweetheart, we know how much Max hurt you," her dad started to say, but Grace turned in her seat, her hand out.

"Do not say his name," she said. "Do not *even* say it. I hate him."

"We just don't want you to get hurt the same way again," her mom said. "We just think you need more time to heal."

"You don't get it!" Grace cried. "I'm not *going* to heal from this! You keep acting like I'm going to explode at any moment, and if you don't say anything long enough, that I'll forget about my baby"—the word got caught in her throat and she had to almost spit it out to get it out of her—"and it'll all be fine! That's what you always do! You pretend like something didn't happen, and then eventually, it's like no one remembers that it *did* happen. You did the same thing with me!"

The silence after Grace's outburst felt especially loud. "What do you mean, Grace?" Michael asked. Grace had almost forgotten that the therapist was even in the room. She wondered if he was regretting agreeing to meet with them in the first place.

"It's like . . ." She tried to find the words that would sum up her feelings. "Like they said that if I ever wanted to know about my adoption, that all I had to do was ask them. But why was that *my* responsibility? Why did I have to be the one who asked? Why couldn't they be the ones to *tell* me about it?"

Grace's mom had tears in her eyes. "We just didn't want to give you too much information."

"No!" Grace cried. "You thought that if I knew about my biological mom, I would try to find her, and that scared the shit out of you."

"Why do you keep those photos of Milly hidden?" her mom suddenly asked her.

"What?" Grace said. "How did you see those?"

"In your desk drawer," she said. "I was putting back some of your pens that I found in my car and I saw them." Her mom's eyes filled with tears as she added, "Why are you hiding them from us? I know you miss your daughter, Gracie, but we miss our granddaughter *and* our daughter. We only wish you'd talk to us."

Grace's dad was nodding his head.

Grace felt the tears slip down her cheeks and she quickly slapped them away. "Why is it always on *me* to talk to *you*?" she asked. "Why can't *you* talk to *me*?"

"Because we don't want you to be sad," her dad said, sounding every bit as sad as he didn't want Grace to feel. "We didn't want you to think that you weren't wanted, and we saw what you were like when you came home from the hospital after having her. We don't want to do anything that would make you feel that bad again." He glanced at Grace's mom before adding, "We've made a lot of mistakes, I think. But we love you more than anything. And God, Grace, we're trying to make it better, but we don't know how to fix you."

Grace tried desperately not to think of the hospital, of that drive home that felt like it was tearing something out of her body, the farther away she got from Peach. "I want to find my biological mom," she said. "I want her to know that I'm okay. And I want you to be okay with that."

"We are," Grace's mom said. "We will be. Whatever you need, Gracie. We're always going to be there for you, no matter what."

Grace remembered how tight her mom's grip had been on her hand during her contractions, how she had never left Grace's side, how her dad had watched Netflix for hours with her without saying a word. The older she got, the more human her parents seemed, and that was one of the scariest things in the world. She missed being little, when they were the all-knowing gods of her world, but at the same time, seeing them as human made it easier to see herself that way, too.

"Grace, have you talked to any other girls who have been through this?" Michael asked. "A support group, maybe?"

Grace shook her head. Talking to strangers about Peach seemed impossible, almost like a betrayal.

"There are a lot of girls who are in the same situation you're in," Michael said, but his tone was gentle. "Is that something we can maybe explore, at least?"

Grace nodded.

"I think we're going to make some really good progress in this room," Michael said with a grin, and Grace sat back in her seat and closed her eyes.

Progress, she thought, sounded exhausting.

* * *

"So let me get this straight," Rafe said. "Elaine from down the street *tattled* on me?"

"And me," Grace said, sipping at the last of her milkshake.

"Elaine from down the street needs a hobby," Rafe muttered.

Rafe had texted her the afternoon after the therapist's appointment. Got running shoes?

What? Grace had responded.

Let's go for a run. Meet you in thirty minutes behind the park?

No thanks, Grace started to reply, then looked at the letters and deleted them. OK, she sent instead. You're on.

Rafe was the kind of running partner that she liked: quiet. Her shoes still fit, and while she wasn't in the best shape of her life to be sprinting up a hill, the stitch in her side and the wheeze in her lungs made Grace feel like her old self, like she still had one thing that was the same even after so many changes. The weather was cool, the autumn air finally feeling like autumn instead of just an extra-long summer, and when she and Rafe made it to the top of the hill, Grace turned to him and smiled. "Not bad," she said.

"Kill me," Rafe had wheezed in response, his hands on his knees.

Grace had just laughed.

Afterward, they sat side by side on the roof of Rafe's car. Grace felt both cleaner and heavier, like someone who had done half their chores but saved the worst ones for last.

Sitting with Rafe on the edge of a parking lot, though, made all of it seem a little *less* heavy, at least.

"You know why Elaine from down the street called your parents, right?" Rafe said, and there was an edge in his voice that Grace had never heard before.

"Because she thinks I'm trying to get impregnated by every boy north of the equator?"

Rafe laughed a little. "Ha. Maybe. But c'mon, Grace. You're a white girl and I'm Mexican. Do the math."

"You think so?"

"I mean, I'm not one hundred percent sure, but definitely ninety-nine percent sure."

"You know that I don't care about that shit, right?" Grace said. "Fuck Elaine from down the street if that's her problem."

Rafe couldn't hide the smile that played at the corner of his mouth. "If it's all the same to you, I'd rather not fuck Elaine from down the street."

"Shut up!" Grace giggled. She had no idea why she always giggled with him. She couldn't decide if it was a good thing or a bad thing. "You know what I mean!"

"Yeah, and you know what I mean, too," Rafe said. "Don't worry, I'm not, like, mad at you about it. But you don't see things the same way I do sometimes. You don't have to."

Grace nodded. "I think we should put a For Sale sign on Elaine's house," she said. "Like a neighborhood cleanup."

Now it was Rafe's turn to laugh. "You go for it," he said. "I'll be right behind you."

"Don't tempt me." Grace rested her feet on the edge of the car's bumper. They were sitting out on the far edge of the parking lot by the mall, the one that looked over the city. From that angle, it almost looked like a big town. Almost.

"Can I ask you a question?"

"Hit it," Rafe said, then sipped at his milkshake.

"So you know my brother, Joaquin, the one I told you about? He's half Mexican, but he grew up in a bunch of different homes with different families. Do you think . . . I mean, I think it's hard for him." Grace wasn't sure what she even wanted to say, or how to say it.

"Are you asking me to comment on this as a Mexican kid? You know that's racist, right?"

Grace waited an extra breath before answering. "I don't know how to ask some of these questions," she admitted. "But Joaquin's my brother, and he's hurting, and I don't know how to help him."

They were quiet for a second. Rafe shook his milkshake. Grace had never seen him so contemplative before. "Some people think you're less Mexican if you don't speak Spanish, and some people don't care. But then there's religion—which church does your family go to, you know? How do you celebrate Christmas? Where's your family from originally? Are you first or second generation? What traditions do you have? All these things go into it, and if you don't have them, and the rest of the world sees you as all in on that, then it's gotta be hard.

"I mean," Rafe continued, then paused. "It's like with Elaine down the street. She made assumptions about me, probably, but at least I can go home and talk to my brother about it and we can laugh about how stupid she is. I'm proud of who I am, and I would never want to be anyone else, and when people are assholes, at least I can go back to my family for support. If your brother doesn't have any of that, then that's got to be fucking *hard*."

Grace listened, then scooted over until their legs were pressing next to each other. It had been a very long day, after all, and she wanted to feel a little less alone in the world. Rafe didn't move away. "Do you think you could talk to Joaq?" she asked.

Rafe smirked. "What, teach him how to be Mexican?"

"What? No! No, I would never—"

Rafe smiled down at her. "Relax, I'm kidding. And yeah, sure, give me his number, I'll text him. Maybe we can hang out. Besides, I'd like to shake his hand after he almost beat up that guy for calling you a slut." Rafe's voice was dark again. "Asshole."

"Adam is definitely an asshole," Grace agreed. "And thanks."

"No problem. But you know, Joaquin just probably needs less people talking to him and more people *listening* to him." Rafe nudged at her shoulder. "And you're a pretty good listener, Grace."

She nodded, not sure if that was entirely true but hoping that it was.

"So now I have a favor to ask you," Rafe said, clearing his throat. "This is important."

"Anything."

"Can you *please* stop chewing on your straw?!" Rafe took her milkshake away from her, inspecting the top of the straw. "Look at this! How are you not bleeding to death right now?"

"Give it back!" Grace cried, but she was laughing as she reached for it. "I just have nervous teeth, that's all!"

"Nervous teeth!" Rafe howled. "What does that even mean?"

"Shut up!" Grace said, but she was laughing, too, and when she made another swipe for her drink, she fell into him.

They both stopped laughing then.

Grace knew what she was supposed to do in the TV-show version of this moment: kiss him. She knew what she wanted to do: kiss him. And she knew what she couldn't do, not just yet.

"I'm sorry," she whispered. "I—"

"I know," Rafe whispered back, and he moved her hair out of her face in a way that Max had never done. "It's okay."

"I need you to know it's not you," Grace said. "I mean, it's not that I don't want to. It's not like you're hideous."

Rafe grinned at her. "That's what I've always wanted a girl to say to me. Thank you for making that dream come true."

"You know what I mean."

"Yeah, I do," he said. His arms still wrapped awkwardly around her, he gave a gentle squeeze. "You want to sit up?"

"Not yet," Grace said.

"You got it," Rafe said, then looped his arm over her shoulders more comfortably. "We've got all the time in the world."

They didn't, of course. Grace chose to believe Rafe anyway, as they sat together, lying in wait at the edge of the world.

MAYA

Nearly a week later, Maya still wanted to pound that kid Adam's face in.

And she wasn't too thrilled with Lauren, either.

She had flat-out refused to speak to her ever since the day Claire told her that Lauren had texted her about their mom. Lauren had pleaded with her, cried, begged, and finally even yelled, but Maya refused to open her bedroom door to her, refused to look at her, refused to acknowledge her in any way. "How long do you plan on freezing out your sister?" her dad finally asked her. "You only have one, you know."

"That is no longer a true statement," Maya said primly. "Can I go back to my homework now, please?"

It wasn't any easier to acknowledge the missing person in their home, either. It wasn't just Maya's mom who was no longer there, but the space that her drinking had taken up seemed to hang over the house like a cloud, reminding Maya of all the time that she had invested in solving a problem that wasn't even hers to fix. Lauren seemed to compensate by watching TV for hours at a time, housewives and fix-it shows and singing competitions flashing across the screen every time Maya came downstairs for a snack. Some of the shows looked interesting, but she felt so betrayed by Lauren, so shattered that her sister would go behind her back and talk to her ex-girlfriend. She had spent so long operating under the idea that secrets never left their house that she didn't know how to handle it when any of them escaped, except to make her walls closer, tighter, hugging her in so that no one else would ever be able to enter.

The pressure finally exploded one night at dinner.

Maya had sort of known what she was doing. She sort of knew that it was a bad idea to bring it up this way, and she sort of wasn't even sure if she wanted to go along with the plan in the first place. But she felt small and mean that day, felt like striking, felt like lashing out.

"So Grace and Joaquin and I think that we should look for our bio mom," she said.

Lauren immediately choked on a bite of her salad and her dad had to thump her on the back.

"You do?" their dad said once they could hear themselves over Lauren's coughing. Her eyes were red and watery, her napkin covering her mouth as she glared at Maya. Maya pretended not to see her.

"I think so," she said, casually tearing off a hunk of bread. Her dad had gotten better with pulling dinner together. They hadn't had pizza in nearly a week at this point. "You know, just to meet her. Learn about our story."

"You have a story," Lauren said. "It's here, with us."

"Maybe I have more than one story," Maya shot back.

"Girls, c'mon," their dad said. "My, are you sure you want to do this right *now*?"

"Yeah, why wouldn't I? No time like the present, right?"

The hole at the table where their mother normally sat seemed emptier than usual.

"Well, it's just . . . it's been a really eventful couple of months. Your mom, finding Grace and Joaquin. Maybe you want to wait until things settle down a bit before you go on another adventure."

"An *adventure*?" Maya glared at him. "Is that what you think this is?"

"Sweetie, no, I'm sorry. That's not what I—poor choice of words, okay? I just think maybe you and your mom and I should talk about this."

Maya laughed. She couldn't help herself. She laughed for an entire minute before she finally got control of herself again. "Well, you know what, Dad? I would *love* to talk to Mom about this. There is literally nothing that I would love to do more right now than talk to Mom, but you know what? I can't, because she can't talk to *anyone*. And then it's Family Day, right? Where we all go up to *rehab* and pretend that everything is fine?"

Lauren sat silent next to her, and Maya couldn't help but wonder if she agreed with her.

"We are not going to pretend that everything's fine—" her dad said.

"Really? Because this family is really good at doing just that."

Her dad took a deep breath and pushed himself away from the table. "I need a moment, girls," he said, then got up and left the room.

"What the hell is your problem?" Lauren hissed at her as soon as they were alone. "*Seriously*? You think Dad doesn't feel bad enough right now?"

"Oh, really? You think? Why don't you go text Claire about it? I'm sure your new BFF would love to chat with you."

"Oh my God. Would you just get over yourself, My? I texted her because I was *worried* about you. You're *good* with Claire. I actually *like* you when you're with Claire." Now Lauren was standing up from the table. "Would you quit acting like this whole family is trying to persecute you? *You're* not the only one who had to dig wine bottles out of Mom's closet, you know? *You're* not the one who found her bleeding to death on the floor. But you're the one who gets to have your little foot-stompy temper tantrum whenever someone does something that you don't like. Well, too bad. I know you like to think that you've got this whole new family that you can just run away to, but you've still got a family here, too."

"Oh, yeah, Laur?" Maya said, and now she was standing up, too. "Tell me something. When Mom and Dad said they were getting divorced, did *you* wonder if they would still want you?"

"What are you talking about?" Lauren shouted.

"Did you ever have to look at the pictures on that staircase and think, *Do they hate me for ruining their perfect family? Am I the reason for all of this? Me and my freak existence?* Let me guess, the answer to all of that is no. So don't try to make me feel bad for trying to find my space in this world, okay? Because you've never had to worry about yours!"

Now Lauren was crying in that terrible way she always did, but Maya was already turning on her heel and running upstairs.

She couldn't get far enough away, though. Not from herself. There weren't enough stairs in the world for that.

Maya couldn't sleep that night.

All she kept seeing when she closed her eyes was Grace's face when Adam called her a slut, Joaquin's face as he described Natalie falling to the floor, Lauren's face when Maya had mentioned the pictures on the staircase. All of them made her stomach feel empty, like it was a pit that could never be filled, no matter how many good thoughts she had to replace the bad ones.

At two o'clock in the morning, she gave up and went downstairs.

Lauren was there, angrily twisting Oreos open and scraping out the cream filling into a bowl. Maya stopped when she saw her, about to turn around, but Lauren saw her, too.

For a few seconds, neither of them moved.

"I couldn't sleep," Lauren finally said.

"Me either," Maya replied. She hadn't realized how tired Lauren had looked lately, but she guessed that now would be a bad time to bring that fact up. "I'll leave you alone."

"I'm just going to throw this cream out," Lauren said. "You might as well eat it."

Maya paused, then turned back around and sat down at the kitchen island, across from Lauren. "I mean, you're the weirdo who won't eat chocolate," Lauren added, scraping another cookie into the bowl.

"You're the weirdo who *eats* chocolate," Maya said grumpily. It was two o'clock in the morning, after all. "It tastes like sweet dirt."

Lauren just scoffed and pushed the bowl toward her. They sat across from each other for a full minute in silence before Lauren finally broke it.

"Do you really hate those pictures on the stairs?"

"I don't hate them," Maya said. "I just hate that it's so obvious that I don't look like you."

"Do you hate me because I look like Mom and Dad and you don't?"

"Why would I hate *you* for that? It's not your fault. You didn't ask to be born."

"You know they would never pick one of us and not the other, right?" Even though she was sitting directly across from Maya, Lauren's voice sounded very far away. "It's not a competition, My. They love us both."

Maya sighed. All she wanted to do was eat her cream filling in peace. "I'm not upset I'm adopted. I love Mom and Dad and all of that, but sometimes, I just have questions that only strangers can answer."

"Like Grace and Joaquin?"

Maya shrugged. "I feel like they understand what I mean when I say things like that."

Lauren's eyes filled with tears.

"Oh, Laur," Maya sighed. "Seriously? Why are you crying?"

Lauren wiped at her eyes, but that didn't help much. "Because you loved Claire so much and then you just pushed her away as soon as you had one little fight—"

"It wasn't little."

"—and now you have these other siblings and this other sister and Mom's gone and it's just . . . I don't want to lose you, too! You're my big sister. I don't care where you came from and I don't care what you look like. You're mine, you know? I don't have anyone else except you."

"Laur," Maya said quietly, "you're not going to lose me as your sister."

"You wouldn't even talk to me for a week!" Lauren sobbed. "You wouldn't even *look* at me. It was like what you did to Claire all over again!"

Maya paused, then hopped off her bar stool and put her arm around her sister's shoulders. "I didn't . . . I'm not . . . fuck, okay. I'm not leaving our family, okay? I'm not," she said when Lauren just cried harder. "I don't want to leave. But I like getting to know

Grace and Joaquin. I'm not sure if I even want to meet my bio mom or not, but that doesn't mean I don't love you."

"It'd be easier to believe you if you'd stop ignoring me," Lauren sniffled.

"Okay, I'm sorry. I was just mad that you texted Claire. It felt like—"

"Like I broke the rules. I know. Will you just promise to tell me if you go looking for your bio mom?"

"Absolutely."

"And will you stop ignoring me?"

"Will you stop texting my ex-girlfriend information about my personal life?"

"That was one time! But yes."

"Okay."

"I love you," Lauren whispered. "Even when you act like a brat sometimes."

"And I love you, even when you call me a brat."

It wasn't the best as far as apologies go, but at two in the morning, with the world spinning faster than either of them could control, it felt like it could be the start of just enough.

JOAQUIN

Joaquin's weekend was not off to the best of starts.

On Friday, just as he was about to leave school and head home, the guidance counselor poked her head out of her office. "Joaquin?" she said. "Can I talk to you for a minute?"

Joaquin glanced around just to make sure that there wasn't another Joaquin standing behind him. He'd had no idea that the guidance counselor even knew who he was. She normally spent her time with the kids who were applying and going to colleges. Joaquin had watched the flurry of college applications from afar, everyone getting ready to leave home for the next phase of their lives.

He thought it was ironic that everyone was trying so hard to leave home, when all he wanted to do was stay in one.

"I saw this," the guidance counselor said to him when he was finally in her office, ignoring all the inspirational posters that told Joaquin that *he could do it!* "And of course, I thought of you. I thought you might be able to use it!" She smiled at him.

Joaquin glanced down at the paper she handed him. It was printed out from the internet, and the date above said that the article was written almost five years earlier. "Tips for Phasing Out of Foster Care" it said in bold letters at the top, and then below, "What You Need to Know for a Successful Adulthood . . . and Beyond!" There was a picture of a rocket next to the headline.

"You thought of me," Joaquin said, trying to keep from laughing or crying or whatever that reaction was that was bubbling up in his chest, pressing down on his lungs.

"I did," she said.

"Of course you did," he replied.

Joaquin knew very well that he was turning eighteen in three months. He didn't need the guidance counselor to remind him of that. He also knew that there were services that he could use until he was twenty-one: rent and food subsidies, possible scholarships for school, job assistance. But Joaquin had spent a literal lifetime in the system, being promised things that were always just out of reach, and he didn't want to spend the next three years chasing the white rabbit down the hole. He had always just assumed he'd join the army, but then he'd think about leaving Mark and Linda's house and his stomach would flip.

As soon as he was out of the guidance counselor's office, he threw the article in the trash.

When he met Ana at their diner, someone was already seated

in their normal booth, and there were kids running around, and Joaquin felt like he wanted to peel off his skin, it felt so tight.

"I told Mark and Linda that I didn't want to go through with the adoption," he said as soon as the waiter brought their drinks. "There, now you can yell at me for the rest of the hour."

Ana widened her eyes but then just started tearing the paper wrapper off her straw. "I'm not going to yell at you," she said, in a voice that was a little *too* steady. "If that's truly what you want, then I'm not upset. In fact, I'd congratulate you on asking for what you want."

"But?" Joaquin asked.

"But," she continued, "I don't think that's actually what you want. I think you think that's what Mark and Linda want instead. I think you're afraid of disappointing them, and afraid that they'll disappoint you, so you shut it down before you could take a chance and get hurt."

"I'm not worried about getting hurt," Joaquin insisted. "I'm worried about *them* getting hurt. I don't know how I'm going to react, so I . . ." He moved his hands farther apart in front of him.

"Distance yourself?" Ana guessed.

Joaquin just took his straw and pounded it on the table until the wrapper was crinkled up at the bottom. He felt like picking a fight with her, and he didn't know why. "You want to know what I did last weekend?" he said.

"Of course," Ana said, smooth as glass as always.

"I saw Grace and Maya. We met for coffee, and while we were

there, some guy Grace knew came up to her and started calling her a slut." Joaquin jammed his straw into his drink with more force than necessary.

Now Ana really did look surprised. "Why?" she asked.

"Dunno. I guess I didn't really get a chance to ask before I slammed the guy against the wall." Joaquin could still feel the pulse against his forearm, how *good* it had felt to scare Adam as badly as he had scared Grace. "We didn't get in a fight. I just told him to leave my sister alone, and he and his friend ran away."

Ana sipped at her lemonade. "Did you use the word *sister*?"

Joaquin nodded.

"And then what did you do?"

"I . . ." Under the table, Joaquin started to bounce his leg, a nervous habit that he had never been able to break. "I ran."

"Where did you run?"

"Into the parking lot."

"And Grace and Maya?"

"They followed me into the park next to the mall. I was . . . my hands kept shaking. I couldn't stop them."

"Joaquin." Ana's voice was too soft for the noise of the diner, but Joaquin heard her loud and clear. "Did you scare yourself?"

Joaquin nodded. He had wanted to tell Ana the story so he could shake her up, make her realize that he was beyond saving, that she was better off having salads and lemonade with a kid who could actually be *fixed*, but her eyes were so gentle, so sad, that it just made him want to cry.

"I told . . . I told them."

Ana frowned a little. "Told who what?"

"Grace and Maya. About Natalie."

Ana reached over, placed her hand on top of his, and didn't say anything.

"They said . . ." Joaquin bit his lip, blinked his eyes. "They said that I was just a kid, you know? They said it wasn't my fault."

"And did you believe them?"

Joaquin shook his head as his lower lip began to wobble.

"Did you want to?"

This time, he nodded, and Ana squeezed his hand and stood up. "C'mon," she said. "Let's go for a walk."

They walked outside until Joaquin felt like he could breathe again. "I'm really proud of you, you know," Ana said as they walked down the main drag. "That's a huge step in your relationship with Grace and Maya. The last time we talked about them, you said you would never tell them about it."

Joaquin shrugged. "It just sort of happened. I didn't plan it."

"Did you hurt the guy who called Grace a slut?"

"No, he just ran off. I just felt so . . ." Joaquin held up his hands in front of him, miming squeezing something. "It was the look on her face, you know? When he said that. She just looked so sad."

"And that made you sad, too?"

"No. It made me angry."

Ana grinned up at him. "Anger is a very—"

"—very valid emotion," Joaquin singsonged. He had heard

her say that phrase at least a million times. "I know, I know. It just *feels* fucking awful."

"And how did it feel when your sisters weren't angry with you for hurting Natalie?"

Joaquin didn't know that there was a word to express that feeling. It wasn't happiness, or relief, or bewilderment. It wasn't confusion, either, or pity for them being stupid enough to trust him. None of those were right.

"In one of the homes when I was six," he said instead, "everyone got bikes for Christmas. Even the foster kids, so that was a big deal. But mine was a two-wheeler and I didn't know how to ride, so the foster dad put training wheels on mine. And I would ride up and down the street, and every time I thought I was going to fall, the wheels stopped me."

Ana had stopped walking and was looking up at Joaquin. He didn't know if that was a good or bad thing.

"And I finally learned to ride, but I wouldn't let them take the wheels off because I liked that feeling, you know? They caught me every time. That's what it felt like with Grace and Maya. Like I was falling, but then I didn't. They were there."

And then Joaquin watched as—to his absolute *horror*—a tear slipped down Ana's cheek.

"Oh, shit," he said before he could stop himself. Joaquin wasn't sure what happened when you made your therapist cry, but it probably wasn't good. "I'm sorry. I am *so*—"

"No, no, it's not . . . *I'm* sorry, Joaquin." She lifted her sunglasses long enough to wipe at her eyes, laughing through her tears. "I'm just really, really proud of you, that's all."

Joaquin eyed her suspiciously.

"I really am okay," she said, then readjusted her sunglasses. "I just want you to think about something."

"Okay," Joaquin said. He would have offered to train circus seals if it meant Ana would stop crying.

"I know you don't believe it now, I know you might not ever believe it, but Mark and Linda are like those training wheels, too. What you described? That's what *parents* do. They catch you before you fall. That's what family *is*."

Joaquin thought of Mark and Linda sitting next to him after a nightmare, easing the darkness away.

"Okay," he said instead. He hoped that one day he would have the words to tell everyone how he felt inside, but *okay* would have to do for now.

"Okay," Ana agreed. "I'm starving. Do you like frozen yogurt?"

"Okay," Joaquin said again, then grinned and dodged away before Ana could punch his shoulder.

There was a strange car in the driveway when Joaquin turned the corner onto Mark and Linda's street. He stopped skateboarding immediately, kicking the back of his board so he could pick it up by the front wheels.

It wasn't his social worker's car, but maybe she'd gotten a new one? Or maybe Joaquin had gotten a new social worker? Either way, he knew that it was there to take him away. He had seen many strange cars in familiar driveways over the years, all of them with backseats big enough for a boy and a trash bag filled with whatever stuff he could manage to grab.

Either way, Joaquin wasn't surprised. He hadn't expected Mark and Linda to keep him, not after they'd offered him a chance to be adopted and he'd turned it down. Who would want a kid that ungrateful? After all, Joaquin basically had taken food, money, and clothes from them for almost three years. He would want a return on his investment, too.

He reminded himself to grab his blue ribbon from the fourth grade art fair. It was always the first thing he packed.

"Oh, shoot!" Linda screamed when Joaquin started to walk in the back door, and he froze, skateboard still in hand. "Mark! Oh, shoot!"

"Sorry?" Joaquin said.

"Oh, not you, honey. No, no, come in. We just thought you'd be home later! Oh, *shoot!*"

Joaquin stayed in the doorway anyway. Linda was holding a huge red bow in her hands, her glasses pushed up on her head, leaning around the front stairs. "Mark, he's *home*! I *told* you!" Then she turned back to Joaquin. "Honey, come in, come in, it's fine. You're fine." She beckoned him in the door.

Mark came jogging down the stairs, a little out of breath. "What are you doing here, early bird?" he asked Joaquin, but he was smiling. "Linda wanted to do a big presentation. She got the special bow and everything."

Linda just sighed in exasperation.

Joaquin was still in the doorway. "What?" he finally said. Was he supposed to put that bow on his trash bag? "Is it a surprise going-away party?"

Both Linda and Mark froze in place. "A what?" Mark asked.

"Well, there's a car?" Joaquin said, jerking his thumb over his shoulder. "In the driveway?"

Linda's face was quickly morphing from exasperated to horrified. "You think we're sending you away?"

If this was a guessing game, Joaquin was definitely going to lose. "Um."

Mark and Linda looked at each other, and then Linda walked over and pulled Joaquin into the house, the screen door slamming behind him. "Joaquin," Linda said, "that car is for *you*."

Joaquin just blinked at her. "What?"

She put her hands on his shoulders, holding him in place.

"Sit down, kiddo," Mark said, pulling out a chair.

Joaquin sat down with a thud, his heart starting to race. It all felt like a trick, like an elaborate stunt that would leave him humiliated and embarrassed, and yet, at the same time, he didn't think Mark or Linda would do that to him.

"You got a car. For me?" he asked.

"Yes," Linda said, then put the enormous bow on his lap. "You were supposed to be home fifteen minutes later. We were going to put a bow on it like in the car commercials."

"We were sort of hoping that we'd make a viral YouTube video," Mark teased, sitting down across from him. "You've just cost us millions of dollars in advertising revenue, early bird."

Joaquin just touched the bow. It was red and soft in his hands.

"We were going to wait until your eighteenth birthday," Linda explained, her hand still steady on his shoulder. "But now with Grace and Maya in the picture, we want you to be able to see them whenever you want. You shouldn't have to depend on us for a ride."

"We think that it's really important for you to see your sisters," Mark added. He spoke softly, like he was talking to a frightened animal. "You okay, buddy? You look like you've seen a ghost."

Joaquin nodded. "I'm fine," he said. "I just didn't . . . I thought it was the social worker."

"Oh, Joaquin," Linda said, rubbing the back of his neck. She wasn't a big woman, but her hands always felt so strong, like they could hold things up instead of tearing them apart. "We're not letting you go anywhere."

"You want to go see it?" Mark said, standing up. "It's got seat warmers."

Joaquin smiled at that. "Yeah," he said, nodding to himself. "Let's go."

It was used, the color of nickels, and there was a small stain on the passenger seat that Linda guessed was melted lipstick. ("Been there," she said grimly.)

Joaquin thought it was the most perfect car he'd ever seen.

"We figured we'd help you out with registration and insurance, at least for the first year, and then with your job at the arts center, you've got gas covered," Mark said after he showed Joaquin the emergency jack, the wool blanket, and the first aid kit in the trunk.

Joaquin pressed the car keys into his palm, pushing so hard that he thought they would pierce his hand, go straight through to the bone. "Okay," he said. He had no idea how much gas cost, but he had money saved.

"And if you ever text and drive, you'll never drive any car again for the rest of your natural life," Linda told him. "At least, not while I'm alive."

"Got it," Joaquin said. "You want to still put the bow on?"

"Yes!" Linda cried.

"No, you need to take the car for a spin," Mark said, reeling Linda back in. "We can put the bow on something else. Like the neighbor's cat."

"Oh, Mark," Linda muttered. Mark hated the neighbor's cat because it peed all over his vegetable garden. Joaquin had heard some epic tirades about that cat in his two years in their home.

"Go, go," Mark said, opening up the driver's-side door. "Drive around. You don't want to hang out with your par— with us." Mark cleared his throat. "Go be a teenager for a while."

Joaquin wasn't sure how to do that, but he would try. For them.

"Seat belt on!" Linda said. "Check your mirrors! The side

ones, too! Those are important. Remember your blind spot!"

Mark pretended to put her in a headlock, pulling her away from the car. "Go," he said to Joaquin. "Maybe I'll put the bow on Linda instead."

"I heard that!" she said, her voice muffled against his shirt.

Joaquin put on his seat belt, checked his mirrors (the side ones, too), and carefully backed the car out of the driveway. He had driven Mark and Linda's cars before, but this was entirely, incredibly different.

After several minutes, Joaquin pulled the car over to the side of the road.

His hands were shaking too hard to hold on to the wheel.

GRACE

I t had been Grace's idea to meet at Maya's house two weeks later.

She didn't have to say much to talk Maya and Joaquin into it. After the Adam incident, she was pretty sure that none of them would be going back to the mall anytime soon.

"They gave you a *car*?" Maya said, breaking through Grace's thoughts. "Are you *serious*, Joaquin? And you're just telling us *now*?"

Joaquin looked both confused and embarrassed by the whole situation as he nodded. "Yeah," he said. "I thought they were sending me away at first. I thought the car was the social worker's."

Grace felt her heart sink into her shoes. She hoped Peach never felt like that, never looked as lost as Joaquin sometimes did. She hoped Peach would never be surprised by the kindness of other people.

She hoped, she hoped, she hoped.

"Do you think Mark and Linda would adopt *me*?" Maya asked.

She was sitting with her feet in the pool again. Grace was glad that Maya never suggested she go swimming. She was still trying to figure out her post-baby body, and a bathing suit wasn't at the top of her list. It wasn't even on her list. She had tried Googling, but everything online was for grown women, actual moms. There wasn't anything about what to do with pregnancy stretch marks when you were sixteen, nothing about trying to make your body feel like yours again when someone else had taken up residence in it for nine months and you still hadn't even finished high school.

"Probably," Joaquin said. He had his feet in the water, too, but he was at the opposite end of the pool, sitting in the shade. "They've got an extra bedroom."

"Score." Maya adjusted her sunglasses a little bit.

"But I told them that I didn't want to go through with the adoption."

Grace saw Maya's head spin in Joaquin's direction almost as fast as her own. "What?" Grace said. "Why? Did they—"

"No, I just thought it'd be a bad idea. You know, because of last time and all." Joaquin shrugged a little. "Things are good now, like they are. I don't want to ruin it."

"Joaquin," Grace started to say.

"Can everyone please stop saying my name like I don't know it?" he interrupted her. "Please? Can we talk about something else?"

"Good idea," Maya said, pulling her legs out of the water and getting to her feet. "Let's talk about snacks. More specifically, cheese and crackers. Most specifically, cheese and crackers in my mouth."

Joaquin got up and followed her inside, Grace a step behind them. The heat was on but Grace felt a little chilled. When she had been pregnant, she had felt like everything was twenty degrees hotter than it was, but now she just always felt cold.

She had spent the past week mostly on her computer, going back and forth between researching Melissa Taylor and researching teenage birth mom support groups. Michael, the therapist, had given Grace a list of suggestions, but when she looked them up, they looked too forced, too false, a bunch of strangers smiling at a camera. Grace couldn't imagine sitting with them, talking about Peach.

The Melissa Taylor research was even more dismal. Even with her parents' help, there wasn't much. All the info that the adoption center had was either classified or no longer valid, and Grace was starting to feel the same way she had when Peach had gone home with her parents, like she was losing something that she would never be able to get back again.

"Grace?"

Her head jerked up. "What?"

Maya gestured toward her, holding a sleeve of Ritz crackers. "You want some, Spacey Lady?"

"Of course," she said, sitting down on the stool at the kitchen island. Joaquin was digging around in the refrigerator, looking for something, and Grace took the crackers from Maya and started to arrange them on a plate.

"New necklace?" Maya asked her, digging out the cutting board from a kitchen cabinet. "Where'd you get it?"

Grace's hand immediately flew to her neck. She had bought the chain long enough so that she could hide it down the front of her shirt, but it had apparently escaped.

She had found the delicate charms online, a tiny gold *M* and a tiny gold peach, and used the money from her old clothing boutique job to pay for them. Grace had wondered if they were stupid, sentimental things to buy, but when she put the necklace around her neck and looked in the mirror, it felt right.

"Oh, it's just this old necklace from my grandma," she said, slipping it down her shirt again. "My mom found a bunch of her old jewelry."

"What's the M stand for?"

Grace just shook her head. "No idea. I guess my grandma had her secrets, too."

The peach *thunked* against her heart before settling onto her skin.

Her phone buzzed just then, and Grace glanced over at it.

Hey, are you around next week? I found some straws that need to be disemboweled.

It was Rafe, of course, and Grace tried to swallow back the butterflies she felt when she saw it. "Who's that?" Joaquin asked.

"Yeah, Grace, who is that?" Maya asked. "You look a little . . ."

"You're blushing," Joaquin said.

"I am not," Grace told them. "He's just a friend."

Maya's eyes lit up. "Oh, he is not *just a friend*," she said. "No one ever says *he's just a friend* when he's just a friend. Joaquin, back me up here."

Joaquin put three wedges of cheese down on the countertop. "She's right."

"Is she?" Grace asked him. "Is she, really?"

"I have no idea. I'm just scared to disagree with her."

"She's your little sister," Grace said. "You have seniority over her."

Maya just preened a little as Grace's phone buzzed again. "Ooh, is it him? Is it him? What's his name?"

"None of your business."

"Well, that's unorthodox," Maya said, "but hey, I don't judge. Let me see!"

"No!" Grace cried. "Oh my God, go away. I thought you wanted cheese and crackers."

"I can eat cheese and crackers *and* help you talk to a boy! I'm really good at multitasking!"

"Get away!" Grace said, using an unopened sleeve of crackers to defend herself. "Oh my God, you're the worst!"

"Get her phone, Joaquin!" Maya screamed, chasing a giggling Grace around the island.

"No way," Joaquin said, calmly slicing up pieces of cheese. "I touched my old foster sister's phone once. Big mistake."

"Listen to him!" Grace said. "Maya!"

"Victory!" Maya said as Grace felt the phone slip out of her grasp.

"If you text him, I'll kill you."

"Oh, you will not."

"I'll maim you."

"I can live with that." Maya, a little out of breath, started to read the message. "'Dear Grace,'" she read, "'it's been another month and Milly is changing so much, so fast.'"

Grace felt all of the breath leave her body.

"'She continues to be the precious light of our lives, and we think of you every day, of course.'"

"Stop," Grace said, but she couldn't make her voice louder than a whisper.

Maya had frozen in place, her face going from gleeful to confused. "There's a picture of a baby," she said. "Grace, what is—"

Grace forced her legs to move forward, and she swiped the phone from Maya so fast that it clattered to the floor. "*Stop it*," she hissed. "I told you to leave it the fuck *alone*, Maya."

Next to her, Joaquin was standing still, the cheese slicer still in his hand, watching both of them.

The silence was horrible.

"Who's Milly?" Maya finally asked. "Is that your baby, Grace?"

Grace closed her eyes, praying that it was a dream, that she could go back in time and wake up in her bed a year ago and have everything go back to normal. "Shut up," she whispered.

"Did you have a *baby*?" Maya asked again, and she sounded

genuinely confused. "Grace, answer me."

"It's none of your business!" Grace screamed at her, reaching down with shaking hands to pick up her phone.

"You had a baby and you didn't tell us?" Maya shouted. "Are you *serious*? I told you about my mom and her drinking and Joaquin told you about Natalie and the accident, and you've been keeping *this* from us?"

"Why would I tell you?" Grace shot back. "So you could just say that I abandoned her, the way our mom abandoned us? Or so you could call me a slut, like Adam did?"

Joaquin's face went solemn. "Oh, shit," he said softly. "That's what that was about?"

"I didn't abandon her, okay?" Grace cried. "I found a really great family for her. And she's perfect and they love her and she's happy! She's going to be *so* happy and she'll have everything I couldn't give her! Did you ever think about that when you were busy hating our mom, Maya? That maybe she did it because she *loved* us?"

Maya looked stunned. *"Grace,"* she said.

Grace was trying her best not to cry. "I just didn't want you two to hate me, or say all these *things* about me like everyone else does. Because I love her so much and I would never . . . I would never just *abandon* her. That's not what I did. I swear to God, I didn't abandon her, but I feel so . . ." Grace was trying to gulp in air and the necklace shifted against her chest, making her physically ache. "It's just like there's this space where she used to be and now I can't fill it, and I keep *trying*, but I'm walking around with this hole inside me and she's not . . . she's not . . ."

Joaquin was the first one to grab her, and then Maya was there, too, Grace's tears wetting her shoulder as they hugged her tight. "It's okay," Maya kept saying, and Joaquin's hand was both strong and soft against her hair, and Grace pressed her face against both of them and quietly, steadily, lost her mind.

When she woke up, it was in a room that she didn't recognize. And then she noticed the Polaroids that were marching down one side of the wall, and the pink curtains that had been pulled shut. She had seen this room once before, what seemed like months ago. It was Maya's, and she was in Maya's bed, the blanket at the edge of the bed spread over her. Someone had taken her shoes off, too, and Grace glanced down to see them neatly lined up next to each other on the floor.

"Hi," Maya said softly, and Grace rolled over to see her curled up on the other side of the bed. "Feel better?"

Grace rubbed at her eyes as she tried to sit up. They felt thick and swollen, and her mouth was dry. She remembered Maya and Joaquin guiding her up the stairs, still weeping, Maya saying, "Shh, sleep," as Joaquin covered her up with the well-worn blanket.

Grace was very touched and very mortified.

"A little," Grace answered. "Where's Joaq?"

"He went downstairs." Maya gestured toward the half-open door. "Here, I got you a washcloth."

Grace took it gratefully, pressing it against her sticky eyes and cheeks. "Thank you."

"Of course." Maya carefully pushed her fingers through Grace's hair, easing out some of the tangles. "Grace? I'm sorry I stole your phone. I just thought it was a boy texting you. I didn't—"

"It's okay," Grace said, because it was. "I know you didn't mean to. I should have told you a long time ago. You and Joaq were brave and I wasn't."

"I think you're very brave," Maya said, still combing through her hair. "Was he your first?"

Grace nodded.

"Did you love him?"

"I thought I did. But now I think that maybe I just loved being in love with him."

Maya nodded. "And he didn't want to keep her?"

"His parents didn't want him to keep her. He signed away all his rights."

"Oh, *boys*," Maya sighed. "You know, none of this would have happened if you had just been a lesbian like your adorable little sister."

Grace smiled a little. "Shut up."

"I'm serious," Maya said, but Grace could tell from her tone of voice that she wasn't. "At least tell me the sex was good. If you *have* to get pregnant and have a baby, the sex should be mind-blowing."

"It was fine," Grace told her.

Maya just wrinkled her nose. "*Fine* is probably the worst word to describe sex," she said.

Grace had never been so happy to see Joaquin walk into a room.

"Hey," he said. "You're awake." He had three bottles of water and he handed one to each of them. "How do you feel?"

"Like shit," Grace admitted. "All the time."

Maya nestled closer to her, pressing up against Grace's side as Joaquin sat down on the edge of the bed next to them. "I'm sorry if we made you feel like you couldn't tell us," Maya murmured. "I'm so sorry, Grace. We both are. We didn't know."

"It's okay," Grace whispered, then sipped at the water. It felt so good and cold and clean that it was almost enough to wash everything else away. "I should have told you sooner." She glanced toward Joaquin. "I didn't want you to think that I left her like our mom left you."

Joaquin just looked at her like she had three heads. "I would never think that," he said. "Not in a million years."

"Can I ask a question, though?" Maya asked.

"Of course." Grace sipped at her water again.

"Is her name Milly?" Maya sounded very, very small. "That's what it said in the email."

Grace nodded, digging around under her shirt until she found the necklace, then pulled it out. "They named her Amelía. Milly for short. But I used to call her Peach when I was pregnant with her." She pressed her thumb against the charms, separating them a little. "It's not my grandmother's. I bought it online."

Maya reached over and took the chain in her hands. "It's beautiful," she said. "She's beautiful, too. She looked like you in that photo."

"Where's the dad?" Joaquin asked. "Is it Adam?"

"God, no," Grace said, sitting up a little bit more. "It was my boyfriend at the time, Max." Grace closed her eyes briefly against the stab of pain, and Joaquin reached over and put his hand on her arm as Maya nuzzled her chin against her shoulder.

"Asshole," Maya murmured.

"His loss," Joaquin said.

"I needed him, you know?" Grace twisted the charms around and around, tangling the chain around her neck. "I needed him and he wasn't there. He got crowned homecoming king the night she was born. He wasn't even with me in the room."

Maya muttered something under her breath that did not sound complimentary.

"What?"

"Nothing. Do you get to see her? I mean, if the parents are sending you updates . . ."

"We agreed to two visits a year, but I don't know if I can do it," Grace said. "I don't know if I can see her again. I don't know if that's what she needs."

"What about what you need, though?" Joaquin asked. His hand was still on Grace's arm, as if he was afraid that she would suddenly sprout wings and fly out of the room.

Grace just shrugged. "It's not about me."

"This is why you need to find our mom," Maya said softly. "That's why you keep bringing it up."

Grace bit her lip so she wouldn't burst into tears again. She could tell that Maya and Joaquin were exchanging a glance over her head. It made her feel small when they did that, and she sort of liked it and sort of hated it.

"I've been trying," she admitted. "But there's nothing. The letters my parents sent through the lawyer got returned; they don't have a working number. She's a ghost."

Maya shifted a little. "No. She's not."

"What?" Joaquin said. "What are you talking about?"

Maya looked at both of them, then started to climb off the bed. "C'mon," she said. "Follow me."

"Maya," Grace said, and the sound of her own voice scared her. "What are you doing?"

"Come on," Maya just said again. "Before Lauren and my dad get back."

Joaquin helped Grace off the bed, then kept his arm around her shoulders as they followed Maya downstairs into what looked like an office. Grace had never seen her look so solemn before, and it scared her. "Maya," she said again.

Maya just ushered them inside, then shut the door and locked it before going over to a file cabinet. "When we were little," she said, "Lauren and I used to play Detectives. We'd hide around the house, pretend that we were finding clues, you know, stupid shit. But then, one time, we found this." She opened the cabinet and pulled out a small black box with a combination lock on it.

Grace felt her heart move from her chest to her throat.

"I knew it was about me," Maya said, setting it down on the

desk. "So one night, after everyone was asleep, I came downstairs and worked on the combination until it opened."

She was spinning the lock as if she had done so a million times before. Grace wondered if maybe she had.

"There we go," she said as it popped open. Then she reached inside and pulled out a small stack of papers, spreading them out on the granite-topped desk.

Grace wondered why everything in Maya's house felt so *cold* all the time.

The three of them leaned in close, heads together, sifting through the papers. Grace saw Maya's birth certificate, her parents' names carefully typed in, and a small set of baby footprints. There was some official-looking paperwork, and then Maya reached for an envelope with a red "Return to Sender" stamp on it. "Here," she said, handing it to Grace.

Grace's hands were shaking as she took it. At first, she couldn't figure out why it was so important, and then she saw it.

The address.

"Your parents sent a letter to her house?" she gasped. Her hands were shaking so bad that she had to hand it to Joaquin.

Maya just nodded.

"How . . . when did you find this? How did they even get it?"

"I was ten," Maya said. "And I don't know. They don't even know that I found it."

"Did you ever look it up? Did you write her? Did you . . ." Grace forced herself to slow down. Next to her, Joaquin looked stricken, and he kept turning the envelope over and over, as if looking for another clue, as if he was playing Detectives, too.

"No," Maya said. "I just put it back. I used to take it out every now and then and look at it, but I just couldn't do it. I guess," she added after a pause, "maybe I was waiting for you two."

Grace reached over and put her hand on Joaquin's, stilling his movements. "Joaq," she said, "do you want to do this?"

"Well, you—"

"No, not me. *You*. Do *you* want to do this? It's okay if you don't."

"Totally, Joaquin," Maya said. "You have . . . we know . . . fuck, I don't know what to say."

"No, I want to," Joaquin said. "I want her to see me." His voice reminded Grace of the ocean, of sand being sucked back into the sea. "It's easier with you two."

"Okay," Grace said. "You're sure?"

Joaquin nodded. "I'm sure."

"Then I'm sure, too," Maya said.

"I'll drive," Joaquin replied. "Next weekend?"

"Damn straight," Maya said.

Grace had never thought that it could feel so good just to breathe again.

MAYA

Maya was really good at keeping secrets.

That's probably because she had so much practice at it.

She never told anyone about the envelope in the safe, at least not until Joaquin and Grace, and she didn't tell anyone that she was going to drive three hours to see if her biological mom was still at the address on the envelope. That secret was making her feel like something was pushing under her skin, desperate to get out.

And that made her think, of course, of Grace.

Even though she had already said sorry, she had texted Grace at least once a day since then, apologizing for stealing her phone.

Did I tell you how sorry I am? Because I am.

My, it's fine.

I'll buy you frozen yogurt next time.

I actually hate frozen yogurt.

Gah! I am so bad at apologizing!!!!!!

Maya still had questions, of course. She wanted to know when the baby (she couldn't call her Peach no matter how hard she tried) had been born, if it had hurt as much as everyone says it does, if Grace had been scared before and after. She wondered if Grace would feel bad forever, if that look on her face when she had first told them about the baby would ever truly go away.

And at three a.m., when that same old insomnia crept back, Maya wondered if her mom, the one who was in rehab, missed her the same way that Grace missed her baby.

She had seen pictures of the rehab place online. It seemed nice, if a little sparse. It advertised sunshine and palm trees and recovery, but Maya thought that behind all the perks, it just looked lonely. She hated to think of her mom being lonely, or afraid, or sad, and at the same time, she was so mad at her. On the one hand, it was her mom's own stupid fault for even being in rehab in the first place. If she really loved Maya and Lauren like she said she did, she would have stopped drinking a long time ago. She would have changed for them.

But on the other hand, Maya knew that the problem was bigger and more complicated than that, and it scared her that she didn't know how to figure it out.

On Wednesday night at dinner (homemade meal again; her dad was really pulling it together), Maya's dad cleared his throat and said, "So. Mom can have visitors this weekend."

Maya's fork froze halfway to her mouth, sauce dripping off the spaghetti and back into the bowl.

"It's Family Weekend this Saturday at the center," he said. He never said *addiction recovery* or *rehab*. It was always *the center*, like their mother had spent the two weeks at a YMCA doing water aerobics.

"I know she'd really like it if both of you were there," Maya's dad continued. "I'm going to go, and I'd like it if you came, too, but it's your decision."

"I'm totally going," Lauren said. Maya wasn't surprised. Lauren had always had a soft spot for their mom. The week before, Maya had spotted her standing in their parents' closet, sniffing one of their mom's blouses. Maya had snuck away before Lauren could see her, but it had made her feel funny and sad for the rest of the day.

She wished she had never seen her sister look so vulnerable. It made her want to zip Lauren into her hoodie and hide her away from the rest of the world.

"Maya?" her dad asked. "No pressure, of course."

Maya raised an eyebrow. "Really? No *pressure*?"

Her dad just shrugged and stabbed (there really wasn't a better word for it, Maya thought as she watched his fork) at his salad. "No pressure," he repeated. "If you want to go, we'd love to have you. But if you still need more time, I understand. And Mom will understand, too." His eyes were gentle as he looked over at Maya, then reached over and patted her hand. "I know it's intense, sweetie."

Maya just nodded. *Dad*, she thought to herself, *you have no idea*.

✳ ✳ ✳

She had absolutely zero intentions of going out to her mom's rehab center, not when she had possibly life-altering plans with Grace and Joaquin.

Maya also had zero intentions of telling her dad about said life-altering plans. She knew he would squash them immediately, or insist on going with her, or sending a letter first before going to the house, and Maya wasn't interested in any of those options.

She had no idea if Grace or Joaquin would tell their parents or . . . whatever it was that Mark and Linda were. Maya could understand why Joaquin had said no to the adoption. The story about Natalie had been frightening, but the idea of Joaquin being yanked out of his home, of being hospitalized, of *hurting*—it was almost too much to bear. It made her teeth ache when she thought about it, so she tried not to think about it too often.

Lauren knocked on her door that night after dinner, then came in without waiting for Maya to respond. "Are you seriously not going this weekend?" Lauren said, her arms crossed over her chest.

"Um, why do you even knock if you're just going to barge in anyhow?" Maya said, folding another shirt from her clean laundry pile. "How do you know I'm not dancing around naked in here?"

"You're not, so it's a moot point."

"PSAT word?"

Lauren ignored her. "You're really going to make me go alone with Dad this weekend?"

Maya wanted to tell her so, *so* bad. She knew Lauren felt left out, that she was worried about the two new people in Maya's life, but there was no way in the world that Maya was going to tell Lauren anything about the envelope, the address, the upcoming trip. She was at least 90 percent sure that Lauren would tell their dad about it, and even if she didn't, Maya would never have asked her to keep such a big secret.

So instead she just said, "Yep. Road trip with Dad, how fun! Maybe he'll get you a slushie from 7-Eleven."

"*Slurpees* are from 7-Eleven!" Lauren corrected her. "Not slushies!"

"You pick the strangest things to get upset about sometimes, Laur."

"Well, okay, how about this, then? I'm upset that my big sister isn't going with me to see our mom for the first time since we found her bleeding to death on the floor."

Maya sighed, setting down her shirt. "I just need more time, okay? You go see her if you want, but I'm not ready."

"Are you mad at her?"

"Yes," Maya said. "I'm mad at her for picking wine over us. I'm mad that she got so drunk she fell down and let you find her like that. I'm mad that she left us here to answer everyone else's questions. We are literally cleaning up her mess, Lauren. So yeah, I'm mad." Maya picked up another shirt and started folding it with way more intensity than necessary.

Lauren just stood in the doorway, watching her. "Well, don't you want to say that to her?"

Maya wanted to say and do a million things to her mom. She

wanted to scream at her, shake her, ignore her forever, crawl into her lap and cry.

"I'll say *what* I want to say to her *when* I want to say it to her," Maya replied. "And not before."

"Dad says that we need to start going to a family therapist."

Maya raised an eyebrow but didn't look up. "Dad's just getting that now? Because I could have told you that five years ago."

"My," Lauren said, and she looked up this time. "Don't make me go by myself. Please."

"You're not going by yourself. You're going with Dad, remember? Slurpees!"

"You know what I mean. Please, Maya. You promised you wouldn't leave me behind."

Maya walked over to her, putting her hands on Lauren's shoulders. "Laur," she said. "I promise I'm not leaving you behind. We're just on different paths right now. They'll meet at the end, okay? I promise," she added again when Lauren looked unconvinced. "I'll see Mom when I'm ready. If you're ready, though, you should go now."

Lauren sighed heavily. "Fine," she said, then flounced out of the room. "Betray me, that's fine!"

"Okay!" Maya said. "Good talk, Laur!"

The only response from Lauren was a slammed door.

By Friday night, Maya thought she would burst.

The problem with keeping secrets, she was starting to realize, was that they were too big to carry by yourself. When the girls had been little, Lauren had always been her secret keeper, but they weren't little anymore.

There was only one person she wanted to tell, Maya realized on Friday night, after everyone else had gone to bed and the house sounded louder and emptier than it did during the day. Only one person would truly understand.

She reached for her phone and texted Claire.

you up?

The wait time was excruciating, and Maya rolled over onto her side, the blue light from her phone illuminating everything in the room. She closed her eyes for a moment, trying to will herself back to sleep, convinced that Claire would never write back.

Her phone buzzed.

Maya almost fell out of bed trying to read it.

are you seriously texting me right now?

I'm going to meet my birth mom tomorrow.

Maya held her breath and waited.

whoa.

I know. can you meet? please?

Why should I meet you, My?

Maya hesitated, then typed.

because I'm scared. and I'm sorry.

i'll be at the park in 20 min.

Maya threw herself out of bed and went to get dressed.

She was almost out of the house when she hit the bottom stair and ran straight into Lauren.

"Where are you going?" Lauren asked.

"What are you doing up?"

"Eating ice cream. Where are you going?"

"You got up to eat ice cream and didn't wake me? I'm hurt."

"Where are you *going*?"

They were both whispering fiercely, trying not to wake up their dad. Maya was pretty sure if the circumstances weren't so dire, they would have looked like they were doing a comedy routine.

"Just . . . somewhere."

"Are you sneaking out?"

Maya nodded. "Don't tell Dad, okay? I'll be back in an hour."

"Are you meeting someone?"

"I'm meeting . . . someone."

Lauren's face lit up. "Are you meeting *Claire*?"

"Shh!" Maya practically fell on top of her sister trying to keep her quiet. "You are the worst at being sneaky, you know that?"

"Only you would think that was an insult," Lauren replied, but she didn't sound too upset. She was even grinning. "Oh my God, are you and Claire getting back together?"

"Just cover for me if Dad wakes up, okay?"

"How do I cover for you?"

Maya was fairly certain that she was going to murder her sister that night. *"Lauren!"* she whisper-cried. "Just be quiet and go back to bed, okay? I'll text you when I'm back."

"Okay, okay, fine." Lauren looked positively gleeful. "Just

apologize for whatever you did and get back together, okay? You've been moping around for weeks, and so has she."

Maya had no idea if this was true, but she wasn't going to waste time arguing with Lauren about it. "Good night," she said. "Also, stop eating all the ice cream. Leave some for me next time."

Lauren threw her a mock salute, then climbed the stairs as Maya slipped out the front door.

By the time she got to the park, everything was a pulsing red behind her eyes, each burst of color in perfect sync with her heartbeat. Maya wasn't sure if it was love, fear, or just plain stupidity, but the colors picked up speed when she saw Claire waiting in the parking lot for her.

Claire had her hands jammed into her hoodie pockets, the hoodie pulled up over her hair so that Maya could only see her face. She thought it was still one of the most beautiful faces she had ever seen. "Hi," Maya said as soon as she was close enough.

"Hey," Claire said. She sounded disaffected, cool, all blues and violets, the opposite of the hot ember glow that burned inside Maya.

"Hi," Maya said again. She suddenly felt as dumb as she had the first time she'd met Claire, tongue-tied and awkward. "I just, yeah. I just wanted to tell you. About my birth mom."

Claire nodded her head toward one of the picnic benches. "You want to sit?"

Maya nodded and followed her.

"So," Claire said. "Talk."

Maya wished she had planned this out a bit. She didn't know what to say or how to say it.

So she told Claire everything.

She told her about Grace and the baby, about Joaquin and Natalie and the failed adoption. She told her about Lauren and their fight, how their mom had looked on the floor with blood coming out of her head, the way her dad had flown home and cried in the hospital when he saw his daughters. She told Claire about the safe and the envelope and the address, their scheduled trip for the next day and how she was missing Family Day at *the center*. She told Claire everything she could possibly think of to say, and at the end, she felt wrung out and exhausted.

"Okay," Claire said when she was done. "But My, how do you feel about all of that?"

Maya blinked. "What?"

"How do you *feel*?" Claire turned to look at her. "Don't you get it? Every time you get scared or feel all these big things, you run."

"I—"

"You pushed me away." There was no missing the wobble in Claire's voice when she said, "You can't just keep opening and closing this door, saying nothing to me and then texting me in the middle of the night. Shit, Maya, you broke my *heart*!"

Maya felt very small sitting in the dark. "I didn't mean to break anything," she said. And suddenly she thought of Joaquin. Why? He was saying he didn't want to be adopted by the two people who loved him more than anything in the world, and . . .

"Oh, no," she whispered. "I'm doing it, too."

"Doing what?" Claire asked, but Maya was starting to cry.

"I'm doing it, too," she wept. "I'm so sorry. I didn't want you to know. About my mom, about any of it. I got scared and I . . . I panicked. I—I don't want to be alone!"

"My, My, calm down." Claire's hands were soft on her face, softer than Maya had any right to feel. "You're not alone. A lot of people love you and care about you—what are you talking about?"

"I'm so sorry!" Maya said again. "I'm so sorry, Claire. I miss you so much and I hurt you and I thought that I was only hurting *myself*, but I hurt you, too, and I'm so sorry . . ."

"It's okay," Claire whispered. "I forgive you, it's okay." But now she was crying, too, and when she leaned in to kiss Maya, Maya could taste the white-hot salt of their tears mingling together. "It's okay," Claire whispered again. "Just don't do it again, okay?"

"Okay," Maya whispered back, then kissed Claire again before wrapping her up in her arms. "I don't ever want to leave you again."

"So don't," Claire murmured against her hair. "I told you last time, I'm not going anywhere."

It was more than Maya deserved, she realized, but she would take it anyway.

JOAQUIN

Joaquin didn't tell Mark and Linda about going to look for his birth mom.

He wanted to, though. He wanted to tell someone—*anyone*—but he didn't know how. Ana would have made him talk about his feelings. His social worker, Allison, would have probably said something about rules or paperwork. Birdie was—well, Birdie was no longer an option. Joaquin was pretty sure that Mark and Linda would have listened to him, at least, but he wasn't sure how to look at two people who wanted to adopt him and tell them that he was going to find his birth mom. And after they had given him a car of his very own?

No way.

Joaquin decided to keep this one to himself.

And that turned out to be a huge, huge mistake.

* * *

That week at school, Joaquin had turned the corner down the hallway toward his English class and come face-to-face with Birdie and Colin Maller.

They were kissing, Birdie's long arm wrapped around Colin's neck the same way that she used to wrap it around Joaquin's. If he thought about it too much, Joaquin could almost feel the warmth of her skin, the heat of her mouth, the way she always smelled good, like soap and shampoo.

Joaquin had thought that nothing would ever hurt as bad as breaking his arm, but he could have broken both arms and legs and it still would have been a drop in the bucket compared to how he felt when he saw Birdie in Colin's arms.

He stumbled backward, not caring if he missed English class, or the rest of school, or even the rest of his life. He had to get out of there, and he was almost out the door when someone called him back.

It was Birdie's friend Marjorie. "Joaquin, wait!" she yelled, chasing after him, and Joaquin stopped with his hand on the door, his chest heaving like it had after he'd pushed Adam against the wall, adrenaline flooding his system and overwhelming his senses.

"Wait," Marjorie said again, even though Joaquin hadn't moved. "Joaquin, she's just trying to make you jealous. She doesn't even like him."

Joaquin laughed. He couldn't help it. "Looks like she likes him a lot," he said, running a hand through his hair. "Tell the happy couple I said congratulations."

And then he was gone, Marjorie calling after him, the school behind him as he started to run.

By Saturday morning, Joaquin was a mess. On the outside, he looked pretty good. He showered and washed his hair and wore the shirt that Birdie had bought for him when they'd first started dating because she said it made his eyes look good. Joaquin had dark brown eyes, so he wasn't exactly sure how a blue-checkered, button-down shirt could make them *pop* (Birdie's word, not his), but Birdie had always been smart about things like that, so he trusted her opinion.

Joaquin wondered if his mom had eyes like his. He wondered if she still knew his dad. He wondered if she even wanted to see Joaquin and his sisters, or talk to them, or if Joaquin would only be a reminder of the worst time of her life. Would she think that he was trying too hard, dressing up for her? The last time he had gone to see her, he had worn his favorite Spider-Man T-shirt (Spider-Man didn't have parents either, just like Joaquin), but she had never shown up, so maybe it didn't matter if he wore his best shirt or not.

Joaquin looked in the mirror, straightened his collar, and wondered if he was the biggest idiot on the planet for trying so hard to find the woman who had left him so easily.

Mark and Linda were in the kitchen downstairs, eating breakfast and reading the paper. (Joaquin suspected that theirs was the only house on their street that still actually got the newspaper delivered every day.) "Whoa, looking fancy on a Saturday," Mark said when Joaquin walked into the room. "Is it Formal Wear Day at the arts center?"

Any other day, Joaquin could have taken Mark's teasing tone without a problem. It wasn't any other day, though. "Why?" Joaquin said. "Is it too much?"

"No, no, you look great," Mark said. "You just never really dress up, that's all."

Things with Linda and Mark had been a little *off* ever since they had given Joaquin the car. Or, more accurately, things with *Joaquin* had been off ever since they had given him the car. He had only driven it twice in the past week, once to work and once to go to the grocery store for Linda, but otherwise, it just sat in the driveway, a huge, metal reminder of all the things that Joaquin would never be able to pay back to his foster parents.

The more they gave him, the bigger the world felt, and Joaquin needed a fence, an edge, something to keep him from falling off the face of the thing. Everyone had a breaking point, after all, and the fact that Joaquin had spent almost three years with Mark and Linda and he still hadn't been able to find theirs made him nervous. He had thought turning down the adoption would do it, that they would put him back in foster care and then Joaquin would know how the fairy tale ended, but then Mark and Linda turned around and bought him a car instead.

Joaquin felt like he was the star of a video game, dodging from one level to the next, swinging from vine to vine in search of some treasure that always seemed to be just out of reach. Some kids didn't make it that far—some ran out of lives, or chances, or hope. But Joaquin had played long enough to know that for every level he managed to pass, for each thread of hope that Mark and Linda gave him, there was just something bigger, even more menacing, waiting for him at the end. Joaquin knew that he'd never get the treasure without first slaying the dragon.

So Joaquin started pushing back. At first, it was just ignoring Linda the first time she asked him to do something, or pretending like he didn't hear her when they both knew that he had. He told Mark he would help him mow the front and back lawn on Wednesday evening, but stayed upstairs instead, listening to music. By Friday night, things were tense at dinner and Joaquin disappeared into his room without helping with the dishes. "You want to give Linda a hand?" Mark had asked.

"Nope," Joaquin said, and they hadn't answered, which made him even more nervous, out of control, teetering on the edge, bracing for a fall.

By Saturday morning, though, with a stomach full of butterflies, Joaquin felt ready for a fight.

"Hey, Joaq?" Linda said, glancing up from the paper. "Can you take a seat? Mark and I want to talk to you about something."

Joaquin felt himself roll his eyes before he could stop himself, but Mark just pulled out a chair and patted it, so he sat. "What?"

"You've been . . . well, honestly, Joaquin, you've been sort of a jerk," Linda said. "To me, to Mark. Is it . . . did we do something? Did we say something to hurt you? We just wish you'd talk to us about it."

"Why do you always think it's about you?" Joaquin snapped.

"Why do you always think it's something that you did? Why can't it just be about me?"

Mark shrugged, pushing his chair back from the table a little. "Okay, let's make it about you, then. Why are you being a jerk?"

It would have hurt a lot less if Joaquin hadn't thought that they were right.

"Do you like the car?" Linda asked. "Or was it too much?"

Joaquin shrugged a little, crossing his arms over his chest. Just thinking about the car made his stomach flip, tossing the butterflies every which way. "I don't really care," he said. "I mean, I didn't even *ask* for it. *You're* the ones who got it for me."

Mark turned in his chair so that he was facing Joaquin. Joaquin wished that Mark would hit him, push him, send him away. Anything but that soft look of sympathy that was scrawled across his face. "Joaq," Mark said, "we're trying here, but you gotta meet us halfway." When Joaquin didn't reply, he added, "Talk to us, buddy. What's going on with you?"

He started to put his hand on Joaquin's arm, and Joaquin, thinking that this was it, instinctively flinched away. Everyone froze when he did that. Even the clock on the wall seemed to stop ticking, its hands stuck in time. "Joaquin," Linda said, her voice hushed. "Sweetie."

"You know I would never hurt you," Mark said, his hand still frozen in midair. "You know that, Joaquin."

Joaquin huffed out a laugh. "You think that's the only way to hurt someone? Seriously?"

"Joaquin—"

He thought that if he heard someone say his name one more time, his head would splinter into a thousand shards. "Just stop it, okay?" he cried, getting to his feet. "Just stop with, with everything! The car, the clothes, the skateboard, just *stop!*"

Now Mark and Linda were standing up, too, a triangle formed between the three of them. Mark looked confused, but Linda just looked scared.

"You always say you're not going to hurt me," Joaquin continued, his pulse fluttering wildly under his skin. "But you don't get it, do you? Hitting someone is the easiest way to hurt them! You could hurt me so much more than that!"

"We don't want to hurt you at all!" Linda insisted. "We just want to help you, we want to be there for you, support you. We want you to have the world, Joaq! We want so much for you!"

"Oh, yeah? You think I don't see how people look at us when we're out?" Joaquin felt his chest tighten just thinking about it. "These two white people who rescued the poor brown kid?"

"You know we don't care what people think," Mark said, his voice low.

"Yeah, of course you don't, because they look at you like you're a hero! They look at me like, like I'm . . ." Joaquin forced the words out. "Like I'm trash."

"Do *not* say that," Linda fumed. Joaquin saw that her hands were clenched into fists. "You are *not* trash, Joaquin. Don't ever say that."

"Yeah, easy for you to say," he scoffed. "You think you can just adopt me and all of that will go away? What, you can teach me about what it's like to be Mexican? You can teach me to speak Spanish? You can tell me where I'm from?"

"No," Mark said, and he sounded somewhere between sad and furious. "We can't do any of that. But we can help you find people who can! We're not here to take anything away from you!"

They were saying all the right things, but it all felt wrong. Joaquin felt himself stepping toward the abyss with no boundaries to keep him from falling.

So he decided to leap.

"You think *I* can make up for the fact that you can't have babies?" he said.

Linda and Mark stood there, stricken, and Joaquin felt himself smash against the ground, shattering wide open. Mark took a step toward him, and then Joaquin was moving, his feet faster than his brain.

He ran out of the house, Mark and Linda yelling after him, and was in the car and halfway down the street before he realized that he hadn't grabbed his phone. "Fuck," he muttered to himself, then saw Mark and Linda's faces again, and he raised his fist and smashed it down on the dashboard.

Mark and Linda would never let him back in their house now. Joaquin wouldn't have wanted to let him back in, either, not after what he had said.

The dragon had won, and Joaquin was just a pile of broken bones and ash on the scorched ground, out of time and out of lives.

Game over.

GRACE

Grace had never kept such a big a secret from her parents for this long. Even when she'd discovered she was *pregnant*, she had told them within twenty-four hours. But she knew that if she told her parents about her upcoming trip, how she planned to just go up to the front door of a stranger's house and knock on it and possibly meet her birth mother?

Grace had a pretty active imagination, but even she couldn't imagine all the ways her parents would say no to that.

So she told Rafe instead.

"Wait, so let me get this straight," Rafe said. They were sitting in what Grace had come to think of as "their" booth at the back of the restaurant near the kitchen supply store. "You're just going to go up to some stranger's door and knock on it and say, 'Hi, Mom'?"

"Well, not exactly like *that*," Grace said. "You're making it sound like we're going to egg her house or something."

"Grace." Rafe set down his fork and looked at her. "Look, no offense, but I don't think this is your best idea."

"It's not my idea, it's *our* idea," Grace said. "Me and Joaquin and Maya, we're all going together."

Rafe didn't look convinced. "So what are you going to do if she's not home?"

"Leave a note?"

"Leave a note?" Rafe repeated. "'Hi, your three bio kids swung by to say hey, sorry we missed you.'"

Grace rolled her eyes at him. This was not how this conversation was supposed to go. "You know, if I wanted someone to illustrate for me all the ways that this could go wrong, I'd just tell my parents."

"You didn't even tell your *parents*?" Rafe lowered his head to the table and started banging his forehead against the edge. "Grace, Grace, Grace. This has disaster written all over it."

"You know, you could be at least a little supportive!" Grace said. "This is really scary, okay? You're supposed to be my friend."

"Yeah, well, sometimes your friend has to tell you the truth," Rafe said. "You should tell your parents, at least."

"They won't understand."

"Grace, you had a *baby* and they seemed to come through that experience just fine. I don't think you're giving them enough credit."

"If I tell them, they'll just give a million reasons why it's a bad idea."

Rafe just raised an eyebrow as if to say *I told you so.*

"God, never mind," Grace said, pushing her plate away. She had barely touched her sandwich or fries, or much food at all, for that matter. Just thinking about Saturday made her feel nauseous in a way that she had never experienced during pregnancy.

"Okay, but can I just ask one question?" Rafe said.

"If I say no, are you going to ask it anyway?"

"Yep."

"Fine, ask away."

Rafe leaned forward a little, putting his hand on the table toward Grace. "What if your birth mom doesn't want to be found?"

Grace sat back against the booth, the leather suddenly cold on her legs.

"I mean, all the letters were returned, her phone's disconnected, she's never tried to find any of you, not even Joaquin. What if she just wants to stay gone?"

Grace fiddled with the napkin in her lap. "I don't know," she said. "I don't. But I just want her to know that I'm okay. Is that selfish?"

"I don't think so," Rafe said.

"Is this a stupid thing to do?"

"Maybe. I'm not really sure."

"What would *you* do?"

Rafe thought for a minute, then pushed his hand farther across the table so that their fingertips were touching. "I don't know," he said. "But maybe this way, either way, you'll have an answer."

Grace raised her hand so that it was covering Rafe's. "I told Joaquin and Maya about Peach."

Rafe's eyes widened almost comically. "Seriously?" he asked. "Why? How?"

"Maya saw an email from her adoptive parents. She was just teasing me with my phone and she saw it, and yeah. Hard to hide after that."

"Wow. Are you good with that?"

Grace was, actually. She felt lighter after that day, like the heavy cloud that had hung over her had finally turned into rain. "They want me to visit her."

"Joaq and Maya do?"

"No. Peach's parents. They want me to visit in a few months, when she's six months old. We had originally agreed to two visits a year back before the adoption."

Rafe waited for her to go on, flipping his hand over so that their palms were pressed together.

"I don't know if I can."

"That's fine. You don't have to."

"But what if she wants to see me? I mean, not now, but in the future."

"You mean like *you* want to see *your* birth mom?"

Grace nodded. "I just don't want her to wonder, you know? I don't want her to have any questions like I do."

Rafe shrugged. "Then go see her. Either way, it's going to be hard, but you've always done the right thing for her. Don't stop now."

Grace didn't say anything. She wasn't sure she could speak.

"You want to keep talking about this?" Rafe asked.

She shook her head.

"You want to talk about that return you've got there?" He nodded toward the package sitting next to Grace, a mail order from the kitchen store.

This time, she smiled, pushing the tears away. "This one's pretty great," she said.

"Your mom's insomnia purchases are *amazing*," Rafe agreed. "Let's see."

Grace pulled it out of the package. "I think it's a pepper mill," she said, holding up the small garden gnome. "You twist its hat and the pepper comes out of his beard."

Rafe put his hand over his mouth. "Wow," he said after a minute.

"Think we should name it?" Grace asked.

"No," Rafe said, then started to climb out of the booth. "It's probably best if we don't get attached. C'mon—if we get back early enough, you can wear my apron."

"Oh, goody," she said, rolling her eyes, but took his hand anyway when he held it out to her.

On Saturday morning, it was a text from Rafe that woke her up.

good luck today, it said. call me if you want later.

Grace looked at it for a long minute before typing back, ok.

Then she went in the bathroom and threw up.

Her parents were already gone for the day, at some gardening show. They had left dinner defrosting on the counter for her, and seeing the Tupperware sweating on the countertop made something tug at Grace's heart in the most painful of ways. They had forgiven her a lot over the past year. She hoped they could forgive this, too.

Maya pulled up in a cab just as Grace was finishing getting dressed. She had tried on at least ten different outfits. She wanted to look pretty, but not overdone. She wanted to seem casual, but not too casual, like she normally spent the weekend knocking on strangers' doors and asking if they were her mom.

Rafe's words echoed back at her, but Grace just pushed them away. Whether it was a bad idea or not, it was going to happen.

"Oh my God, I think I'm going to puke," Maya said, wheeling her bike into Grace's garage.

"I already did," Grace admitted. "Twice."

"Seriously? Are you pregnant again?"

"Ha. No."

Maya just grinned at her, but the smile quickly fell from her face. "I don't know. Is this a bad idea? Are we idiots?"

"I don't know, and probably."

"Oh God, I really am going to barf."

"Please stop saying that," Grace said. "Do I look okay?"

"You look amazing. You look very . . . *you*. What about me?"

"You look great. Wait, what do you mean, very . . . *me*?"

Maya smiled. "You look very clean."

"What does *that* mean!" Grace yelled, and was about to turn around and run back up the stairs so she could change her outfit for the eleventh time, when Joaquin's car swung into the driveway.

Even before he got out of the car, Grace could tell that something was off. The way he parked the car was all wrong, in one fast motion that ended too sharply.

"Whoa," Maya said next to her.

"I'm not going" was the first thing Joaquin said when he got out of the car.

"Ha!" Maya cried. "Nice try. Anyone else have to pee before we get on the road?"

"No, I'm serious," he said. "Take the car if you want, I don't care. But I'm not going."

Grace felt like she had missed the second act of a three-act play. "Wait, what are you even talking about?" she said. "What happened? Why are you being like this?"

Joaquin was now pacing in front of the car. "I can't go. I'm not."

"But *why*?"

"Because!" he cried. "I ruin fucking *everything*!" He ran a hand through his hair, but it just flopped back into place like he had never touched it. "I'm the worst thing that could have happened to you. Either of you. Don't you understand?"

Maya just crossed her arms and watched Joaquin pace. "Are

you done?" she said. "Because we should get going."

"I just told you. You're going without me."

"Nope," Maya said. "This is an all-or-nothing thing." She grabbed her bag and started to walk toward the car, then turned around when Joaquin didn't follow her. "C'mon, Grace," she said.

Grace stayed where she was. "Joaq, what happened?" she asked again. "You're practically shaking."

"I just . . . I can't go back to Mark and Linda's."

"What? Why?"

"We had a fight. I ruined it. I pretty much obliterated it. Burned it to the ground." Joaquin was chuckling to himself, but Grace thought it sounded more like a sob. "They're not going to let me back in."

"Did they say that?" Maya called from where she was standing by the passenger-side door.

"They didn't have to."

"Well, we're not going without you," Grace told him. "C'mon—we can talk about it in the car."

"No!" Joaquin said. "Are you not listening to me? I don't want to ruin this, too. Not for you."

"Can you open the doors, please?" Maya called.

Joaquin ignored her. "Here," he said, tossing the keys to Grace. "Just text me when you get back." Then his face changed. "I left my phone at their house. *Shit*."

Grace felt like she was scrambling to stay ahead of a tornado. "Joaquin," she said, then stepped forward and put her hand on his arm. "If you don't want to meet our mom, that's fine. That's totally fine. But if you're not going because you think you'll ruin it? Then that's not fine. And it's not true, either."

Joaquin shook his head. "Look, you two are my sisters, right? You're my family. I won't hurt you like that."

"Oh, for fuck's sake!" Maya suddenly screamed, and they both turned around to see her still standing next to the car, hands on hips.

"That's exactly what family *is*, Joaquin!" Maya shouted at him. "It means that no matter where you go, no matter how far you run, you're still a part of me and Grace and we're still a part of you, too! Look at us! It took us fifteen *years* to find each other, but we still did! And sometimes, family hurts each other. But after that's done you bandage each other up, and you move on. Together. So you can go and think that you're some lone wolf, but you're not! You've got us now, like it or not, and we've got you. So get in this fucking car and let's *go*!"

Grace looked at Joaquin.

Joaquin looked at Maya.

And then he got in the fucking car.

"*Thank* you," Maya sighed, then looked toward Grace. "Oh, yeah, one more thing."

"What's that?" Grace said, picking up her backpack.

"Shotgun!"

They spent most of the three-hour drive in silence, Grace sprawled out in the backseat and Maya curled up against the passenger-side window while Joaquin drove, her camera snapping a picture of the landscape every so often. Joaquin's grip on the steering wheel was tight, but Grace could see the sad slope of his shoulders and neck, the way he seemed to almost hang his head. At one point, Maya looked up from the window. "Do you want to talk about it?" she asked him.

"Nope," he replied.

"Okay," she said, and rested her cheek against the pane of glass once again.

They listened to the radio for a while, pop songs that Grace hated but always seemed to know the words to anyway. As they got closer to the desert, the station faded into crackling noise and Joaquin eventually turned it off. They passed the giant dinosaurs at the rest stop and then drove through what seemed like a sea of windmills. It made Grace think of *Don Quixote*. She wondered if she and Maya and Joaquin were on the same ridiculous quest as Quixote, racing toward something that was different from how they imagined it would be, destined for disappointment, for humiliation, for failure.

Her phone buzzed in the backseat, and she glanced at it.

how goes it? Rafe asked.

it goes, Grace wrote back.

you scared?

terrified.

it'll be okay. everything always works out.

She wasn't sure if that was true or not, but she was glad that at least one person thought so.

By the time Joaquin pulled onto the street, Grace's palms were sweating. Maya was no longer slumped against the window and was instead sitting straight as a jackrabbit, her sunglasses pushed up onto her forehead. "There it is," she said, pointing toward a small house.

Joaquin parked across the street and they sat there in silence, the three of them breathing in unison, looking at the house. It looked freshly painted, the trim a bright white against the bluish-gray of the house, and there was a pot of geraniums near the front door. A dark-blue sedan was parked in the driveway.

"It looks nice," Grace said after a minute.

"Yeah," Joaquin said. He had gone utterly still, not even flinching when Grace put her hand on his shoulder and started to get out of the car.

"Wait, wait, wait," Maya said. "Not yet. Just . . . let's just agree that no matter what happens here, that it's the three of us together, okay?"

Joaquin's jaw was clenching and unclenching, but he nodded and Grace said, "Agreed."

Maya glanced out the windshield again, then took a deep breath. "Okay," she said. "Let's do this."

Grace would later wonder what the three of them must have looked like as they walked up the front steps of the house toward the front door, huddled together like a scared flock of ducks. Her own heart was beating so hard that it actually hurt. She was more scared than when she'd told her parents that she was pregnant, than when the doctor had told her it was time to push, than when Peach first rested in her new parents' arms.

Grace wondered if Melissa was even home.

She wondered if she even still lived in that home.

What if no one answered the door?

What if someone did?

"You knock, Grace," Maya whispered. Joaquin was standing behind them, almost like protection, and Grace steadied herself and reached out to the tarnished brass knocker shaped like a lion. It seemed almost to snarl at them, like they were intruders.

Grace hoped that wasn't a bad omen.

The knock seemed to echo down the street, and after a minute, a woman opened the door. She was wearing nurse's scrubs, her dark, curly hair pulled back into a ponytail, and when she saw them, she smiled. "Magazines or cookies?" she said.

"Wha—I'm sorry, what?" Grace stammered. She could feel Maya trembling next to her, her eyes gone wide as she stared at the woman with Joaquin's nose, with Maya's eyes.

"Oh, sorry!" The woman leaned against the door. "Just the high school always has kids selling stuff for fund-raising. I'm happy to just write a check, I told them, but you know, people like their stuff." She smiled wider and Grace thought she saw a glimpse of Peach. "I hope it's cookies, because I have a ton of magazines I haven't read."

"We're not, um." Grace realized with horror that maybe she should have practiced this. "Are you Melissa Taylor?"

The smile fell from the woman's face as if Grace had slapped it away. "No," she said. "Melissa passed away a long time ago. I'm her sister, Jessica."

Grace didn't even realize she had swayed on her feet until Joaquin was stepping forward to prop her up. She fumbled for what to say next, her head a clanging rush of noise and pain and shock, when the woman suddenly gasped, clasping a hand over her mouth.

"Oh my God," she whispered, and then she was crying. "You're her kids. You're *Melissa's kids*." And then she was stepping forward, pulling the three of them into her arms.

That's when Grace started to cry, as well.

MAYA

The inside of Jessica's home was as neat as the outside.

Maya sat between Grace and Joaquin at the kitchen table as Jessica fluttered around them, getting sodas out of the refrigerator, setting them down along with paper napkins. "We would have called," Grace said, her voice still thick and papery-sounding from crying, "but we didn't have a number."

"Oh, it's okay," Jessica said. She was smiling even though there were still tear tracks on her cheeks, her mascara pooling under her eyes. Every so often, Maya would see Joaquin in her features, and then Grace, and sometimes herself. It was like looking at a funhouse mirror, the image in it constantly shifting, and Maya was fascinated. "I got rid of the landline a few years ago," Jessica added as she sat down across from them. "Didn't make sense to have one when I'm always using my cell. They keep calling me and offering me a great deal if I get a landline, but I told them why would I—"

Jessica suddenly stopped and smiled sheepishly. "Sorry. I babble when I'm nervous."

"Me, too," Maya told her.

Joaquin was very, very quiet as he sat next to Maya, but she could see his head following each of Jessica's movements.

"So," Jessica said, giving them all a watery smile. "I bet you have some questions for me."

"How did she die?" Maya whispered. It felt like she had both lost and gained something huge. Melissa was gone, but Jessica was still here. A door had been closed, but another had been opened.

Jessica nodded to herself as she looked down at her untouched glass of water. "It was a truck accident," she murmured. "She was twenty-one, crossing the street, and she got hit by a trucker who ran a red light. He said he didn't even see her. She died instantly, they said. She didn't suffer. I worried about that, but that's what they told us."

"Did you know our dads?" Grace asked.

"Maybe I should just start at the beginning," Jessica said, looking at each of them in turn as her eyes overflowed again. "Oh, I am *so* sorry," she whispered. "I just haven't seen Melissa's face in so long, and now I'm looking at three versions of it and it's so . . ." She fumbled for words. "All three of you are just so beautiful. You look just like her."

Maya felt Grace's hand press against her own, and she wrapped her fingers around Grace's and squeezed tight. She was afraid she would start crying if she didn't hang on to something, and Maya wanted to remember every single word of this conversation. She wanted to breathe in each memory of her mother until it filled her up and made her fly across a pink-streaked sky, warm with fading light.

"Do you," Joaquin started to say, then cleared his throat. "Do you, um, have any pictures? Of Melissa?"

Jessica shook her head, her lower lip trembling. "Your grandfather, our dad, he disowned her when she got pregnant with you, Joaquin. She was seventeen, and our parents were just beside themselves. They kicked her out. Our dad, I think it just broke his heart. He burned all of the pictures of her."

Maya thought of her own home, her parents, her bedroom, the photos on the stairs. She couldn't imagine leaving any of them without having somewhere else to go.

Joaquin leaned forward, and Maya felt herself reach up and put her hand on his arm, anchoring him to her and Grace. "Did you know my dad?" he asked.

Jessica nodded, her eyes lighting up. "You should know, your parents were in love. They were high school sweethearts, they were so head over heels with each other. It was a little disgusting, actually." Jessica chuckled to herself, wiping at her eyes. "She used to plan their wedding during study hall. He was so good to her, he just adored her.

"But he got deported. Melissa didn't know she was even pregnant at the time. I would hear her cry in her bed every single night, and then she started throwing up. At first, we both thought it was just because she was so sad, but then, well . . ."

Joaquin nodded, his jaw set tight, his shoulders up around his ears. "Okay," he said. "Do you remember his name?"

Jessica looked at him. "Did you not know? Your dad's name was Joaquin. Melissa named you after him."

"Oh," Maya said softly, squeezing his shoulder. She couldn't even imagine what that meant to him, but next to her, Joaquin was still, unmoving.

"Did he, um, did he have a family?" he asked.

Jessica nodded. "Yes, two parents and a little sister. They adored Melissa—she was always over at their house. They were all deported, just *gone* one day." Maya could tell that Jessica was trying not to cry again. "Your mom, she just . . . it shattered her."

Maya watched Joaquin's jaw start to tense and flex. She tried not to think of what his life would have been like with this other family, rooting him to the ground, sheltering him in their wings.

"What happened when your dad kicked Melissa out?" Grace asked.

"Well, she met another boy at this restaurant where she was a waitress, and then she got pregnant with you, Grace. I was only fourteen at the time, but I used to go into the restaurant and she'd give me free Cokes. They agreed to give up the baby— you, I mean—for adoption. I think *he* only stuck around because Grace's parents paid for rent, utilities, all of that while Melissa was pregnant with Grace. And then when Grace was gone, things got worse, and social services showed up, and yeah. It wasn't a safe place for you, Joaquin." Jessica looked down at the table, her finger tracing an invisible pattern.

"Is that when she gave me up?" Joaquin asked. "After that?"

Jessica nodded. "She was trying to get it together, get you back, but then she met Maya's dad, who wasn't great"—Maya suspected that Jessica was leaving out some important details, trying to spare them—"and then she got pregnant with Maya, and it all fell apart again. She couldn't keep any of you. She couldn't keep her own life together. I think losing you broke her." Jessica wiped at her eyes, and Maya thought of Lauren possibly hurting and hopeless. Next to her, Grace sniffled quietly, and Maya held her hand tighter.

"Did you get adopted?" Jessica asked Joaquin, her eyes hopeful. "Were they a good family?"

Joaquin shifted a little in his chair. "Um, no. There was one family, but they got pregnant right before the adoption went through, and they only wanted one kid, so . . . yeah. Ended up back in the system for a while."

Maya watched as Jessica's face fell. "For how long?"

"My entire life."

"But he's with a really good family now," Maya interrupted as Jessica started to cry again. "They're *crazy* about him. They really love him a lot. They even bought him a car!" Maya wasn't sure who she was talking to at this point, Jessica or Joaquin, but she knew they both needed to hear it. "Mark and Linda are really great people."

"I'm okay," Joaquin said softly. "Really. I'm fine now."

Jessica got up and came back with a box of tissues. "This is for all of us, even though I may use most of them," she said. "God, I just can't believe that you're all here. She wanted so badly to know the three of you. I know she wanted your parents to take Maya, Grace, but they couldn't."

"No, my grandma, she died from cancer right before Maya was born," Grace said. "But they helped me find her and Joaquin after . . ." Grace's voice faded out for a few seconds. "I had a baby a couple of months ago. I gave her up for adoption, too."

There was a moment of silence as Jessica stared.

"But my parents are wonderful," Grace said immediately. "They've been really supportive of me, nothing like what happened to Melissa. I'm very lucky. I have great parents. They love me a lot."

"Oh, thank God," Jessica sighed.

"And I have a good situation with her adoptive parents," Grace said. "They send me pictures." She opened up her phone, flicking to the photograph that Maya had seen the week before and holding it up for Jessica.

"She's beautiful," Jessica said, and Maya watched as Grace beamed, the pride shining through her like the sun.

"Did you ever meet my dad?" Maya asked. "Did you know him?"

"No, I never met him. I think after losing both Grace and Joaquin, Melissa was just untethered, you know? She couldn't come home; our parents wouldn't even speak to her on the phone. I think she was lonely, and she kept meeting men who promised her the world and never followed through.

"But she would always refer to you as 'the baby,'" Jessica added. "And she remembered all your birthdays." Jessica's eyes started to fill again. "I know it doesn't seem like it, especially for you, Joaquin," she whispered. "But God, she loved you. She did. I can't tell you what it would mean to her to see the three of you sitting next to each other like this."

"What about your parents?" Joaquin asked, and Maya knew him well enough by now to hear the quaver there. "Are they still alive?"

"No, they passed away a few years ago. Heart attack and stroke, both within a year of each other. I don't think our dad ever forgave himself after Melissa was killed. I think he regretted a lot of the decisions that he made. He would return all the letters that your parents would send to her."

Maya reached into her back pocket and pulled out the envelope from the safe, sliding it toward Jessica. "Like this one?" she asked.

Jessica smiled sadly. "Like that one."

"And there's no one else?" Grace asked. "You don't have any other brothers or sisters?"

"Just me," Jessica said, smiling a little.

Maya felt her own eyes spill over. "You're all *alone*?" she asked.

"Oh, sweetie, please, don't," Jessica said, then pushed the box of tissues toward Maya. "I'm not *alone*. I have a boyfriend, I have wonderful friends. I inherited this house when our parents died and remodeled it a little. I'm *so* not alone—please don't be sad for me."

Grace was crying now, too, and Maya pushed the tissue box toward her.

"And," Jessica added, her mouth quivering a bit, "I'm an *aunt*. I've thought about all three of you every single day. I didn't know how to find you, but I never forgot about you."

Now even Joaquin had tears on his cheeks, and Maya steered the tissue box back in his direction.

"Having a new aunt would be very, very nice," Maya said. "We could use one."

Jessica stood up, then reached up to cradle each of their faces in her hands. She lingered on Joaquin for the longest. "She *loved* you," she whispered to him again. "She loved your dad and she loved you like crazy. I know it may not seem that way, but she did. I promise you that, Joaquin. She wanted the world for you."

Joaquin brought his hands up to hold on to Jessica's wrists, and she ran her thumbs under his eyes and then kissed the top of his head. "Oh!" she suddenly gasped. "Oh my God, I can't believe I forgot! I'll be right back."

She hurried out of the room, leaving the three of them tearstained and dazed. "You're named after your dad," Maya whispered to Joaquin. "How crazy is *that*?"

He just shook his head, then wiped his eyes on his shirt sleeve.

"Are you okay?" Maya asked him.

"I think so," he said, then cleared his throat. "Just . . . it's a lot."

Next to them, Grace nodded. The photo of Peach was still looking up at her from her phone.

"Okay," Jessica said as she came back into the room. "God, I can't believe it took me this long to think of this, but this is for you, Joaquin." She held out a key and he took it from her. "It's a safe deposit box. Melissa set it up after you were born, and then after she died, I continued to make the payments on it. She always said it was for you, Joaquin. I never opened it up—I don't know what's in there. I figured that it was your business, not mine."

Joaquin just blinked down at his palm, then back up at Jessica. "Melissa did this?" he asked.

"Yes. For you. She just said that it was for you."

Maya felt the hairs on the back of her neck stand up.

"So," Jessica said. "Are you hungry? Talk a little, eat a little?"

Maya wasn't sure if she could eat anything, but when she saw the look on Jessica's face, she answered for all three of them.

"I like talking and eating," she said.

And next to her, her brother and sister nodded.

JOAQUIN

Grace ended up driving them to the bank because Joaquin didn't trust himself behind the wheel.

His hands were shaking too badly.

He had been okay at Jessica's house, sitting in the same rooms where his mother had eaten dinner, watched TV, gone to sleep. They had sat in the backyard, had some sandwiches and potato chips; and Jessica was so nice. Her laugh sounded like Grace's, high-pitched and free, and she had the same small dimple as Maya's. A couple of times, she reached over and took his hand, simply holding on to it, and if Joaquin thought about it hard enough, it almost felt like he was holding his mother's hand, that she was somewhere in the universe watching him.

Joaquin wasn't quite sure what to do with that information.

They left Jessica's house with hugs and promises to stay in contact, Jessica touching each of their faces as they got into Joaquin's

car, her number written on a piece of paper and tucked into Joaquin's pocket next to the mysterious key.

"If you want to get going home—" Joaquin said as Grace
started to pull away from the curb.

"No way," Maya said from the backseat. (She hadn't put up a
single shotgun argument this time, which made Joaquin feel even
weirder.) "You're *going* to that bank."

Joaquin couldn't argue with that.

They rode in silence, then got out of the car and walked into
the bank in a single-file line, Joaquin leading their pack. "Hi," he
said to the teller. "I, um, there's a safe deposit box here? Jessica
Taylor called and said . . ."

"Name, please?"

He swallowed hard, said his dad's name, said his name. "Joaquin Gutierrez."

The woman looked him up in the computer. "And do you have
your key?"

Joaquin pulled it out of his pocket and tried to ignore his shaking hands. "Right here."

The woman started to lead him down the hall, but he stopped
and beckoned to Grace and Maya, who had been settling themselves in the waiting area. "No," he said. "The three of us together,
no matter what, right?"

They stood up and followed him down the hall. Joaquin
reached back and took each of their hands.

The room was small, not like all the times in movies when

people went into huge, marble-covered rooms to retrieve their safe deposit boxes. The lighting was a little flickery, too, but Joaquin didn't care. He and the banker turned their keys at the same time and the box slid out of the wall, long and thin, the same size as a piece of notebook paper.

"You can view it in here," she said, pointing them into an even smaller room, and then she shut the door behind them, leaving the three of them alone, the box on the table between them.

Joaquin took a deep breath, then another. "Any bets on what's in here?"

"Cash," Maya said.

"Apple stock," Grace said, playing along.

"Sticker collection."

"A pony."

Joaquin started to laugh despite himself. "Weirdos," he said. "Okay, here goes nothing."

He lifted the lid.

At first, he thought it was just a bunch of postcards, photographs of people he had never met in places he had never been, and then Grace let out a strangled gasp as Joaquin's eyes focused on one postcard of a woman holding a laughing, curly-haired baby boy. She was laughing, too, and their eyes were the same, and Joaquin realized that they weren't postcards at all, that it was a photo of him and his mother, and the entire box was full of them.

The tears started before he could stop them, his hands digging into the photos and turning them faceup. There was one of him as a newborn in the hospital, red and wrinkled like a raisin, and another of him sitting in a playpen, grinning up at the camera.

Joaquin felt the emotions rush up and over him again and again with each new picture, each one a heartbreak and a joy. His mom looked just like Grace and Maya, bright-eyed and cheerful, and it wasn't until he realized that his tears were splashing down onto the photos that he tried to wipe his face. Next to him, Grace was quietly sobbing against Maya's shoulder blade, and Maya had her forehead pressed against Joaquin's shoulder, and he reached out and gathered them to him, their past spread out on the table like an invitation to something more, something better, something true.

"Look," Maya whispered, reaching down for a photo. "Look."

Joaquin took the picture from her, holding it up. His mom was holding him on her hip, pointing toward the camera, an obvious bump in her stomach. "It's Grace," he said, smiling.

Grace leaned forward to look at it. "Wow," she said.

Joaquin started to sift through the photos again, looking at the baby in each of them, looking at himself. It was easy to forgive a baby who looked like that, all wide-eyed and apple-cheeked. Joaquin had to keep reminding himself that it was him, that someone had once loved him enough to save his pictures for nearly eighteen years. They weren't on a wall or in an album, but they had been kept safe.

Someone had thought that he was worth saving.

There was one that didn't have a baby in it, though, a

professional one taken at what looked like a high school dance, and he realized that he was looking at a picture of his mom and dad at the prom. They were both the same height, dressed in cheap-looking formal wear, but his dad's eyes were focused on his mom, gazing at her with the exact same adoration that Jessica had described. On the back, someone had written "Melissa hearts Joaquin xoxo."

Joaquin felt something crack open in his chest, and at the same time, another fissure started to seal itself back up. He felt like he was flying apart and coming together at the same time, and he sank down in a chair as his sisters sat on either side of him, the three of them quietly sorting through their past.

It was the greatest gift anyone had ever given to him.

When they finally left, it was closing time, and they had to borrow a paper bag from the teller at the front desk to transport all the photos. "Do you want to keep the box?" she asked Joaquin.

"No," he said. "I've got everything I need."

Grace drove home, too, Joaquin curled up in the front seat with the bag of photographs between them. A couple of times, he peeked inside the bag, just to make sure they were still there.

His younger self gazed back up at him every time.

"Good day," Maya murmured, leaning forward from the backseat and resting her head on Grace's shoulder, her arm stretching out to wrap around Joaquin. Grace just hummed in response, the setting sunlight and wind hitting the girls' hair so that it swirled like a dark flame around their faces, and Joaquin thought that they were beautiful, like their mother.

Joaquin reached up to hold Maya's wrist in his hand, their skin and blood the same, and they drove home, the three of them together, just like they had promised.

By the time they exited the freeway, though, Joaquin started to worry. The fight with Mark and Linda felt like it had been a million years ago, not just that morning, and he wasn't sure what he was going to do. Maybe they'd let him come home long enough to get his stuff? Or was it their stuff now? Joaquin hadn't paid for any of it, after all. He had no actual claim to it. Maybe he should just find a phone and call Allison and tell her that he needed a new placement. Maybe he could crash at Grace's or Maya's house, just for a night or two until he knew where he was going.

He was so busy thinking about it that he didn't even notice Mark and Linda standing in Grace's driveway, their car parked out front, their faces full of worry.

"What?" he said once he saw them. "Wait, what? What are they doing here?"

Maya didn't even bother to look apologetic. "We called your phone," she said. "When you went to use the bathroom at Jessica's. They answered and we told them that you were with us. They were really worried about you."

Joaquin was so shocked that he couldn't even get out of the car. He had left many houses many times, but no one had ever come looking for him. Not even, he suddenly realized, his mother.

He stayed in the car for so long that Mark had to walk over and open the door. "Hey, bud," he said. "Heard you had an adventure."

Joaquin had thought he had cried enough for a lifetime, but seeing Mark standing there was too much. "I'm sorry," he said. "I'm so sorry, Mark."

But then Mark was reaching into the car and undoing his seat belt and pulling Joaquin to his feet, and then Linda was there, too, wrapping her arms around both of them, and Mark held him steady and said, "It's okay, it's okay, we're not angry," and Joaquin hung on to them so tight that his arms ached and he thought that this must be what forgiveness felt like, pain and hurt and relief all balled up together, pressing against his heart so that it might burst.

"Dad," he whispered. "Mom."

Joaquin's parents just held him tighter.

And they never let him go.

LANDING

MAYA

The inside of the rehab center feels chilly after she's been out in the late-February sun of Palm Springs. Maya feels her eyes relax once she steps inside, the bright blue sky no longer bearing down on her, and it's so quiet in the front lobby that she can hear her own footsteps as she walks up to the front desk.

"I'm Maya," she says. "I'm here to see my mother, Diane?"

Maya's dad dropped her off out front, after she had sworn numerous times that she didn't need him to come in with her, and drove to a nearby Starbucks to wait for her. "Just text me if you need me," he told her at least fifteen times. "I can be there in five minutes, no problem."

Lauren stayed home. She's already been to visit their mother three other times, but Maya hasn't been ready. She still isn't sure if she's ready, even after months of family therapy and one-on-one therapy and talks with Claire and Joaquin and Grace—but it's her mother. There's no way to avoid seeing her *ever* again.

The man at the front desk leads Maya down a linoleum-tiled hallway and into what looks like a rec room. There's a pool table and foosball table, as well as several couches and, tellingly, boxes of Kleenex.

Her mom's sitting in a chair over in the far corner of the room, and her face lights up when she sees Maya. *She's gained weight,* Maya thinks with a start. Her cheeks have filled out a little bit, and her hair looks darker and longer. She looks, Maya realizes, healthy. It's been a long time since her mom has looked that way.

"Sweetie," her mom says. She stands and reaches out for her, but Maya takes a step back. She's not ready for a hug yet. It's been three months, but she's still angry, still resentful. Her therapist said that it would take time, and Maya decided to believe her.

"You're so tall!" her mom says instead, clasping Maya's hands in hers. "Did you grow? You look so big to me, Mysie."

"Mom, seriously? You're making it sound like it's been years since you saw me."

Her mom's face doesn't change, though. "I can't believe you're almost sixteen."

"Believe it," Maya says, blushing.

"Lauren told me a few things," her mom says. "You and Claire are back together?"

Maya nods. "Three months now. I really love her, Mom."

"Well, I think that's wonderful, honey. I'm so happy for you. And for Claire, too, of course."

"Do you want to sit?" Maya asks her. "There's, like, a thousand couches in here."

They choose a couch near the back of the room, sitting next to each other. The silence is awkward, and they both know it. It's been a long time since they've talked to each other, even before rehab.

"So I want you to know——" her mom starts to say.

"So you should know——" Maya begins, and then they're laughing. "You first," she says. "Go ahead."

"Okay. Well, then, I just wanted you to know . . ." Her mom's voice breaks a little, and she glances down briefly at her lap before looking Maya right in the eye. "I want you to know that I am very, *very* sorry for all the things that I've put you and our family through. You and Lauren, you were my secret keepers, and I want you to know that it's not going to be like that anymore. I've done a lot of work in here, I've made a lot of changes, and I'm ready to come home and make things right."

Maya nods as her eyes well up. She's fairly certain that there isn't a family in the world that cries as much as hers. "I know," she says. "It's okay."

"No, sweetie, it's not." Her mom leans forward and puts her hands on Maya's shoulders. "It's not okay, but we're going to try and make it better, Dad and me. I want you and Lauren to have that. I don't want"——her mom's voice wavers again——"I don't want you to look back and remember me like I used to be. I want you to be *proud* of me."

Maya nods again, too overwhelmed to speak at first. "I *am* proud of you, Mom," she finally says. "You've worked so hard, you really have."

"Okay, enough about me," she says, laughing as she pats her cheeks dry with her hands. "What were *you* going to say?"

Maya takes a breath, steadies her nerves. She wants to get it right because there won't be a second chance to say it.

"I haven't talked to Dad about this at all," Maya says. "Or Lauren. I wanted to tell you first. But a couple of months ago, I went with Joaquin and Grace to visit our birth mother."

The color drains from her mom's face as her hand comes up to cover her mouth.

Maya forges ahead anyway.

"I found an envelope a long time ago in your safe, so we went to the address that was on it," she said. "And she—Melissa—she died a long time ago. A car accident."

"Oh, sweetie." Maya's mom is holding her hands so tight that Maya can feel her wedding ring branding itself into her skin. "Oh, sweetie, oh no."

"No, no, it's okay," Maya says quickly. "I'm not— I mean, yes, I'm sad about it, but she has a sister, Jessica, and she's really nice. And there are pictures. And I just . . ." Maya can feel her mouth quivering. She hates it. It makes her feel like everything, including her own body, is out of her control.

"I just wanted to tell you first," she says, and now her voice is quivering, too. "Because you're my mom, okay? *You* are. *You're* my mom. And I love Melissa because she had me, but I love you because you raised me, and I just wanted you to know that even though I'm still really mad at you, you can screw up a million times and I'll still love you, no matter what. Just like you love me, no matter what. Right?"

Her mom is crying silently now, rivers of tears running down her face as she nods. "Yes, sweetie," she says.

"So . . . when are you coming home?" Maya asks, hanging on tight to her mom's hand, like she could levitate and float away.

"Soon," her mom whispers back. "I'll be home soon, I promise."

"Home with us," Maya murmurs, and then smiles a little to herself. "Where you belong."

JOAQUIN

The adoption party ends up becoming a combination adoption–eighteenth birthday party.

Joaquin doesn't mind one bit.

At the courthouse this morning, it was just the three of them, plus a photographer who Linda hired for the day. Joaquin wore a new suit that made him feel like an adult, and a tie that matched Mark's. Linda wore a dress in the same colors as the ties, and the three of them looked at themselves in the mirror before leaving the house.

"We," Joaquin declared, "look like huge dorks."

Mark just laughed. "Too bad for you, kiddo," he said. "Because in an hour, you're going to be related to us. There's no turning back now."

Joaquin thought that sounded like a pretty fair deal.

Linda cried during the brief ceremony, and Mark got teary but later swore it was allergies. Joaquin still wasn't sure it would actually happen, that a lightning bolt wouldn't strike the court-house, but the skies were blue and nothing went wrong and then the judge was saying, "Congratulations, young man," and the photographer took all their pictures together, and Joaquin's face hurt for the rest of the afternoon because he was smiling so much.

The backyard is pretty busy and the party's in full swing by the time the sun sets. Mark and Joaquin strung up lights all throughout the trees yesterday (and only ended up needing two Band-Aids in the process), so the backyard looks almost magi-cal. The bougainvillea and morning glories are in full bloom, too, along with the jasmine that makes everything smell as good as it looks. Joaquin and Linda planted those plants together a month ago. (They only needed one Band-Aid after that project.)

Mark and Linda are there, of course, dancing to the mariachi band that's playing in the corner of the yard. Their next-door neigh-bors are there, too, mostly because Mark and Linda were afraid that they would call the police because of all the noise, but they seem to be having a great time. They're chatting with Bryson-the-pencil-holder-maker-from-the-arts-center's parents while Bryson stands a little *too* close to the horn section, staring up in fascination. Joaquin hopes he doesn't accidentally get bonked with a trumpet.

In the corner, Joaquin can see Maya and Claire chattering away, their heads together, while Lauren and her dad peruse the barbecue buffet that Linda's set out. Claire and Maya look like they're up to a serious conversation, but then Maya's face breaks into a grin, and she looks so much like Melissa in that moment that Joaquin feels his chest swell.

Jessica—Jess now—is there too, along with her boyfriend. Joaquin's not sure what he does, something with numbers and math and other people's money, but he seems nice, so Joaquin decides that he's good enough for Jess. She's got her hair piled up on her head, and she's talking to Linda as she and Mark—swing dance? Salsa? Joaquin has absolutely no idea what they're doing—past them.

Grace is over by the drinks table, her parents talking to their other next-door neighbors, her hand entwined with Rafe's as he stands by her side. Joaquin and Rafe have hung out a few times, and Joaquin has decided that he's good enough for Grace. Not many people are, but Rafe is one of them. They're going skateboarding next week.

Dr. Alvarez is there, too, Joaquin's professor from the Intro to Sociology class he's taking at the local community college. He thinks he might want to become a therapist like Ana, or maybe a social worker like Allison. He's not sure yet, but he likes having options. He likes thinking about those things now. He also thinks about his dad's family, where they might be, if they'll be happy to meet him. He imagines grandparents and another aunt, a father who never got a chance to know him. He thinks about how a year ago, he barely had one family, and now he has three: Maya and Grace and Jess; Mark and Linda; and a family across the border, lost but not gone. Three branches on his family tree that won't break or collapse or let him fall.

He's talked to Dr. Alvarez a lot after class about where his dad's family might be, and Mark and Linda have been trying to help him sort through the mountains of paperwork to see if he might be able to track him down. "It's like a needle in a haystack," Mark said at one point as they stared at the computer, but Joaquin didn't mind. He knows by now that if you look hard enough for something, you'll eventually find it.

He's also taking Spanish classes at the college. Those aren't going as well as he would like, but he's trying. It's something, at least.

Ana's standing under the tree, chatting with her husband as well as Gus from the arts center, and Joaquin tries to sneak past them in order to grab more drinks, but they manage to wrangle him into a conversation about college and his birthday and the white-water rafting trip that Mark and Linda took him on last month. Joaquin has photos from that trip still saved on his phone, and he shows them, especially the one where Linda's screaming bloody murder. Mark has plans to get that one blown up onto canvas for Linda's birthday. Joaquin thinks Linda might become a single parent if that happens.

He finally goes inside to grab drinks, but then he hears voices on the stairs, and he pokes his head around the corner to see Grace and Maya sitting on the stairs. Maya's arm is slung around her shoulders and Grace looks teary. "She's fine," Maya tells Joaquin. "She's just a little emotional."

Grace nods and points up at the framed photo of Joaquin and Melissa that's now hanging above the staircase. Linda and Mark had it professionally framed, along with several others from the safe deposit box, and now Joaquin sees himself every time he goes up and down the stairs, or past the refrigerator, or out the front door.

"It's just a great photo," Grace sniffles, and Joaquin leans against the banister next to them.

"It is," he agrees.

"She's worked up because of tomorrow," Maya explains as Grace dabs at her eyes with the edge of her sleeve.

"Oh, that's right!" Joaquin says. "You ready? You need backup?"

Grace just laughs and shakes her head. "No, I'll be okay. I need to do it by myself. And I'm going to see Rafe afterward."

"Are you two dating now, or what?" Maya asked. "Claire and I have a bet going."

"You bet money on my love life?" Grace gasps.

"*Love* life? Woohoo!" Maya raises her fists triumphantly and pumps them in the air. "Claire owes me twenty bucks!"

Joaquin just grins and tries to avoid getting accidentally punched by Maya's victory fists as Grace groans and covers her face with her hands. "We're figuring it out," she says. "It's a process."

But Maya's dance ends as suddenly as it begins, and even Grace looks up, surprised and sober, and Joaquin turns around to see Birdie standing there, along with her little brother and her parents. She looks as nervous as Joaquin feels. "Hi," she says. "We got invited to the party. Hope it's okay."

Joaquin can't say anything at first. "W-Who?" he manages to stammer out.

"Hi," Grace says, standing up. "I'm Grace; this is Maya."

"Hi," Birdie says, but she's still looking at Joaquin.

"Did you—" Joaquin starts to say to his sisters, but they're already guiding Birdie's parents and brother out into the backyard. "Right this way," Maya's saying. "Have you seen the lights in the trees? Beautiful. It's like a fairy garden out there!"

The house seems even quieter with the party in full swing outside, and Joaquin stands and looks at Birdie. "Hi," he finally says.

"Hi," she says again, then holds out a present to him. "Oh, sorry! This is for you. Happy birthday and adoption."

"Thanks," Joaquin says. "Can I . . . ?" He feels as nervous as he did the day he met Birdie at school. It seems like a million years ago now, a different lifetime, a different person entirely.

"Yeah, of course," Birdie says, and Joaquin carefully pulls off the bow and paper to reveal a framed poster. "ON THIS DAY" it says at the top in huge lettering.

"It's this thing I found online," Birdie says. "It tells you all the things that were popular on your birthday, like the top books, the top songs, the biggest movies. It just made me think of you when I saw it, so . . ." She trails off, her hands clasped in front of her.

"I love it," he says, because he does. "Thanks, Bird."

"Of course," she says, and then she hesitates before saying, "It looks like a great party."

"Joaquin!" someone yells from outside. "We're taking a group photo, c'mon."

Joaquin looks at Birdie, and she looks up at him.

"I'm sorry," he whispers.

"You really hurt me, Joaquin," she whispers back. "I mean, *really* hurt me."

"I know," Joaquin says. "I'm so sorry, Bird."

"It's just that every time I think about not having you in my life, it doesn't feel right, you know? It's like there's a piece missing." Birdie is wringing her hands in front of her. Joaquin wonders if they're still cold, wants to reach out and hold them in his own hands. "I don't know how you fit back in my life, if you're a friend or my boyfriend or what, but I just know that you *fit*."

Joaquin nods. "Okay," he says, because it *is* okay. It will be okay. "We can talk, maybe? Tomorrow?"

"Joaquin!" Mark's yelling from outside. "C'mon, group photo!" Both of their heads swivel toward the back door.

"Go, go," Birdie says. "It's your party—we can talk later."

Joaquin just holds his hand out to her. "C'mon," he says.

She smiles as he reaches down to take her hand, then leads her out to the lawn. The photographer arranges their whole group, even the mariachis, and Joaquin stands between Birdie and his sisters and his aunt and his parents, and he thinks of Melissa.

He hopes she can see him, because he sees her now. He sees her every single day.

He hopes he can make her proud.

"Okay, on the count of three!" the photographer shouts. "One, two—"

"Three!" everybody cries.

Joaquin thinks it just might be a photo worth saving.

GRACE

Grace pulls into the parking lot of the park two minutes early. Her phone buzzes. It's Rafe.

They bet $20?!?!?!

I know, right? Grace texts back.

I want a cut.

I'll let Maya know.

You there yet?

Just parked.

Okay. Call me later if you want.

Okay. I like you.

I like you, too.

Grace gets out of the car and tucks the phone into her back pocket. She doesn't know if she's scared or nervous or just plain terrified, but there's no going back now. She met with her birth mother support group a few days earlier, telling them about the upcoming meeting with a voice that didn't shake or tremble. She had thought that she would never be able to talk about Peach with strangers, but the girls in her group understood.

At first, her parents were speechless that she had gone looking for Melissa without telling them. "We said that we would help you!" they cried the next day, after Joaquin had gone home with Mark and Linda and Maya had disappeared down the street, refusing a ride from everyone.

But then they talked, Grace's guard worn away by exhaustion and relief and gratitude. She had taken a picture of Melissa from Joaquin's collection, and when she put it on the table between her and her parents, their anger died away and they looked at the photo, silent.

They started talking more after that.

Grace's parents told her what it had been like to bring her home as a brand-new infant, the worry that Melissa would take her back. "We had to wait ninety days before the adoption was official back then," Grace's mother said, and Grace noticed for the first time that the straw in her iced tea was chewed into ribbons. "We just didn't want to lose you, not after finally getting you."

Grace understood. She knows what it's like now, to lose one thing and gain something else entirely. She knows how hard she will hold on to the things she has, the brother and sister who fill a new place in her life. The spot where Peach was is still there, still open and hollow, but there are new chambers in her heart that fill her up, make her feel whole in a way she didn't before.

Every night, she sends a small thank-you to Melissa for choosing these two people to be her parents.

Grace hasn't seen Max in months, hasn't heard much about him, either. It's still hard to think about him, but mostly she just feels sad for him. She's thought about what she would say to him. She sometimes makes epic speeches in the shower about how "one day, she might come looking for you, and she might have questions, and then you can explain everything to her, so save your apologies because I don't need them, but you might!" Sometimes she cries, and sometimes she's angry, but mostly it just feels good to let Max go, to move forward, to move on.

Grace sits in the parking lot, looking out at the grassy park in front of her. Her phone buzzes again and she looks down at it to see a text message from Maya.

Good luck! it says, followed by two thumbs-up symbols.

Yeah, good luck! Joaquin's message follows right after. Call us later.

I will, Grace types back, her hands shaking a little and making it hard to press the correct keys. She sends three hearts back to them, then gets out of the car. Her hands are sweaty, and she wipes them quickly on her jeans before walking with trembling knees toward the park. It's a beautiful day, at least. Grace doesn't think she's ever seen such a blue sky before.

The park is massive, but at the far edge, she sees Daniel and Catalina. Catalina spots her first and waves her over. As soon as Grace is close enough, Catalina jogs over and immediately grabs her up in a huge hug. "Grace!" she says. "I'm so glad you could come!" Grace hugs her back and feels so grateful that Peach has someone to hug her like this every single day. "You look wonderful."

"Thanks." Grace smiles. "Sorry, I'm just really nervous."

Catalina's smile is warm and steady. "Of course," she says, "but there's no need to be."

Grace takes a deep breath and lets it out slowly, nods. Daniel's crouched on the ground a few feet away, babbling something, and he turns and stands when he hears Grace.

Grace sees her hair first, dark brown curls gathered at the back of her neck, the sun shining through the trees and dancing across her shoulders. She's wearing a tiny, blue-checked dress and tights, plus a small white sweater. From this angle, Grace can see Maya's eyes, Joaquin's nose and jaw, Melissa's hair.

Grace gathers her courage, finds her voice.

"Milly?" she says.

Peach looks up.

She sees Grace.

And she smiles.

ACKNOWLEDGMENTS

As always, my immense gratitude to my family, who encouraged me throughout the process of writing this book. Thanks for being such troupers. I owe you coffee.

Thank you to my agent, Lisa Grubka, who talked me through every chapter of this book, including the wrong ones. Her belief that I would eventually finish this story was sometimes the light in a very dark tunnel, and I am forever grateful for all the times she read pages, gave notes, and answered my desperate emails. Thanks for being such a partner in crime over the past ten years.

I got the first ideas for this novel while sitting in a Costco parking lot, and I immediately tapped out a rambling email to my editor, Kristen Pettit. She responded, "I am loving this direction. Loving. It." Little did we know that it would take another year before that random idea became a coherent story, but Kristen was there every step of the way, including when I lost the plot altogether (pun very much intended) and had to start over from scratch. Thank you for having my back, for letting me take my time, and for calling me the weekend before Christmas just to check in on me. I owe you a lot more than just coffee.

Thank you to the Harper team, including Elizabeth Lynch, Jen Klonsky, Kate Jackson, Sarah Kaufman, Gina Rizzo, Renée Cafiero, Kristen Eckhardt, Bess Braswell, and Claire Caterer, for taking my words and turning them into an actual, physical book. Thank you also to the whole Simon & Schuster UK team, especially Mattie Whitehead, Jane Griffiths, Jade Westwood and Jenny Richards.

This book would not exist if it weren't for the people who let me talk to them about my characters and their stories. They graciously brought me into their lives and discussed their families, jobs, and experiences with me, and I'm both humbled by and grateful for their generosity: Noemi Aguirre; Dr. Linda Alvarez; David H. Baum; Marie Coolman; Roy, Trevor, and Jacob Firestone; Jessica Hieger; Kate Lamb; and Kim Trujillo. Thank you also to the people who chose not to be named here—your kindness does not go unnoticed. Any mistakes or inaccuracies in this book are mine and mine alone.

I'm lucky enough to be part of an incredibly generous, talented, and funny-as-hell group of YA writers here in Los Angeles. It's possible I would still be working on the first draft if it wasn't for our group writing dates, so thank you for that. Thank you also to Brandy Colbert, Ally Condie, Jordanna Fraiberg, Gretchen McNeil, and Amy Spalding for reading drafts, offering thoughts, and helping me with research, and to Morgan Matson for coming up with the store name Whisked Away. You are all delightful.

Approximately two-thirds of this book was written while I sat at the counter of Dinosaur Coffee in Los Angeles, so thank you to the staff for providing me with excellent coffee and a makeshift office for the better part of a year, and for not judging me when I cried in the back that one time.

An extra-special thank you for my mom, who kept the faith in this book, and in me, when I could not. She supported me through every single version of this story, listened to me ramble about it for hours (sorry for spoiling the ending!), and never once doubted that I would finish it. She is the best, and I love her so much.

And finally, thank you to Joaquin, Grace, and Maya. I've spent more time with them than with any of my other characters, and even though they may be fictional, their struggles and triumphs feel so very real to me. I am endlessly grateful that they chose me to tell their story, and I hope they're doing well, wherever they may be.